I0603112

FOREVER IN YOUR SERVICE

Sandra Antonelli

Forever In Your Service

Copyright 2019 Sandra Antonelli

All right reserved.

This is a work of fiction. Names, characters, businesses, places, events, locales, and incidents are either the products of the author's imagination or used in a fictitious manner. Any resemblance to actual persons, living or dead, or actual events is coincidental.

For my champion, Susan Garbanzo.

CHAPTER ONE

If anything were to be the death of him, it would be this damned tree.

Dripping wet, Kitt shoved open the front door of his Maresfield Garden flat and dragged the spindly thing inside. A bough sprang up and snagged the chair beneath the coat rack. Tree and chair thumped onto the edge of the Persian carpet and polished wood floor. A puddle formed. He righted the chair and swiped his wet chin with his shoulder.

He'd sent Mae a message in the wee hours of the morning: *Breakfast at 7.* She had been here for some time, the heat on to counter an unseasonal October cold snap. Breakfast things were set near the big bay window in the sitting room, the table laid with his vintage blue and white Minton. The Jersey butter, the little crystal pots of her homemade orange and ginger marmalade, the spicy scent of Chelsea buns, the splendid aroma of coffee, it was all there, welcoming him home. He ambled into the kitchen, wet and grimy, rainwater dribbling down the back of his neck.

Clad in an atypical butler's uniform of crisp navy-blue shirt-dress and Doc Martens, her blonde hair in a French braid, reading glasses hanging from a long gold chain, she turned, smoothing her short white apron. If anyone were to be the death of him, it would be this damned woman. Efficient, intelligent, contrary, clever, she was a bloody nuisance.

And he loved her.

"Good morning, Mae," he said.

"Good morning." She put on her glasses, peering at him, her hazel eyes surveying the slice on his chin, the raw, red state of his knuckles, the rope-burn on his wrist, the pine needles and black dirt smearing his neck. She knew his job as a Risk Assessment Specialist for Regent's Park Consortium sometimes sent him to remote and often dangerous parts of the world, places where people tried to kill each other for land, valuable commodities, or different religious beliefs. She was aware Risk Assessment Specialist was a euphemism for *Intelligence Officer* and Regent's Park Consortium was *Her Majesty's Government*. He'd returned from trips in far worse condition, battered, bruised, lip split, eye black. However, soaking wet and spattered with pine needles was new.

She reached for the coffee carafe and poured a cup. Then she smoothed her apron again and handed him a towel rather than the coffee. "Trouble with your girly sports car?"

"Trouble with a girl *in* a sports car." He blotted his face and rubbed his head with the cloth. "Did you miss me, Mae?"

"Not in the least."

With a laugh, he traded the towel for a cup of her blessed coffee.

She draped terrycloth over her shoulder. "Now then. You have coffee. Do get on with frying my eggs."

"You did miss me. I'm so pleased." He had a long, savouring sip of the black brew she'd made, voicing his appreciation with a low sound.

"I'm very hungry and," she removed her reading glasses, tucking them on the chain around her neck, "you've been away for two weeks."

"Yes, two whole weeks of having to fry your own eggs."

"You know you *could* make that sound dirtier."

"Aren't I dirty enough?" He peeled a tiny leaf from the side of his neck and spread his arms wide, cup in hand. "Just look at me."

"I haven't stopped looking at you since you came into the kitchen."

He smiled widely, genuinely. "I suppose you'd have kissed me already if I hadn't been covered in gutter waste and snow."

"It's snowing?"

"It was in Geneva."

"Switzerland. I see. Tell me about the girl in the convertible."

"Ah. The girl in the convertible. That's why you haven't kissed me yet."

"Oddly, I see it as *you* haven't kissed *me* yet."

"Why, I'm covered in filth, Mae."

"It's the filth I'm curious about."

"As long as you stay curious." He set his coffee on the worktop. "I drove all night to come home to you. Shall I bathe or would you prefer my grubby, oil-stinking hands on you first?" Kitt took a step toward her and began to strip, pulling a wet, blue shirt over his head.

"Perhaps I'll make your breakfast instead of you making mine." Mae took the dirty shirt from his red fingers, ignoring the scrapes and raw scratches across his abdomen.

"Oh, scrambled eggs, the lady loves me."

"Yes, and you love my scrambled eggs."

"The eggs. Mae. The eggs in Switzerland were all boiled. Boiled eggs are so...boiled." He unbuttoned the waist of his muddied trousers and then toed off his shoes. "I'll be leaving again this morning, so I hope to make the most of the time we have before Bryce arrives." He kicked his shoes aside and looked down at his sodden feet. He'd left streaks of grime across the white tiles. "I've made a mess on your floor, Mrs Valentine."

"You live here. It's your floor."

"It's your flat I rent," Kitt glanced over his shoulder, "and I've trailed the mess through your house, my dear landlady."

"You were that eager to cook my breakfast?"

"I was more eager," he reached out and took her hand, "to have your coffee."

She closed her fingers around his.

Kitt smiled again. He had smiled a lot in the last few months. "I want to show you something," he said, smiling.

Mae snorted, and as expected, he drew her out of the kitchen, toward his bedroom, along the mucky trail he'd made across the floor, over the tiles and blond polished wood, along the muddy footprints that dotted the green and cream Persian hall runner. When he halted outside the bedroom, she pulled her hand from his. "Is there's something you want to tell me?" she said.

With a chuckle, he slid an arm around her waist, pulling her near, pressing her warmth to his bare, cool chest. "She was a pretty girl in a classic little Triumph TR3, but she had no proper idea how to change a flat tyre. She neglected to shove a chock behind the rear wheel and the car rolled back and into my Bentley. Despite how I'd lashed it, the damned thing blew off the roof, into a pothole full of mud, and got run over by a lorry. I salvaged what I could. It's half its original size."

"You lashed a little sports car to the roof of a Bentley Continental GT?"

"No. I lashed *that* to the roof of my Bentley." Kitt turned Mae toward the front door, where the ragged spruce tree lay upon the rug, and pointed.

Laughter sputtered from her nose then burst from her mouth.

"Where did you find a Christmas tree in the middle of October? Wait." She held up a hand. "Do spies even celebrate Christmas?"

He slipped his hands around her waist, his chin on her head. "This one does now. And I want to have a happy Christmas. Marry me."

Air rushed from her in a half-laugh, half-gasp, and she twisted about, her bright smile lighting up what passed for his silly dark soul, as she had for the last three years. She laid a hand on his cheek, smiling that brilliant, beautiful smile, laughing, "No."

"*No*?" Kitt laughed too. He'd spent hours thinking this through, but, somehow, he'd forgotten Mae wasn't one for grand gestures or extravagant productions. As a butler, she'd worked in a world often filled with pretention and ostentation, but in her own life she preferred simple. She liked good manners and old-fashioned customs. A spontaneous proposal wasn't simple, traditional, or even good manners.

"Yes. I understand," he said, pulling away to kneel, damp trousers pinching.

She narrowed her eyes. "Don't you dare."

With a faint grin, he straightened. "I may fail at being romantic, but I do have a ring."

Still squinting, her mouth pursed. "Show me."

"It was my great-grandmother's. My sister wanted it. As far as she's concerned I'd never have use for it, but it was my father's grandmother's, not her father's grandmother's."

Mae picked errant pine needles stuck to one of the gilt-framed, hand-painted maps of eighteenth-century Europe on the wall. She snorted, wiping her fingers on the towel over her shoulder. "You once said you had a brother, now there's a sister. This is what you do, feed me tiny morsels about yourself at the oddest times, and tell me nothing if I ask, so I'm ignoring that bit of historical bait."

"I'm not accustomed to sharing things about myself. I'm out of practice. I can tell you more when I no longer have secrets to keep. It's for your own good, for your safety."

"Let me see the ring."

Kitt sighed. "She's my half-sister, but still, she's the only sister I've ever had."

"There's no ring, is there?" Mae crossed her arms.

"I have a ring."

"May I see it?" She pulled the towel from her shoulder and tossed it on the chair by the door.

Kitt rubbed a bit of grime from his throat. "It's Edwardian. Filigreed platinum and diamond. It's very different from the ring Caspar gave you." He grimaced immediately. Why was he being so ham-handed? He'd never been this sure about something in his life, yet his clumsy performance contested his confidence. This particular manner of nervousness was new to him. "Forgive me. I know it's very poor taste to mention your deceased husband. I'm not quite sure of the etiquette when it comes to proposing to a widow. Etiquette is your domain."

"And lies and secrecy are yours. I don't believe you have a brother or sister any more than I believe you have a ring."

"You wound me. I said I would never lie to you. I have both half-siblings and a ring. Perhaps I ought to take you to bed to continue this discussion."

"Perhaps it's best we go on as we are."

"Meaning?"

"We go on as we are."

"Meaning me in my rented flat, you living next door as my landlady. Me doing intelligence work, you renovating the flat downstairs? Me frying your eggs, you making my coffee?"

She inhaled, as if she were about to agree, but said nothing, eyes wandering to the leather-bound collection of antique atlases on the bookshelves near the window-seat.

"Yes, yes you would prefer to go on that way. Why?"

She sighed. "How can you speak of marriage when you are already committed to country and Queen?"

"I don't sleep with *her* and it's you I love. Very much."

A groove appeared between her brows as she looked at him, chin tilted, index finger rubbing over her thumbnail.

"Ah, an expression that says 'yes, *but*.' I hadn't thought there'd be one of those."

"Are you surprised?"

"No, I'm curious."

"As long as you stay curious."

"And the rest?"

"I haven't quite come to terms with certain things yet, Kitt."

"Such as?"

She squinted. "You mean aside from your history with women?"

"Right. Of course." Kitt clamped his back teeth together. He'd never considered she'd still be thinking about his philandering past. Had he somehow given her recent cause to? "My history concerns you."

Her squint faded. "Yes." She looked at him, her expression serious.

He refrained from reaching for her hand, placing a palm on the back of the chair beside the door instead. "All right. I suppose that's fair. Based on what you would consider my chequered past with women, you might believe I'd stop wasting my time and move on to someone younger than you soon—or look for someone younger than you later. I promise you. You have the lump of stone that is my heart."

Her brow arched.

"Too trite?"

She gave an airy laugh. "This is not about your playboy past with women, or an anxiety that you'll run off with another woman half my age. I don't doubt that you love me, and you should never doubt that I love you."

"Then marry me."

"For a man highly-trained to listen, you haven't listened at all."

"I've listened. You would prefer to go on as we are." He nodded once. "Here are the important facts."

"And there's the you I know. Do go on."

"I love you. You love me. You're afraid of that. I admit I find it rather daunting myself, but again the facts. I love you. You love me. However trite it sounds, we can face the fear together. Marry me. Please."

"Kitt."

Kitt looked at her for a long moment. "What is it?" he said, softly. "The nightmares?"

"Yes." She chewed her top lip for a moment, her gaze blunt. "I've written about what happened, like you suggested, made a chronicle, and that's helped. But I still struggle with having killed two men, whereas killing is an everyday reality for you."

His finger tapped the back of the chair. "I don't kill people every day."

Her gaze remained direct, arms unfolding. "My writing it all down or not, what you do for a living isn't quite yet fathomable, and it's even less fathomable in terms of marriage."

"Bryce is married," he said, as if he were five years-old with a five-year-old's logic, and ever so casually, so coolly, he shrugged one shoulder. "James Bond was married."

"James Bond's wife died."

"Ah, you're afraid you'll die, be killed by villainous henchmen, is that it?"

She scraped bottom teeth over her top lip, brows arching.

"Yes, let's forget I said that."

"Bryce is not a field officer, you are not a desk man, and I can't get beyond how much I liked killing the Sicilian who was trying to kill you. And I did like it. But my nightmares aren't about that. I did what I had to do. However disturbing, I know that. What I write about now, the nightmares I have, are about you."

"Me?"

"Three months ago, I knew nothing of what you really did for a living. Now I live in this dichotomous world of loving you and hating what you do—not to mention hating what I did. Three months ago, I expected you'd return home when you finished a job because I didn't know better. Now I know better. Now I know there's a chance you might never come home."

"I've always come home to you. I'll keep coming home to you."

She looked at him dully. "I am aware you are not...without skill, yet I can't help but think about the time when men kept Tasering you, or when men tried to drown you with a fish named Shirley Bassey, or when you were handcuffed to a chair and a Sicilian almost strangled the life from you before I killed him."

"All of those things happened on the same day."

"Yes, they did, and that day I thought you were dead."

"What makes you think something like that will happen again?"

Mae burst out laughing. "I know what a terrible spy you are."

He pursed his mouth briefly. "I'm a very good intelligence officer and I am very good at what I do—unless you're there."

She whispered his first name, which meant she was gravely serious. Goody. "I understand," he said. "This is my last field assignment, Mae. I've decided that already."

"You think you're getting too old for this work, but you're far too young to retire."

"I began working on this before you and I became *us*. I have to finish what I started and, realistically, it's time to get out. I have to retire sometime."

"Thank you for not saying 'you had to die sometime.' Time to get out and do what, exactly? You get bored sitting in your office doing paperwork; it makes you feel sluggish, old. Inactivity would make you snap."

"Paperwork is one of Dante's lesser-known sub-circles of Hell. I'm five years younger than you and you retired when you were my present age. So I can retire from fieldwork or I can resign."

"And we're back to inactivity. I retired and then went back to work. For you. I'd never ask you to retire or resign." Mae shook her head.

"No, you wouldn't, and you haven't. This was my choice to make. Trust me."

"We both know no one in your profession ever really resigns or retires. The job is, so to speak, yours for life." She looked away for a moment, heaving a breathy half-laugh. "I do trust you, but I'm not so sure you trust me, or anyone for that matter, and doing what you do, that makes sense. I trust you with my life, yet I don't trust you with yours."

"I trust you, Mae, and I assure you I have a very keenly developed sense of self-preservation."

"I lost Caspar," Mae shook her head again, "and I can't...*I can't*... Do you understand?"

"Yes," he said. It had been a very long while since she'd mentioned her deceased polygamist husband and Kitt frowned. "You don't want spend your life loving dead men in silver-framed photos you keep on the desk in your sitting room."

Mae nodded. "I had to be honest."

"You are always honest. It's part of your charm."

"It doesn't feel charming."

Kitt believed he'd thought this through, made plans accordingly. He'd complete this assignment. It would be his last before he moved into support and consulting. He'd wind up teaching or operating in the same manner as Bryce, and eventually retire at seventy-six, like Llewelyn said he planned to next year. Only he realised he was the same quixotic fool he'd been three months ago.

Resign, retire, take a step sideways, the job was his for life, and Mae was a nuisance, a thorn in his side. Under his skin, embedded in his being, however hackneyed, she was his thorn for life. Christ, what a bizarre and rather wonderful devotion.

No one had ever accused him of thinking with his heart before, yet that's exactly what he'd done. His head had never played a part because this was love. Love was what addled his brain, made him lose focus, quashed his logic, turned him sloppy, slowed his reflexes, sent him blind, and love was what kept Mae's heart chained to a dead man for a decade and a half. Love was why she still had that silver-framed photo of Caspar on the desk in her sitting room. It was her bizarre and wonderful devotion, and how hilarious that he understood the nature of that devotion now that he was devoted to her. He was a man in love with a woman who would always love a dead husband. Was it funny that he considered loving her a sort of penance for some of the things he'd done or was it funnier how she understood what he'd completely failed to see? Whether he continued with field assignments, whether he moved to a support and consulting position, whether he retired or not, to The Consortium, Mae would always be his loyal butler, a trusted employee whose life he'd once put in jeopardy. Her safety was crucial, meaning this was, this would always be, impossible. The depths of his idiocy were astounding and his laugh was bleak.

"I've hurt you," she said.

"Well, it doesn't tickle." Exhaling, jaw set, his frown deepened. "But it's my own damned fault entirely." Kitt looked over at the frail Christmas tree. He closed the space that lay between them and drew her near. "You must know. Whatever, however we are, I love you," he said. "I am devoted. To you. My funny Mrs Valentine."

"At last we move back to the seduction, where I change my mind in the throes of passion at your dirty hands," she said, untying her apron as he began to unbutton her dress.

"Perhaps my dirty hands may present a convincing argument." He undid buttons across her breasts. The apron wafted to her feet.

She tugged at the waist of his damp trousers, unzipping him. "I don't care if your hands are dirty. I don't care if they're filthy. I don't care if they've been all over another woman's car."

"It was such a pretty little Triumph TR3 too." He pushed the dress down her shoulders and his grubby, stained hands paused. He took a moment to gaze at what he'd unwrapped. She was beautiful. The most beautiful thing he ever saw. He went on looking at her, at skin he knew was soft, at the curving swell of her breasts, at the tiny mole at the base of her left collarbone, at her throat, at her mouth.

"Miss me, did you?"

"Not in the least," she said and stubbly whiskers grazed her skin when he pressed his cheek to hers. His nose bumped the tip of hers, her laugh soft and warm and coffee-scented puffed over his lips, as the doorbell rang with a short burst followed by a longer one. Kitt let loose a string of obscenities, his mouth hovering above hers. "Bryce is early."

Mae stopped unpeeling damp fabric over his hips. "The door is locked."

"He's already on his way up. And he knows the key code." Kitt kissed her quickly, drew her dress up to her shoulders, and took a step back. "Good God, Mrs Valentine, look at yourself. Wherever is your apron?" He hitched up his clammy trousers and snatched the towel from the chair, draping it around his dirt-streaked neck.

Dress already buttoned, she retrieved the apron at her feet, tying the strings about her waist as knuckles rapped. The door swung open and Bryce stood on the other side of the threshold with Roger Llewelyn, the head of Special Operations Division.

Llewelyn smiled his genial smile. Kitt uttered more filthy words under his breath. Something had gone or was about to go, as Mae liked to say, *arseways*.

Bryce moved inside, scratching his chin, green eyes glinting. "Why is there a Christmas tree on the floor, Kitty?"

Kitt gave his colleague and friend Timothy Bryce a tight smile. "You're early." He turned his attention to the older man. "Sir. I didn't expect you."

Llewelyn cast an eye over the pine tree mess beneath his feet before giving Mae a pleasant nod, dark hand brushing raindrops from a salt patch in still-black hair. He glanced at the table set for breakfast in the sitting room and his mouth pursed. "Dear boy, I do apologise for arriving unannounced. Plans have altered. Geneva proved advantageous and in line with Keppel, so you're being relocated. Bryce has your amended itinerary. You're booked on the next flight out, which departs in ninety minutes. Professor Molony, that chap you know from the Mikhail-Freudenstein thing, will join you and brief you en route to Heathrow. Dalton will meet you at your hotel."

Dalton. There was the *arseways*. Kitt bit his molars together. "Sir."

Automatically, Mae shifted into the role The Consortium would expect. "May I take your coats, gentlemen?" she said, her manner professional.

"Ah, the housekeeper." Llewelyn smoothed his moustache and smiled like a matinee idol from a '40s film.

"The butler, sir." Bryce's mouth twitched.

"Oh, yes. How clumsy of me, thinking butlers are always men. We've never been formally introduced."

Kitt refrained from grinding his molars together. He grabbed the ends of the towel around his neck. "Mrs Valentine, this is Brigadier Roger Llewelyn, my employer. Sir, Mrs Valentine." Kitt looked at Bryce, flicked his gaze to Llewelyn and shifted his eyes back to Bryce. "You already know Bryce."

Bryce gave a barely perceptible shrug and hung his jacket on the coat rack above the chair, mouth twitching again. "Good morning, Mrs Valentine."

"Good morning, Sergeant Bryce."

Llewelyn handed his heavy wool coat to Mae. "Thank you, Mrs Valentine. I'm so happy we're finally acquainted." He turned to Kitt. "Apologies again for an impromptu arrival, Major Kitt, but time flies and we're short on it."

Kitt recognised *impromptu* as a cloaked direction to 'move his arse.' "Sir," he said and left Mae in the foyer with Bryce and the Brigadier.

Handsome, mid-seventies, of Kenyan-Welsh extraction, Llewelyn dressed fashionably and had the air of a worldly old English gentleman, one who was well-bred, affable—and calculating. Kitt left the door ajar as Mae led the two men to the sitting room across from his bedroom, and he stripped off his wet trousers, listening to the exchange, a simple task considering Llewelyn had a voice rivalling any Shakespearean stage actor.

"As I was saying on the way upstairs, Bryce," Llewelyn boomed to the cheap seats, "Shiraz and Syrah come from the same grape varietal. The name depends on the vineyard or region where the grape is grown, as well as the environment, the soil, the climate. Isn't that so, Mrs Valentine?"

"That it is, Brigadier."

"Might I trouble you for some tea, Mrs Valentine?"

"Major Kitt doesn't drink tea," Mae said.

"And he calls himself an Englishman." Llewelyn chuckled. "Coffee then."

In under a minute, Mae organised cups and served the coffee

she'd brewed for Kitt, setting a folding table and tray in front of his superior.

"So then, Mrs Valentine," Llewelyn said, voice velvety, "I take it you—oh, *do* spare some milk for me, Sergeant—I take it, Mrs Valentine, you're still working part-time for Major Kitt?"

"Would you care for a biscuit, Brigadier?" Mae offered a plate and smiled pleasantly.

Bryce piped up. "Have one of the chocolate ones, sir. They are rather good."

"Yes, Bryce, I will have *one*, since you've managed to grab the other five. See, I knew the Major's butler would know something about wine, Bryce, while you know nothing, and Major Kitt, well, he'd drink tea or poison before he'd sully his palate with wine." He bit into the sweet. "Oh, top marks, this is quite a good biscuit, goes well with your excellent coffee." Llewelyn *mm-mmed*. "Please, sit down, Mrs Valentine. You needn't wait on us."

"Thank you, you're very kind, but please, excuse me. I must tend to the Major's breakfast. May I offer you some as well?"

"I do love a good fry-up, but there isn't time for breakfast." Llewelyn sighed. "May I ask you something, Mrs Valentine?"

"Brigadier?" Mae said evenly, hair prickling at the back of her neck, the man's grin sly and diabolic beneath his trim moustache.

Llewelyn coughed. "Do you like dogs, Mrs Valentine?"

"I do."

"Ever have one?"

"Several."

"You worked for Ettore Gelsomino? I believe he had a few hounds?"

"He did. Please, excuse me."

"Gelsomino spoke very highly of you, said you were always professional; good with his cellar, dogs, and daughters. He couldn't have been more glowing." Llewelyn said, his tone cheery.

"I'm pleased to know that."

"What sort of dogs did you have as a child?"

Mae smiled blandly. "We kept ratters, mostly English Toy Terriers—Black and Tans."

"Like the Manchester Terrier?"

Mae smoothed her apron over her hips. "Yes," she said, "but the Toy is smaller."

"I have two dogs, Pointers; Thumper and Bambi—smart as a whip they are. Smarter than Bryce here. Crumbs, Bryce, crumbs. The lady will have to vacuum you before, and the carpet after we go. Do large dogs put you off at all, make you nervous, Mrs Valentine?"

"Forgive my impertinence, Brigadier, but what do you want?"

Llewelyn's laugh cracked the air, and his smooth, unruffled honeyed tones would have impressed Branagh and Olivier. "Oh, you are sharp. Indeed, you might believe that the fraud, tax evasion, money-laundering events that touched your life this past summer could be why you'd be fresh in my mind. I admit I am rather curious about what appears to be a sad-looking Christmas tree over there, and that, combined with your years in service and practical experience with dogs, I'm after a little," he paused, "Christmas favour."

"More coffee, Brigadier?" Mae mimicked the man's silky tenor.

"Your loyalty to the Major is commendable. I'm sure you're grateful for his assistance with the money-laundering mess, but come now, Mrs Valentine, you work part-time for a man who is seldom here."

Mae stood in front of Bryce, hands clasped behind her back, cool, polite, professional. "Three months ago," she said, "I was mugged, nearly killed, kidnapped and drugged. Your office accused me of murder, theft, money laundering, and informed me my deceased husband, a man I loved very much, was a polygamist.

Forgive me, Brigadier, I have no interest in doing you a favour of any sort."

"Sorry to keep you waiting, sir." Kitt suddenly appeared at the end of the leather Chesterfield sofa, pulling pale-blue shirtsleeves from the cuffs of a brown jumper, adjusting the leather band of his battered Citizen watch.

Mouth flattened, Llewelyn set his coffee on the tea table.

With a respectful nod, Mae said, "Would you gentlemen be needing anything further?"

Bryce laughed.

Llewelyn glared. "What's so amusing, Sergeant?"

Kitt rubbed his chin. "Thank you, Mrs Valentine. There's nothing more we need."

Bryce chuckled again.

Mae collected dirty cups and put them on the folding tray, along with a plate of biscuit crumbs, a milk jug, and crystal sugar bowl. She turned to Kitt, hazel eyes full of warmth for him. "Sir, your extra shaving kit is in the cupboard behind your Christmas tree. There's a bag packed with fresh clothes in the study. Shall I fetch it?"

"Thank you, no. I'm sure by now Bryce has transferred my things from the Bentley."

The two men rose. She set the tray aside and retrieved Llewelyn's coat, helping him into it. "Good morning, Brigadier, Sergeant Bryce. Have a good trip, sir." She returned to the tea table and lifted the tray.

Bryce put on his jacket, had another look at the pitiful Christmas tree, shook his head, and went to open the door. Scowling, Llewelyn joined him and started down the stairs.

Kitt grabbed his navy pea coat from a hook above the umbrella stand. Instead of slipping it on, he tossed it on the chair beside the door, watching Mae carry the tray into the kitchen. He crossed into his bedroom, snatched a small coin purse from a drawer in the bedside table, shoved it in his pocket, and went to the kitchen.

Mae stood in front of the cooker, Chemex coffee carafe in one hand. "Forgotten something?" she said, back to him.

"I never quite kissed you hello."

"And now you want to kiss me goodbye."

"What if I just kiss you?"

She set the carafe on a trivet and turned. "What if you just come home?"

"Of course." He smiled softly, refastening the pinching clasp of the watch he'd hastily strapped on when he'd overheard Llewelyn questioning Mae. "Of course."

Mae wiped both hands on her apron and sighed. "Does Llewelyn know about us like Bryce does?"

"You are the consummate professional, Mae. My employer believes you are my trusted and highly-valued employee, as I am his, and what he's trying to do is called *poaching*." Kitt chuckled suddenly. "Listen, regardless of why he was here, I am glad you said 'no.' I was selfish and not at all rational. My feelings for you cloud my logic. I ought to let you go, you ought to walk away, yet here we are, caught up in a fantasy of sorts, and it makes sense to go on as we were, you 'working' for me. It's safer for you." He put a hand in his pocket and drew the sprung purse from inside, squeezing the sides apart before he tossed it on the worktop.

This she time murmured his name.

"I know there are concerns, but there is another option." He took her hand, turned it, and opened her fingers. Rather than kiss the inside of her wrist or centre of her palm, he placed a small circle of filigreed platinum with a glittering diamond. "Yes, it's conservative, traditional, and very beautiful, but full of fire and spark. In other words, it's exactly like you. What are your thoughts on a very long engagement?"

NINE DAYS LATER, Kitt knew their very long engagement was likely to last an eternity.

The container was stifling, the air stagnant, rank with the stench of corpses that had been there when the two dockers had cut off the lock and swung the doors open.

Nauseous, Kitt was nauseous, dizzy, his muscles cramped, as if he'd been poisoned with strychnine. His head ached relentlessly. His joints ached and the wire that sliced his flesh had left a festering injury. Intermittently confounded and lucid he remembered the Singaporean NCB officer vomiting outside the container. He remembered checking his watch when Dalton asked the time, and Molony's shout, the flash of knives, the NCB officer choking on his own blood. He remembered Molony's silly penknife, the woman screaming, the bolt cutters swinging, Dalton's scarlet-spattered teeth, and the lad falling dead without a sound. He remembered the crack of cartilage, the slice of wire through flesh and bone, the explosion inside his head. He remembered *chichiltic*, a language that wasn't Malay, Chinese, or Singlish. He remembered the container going dark, trying to stand in the blackness, stumbling over rotting bodies, slipping, tumbling, collapsing. And as he tried to lift his head, he remembered biology.

With severe dehydration cells shrank, blood vessels connecting grey matter to the inside of the cranium pulled away and ruptured, organs failed. With hyperthermia, he'd simply roast in his own skin. As unsteady as his thoughts were, he knew his throbbing hand had turned septic, he'd lost a substantial amount of blood, and he'd stopped sweating long ago. Soon, he would die from dehydration or hyperthermia.

Just come home, Mae whispered, above the buzzing of blowflies that would lay their eggs on his corpse.

God damn it. He was going to wind up in a plain silver frame on the desk in Mae's sitting room, right beside her dead husband, only she didn't possess a single photograph of him.

Listless, head pounding, his attention shifted to a narrow beam of sunlight, slipping lower and lower until it crossed the woman and reached the mangled face of the fellow who might have been Professor Molony or Dalton. Flies swarmed, laying eggs in the eyes, gaping mouths, and nostrils of the dead who had been dead for much longer.

Come home.

Home. Mae. They were one and the same. Dark and light. Heaven and hell. Mae. Wasn't it funny that she made him believe he had more than a minuscule scrap of a soul? His eyes settled back on the beam of light again and he watched it, thinking of Mae until she began to disappear along with the fading light, and he slid into a cushion of soft, seductive, lethal blackness.

CHAPTER TWO

Three small deer darted across the driveway as Felix lifted a leg and peed on a sand-filled bag, the brown paper *farolito* wilting over the little candle inside. The *farolitos* that the landscaper had set up ran from the bottom of the long private drive to the front of the curving house. On Christmas Eve, a candle would be lit inside every bag and bathe the grand house with a warm glow—unless the deer trampled them or the dog peed on all the bags, as he had all the *farolitos* beneath the vine-covered pergola. Mae looked from the current wilted paper bag to the house.

Cosmologist Dr Julius Taittinger's 'smart home,' a contemporary take on New Mexico's adobe architecture, sat between Los Alamos, its nuclear research laboratory ten miles to the northwest, and the Bandelier National Monument, a historic preservation site of the Ancestral Puebloans. The curving design of the two-level house was inspired by the concentric building layouts of the ancient Anasazi. The architecture might have been inspired by the ancestors of modern Pueblo Indians, but all Mae saw was the villain's lair from a '60s spy film.

Fuzzy yellow tennis ball in the pocket of her coat, she led the dog down the *farolito*-lined driveway, past the refurbished adobe barn that doubled as a garden shed and garage for the old sports car Taittinger was restoring. Hector, the landscaper, waved at her as he and baseball cap-wearing Mr Coyote strapped a woodchipper in the back of a pickup. She waved back and threw the ball. Felix shot off after it, grabbed the bright yellow fuzziness, shook the living hell out of it, and then ran circles around the barn with the ball in his mouth.

Fifteen minutes and one dead, chewed-up tennis ball later, a blue and white UniDel delivery vehicle halted in front of the house. Taittinger received all sorts of deliveries of various sizes, typically wine, crates of automotive parts, and antiques he bought at auction. This morning, Mae signed for a shoebox-sized, shrink-wrapped package. The parcel had no return address. She took it, and the dog, inside.

In the kitchen, she tied on a fresh apron and ground coffee for her new employer. Once the pour-over filter had finished dripping through the fair-trade Ethiopian brew, she ferried the box and a cup of heavily-sugared coffee to the study, Felix trotting behind.

Unlike the über-villain appearance of his smart home, goateed, bespectacled Taittinger bore a resemblance to a fictional boy wizard, only without a scar on his forehead or the ability to cast spells. "Hey, Valentine!" he said, with great enthusiasm, rubbing the chin of his pale brown goatee before reaching for his coffee.

"Good morning, Dr Jools." Mae lay the box on his desk.

He swivelled back and forth in his chair. "This weather is insane. It's late December, and it feels nothing like the most wonderful time of the year. It's *snow* Christmas without a blanket of white, so we need Bowie. We need Bing. We need to make it feel holly-jolly!" His fingers flew across his mobile's screen. Bing Crosby and David Bowie began to sing *White Christmas*.

She'd grown accustomed to Taittinger's taste in music. Daily, easy listening favourites played in the background in every part of the house, inside and out, Sinatra, Andy Williams, Doris Day, crooning from tiny hidden speakers. Today, festive easy listening holiday classics played in the background.

"Hans, my previous butler, chose you as his replacement. He said your references were impressive, but he never mentioned why you left your last position." Taittinger's mouth compressed for a second.

"My employer died," she said. Two and a half months had passed since Kitt's death and saying those words still showered her skin with stinging nettles.

"Oh." Taittinger nodded. "You with him long?"

"A few years." Mae rubbed her forearms.

"He was in the Army, a Marine or something, right?"

"Yes."

Earnestly, he offered a platitude about life, death, history, and wine, and she tipped her head and pretended to appreciate his meant-to-be kind sentiment. Then he had a gulp from his mug. "Oh, wow, Valentine, I cannot *espresso* how good your coffee is."

"Thank you." She gave him her best amused smile and he looked at the dog.

"Here Felix, c'mere boy!"

The lean, ginger Italian Greyhound bent around and proceeded to lick his own arse.

"Sheesh." Taittinger snorty-chuckled and reached for the package. "When did this arrive?"

"About fifteen minutes ago."

Taittinger began to half-hum, half-sing, "*Hmm-hm* earth *hm-hm* to men...*" He peeled off the plastic wrapping and shipping label and used a letter opener to slice into the tape around the edges of the box, He lifted the lid and screamed, the box flying. A whole, rather large desiccated rat *plopped* onto the parquetry flooring, right at Mae's feet.

With a start, she stepped back from the withered rodent and grabbed the dog before the dog grabbed the rat.

"*Shit! Shit!*" Taittinger pressed the heels of his palms to the side of his head. He looked at Mae and lowered his hands, scraping his bottom teeth over his top lip. "Oh, man, *oh, man*, I'm sorry." He swallowed, face reddening. "Ex-girlfriend. Bad break up. Guess Judith's still a little..." he laughed insipidly, "cheesed off. Guess it's what she thinks of me."

Mae glanced down at the big dead rat and refrained from making a face. "I'll take care of it, Dr Jools." She handed him the dog and scooped up the preserved rodent with the box. Felix squirmed free and followed her out of the study.

Rodent corpse disposal complete, Mae tended to more typical housekeeping. A Persian rug had been delivered yesterday. She hung the bright red, star-shaped Tabriz on the wall in the foyer, then moved on to polish the glass case holding a collection of antique wind-up tin toys, die-cast cap guns, and sheriff badges. Bing and the Andrew Sisters harmonised the Hawaiian Christmas greeting *Mele Kalikimaka* while she dusted items from *nichos*, small niches displaying fuzz-collecting, centuries-old astrolabes and Neo-Babylonian planispheres.

The dog yawned and Mae sighed, wiping a sundial, gazing out a wall of glass. The morning's rat incident aside, as villainous-looking as the house was, she hadn't come across anything villainous on the estate. Huge glass panels framed the beauty of the high-desert setting, giving panoramic views of the spectacular Sangre de Cristo Mountains and Rio Grande in the valley below. The foyer opened to vaulted ceilings and a massive, glass-walled great room that jutted out over the canyon. A staircase curved upstairs to seven bedrooms, with the same panorama as downstairs. To the right lay a formal dining room, kitchen, and domestic quarters. To the left lay Taittinger's study, and beneath it all sat the wine cellar.

A marvel of engineering and construction, carved into rock, the subterranean wine cellar had a rather boring entrance no one ever noticed because of the almighty view. Any time she looked up from dusting, something about the bloody view—the sky or a craggy rock—made her think of Kitt, of his blue eyes, of the cragginess of a scar on his shoulder and she'd stop dusting, stop working. Mae set her gaze on the uninspired entrance to Taittinger's wine cellar, then on the small, slim dog chewing a fuzzy yellow ball near the cellar door. The dog had focus, all directed on that ball, and she had distracting views that set her mind wandering.

She left Felix to gnaw, put away the dusting things, and went to remove mineral stains from the electric teakettle, dumping two denture-cleaning tablets into the stainless-steel pot, filling it with water. An unorthodox cleaning product, the tablets came in handy. Later, she'd use them to rid hard water stains from a guestroom en suite toilet. She'd drop a few tablets in the bowl, leave them to dissolve, and toss a strip of Dent-o-clean on a shelf at the back of the vanity, for later use. The tablets in the kettle hissed and effervesced like the fizzy upset-stomach-headache remedy Kitt had occasionally used to combat particularly beastly hangovers. She swirled the fizzing liquid in the kettle and left it to de-scale.

Mae buried herself in holiday preparation. From a kitchen with distracting, spectacular views of the Rio Grande and mountains, grey clouds played peekaboo with a bright blue sky and she rolled out dough for the cardamom Christmas biscuits. Chestnuts roasted on an open fire, sleigh bells rang, and Nancy Wilson sang about wives being lovers. Mae cut out star shapes while Rudolph had a red nose. When she turned to slide the biscuit trays into the oven Engelbert Humperdinck crooned *Quando Quando Quando*.

"Would you like to dance?" Kitt stood a mere half-metre away, his shirt sky blue.

The tray sagged and fell from her grip. Felix scrambled across the floor tiles and gobbled the spoiled bits of biscuit dough. Mae didn't stop him.

"Are those...Chelsea buns?" Kitt's blue shirt had turned into a sweat-dampened grey sports tee, dark blond hair tousled from a run, nose sunburnt.

Engelbert went on singing.

Kitt went on talking. "I do love your Chelsea buns, Mrs Valentine, almost as much as I love your scrambled eggs. Now that I think about it, I confess I fell in love with your baked goods before I fell in love with you, although, if I am honest, those two things did happen within seconds of each other."

Mae didn't know which was worse, the singing or the phantom. A glob of dough stuck to her apron. She pulled it away, squeezing it in her hand, and moved to the touch control near the kitchen entrance, stabbing an oily finger on the pad, killing the music. Fingers dough-sticky, she looked down at the watch swimming on her wrist, at the ring on the chain around her neck. She pulled off her glasses and rubbed her face, smearing butter on her skin. When she looked up, Kitt smiled softly, his neck speckled with pine needles. "I want to have a happy Christmas," he said.

"Well, feckin' Happy Christmas," she muttered, oily-faced.

The ghost of a Christmas that never came to pass vanished as she cleaned away greasy smears and gooey bits. She rolled out another tray of biscuits, shoved them into the hot oven, and sat in a chair rubbing the dog's ears until the biscuits were baked. She'd been on the verge of brooding when Taittinger entered the kitchen.

He'd been hiding his post-rat embarrassment in the barn for a while, tinkering with his old sports car. He adjusted his round glasses. "Again, I'm *really* sorry about the rat. I guess Judith hates me, you know?" With a sheepish laugh, he shook his head. "Anyhow, I like where you placed the Tabriz rug in the foyer. You have a good eye."

"Thank you, Dr Jools."

The not quite boy-wizard snagged a still-warm cardamom biscuit from a cooling rack. "Ho-lee shit." He closed his brown eyes the way Kitt sometimes had when he'd eaten scrambled eggs. "This cookie is incredible!" Taittinger said, mouth full. "I have a *confection* to make. My veddy English mother never made Christmas cookies like this."

"You're quite amusing. I'm pleased you enjoy my baking."

He reached for another biscuit and, munching away, glanced around the kitchen, at the turkey she'd roast later, at the place cards she'd already made, at the bowl of mushrooms on the table, at the dog curled on a rug near the sink. "Here, Felix." He patted his leg.

The dog didn't move, he simply looked at Mae.

"Hey," Taittinger snapped his fingers, "come on."

The dog remained on his rug.

"Felix, come...gahhh! Why won't he listen, Valentine?"

"Your tone, Dr Jools."

"Oh, yeah, my tone, and my hands, and then praise." He moved both hands, bringing them from his hips to his chest, and pitched his voice a little higher, "Felix, come!"

The dog rose, stretched his long front legs, and trudged over to Taittinger. "Good boy, good dog." He offered a bit of cookie, crouched down, and rubbed Felix's head as the dog ate the sweet scrap. When Taittinger straightened, the dog latched on and began to hump his leg. "Oh, for the love of... Down. Get down. Off!"

Mae swallowed her laugh and pointed. "Felix, off! On your mat."

The dog disengaged and returned to his place, plopping down to gnaw his furry yellow tennis ball.

Taittinger brushed off his trousers, removing more cookie

crumbs than reddish dog hair. "I should be back with my mother, sister, and her kids by noon-thirty. Their rooms ready?"

"Yes, Dr Jools."

"Cool. Is that the turkey for tomorrow, right?"

"It is."

"I did mention my sister is vegetarian, didn't I?"

"You did. I've prepared several dishes for her Christmas dinner. I'll do the same for Mr Nash next week. I've also informed the caterers there are vegetarians attending your New Year's Eve party."

"Oh, yeah, 'bout that. Add two more to the houseguest list for New Year's Eve. Met this Aussie at Tuesday night's dinner. He has a real palate for Napa Valley Cabernet Sauvignon. At dinner, he opened a '41 Inglenook—minty, cherry, brown sugar, and dried plums—it was freakin' Christmas in a bottle." His expression turned dreamy for a few seconds. "Anyhow, the guy's hot to collect. I invited him to stay. So it'll be Ruby Bleuville, Ari Basil, Bob Nash, this Aussie David Case and his fiancé, Ian. With Milt Foley and the Chungs not coming until New Year's Day, we'll still have a spare room."

"I'll have all the rooms prepared, in case anyone should overindulge."

"And you know someone will." He straightened and sat on the table, legs dangling over the edge. "You're always on top of it. And you understand the calamity of human beings displaced by war and persecution, and the moral obligation we have to these people. Hans never got that. Anyhow, I'll do the speech thing at the New Year's Eve party, pass the hat, and my guests will be generous, but when it comes to wine, these people can be a little ruthless; kind to your face, but they'll send you a dead rat if they don't get what they want."

"You have something they all want, Dr Jools?"

A grin blossomed on his baby-face, cheeks bunching, eyes squinty. "A 1982 Château Lafite Rothschild."

Mae gave an appropriate impressed nod.

"Bob Nash and David Case both claim to have something even rarer." Taittinger picked a mushroom out of the bowl and turned it in his fingers.

Her employer played with the pale, grey-brown cap and Kitt leaned against the sink. "I hope you're not going to put that dirt in my spaghetti," he said.

"My mother was right." Taittinger twirled the mushroom. "I thought it would be hard to replace Hans, but there isn't any further need for a trial. You're working out well for me. I'd like you to stay on."

Mae drew her eyes from Kitt at the white porcelain sink. "Thank you, Dr Jools."

"I bet you'll like working for me more than your last guy." He held up the portobello mushroom. "I'm a real *fungi*." He grinned like an eejit, snagged two cookies, and left for Santa Fe to pick up his British mother, his sister, and her two children. Tomorrow, Christmas Day, he'd play Santa Claus.

MAE PLACED her coffee on the table and looked about Central Avenue, at the town's high street and weird mix of architectural styles, from Santa Fe adobe, flat-faced facades of the 1990s, to the Fuller Lodge, a massive log cabin that had once been the dining hall of a ranch school.

The Lodge was now an Art Centre and gallery that showcased local artists, like Taittinger's mother, Evelyn. Before WWII, Los Alamos had been little more than homesteads and the ranch school. During the War, the US government took over the school and homesteads for the secret Manhattan Project, the plan that gave birth to the first atomic bomb. These days, the town was known for its nuclear research facility, a population heavy with PhDs and, per capita, the highest number of millionaires in the USA, just ahead of Naples, Florida, where Evelyn Taittinger lived during the winter. Except there hadn't been much winter. The two days after Christmas still felt like spring. Without a blanket of wintery snow, the green garlands and wreaths wrapped around the wooden pillars of the Fuller Lodge looked out of place. Mae felt just as out of place.

She leaned over and adjusted Felix's little blue coat. In spite of the balmy nature of the weather, Italian Greyhounds had little body fat and got cold easily. She re-tied his lead to a leg of her wrought-iron chair and the toes of dark brown suede boots came into view.

"You've picked a nice sunny spot, Mrs Valentine."

She glanced up. Bryce held an enormous iced coffee topped with a snowdrift of whipped cream, a long, green plastic spoon sticking out. "How nice to see you, Sergeant."

Bryce put coffee and spoon on the table, a handspan away from hers, leaned down and kissed her cheek. "You too. Happy Christmas."

Mae smiled softly. "You seem out of breath."

He tugged the paper covering from a straw, inserted it into his drink, and began patting the outside pocket of a field jacket a green darker than his eyes. "It's the altitude. It's nearly two and a half thousand metres here."

"How was your Christmas?"

"Santa Fe is pretty this time of year. Nari loved it." Bryce had a seat and gave Mae a smile. "Here's your post. Your tenant Stephens collected it for you." He lay a small stack of rubber band-bound paper on the table.

"Thank you for bringing it all this way, but I doubt it's anything important." Mae pulled off the band to sift through bills and a couple of postcards—advertisements from the UK Egg Council. The first, two fried eggs holding hands, told her to *Have a cracking breakfast*! Postmarked Helsinki, Finland. She turned it over. On the back, beside the address label and printing declaring the health benefits of eggs, an unfamiliar hand had written *Quando*? The second postcard had a later date stamp and postmark from Santiago, Chile. A grinning cup of coffee and beaming egg in an egg cup suggested she *Beat 'em and join 'em*! It had different handwriting, but the question remained the same: *Quando*?

A twinge of shock gave way to anger. They'd been sent weeks apart and two did not make a pattern, but a pattern is what Kitt had planned. Had he lived, there would have been another postcard, perhaps one with an image of laughing scrambled eggs on toast saying, *Crack Up for Breakfast*. The postmark might have been from Dakar or Kathmandu, another *Quando* written by another hand. It would have made Kitt's intention crystal clear.

Quando, Quando, Quando, the Italian pop song from the early '60s, the damned song Engelbert Humperdinck made her lose a half-dozen Christmas biscuits over. She'd danced with Kitt to that song one evening in Sicily, months ago. Before she'd known he'd spoken flawless Italian, before she realised she loved him, before he'd confessed he'd loved her for years, she'd translated the words. *Quando*, Italian for *when*. Kitt had wanted to know when they might end their very long engagement.

Razor-edged pain slashed at her, but rage sliced sharper, deeper and went on forever. It was her fault, despite everything she knew about him, despite his being a flashing neon warning of eventual sorrow, she'd loved Kitt, but there was no cause to be sentimental, no reason to hold on to a scrap of something that never would be. She looked up. Bryce had been watching her. She smiled faintly and handed the postcards to him. "Kitt was quite fond of scrambled eggs."

"Was he?" Bryce licked a fat glob of whipped cream from the spoon, looked at the cards, front and back, then looked at her again. "Cute," he said, placing the postcards on the table beside her untouched cappuccino.

She'd skipped the typical plastic lid on her coffee and as she looked at grinning egg and smiling cup, an unseasonably warm breeze puffed foam from the cappuccino, dusting the postcard's smiling egg with a milky, cocoa-blemish. She glanced at Bryce, blew the foam away, and the dog lifted his head, tongue licking chops. She looked at the animal's brown eyes. What was she doing here?

"Perhaps," Kitt pulled out a chair and sat beside Bryce, eyebrow arched, "now would be a good time for a holiday. You once mentioned a spa in New Mexico. What was the name?"

Bryce licked more whipped cream.

"*Ojo Caliente.*" Kitt leaned forward, his expression seductive. "That's it. It's not just for distinguished gentlemen, and it's not far from here either. Shall we go there together?"

Mae shifted her gaze to the Jemez Mountains and Caballo peak, the distant, sloping, patch that was bare of trees and the snow it should have had this time of year.

Bryce coughed softly. When she looked at him he gave her a fairly sardonic smile. "Tell me again. Explain it to me."

"You said the word *remains*. You said remains had been recovered in a shipping container and analysis verified those remains were Kitt's. Instead of ruminating on what that meant and facing a Christmas that would have been ours, I thought of myself, or what remained of me. I opened the envelope you gave me, the one with his things inside, and I put on his watch." She glanced down at her wrist, at the beaten-up Citizen timepiece that had belonged to Kitt, the sturdy leather band darkened by sweat. The crystal had a crack that marred the face and distorted the number 10. "A watch has one purpose. It tells time. Despite what had happened to this watch, how it cracked, it continued to do its job. It continues to do its job. When I realised that, I understood I needed to do what I had always done. I had to work. I had to be productive. I *needed* to be productive. Productive is my way through grief." Mae rubbed the dog's soft ears as he rose and dropped his head into her lap.

"I said it before. Kitt wouldn't like it." Bryce exhaled. "I don't like it." His eyes narrowed as he glanced at the postcards, and then at her. "Yet here I am."

"Thank you for stopping in town to visit on your trip to Disneyland," she said.

"It's on the way." He sat back in his chair, blob of whipped cream at the edge of his mouth. Global warming wreaked feckin' havoc with the seasons. London had been unseasonably cold in October while Los Alamos was positively balmy in late December. The winter sun shone robustly, heating the brick wall behind them, warming their bodies, and accentuating the colour of Bryce's eyes.

Bryce had the greenest eyes she had ever come across. With sooty lashes, black hair sprinkled with bits of silver, and those green eyes, he was one of the most handsome men she had ever known—although the cleft in his chin gave his looks a cartoon superhero quality. When the Welshman turned serious, as he just had, Mae pictured him wearing blue spandex and a red cape. She looked back at the shabby, but expensive timepiece. "Perhaps this watch ought to go to Kitt's next of kin," she said softly.

He licked away the cream blob. "Even if he's dead, information about Kitt is still classified, but I can tell you, you were listed as his next of kin. It usually takes a few months to clear, but you'll hear from the solicitor with instructions on how to dispose of his estate."

Air popped from her lips and Mae shook her head. It was a little late for instructions. "I've disposed of some of it already."

Bryce exhaled unhappily and laid his big hand over hers. "He asked me to look after you. He loved you, you know."

"I know." The dog moved to stretch out on sun-warmed concrete and Mae's gaze wandered to the left, to the west, to the highest still-snowless peak of the Jemez. "Five months ago, I spent a lovely two weeks in the Sandia Mountains of New Mexico with you looking after me because Kitt asked you to."

"You know my duty didn't end when that business was over, Mrs Valentine."

"Your duty?" She returned her attention back to Bryce.

"Yes." Bryce took his hand away and smiled. It made him look Supermanly.

"I thought we were friends."

"We are friends, you and I," he picked up the spoon again, "but Kitt and I served together. He was my commanding officer. I had orders. They still stand."

"Orders. All that time you and I spent together we never talked much about your wife. What does Nari think about your orders and your duty, Sergeant?"

"My wife is a Lieutenant Colonel in the Italian Army, senior staff to the Italian Military Representative on the NATO Military Committee. She understands duty." Bryce rubbed his holey chin for a moment and sighed. Then he dug out a fluff of cream and sucked it from the long-handled green plastic spoon. "I'll check in with you again on my way back from Disneyland, and wish you'd call me Timothy, Mae," he said.

She picked up a postcard to stare at the *Quando*, running a fingertip over a silly Italian word that connected back to a man she loved, waiting for something, for anything other than anger to register. Things might have been different if she had simply said *yes* instead of agreeing to a *very long engagement*. Maybe *yes* would have changed the outcome. Maybe then and there Kitt would have changed his mind about one last assignment, maybe moved into a different area of operation, or maybe quit the job that was his for life, the goddamn job that had taken his life. *Maybe, maybe, maybe.* Kitt was dead. There was no point in *maybe* anything—except that maybe she'd gone a little insane.

Her eyes went to the dog. As instructed, he'd been microchipped this morning, but what was she really doing here? What lunacy had compelled her to agree to do a favour for a man who had once accused her of crimes? She looked at Bryce and his Superman jaw. He said her name again, her brain registered that his lips moved, and for a few seconds, she saw him the day he'd come to Kitt's flat and told her he was dead. That day, she'd clung to unlaundered clothes that held the scent of a man she'd been eejit enough to love. Hours later, when Bryce had returned with a crew of men to inspect the flat for sensitive material and dispose of some of Kitt's things, she clung still to unwashed garments that smelled of the man she'd loved, sinking, going down, about to drown in immeasurable grief.

That day, with Bryce and his fecking gobshite team, was the instant she saw how to save herself. That day, envelope of Kitt's belongings in his hands, green-eyed Bryce looked at her with a moment of his own grief and distress before his expression shifted to the same practised, calm, detached expression Kitt had often worn. That day, Bryce had never been a superhero, but a flotsam reminder, a buoyant fragment of something she could seize to try to rescue what was left of her own life.

And today Bryce was the man who was trying to be her friend. She lifted her cup and had a sip of coffee. The foam tasted sour and her expression turned sour.

Bryce had put down his spoon to gaze at her earnestly. "I know you're angry, Mae."

"Angry? No, I'm not angry. I'm *livid*. With him. With myself. And I see him. Everywhere. Clear as day. The barista in the café was Kitt. The postman across the street is Kitt. Taittinger shuffling into the kitchen this morning was Kitt. It's not uncommon. The same thing happened for a year or so after Caspar died. Every man turned into Caspar."

"In other words, it's grief."

"Yes." She shoved the smiling egg and coffee cup postcards aside and raised her burning eyes to Bryce, exhaling a half laugh. "I don't need you to save me from this, Timothy."

"You're doing that all on your own. And I don't like it." Bryce huffed, had another mouthful of whipped cream, and got back to business. "What's it been like here?"

"I wrote you all about Taittinger in your Christmas card."

"I'm making conversation." Bryce mined a bit of fluffy whipped cream and spooned it into his mouth. White flecked his top lip.

Mae chuckled softly. "I've spent two months minding a dog and planning family Christmas and a New Year's Eve party. My employer drinks a lot of wine, talks about wine, art, and car restorations, but says next to nothing about his work at the Lab in Los Alamos.

"Did you ask him about his experiment on dark matter simulations to constrain the low mass end of the mass function of dark halos?"

"You read the article about him in *Wine Enthusiast*."

"How do you think I knew about 'dark matter simulations to constrain the low mass end of the mass function of dark halos'? Does he really collect bottles?"

"For his mother. When he drinks a bottle of wine, he sets it aside for the sculptures his mother makes. You know Evelyn Taittinger is an artist. She flew back to Florida with three crates of empties this morning and left two in the studio on the estate, for when she's here in summer. Have you ever seen her work?"

"Yesterday, at a gallery in Santa Fe. She makes dragons, lizards, birds, small animals out of broken wine bottles. It's sharp."

"Very funny."

"You've settled in, then?"

Mae slid a hand around her coffee cup. She studied Bryce for a moment. "You know, Taittinger has a friend who helps him restore cars. He's a landscaper and mechanic. You look a bit like Hector, only twenty years younger and without the long hair and Native American ancestry."

Bryce chuckled and tipped his chin at Felix. "The dog appears to be well-behaved." He spooned more whipped cream.

"Yes, now Felix can sit, stay, and drop, although I have a bit of an issue with breaking one unwanted behaviour."

"Which is?"

"He likes to hump men. I wonder if Llewelyn knew about the humping when he asked me to do him a favour." She gave a little cough, sipped her coffee. "It's been two months of dog training, and party planning, and rodent disposal."

"Infestation?"

"Vindictive ex-girlfriend sent a dead rat for Christmas."

"A dead rat?"

"M-hm. It was freeze-dried."

Bryce chuckled.

Mae did not. She drummed fingers on the table. "Have you ever seen the Cary Grant Hitchcock film, the one with Ingrid Bergman, about the wine cellar and uranium sand?"

"You watch a lot of films, Mae?"

"I have lately and it's disappointing. There's no uranium sand anywhere, not in Taittinger's wine cellar, not even in the barn where he's restoring another sports car. One sort of expects espionage at the Los Alamos Lab, nuclear secrets being sold to North Korea, uranium sand, and such, not dog minding, an art-collecting oenophile, and private wine auctions."

"Private auctions are similar to home poker games; money

changes hands with no taxable income recorded and no money trail to follow. Do you like your new position, Mae?"

Her lips pursed. No butler worth their salt talked about their employer this way. It grated. She did it anyway. "I admire Taittinger's social conscience. He donates a good deal of money to charities dealing with refugees—his New Year's Eve party is a charity event for refugees—but he likes his Xanax and marijuana, and I hate how it smells." Mae cracked a smile. "Aside from that, the routine has been good for me. The work has helped me manage the...loss. That's what this is, Timothy, loss management." She sighed and watched a tall man waiting for traffic to pass on the other side of the street. When it was clear, he crossed, heading for post office. For a few beats of her heart she saw blue-grey eyes that were sometimes cold and hard, a cruel mouth that could blossom into a summer smile, short, dark blond hair the sun turned gingery. Her fingers strayed beneath the pink Hermès scarf Taittinger had given her for Christmas, to the chain where Kitt's ring hung alongside her reading glasses. She slipped the diamond on and off the tip of her finger.

"When you see Kitt, does he talk to you?" Bryce said softly. "Or do you talk to him?"

"I'm not delusional."

Bryce smiled. "Well, I don't know. That man you're watching looks nothing like Kitt."

CHAPTER THREE

Three hours before sunrise on New Year's Eve, tucked beneath a shelter of blankets, Mae woke on the sofa, the dog snuggled into the back of her knees. She got up and stretched her arms overhead. Felix hopped off the couch, stretched his long legs forward and yawned. Mae put on water for coffee and organised breakfast for Felix, and scooped coffee into a filter. She watched the dark brew drip into the glass carafe. The routine of arranging coffee and breakfast hadn't altered since Kitt's death, except instead of scrambling eggs for a man, she prepared kibble for a dog.

Felix ate, she reached for the carafe of coffee, poured some into a mug. She'd made enough for two.

"*Coffee*, thank Christ. I drove all night to come home to your coffee." Kitt sat on the edge of the kitchen worktop, swinging bare feet, a bandage covering an injury just below his right clavicle.

Mae stared at the bandage and gulped too-hot Tanzanian Mondul. The coffee burned all the way down.

"You've lit the very corner of my dark soul and I've moved into yours. I'm nothing like you wanted and everything you needed and loved."

She coughed, went to the sink, and guzzled a handful of cold water.

"What *are* you doing, Mrs Valentine?"

More water. Yes, what was she doing watching Taittinger, looking after his dog, disposing of dead rats, organising wine tastings, family Christmas gatherings and New Year's Eve parties?

Kitt wore a wry grin. "You know the heart of intelligence consists of gathering information. Most intelligence work is not exciting or even necessarily life-threatening. It's mostly drinking, networking, socialising, more drinking, managing to stay upright with all that alcohol, and paperwork. There's an incredible amount of paperwork. Paperwork needs to be done to ensure that everything was properly cleared and authorised. All that information gathered leads to paperwork. I hate paperwork. Who's doing your paperwork, Mae?"

Mae watched Kitt's feet swing, followed the motion of his legs, the rippling of muscle along his bared thighs, to the black terry-towelling dressing gown tied at the waist and open at the chest. She snorted. The wound he'd sustained last August, when he'd found Mafiosa Godmother Vivi Gallia, had been on the left side, not the right.

Kitt's mouth quirked. "I'm a mirror image, Mrs Valentine."

She set the coffee carafe on the cooktop. She'd loved one dead man for sixteen years and she'd go on with the rest of her life loving another dead man. Tongue scalded, she snorted again in irritation, and spent the next forty-five minutes running on the treadmill in the corner until her throat was raw, she was soaked with sweat, and the feet-swinging, smirking apparition disappeared.

Morning progressed in preparation for the evening's party. She moved from one task to another until it was time to exercise Felix.

She took him outside. A front the previous evening had finally brought snow. Seven or eight centimetres had accumulated, sticking to piñon and ponderosa pine boughs, covering the front walkway, the driveway, the garden that turned rocky and dropped away to a canyon. Felix sniffed the white stuff cautiously. Suddenly, he took off like a shot, biting at the snow, spinning, bounding through drifts, his winter jacket a blur of blue against white. He leapt over the low wall along the driveway and shot left, zigzagged, biting at the snow-covered ground half a metre from Mae's feet. He gave a bark, turned tail and took off, all four legs off the ground at once. He disappeared into a ridge of snow-laden trees, reappearing and vanishing again, only to appear again at the top of the driveway. In a flash, he was off toward the barn, streaking toward Evelyn Taittinger's art studio.

Jaysus, he was fast and she'd forgotten his yellow ball. She knew better than to give chase; it would only turn things into a game, make Felix run faster and farther away. She sat on the cold ground. Snowflakes fell on her face, soft as the brush of Kitt's mouth on her cheek.

Snow. Kitt said it had been snowing in Switzerland the morning he came home with a Christmas tree. Did he like snow? She'd never asked him. He'd liked vintage china patterns, scrambled eggs and coffee and bourbon and kissing the centre of her palm and her honesty and... Damn him.

God damn him.

He was a bleedin' spy, heartache hovered above him, and she loved him anyway. How was it a surprise that his profession had taken his life when she'd known it would all along? She should have had the good sense to walk away from him before all the heartache came crashing down. Instead, she'd ignored intelligent thinking, ignored his certain fate, ignored the impending catastrophe of a man with a condensed lifespan for love. *Eejit. Fool.*

Kitt stood in ankle-deep snow, in front of a gas cooker, spatula in his hand. "You want me...to cook breakfast?"

The look on his face, the words he said, they were the same as when she'd confessed that she loved him. That morning had been the only time she'd ever seen him flustered, and that moment's tousle of his confidence had only made her love him more. *Eejit. Fool.*

"You'd prefer to go on as we are," he said softly.

Eejit. Fool. Love was undeniable. Leaving him would never have lessened how much she loved him any more than his dying did. Plainly, she excelled at two things in life: being professional and loving dead men, and as she lay there in the snow, flurries drifting down into her face, she raged at the two men she had loved. One more secretive than the other. Both just as dead.

Felix licked her ear, nosed into her neck, tickling. She took hold of him and cuddled him close. "Good boy, good little man," she murmured. Then she slid on his collar and lead and rose. She wiped cold snow from her arse and furious hot tears from her cheeks. She'd fry her own damn eggs for the rest of her life and not cry about it.

Focus on work. Be professional. Professional, productive, that was the way through this, it was how she'd survived after Caspar. She'd done it before and—God damn Kitt—she'd bloody well do it again.

Her mobile *buzz-buzzed* in her pocket. A message from the landscape gardener; Hector Rodriguez was coming to plough the snow. Rage a vexing rash, she stuffed the dog's yellow ball into her coat pocket and put Felix indoors. Then she went to the barn, keyed in the code to unlock the side entrance. She slammed a hand against the control for the garage-like door. Metal rolled upward and she stood shaking amid the bags of potting mix, ride-on tractor, and cloth-covered, half-restored British sports car. A burst of sunlight streamed in through the windows, security bars across the glass painting lines down the fabric draped over the convertible and the large wooden crates Hector had dropped off yesterday.

Heated by solar panels on the roof, the barn's warmth accentuated the smell of old car, garden soil, and the black rubber mat beneath her feet, the stink of it fuel for her fury. Mae stomped toward the potting mix, gave the bags a swift kick, then another and another, swearing, kicking and swearing in a full-blown tantrum until she was gasping for air the mountain altitude made thin.

"Breathe, Mae," Kitt said.

Mae took a breath of earthy, grease-tinged air, blew it out slowly, and inhaled again.

"Yes," Kitt said, "just like that. Breathe."

Heart slowing, breathing, in and out, Mae heard the sound of Hector's pickup truck rumbling outside. She moved to the open door, collecting herself.

Handsome, fifteen years older than Bryce, Hector waved a rosy brown hand and hopped out of his big Dodge. With him again was Coyote. "Hiya, Ms Valentine," Hector said, smiling. "About time we had snow."

"Hello, Mr, Hector, Mr Coyote," she said, hoped her glued-on smile wasn't maniacal.

Stocky Coyote, the Central American cousin of a cousin, spoke little English. He nodded a greeting, flashed a toothy grin, and went off to shovel the front walk.

"I'll be quick with the tractor." Hector said. "Tell Jools when he's done with those crates, Coyote'll take the wood and chip it." He turned, hesitated and swung around. "You know, I'm giving the Sunrise Lecture at the Fuller Lodge the day after tomorrow. It's called 'Drunken Rabbits and Oenology.' I invited Jools and his friends. Hope you can come too."

The plastered-on smile began to ache. "Thank you. I'll be

driving guests into town. Hearing you will be nicer than waiting with the car. Stay warm."

Long, salt and pepper plait swinging between his shoulder blades, Hector attached the snow-throwing implement to the tractor, hopped on, and powered up the engine. She watched the man clear the long driveway, piling up small mountains of snow along the pavement, and cursed Kitt's name, the noise of the tractor's motor drowning out her swearing in between all the breathing.

When she returned to the house, she began preparing the afternoon's lunch. Soon, five guests would arrive for a pre-party wine tasting. They would stay on after the New Year's Eve party too, for more wine tasting and skiing or snowboarding the slopes above Los Alamos. With lunch ready to go in the oven, nibbles organised, and guest rooms in order, she readied bottles of Beauséjour Duffau Saint-Emilion, Sine Qua Non Midnight Oil Syrah and Araujo Estate Eisele Vineyard Cabernet Sauvignon for the tasting in the great room, arranging a table in front of the spectacular backdrop, the sky outside heavy with blue-grey clouds the colour of Kitt's eyes.

The mobile in her pocket *buzz-buzzed*, indicating her new employer had returned. She went to the garage at the opposite end of the house. Despite its heated floor and vaulted ceiling, the garage didn't quite match the lavishly villainous scale of the rest of the home. Four British convertibles from the '50s and '60s—cars he'd restored—sat in the garage, but Taittinger's taste for what he drove every day was more practical. His bright green Jeep Cherokee, spattered and caked with reddish ice, pulled into the space beside the two-toned Austin Healy and the beige Volvo SUV Mae drove.

Cold air wafted in. Ruddy water dripped on tidy grey concrete as Taittinger jumped from the Jeep, stretching his arms overhead, shirt-tails un-tucked from his jeans. The man's neck gave an audible crack when he rolled his head and lifted his chin to the ceiling. His sandy brown hair stuck up on his head the way Kitt's had when he'd climbed from bed in the morning.

Bleedin' feck, did *everything* have to be a reminder of Kitt? Mae moved to close the garage door and shut out the wind that had turned frigid.

"Hey, Valentine. Better leave it open." Taittinger's neck cracked. "Ruby's right behind me."

A champagne-coloured Cadillac slid in front of the open garage door. Engine running, the driver, a fair-skinned middle-aged man got out and opened the rear passenger door.

Red-soled Louboutins flashed. Ruby Bleuville, a Fine Art and Collectables Specialist at Smythe & Dexter Art and Auctions in Santa Fe, took the chauffeur's hand and climbed out. Long, strawberry hair drawn back with clips accentuated eyeliner that gave large, pale green eyes a doll-like appearance. Petite, all sleek-bodied in a pink Givenchy floral print with long sleeves, she stood a foot below Taittinger and was ten years younger. She was exactly Kitt's type.

"Criminy, am I the first?" the Texan woman drawled, adjusting the coat over her arm.

"You are." Taittinger went to her, paused and, somewhat shyly, kissed her cheek.

"I'm starvin' and," she put a hand on his arm, "it's dad-burn freezin' out there. Mind if I cuddle up alongside you for a sec?"

Taittinger's face took on a school-boyish flush.

Mae swallowed her amusement.

The driver had taken luggage from the boot and set it beside Taittinger's Jeep. Ruby glanced at him. "I'll let you know when I need you again, Wally."

"I'll be at the Hampton Inn, ma'am." The English-accented chauffeur smiled amiably and nodded, silver-shot brown hair flopping over his forehead the way Hugh Grant's used to. He got back in the Cadillac and pulled away. Mae shut the garage door.

"Howdy. It's Valentine, right?" Ruby said above the humming automatic door.

"Yes. Good afternoon, Miss Bleuville. May I show you to your room?"

"You can just take my bag, honey." The woman smiled dazzlingly.

Taittinger took off his round, tortoiseshell glasses and cleaned the lenses with the bottom of his shirt. Perhaps they'd fogged up.

Ruby handed her coat to Mae. "Oh, Jools, that blue car," she pointed, "is *adorable*. Will you take me for a ride in it with the top down?"

Taittinger set his glasses on. "That's a Morgan Plus 4," he looked at the blue car, "that's an MG-A, the green one is an Austin Healy Sprite, and we don't drive these in this weather. Any time you want a ride when it's clear, you let me know."

"Aw, thank you, sugar." Ruby slipped her arm through his.

Taittinger's ears turned rosy. "Have any of the others arrived, Valentine?"

"Not yet. I expect within the half hour, Dr Jools." Mae glanced at Kitt's watch and lifted the bags from beside the Jeep.

Laying a hand over Ruby's, Taittinger began to hum. "*Hm-mm you be mine, tell me quando hmm-hmm quando...*"

With a grimace, Mae jerked up the handle on a wheeled red case, steeling herself for more of the doctor singing that song. Her shoulder began to bunch until a ringing mobile cut the performance and she thanked God and the baby Jesus for the small mercy.

Taittinger answered the call and began to lead Ruby away, chatting, "Hey, Baz... Yeah, I know the cell coverage is spotty in places...

Uh-huh, that's right... You're nearly here. Past the elk sign, turn right, and then up the hill. Keep going 'til you run out of road. Valentine will meet you out front. It'll take about four minutes from where you are."

Mae ferried Miss Bleuville's things to a guest room, then pulled a coat from a rack beside the front door, slipped it on, and met the black Mercedes Maybach halting in the driveway.

Turkish Ari Basil, the Basil in Basil & Vallance, the London upscale grocery store chain, had flown in to Los Alamos on a private jet from Toronto with his man. Dark-haired, mid-thirties like Taittinger, his man swivelled out of the luxury car, shoes a highly-polished black. Overcoat flapping in the breeze, he gave Mae a nod and opened the rear passenger door. A man, sixtyish, exited from the rear of the Mercedes.

"Good afternoon," she said.

Expensively dressed, tall and quiet-spoken, Basil sounded like the actor Omar Sharif. "Good afternoon to you, Valentine, how lovely to meet you." He looked over to his butler. "This is Mr Grant."

Tall, the end of his long nose red-tipped, Grant nodded politely. He removed a Louis Vuitton suitcase from the boot, his black pony-tail fluttering in the breeze when he pulled out a leather valise and handed it to Basil.

Mae led the men inside. Taittinger's easy listening music played throughout the house, soft and ambient, Vince Monroe aptly crooning *Let It Snow*.

Mr Basil came to a dead halt. "Breathtaking," he said, admiring a seventeenth-century sundial, rather than the view from the rear of the house. Upstairs, he gave an approving nod to the understated furnishings of his black and white room and sat on the edge of the king-sized bed. He glanced around the room and up at the ceiling. "This is splendid, but how do I turn off the music?"

"Just here, Mr Basil." Mae poked a finger at the touchpad that controlled the lights, the window shades, and music.

"Thank you. Tell me, where would I find the sunbeam?"

"The sunbeam?"

"The little car Jools is restoring, the Sunbeam Alpine."

"Oh, yes. That one is in the barn. Would you like me to show you?"

"No, no. I'll wait for Jools. Thank you." He smiled politely. "And where will Grant be tonight?"

"Mr Grant is in staff quarters. I hope that suits you, Mr Basil."

"Thank you, Valentine. I'm sure Grant will be happy wherever you have him." Basil glanced at his man and frowned.

"Dr Taittinger would be happy to have you join the party this evening, Mr Grant."

"That is very kind of him, Valentine." Grant, an American, placed the suitcase on a low rack and wiped his nose.

Basil glanced at his man again. "I don't wish to keep you from having a little holiday fun tonight, but you look terrible, Grant. I think you need something to tame that beastly cold. Valentine, is there a pharmacy nearby, where Grant can go to fetch something medicinal for himself?"

"There's a pharmacy in the supermarket in White Rock," she said.

"Thank you, sir." With a slight smile, Grant set to work unpacking and arranging his employer's things. "Before I go, sir, the Prada or the Zegna for tonight?"

"Zegna. And the blue shirt," Basil said, looking at exquisite mandala hanging on the wall.

Grant sneezed convulsively.

"Goodness, Grant. Valentine, please see to Grant. Go settle in, man, and get something for that nose."

"Thank you, sir."

Mae ushered the sick man through the house, the kitchen and to the staff quarters where Felix greeted them, pawing at Mae, sniffing the butler's shiny shoes. Within half a second, front paws latched around Grant's leg, and the humping commenced.

Messenger bag across his chest, small suitcase in one hand, and Mr Basil's suit over an arm, Grant shook the dog free. Felix scurried in a circle around an overstuffed chair and sat.

"This is Felix, Dr Taittinger's dog. And you did that well."

"I've had employers with dogs before." Grant sneezed, then took in the sitting room, kitchen, and folded bed linen Mae had left on the broad back of the sofa. Tired brown eyes filled with a hint of despair. "I'm on the couch?"

"No. You're in the bedroom on the right."

"Who's on the couch?"

"I often fall asleep reading out here," she said. Dog following, she moved into the kitchen and pulled open a drawer. "Here's your key," she said, laying it on the worktop. "Now, once you're settled, you'll want to see to Mr Basil's things. The laundry is just outside the apartment."

He sneezed again. "Sorry. Of course." He put the dinner suit on the little dining table, eyes settling on the ceramic bowl of apples next to the new iPad Bryce had given her. She used it to stay in contact with him, make notes, read books, and keep her journal.

"There's chicken soup in the refrigerator. Do have some."

"That's real nice of you, Valentine," he said, wiping his nose.

"Mae."

"I'm Russell."

"You should be in bed. I'm sorry I don't have anything more useful than aspirin and a slug of Irish whiskey to give you."

"I'll take you up on the whiskey later. Thanks."

"You do look awful."

"I've worked when I've been worse. Bet you have too."

"Not for quite some time. Have you been in service long, Russell?"

"Fifteen years."

"Have you worked for Mr Basil all that time?" She opened the door to the second bedroom.

He sneezed and dumped his bag on the bed. "Three years. Before that I worked for the British High Commissioner to Malaysia." Eyes bleary, he sat on the edge of the mattress. "What about you? Been with Taittinger a while?"

"A few months." Mae pursed her mouth. "Now, give me that dinner suit. You settle in and have a little lie down."

Mae left Grant and pressed Basil's dinner suit. When the next guest arrived, she darted out of the house without a coat and wished she hadn't. The temperature had dropped. The wind had picked up. The glasses on the end of her nose went cold.

A red sedan dulled by crusted ice and dirty snow pulled away, revealing a lean man. Robert Nash was a retired Premier League player, a restaurateur, and Irishman whose good looks were spoiled by a fashion sense from the '80s. Mullet-style blond hair and electric blue parachute jogging bottoms flapped in the wind. He handed over a brown box. "Shall we get out of this wind?" he said, sounding vaguely like her brother. He hoisted on an enormous backpack, grabbed a yellow snowboard, and followed her indoors, pausing to inspect various antiques and artefacts, sniffing disdainfully.

When they'd reached his room, he tossed the snowboard and backpack on the floor at the foot of the bed and took the box from her. Then he yanked his shirt overhead, revealing a pale blue tee stained with chocolate. He tossed the shirt aside, opened the bag, and began pulling out one dirty garment after another until there was a mound of soiled things. He grabbed the pile and tossed it at her. "Don't shrink anything."

The trumpet of a car horn heralded the next arrival. A smallish Ford SUV stood in the driveway, sky-blue body glazed with red soil the state used to neutralise icy roads. This would be the Australian Private Equity Investors, David Case and Ian Somerset, but a lone man in a brown beanie hopped from the SUV. He dragged out an ugly, down-filled parka, and put it on quickly. He tucked a shoebox-sized container under an arm, grabbed a small duffle and garment bag from the rear seat.

Mae stared at him, at the way he moved with easy grace, and the man became Kitt; Kitt lifting the duffle he'd left on the chair by the door. Kitt hoisting a garment bag over his shoulder. "G'day," he said.

Her mouth went dry. She ran her arid tongue over parched lips, took a breath, blew it out softly. "Good afternoon. Mr Somerset or Mr Case?"

"David Case. Ian's plane was delayed." Late forties or early fifties, and handsome in all the ways Kitt was not, the Australian stood six feet, maybe more. He had crow's feet around eyes that were bright blue-green. Ginger hair poked from the edge of his beanie. "Valentine, I assume?" He cocked his head, a darker ginger eyebrow arched.

The gesture, the expectant expression, was so like Kitt and Mae swallowed. "Yes. Dr Taittinger would like you to join him and the others in the great room, after you settle in, or before if you like. May I take your things to your room?"

"You can take me to my room. I'll keep the bag and box, you can have the suit." He held out the garment bag.

With a nod, she took his suit, led him into the house, and pushed her fogged-up glasses down her nose. Mr Case trailed behind. When they reached his room, he tossed his duffle on the king-sized bed. It left a rusty smear on the cream coverlet, one she'd have to soak out. She hung his garment bag in the walk-in wardrobe, returned to the bedroom and demonstrated the room's touchpad controls. "May I assist you with anything further?"

"Ari Basil here yet?" He pulled a black and red paper ring from a cigar he'd already clipped.

"Mr Basil arrived a short time ago, with his assistant. I believe Dr Jools is showing him, Ms Bleuville, and Mr Nash the sports car he's restoring. It's a Sunbeam. Would you like to see it?"

"Nah." The flame of a gold DuPont lighter flared near the end of the Arturo Fuente between his teeth.

"I beg your pardon, Mr Case. Dr Jools asks that smoking is confined to outdoors. May I take you to the patio where you can enjoy your cigar?"

MAE COVERED Taittinger's four bottles with a tea towel and placed a box over the top of the towel. Sunlight spilled into the great room and shone upon the sculpture made by Taittinger's mother. A green glass lizard, the size of a ten-year-old boy, glittered and refracted sunlight, dappling the bottles of wine for the afternoon tasting. Glasses and the wines, all a 2001 vintage, sat alongside bread and crackers on the table. Spittoons had been placed in discreet locations around the great room. By the time guests began to filter out of the cellar, she'd uncorked the Sine Qua Non Midnight Oil Syrah and filled glasses on a tray. She offered the tray to Mr Nash.

Wine in hand, Nash shuffled around the dragon, sniffing wine, ragged hem of his purple trousers scuffing the floor. "That's quite a cellar, Jools."

"Took six months to tunnel in, three months to fit it out, and nine years to build my collection. I'm happy with it." Taittinger beamed.

Felix wove his way around the furniture and glass dragon, sniffing everything and everyone. David Case nodded, taking a glass, avoiding the dog. "You should be. Ian will be impressed—if he ever gets here."

"Let's hope that's soon." Taittinger nodded and clicked fingers together, in time with Harry Connick Jr singing something old and up-tempo. "If you're interested, Hector can tell you more about designing the cellar at his *Drunken Rabbits and Oenology* lecture, day after tomorrow. You're all invited and he'd love you to come. But firs—"

Case pushed the small dog away from his legs. "Hector?"

"My old friend. He's a landscaper with the most developed palate you'll ever come across. He's starting up a small, private winery, and his Côt Noir is astonishing."

Well, that was an interesting bit of news. Mae handed Taittinger a glass and Connick stopped crooning. Wine swirling, her employer spread out his hands, Gene Krupa's hammering beats of the swing classic *Sing Sing Sing* a stage introduction to his excitement. "Who wants to find out what fucking incredible tastes like?"

"Jools, sugar," Ruby grasped his arm and smiled up at him, "would you mind turnin' that music down a little?"

"Yes, please turn it down." Basil had a seat on a leather ottoman, lifting his wineglass away from the dog. "I was wondering if I could see the Sunbeam again?"

His perfect moment of music and staging gone, Taittinger's shoulders slumped slightly. He took a mobile from his pocket, lowered the music's volume. "Later, Baz."

"Sunbeam?" Case swirled garnet liquid in his glass. "Is that the winery your landscaper's starting?"

"No, no." Taittinger chuckled. "The winery is *Drunken Rabbits*; the Sunbeam is an old sports car."

"What's for lunch, Jools?" Nash shoved his nose in the top of his glass.

Taittinger rubbed his goatee and glanced at Mae. "Sand-crab lasagne, Dr Jools," she said.

"You know I'm vegetarian, Jools. Vegetarian means no seafood or chicken."

"Mr Nash," Mae handed Ruby a new wine to taste, "I've a *pasta alla Norma* for you. That's aubergine with tomato and pasta."

"You know, Bob," Taittinger shook a finger, "catering for you sure cost me a *pretty penne*."

Germy Mr Grant blew his nose with a honk.

Case shot a look at the sick butler. "Ian will love to see the cars you've restored, especially a Sunbeam."

"Boys and old cars you fix up and never drive." Ruby tore a chunk of bread in two. "My, you are pretty, but," she pushed the curious dog, "this is my bread."

Taittinger patted his thigh. "Sorry for the *inter-ruff-tion*. Everybody, this is Felix." The animal ignored the man and roamed about, smelling every new smell in the room.

Basil rose, expectorated wine in the spittoon, casting a wary eye over the slim animal attempting to mount his knee. "Is he a Whippet?" He pushed the dog away, unamused.

"Felix, off," Mae said softly. The dog moved on to sniff Mr Case.

"Italian Greyhound." Taittinger grabbed a water cracker from the table. "He's a rescue. Can you believe someone abandoned him? Italian Greyhounds were once the favourite companion of noblewomen in the Middle Ages." He looked around at his guests. "Hope no one's allergic to dogs," he said as Grant sneezed.

Case took the glass Mae offered, nodding politely. "Is this a 2001?"

"It is." Basil chose a plain cracker. "Grant's a sommelier. He can tell us about this vintage. Grant, if you would."

Grant blew his nose, tucked the handkerchief into a pocket, lips tipping into a weak, polite smile. "Thank you, sir." Clothed in the traditional white shirt, tie, tailored black jacket, and grey waistcoat, the uniform worn by many butlers, he stepped from the side of the great room, where he'd taken an unobtrusive position. "Autumn weather transformed a dismal growing season into an exceptional vintage. This Syrah Valentine has ope—"

"Hey," Ruby said. "I think all of us here are experienced enough to know vintage characteristics." She gave the butler a smile. "No one here wants whatever it is you've got. No offence, honey."

"None taken, ma'am," Grant returned to the edge of the room, swabbed his nose, and avoided the pooch interested in sniffing his soiled handkerchief.

Taittinger glanced at Mae before holding out the cracker. "Felix, come."

The dog trotted over and sat beside the Taittinger, eyes on the cracker, licking chops, waiting. *"Bone appetit!"* the man said. Cracker barely down his throat, Felix wrapped white-tipped paws around Taittinger's leg.

"Down! Off!" The man pushed at the dog, driving him into Mr Nash and the box beside him. "Sorry. You can see he's still learn-ing." Taittinger gave a sheepish grin. "Still working on the training and stuff."

Nash snorted. "You need to get that animal neutered."

Ruby leaned over and examined the dog's hind end. "He is neutered."

In an instant, the discussion turned to neutering, gelding, castrati opera singers, and meandered to one about phalluses, Venus figures, and *Vinalia*, Roman festivals of wine. Felix grew bored and flopped down on a warm, sunlit patch of Persian rug.

Mae went on listening and watching, filling glasses with Chateau Peby Faugeres, Saint-Emilion Grand Cru. The hour slid into the usual friendly chit-chat, tasting, nibbling on finger-food. Another bottle was uncorked for tasting, then another, and another.

Mae went about usual business, alert to guests. Sober turned to tipsy and Taittinger got down to the business at hand. "Now that we've tried a few of the bottles I'm serving tonight, how about we get to seeing what's up for tomorrow and then move on to lunch?" He placed his glass on the table. "Didn't know 'til half an hour ago, but Milt Foley's decided to come tonight with—are you ready? A 1996 Krug Clos d'Ambonna. Looks like Milt wanted to get in ahead of the Chungs. In the meantime, as always, Ruby's representing a buyer."

"Ya'll." Ruby reached for a velvet bag she'd set at the side of the sofa, "My client has this here Jacques Selosse Grand Cru Blanc de Blancs Brut 1990." She moved to the table, and unzipped the bag, pulling out a white, blue, and yellow-labelled bottle from a padded interior. "Now, I've only got one with me, not exciting I know, but this is luscious, salty caramel, stone-fruit, umami and, heck, even a little pixie dust. There are six bottles in total and I can have 'em here tomorrow." She set the bottle on the table. "Basil?"

"Thank you, Ruby." Basil gave a nod to Grant. Bleary-eyed, the man found his employer's leather case and placed the bottle inside it on the table. "Very good, Grant. Now, have a seat before you fall down." Basil waved his butler away.

Grant found a chair. The guests gathered about Basil's dark green magnum bottle, its label age-speckled brown. "A 1947 Château Lafleur. I have seven others, eight in total. And this is all so exciting," Basil said.

Taittinger began to hum along with Peggy Lee and *Fever*.

Case got to his feet, wooden box in hand. He opened his hinged box, removed a layer of moulded rubber padding, and lifted out a hand-blown, dark green bottle. The top was secured with a thick, black wax seal, the label handwritten and brown with age. The level of the contents sat just below the curve of the bottle's neck. "Kids, I've got a Bordeaux, from American history's greatest wine connoisseur: Thomas Jefferson."

A hush fell over the group.

CHAPTER FOUR

Mae knew wines were expensive because they could be, but value was subjective and the afternoon was less about tasting wine than it was about *owning* wine. Owning a rare bottle had prestige. Ensconced beside the table, she watched covetous guests gather around the old bottle Case put on the table. Taittinger rubbed the lenses of his glasses on the bottom of his tee, swallowing as if salivating. Ruby gnawed a thumbnail. Basil wore an amused smile. Nash scowled at Case.

"Ho-lee shit." Taittinger raised a sceptical eyebrow, moved forward to examine the bottle, and slid his spectacles back up his nose "You're the guys with the 1787 Jefferson Lafite, the *actual* Jefferson Lafite."

"We tried to keep it quiet, but you've heard rumbles, and it's verified by Jefferson scholars." Case nodded. "The label, the capsule, and the wax all match records and letters written by Thomas Jefferson held in the collection at Monticello. *This* bottle came from a property restoration outside Simeon, Virginia. That's a few miles from Monticello. The estate scholars can provide further provenance if you want it. Why don't you show us what you've got, Jools?"

After chewing his lip for a moment, Taittinger moved. He lifted the box Mae had placed over his bottles earlier. "Let me introduce you to four legendary beauties." He said and with a flourish, he whisked away the tea-towel to reveal a 1982 Château Lafite Rothschild, a 1961 Jaboulet Hermitage La Chapelle, a 1964 LaTâche, and a 1964 Romanée-Conti.

The Irishman cleared his throat. "Impressive, Jools. That '61 Jaboulet Hermitage is, no other words for it, fucking delightful, but this, this is *beatific*." Nash opened his padded case. Set inside a cushion of moulded blue foam were two bottles. With the utmost of care, Nash drew one bottle forth, turning the 1945 Mouton Rothschild.

Taittinger shifted his glasses and shrugged. "Okay, you have one," he said, eyes on the un-yellowed label of the bottle.

"No, I have two." Nash pointed to his valise.

Ruby leaned closer to the table to examine the wine, her, "Bless your heart!" sounding more like *fuck you*.

"And like Mr Case, I have ironclad documentation, as I'm sure you have as well, Jools." Nash said, his smile of triumph a very plain *fuck you all*.

Basil clucked his tongue thoughtfully. "Each bottle here is valuable—or has the potential to be. I'm not captivated by your Rothschild, Bob, but Jools, throw in the Sunbeam and I'd be happy to deal."

Case's phone jangled. He spoke quietly into the mobile, moving away from the table.

"Spend all the time you want talking about worth." Taittinger bent forward to run a finger over the dark green Jefferson bottle before peering even closer at Nash's Mouton Rothschild. "I can't wait to uncork this. I can't wait to taste it. The complexity, the richness, the anticipation of what history will be like on my palate. Jesus, what a thrill!"

"As you Americans say, 'money talks and,'" Nash sneered in Case's direction, "bullshit walks.'"

Ruby caught the Irishman's look and rolled her eyes. "Spend all the time you want talkin' 'bout worth and anticipation. Even if I don't smell what you're steppin' in, y'all remember that Koch got ripped off with his Jeffersons." She set aside her empty wine glass.

Taittinger exhaled. "Okay. We have a responsibility as collectors regarding connoisseurship, provenance—particularly with Jefferson bottles, but don't you want to know what it tastes like?"

"Thank you for saying that, Jools." Basil clasped his hands together. "Yes, we have a responsibility. I too have documentation. Grant can fetch it." Basil turned to his man.

The butler had fallen asleep, chin bowed on his chest, handkerchief in hand.

Ruby gave a musical chuckle. "Oh, my, that man is positively *dead*."

"Oh, dear, dear." Basil shook his head, a concerned rumple in his brow.

Taittinger patter his shoulder. "We can examine provenance later, Baz."

"Yes," Nash hissed, eyes on Case returning to the room. "We're damn well going to examine provenance before anything changes hands. The Jefferson is an anomaly, too specific, too problematic. I'm not interested." He had an angry slurp of wine and sloshed it about in his mouth.

"Apologies for the call. Ian's flight's been delayed again. What did I miss?" Case slid into an armchair, glancing about at the others before he grinned at Mae.

For an instant, she saw Kitt, a flicker of his smile, as she had once before, but the Australian redhead looked nothing like him and her attention shot to the hacking, spitting Nash who missed the spittoon, gobbing wine onto the cream part of the rug. "Who shat in this bottle?" he grumbled.

Mae blotted the stain and listened to Nash insult Taittinger's wine choices for the afternoon. Some collected wine for the status, some as an investment, some because they truly loved wine and saw it, like Taittinger, as a piece of history. Nash fell into the first two categories. The tasting had kept her occupied, left her no time to have a wandering mind, or be distracted by anything that might give cause for her to think of Kitt for more than two seconds. She counted on lunch and the rest of the night to be the same. Her life was getting back to a semblance of normal—if normal meant determining if any of those bottles on the table were fake, or if any of the guests were counterfeiters. Mae's money was on Nash, but only because he was an arsehole.

THE CATERER and her black-clad crew moved into the kitchen. The team, six women and three men, were waiters, barmen, and a young kitchen lackey. Everything fell into place. Mae went over the evening's schedule before relinquishing the kitchen to the very capable caterer and her team. Over the course of the night she'd give direction as necessary.

She went to her quarters to dress. Felix jumped upon the couch, scratched at the blankets, turned in a few circles and snuggled down into the bed linens. Mae plugged her phone into the charger on the end table beside the couch and changed into a simple, black taffeta cocktail dress.

A little before seven o'clock, one-hundred and two of Taittinger's closest friends, colleagues, and wine-loving acquaintances began to filter into the house. She watched. People laughed, drank wine, danced, and spilled things as Taittinger's easy listening music played. Like his taste in music, her new employer had an eclectic mix of guests. An indiscreet periodontist disclosed the names of his famous patients with gum disease. A fashion designer boasted about his collection of erotic Japanese art.

Another guest, a collector who would be at tomorrow's private wine auction, had a shining bald head, bushy white beard, a heart-shaped port wine-stain birthmark at his left temple. "Show 'em, how it fits, honey," Milton Foley said to his wife.

Young, ample-bosomed, and golden-haired, Emmy Foley twirled the full skirt of her low cut, red-trimmed, pine-green gown designed by the erotic art collector. Foley *haw-haw-hawed* raucously, his laugh cutting through the music. A skinny actor known for playing weasels watched her spin and nudged Mae, muttering through smiling teeth, "Look, it's a Christmas tree with tits."

Diplomatically, Mae turned her attention to the crowd, moving on to chat with archivists, art collectors, exhibit designers, academics, nuclear physicists, museum curators, and wine enthusiasts. She circumnavigated the room, mixing in the crowd, chit-chatting pleasantly, withstanding a blast of laughter from Foley, an elbow in the back. At the front of Taittinger's collection of tin toys, cap guns, and sheriff badges, she caught the haggard look on Mr Grant's face. He bore Mr Case's heavy arm draped along his shoulders as the twenty-something photographer zeroed in to take pictures.

"You there," the photographer jerked his head at Mae, "come and squish in with these two." Clad in a blue velvet suit, and sporting a handlebar moustache, he grabbed Mae's shoulder and shoved her in between Grant and Case. "Closer. A little closer. A... little *closer...annnnd...Happy New Year!*" he said, angling the camera for a few photos before whirling about abruptly to Taittinger and Miss Bleuville. "Show him the love, sweetheart!"

With a nod, Mr Case excused himself and Grant turned to her. Pale, except for the red tip of his long nose, the butler coughed into a folded handkerchief he'd taken from inside his jacket. His hacking had grown worse since the afternoon. "How are you holding out?" Grant rasped. His traditional white shirt, tie, tailored black jacket, and grey waistcoat accentuated his pallid complexion and blood-shot eyes.

"Much better than you."

With a swallow and grimace, his eyes flicked to Case crossing to the other side of the room. "Yes. I can see you are. Thankfully, Mr Basil has sent me to bed."

"I hope you feel better."

"Thanks, so do I. Happy New Year." He leaned in, kissing her mouth.

Mae gave him little push. "Mr Grant," she glared.

"I'm sorry. That was out of line. I best say good night." With a wavering, sickly smile, he left her and escaped the great room.

Mae wiped her lips, signalled wait staff to move in with drinks and canapés. For an hour, she tended to work, conversations swirled around her. "...it's only the largest private collection of Georgia O'Keeffe paintings..."

"...say that when you worship idols *haw-haw-haw!*"

"...hysterical to stomp out the lanterns at the Farolito Walk on Canyon drive..."

"...the wine the Aztecs drank was made of agave, more like a cider..."

"...and California reds will never match the quality of a Bordeaux..."

An attractive, white-haired woman, the companion of a Lab colleague of Taittinger's, paused to adjust the strap of her shoe. Belle, Bella, Mae couldn't quite recall her name— "What," the woman said, "is this music playing?"

Mae tilted her head, listening. "It's Nancy Sinatra."

"Jools is stuck in the '60s."

"Well," Mae chuckled and glanced about the great room, "he does like antiques."

"And I like that tall drink of water over there, the one with the whole Hugh Jackman Australian thing going on." She waved a finger to the far side of the room, eyes fixed on Mr Case and the back of a slightly taller man wearing a dinner suit and black cowboy hat.

The Aussie wrapped his arms around the cowboy and kissed him firmly.

"Well, shit." Belle or Bella planted a hand on her hip. "So much for my kissing him at midnight." With a laugh, she moved on and Mae watched Mr Case and his fiancé head off into the hallway toward the stairs, hand in hand, Mr Somerset's cowboy hat bobbing.

The photographer snapped photos. Taittinger's lounge music serenaded. Guests chattered about wine, art, auctions, pornography, and how the Saint Denis civil suits had recently settled out of court. Kitt had mentioned that intelligence work was occasionally dull, particularly when it came to observation, but for Mae it was part and parcel to being in service, a necessary skill for housekeepers and butlers to be attuned to the household, to the hostess or host, to guests. It was vital to keep a low profile, to remain in the background until required. Her proficiency at observing was why she'd been offered this position.

Observation was easy. So was record-keeping, particularly since last summer when she'd started keeping a journal to chronicle the bizarre events and nightmares she'd survived. Made up of random thoughts, stream of consciousness, memories, full stories, whatever had come to fill or disturb her mind she'd written, and added even more after Kitt had died. There were occasions, like today, where her entries were more like a diary documenting an event. Accounts of this sort were the boring paperwork Kitt had always loathed, and Mae kept things brief; she would note the concern over the authenticity of a Jefferson Lafite brought by Mr David Case and mention that party guests danced, drank and ate the wine and food provided by their host, Taittinger.

She made a circuit around the room, scanning it, pausing near Mr Nash, his rumpled trousers too tight in the crotch, bunched at the top of dirty brown hiking boots, dinner jacket too short in the sleeve. Squirrel-like, he dug almonds from a bowl on the table, crunching one nut at a time, listening to a chubby African man. "The first South African wine was made in 1659 from French muscatel grapes. Not man—"

"Can I get a photo, guys? The hipster photographer hefted his camera.

Mae shimmied by Mr Nash and the African man smiling for the camera. She squeezed behind the photographer and tried to move out of the way for Hector Rodriguez. She went right. So did he. Then she went left. So did he. Mae turned side on. Hector stepped on her toe.

"Sorry, Ms Valentine." He tucked flowing, silver-and-black hair behind an ear.

"No harm done, Mr Hector." Mae said, eyes level with a chin cleft like Bryce had. "Leaving already?"

Hector made a face. "To be honest, some of the people here are an acquired taste, and two or three of them I've never found palatable, like that Nash guy. Don't know how Jools—or anyone—puts up with him. 'Course, my wife finds Milton Foley's laugh irritating and his fundamentalist biblical literalism and ultra-right-wing take on Christianity offensive." He glanced back at the bald, bearded man chatting up Miss Bleuville. "He once told her all Catholics were going to hell for idolatry, but we're all damned for something, and he's really a generous man." He laughed. "Well, Jools said he put out the invitation, but do you think anyone of these people here will come to my lecture at the Fuller Lodge?"

"His guests seemed interested."

"Yeah," he nodded. "Nice of Jools to invite an old man like me to these parties. He must like me or something."

"How long have you been friends?"

"Since he was twelve and worked for my landscaping company." He chuckled. "You have a Happy New Year, Ms Valentine."

"You too, Mr Hector."

The music stopped. Taittinger clinked a spoon against his wine glass. It was speech time. Heads turned in his direction. "Thanks for coming tonight to ring in the New Year. Some of you have already mentioned you thought the Richebourg would be a little more opulent and have a little more finesse instead of tasting like a two-day-old bacon cheeseburger. You can thank Milton Foley for donating the Richebourg to taste. I appreciate you telling me about your experience of the wine but direct your displeasure at Milt because it's not good to keep things bottled up."

Laughter and a few groans came from the guests.

Taittinger continued, "You've all already been very generous in your donations. It's not even nine o'clock and we've hit one-hundred and fifteen-thousand. That's a nice start. I'll match that, but I know we can do better. I know we can hit a half a million by midnight. And I'll match that too... Just like I bet Foley will, won't you, Milt?"

Foley *haw-haw-hawed* and tapped a finger against his birth-marked temple, hairless skull reflecting twinkling Christmas lights. "I see you've let Jesus save you, Jools!"

"Now, now, Milt, atheism is a *non-prophet* organisation." Taittinger dropped his head for a moment. "We are privileged, every one of us here. In the eighteenth century, Edmund Burke suggested society as a partnership between the living, the dead, and those who are yet to be born. We need to see society as a chain of human continuity. We need to demonstrate a tradition of philanthropy that comes with the privilege we enjoy and not see giving as a tax incentive or means to protect our wealth."

"Hear, hear!" the O'Keeffe collector shouted.

"Thanks, Felix, you know I named my dog after you." Taittinger laughed. "So, I'm asking you all to give big, give small, but give, and give with your heart, give with the idea that you are continuing to add links in the chain of human continuity, of human history. The displacement of the Syrian people is the displacement of human history..." Taittinger went on, championing the need for altruism, philanthropy, responsibility and social justice in a world full of war, and his guests went on listening, drinking, and nodding, agreeing, clapping. "Now, drink, dance, roll on midnight, and *love the wine you're with!*"

The music kicked in again, Big Band Sinatra this time. Mae wound her way to the other side of the room, sifting by the older man in white dinner jacket, the photographer, Miss Bleuville and Foley, the man's shiny head dipping as he rubbed the purplish-red patch at his temple, Ruby flashing a him a smile. Over the next twenty minutes, Mae prompted a waiter to circulate food to the guests near the windows, gave directions to the powder room, led two men to the front pergola where they could smoke, and detached a necklace snagged in a woman's lace dress. Then a finger poked into her back.

The kitchen lackey, a young Asian man with a topknot, began spewing words. "Your dog got into the kitchen, knocked stuff from the table, took a big hunka Italian cheese, and tore off outside. I was taking flat champagne and stuff out to the garbage on the patio. Holy shit, that dog is fast—even with a big hunka cheese in his mouth, he just shot out the door. I tried to sto—"

Mae turned heel and made her way to the kitchen. The caterer and another staff member were cleaning up dozens of gooey smashed eggs and an upended serving tray of *arancini*, the squashed balls of rice like dead maggots across the tiles.

She picked her way over the mess. The swinging door into the laundry had been folded back into the kitchen, the sliding door to the patio gaping the way the lackey had left it. The entrance to her quarters gaped wide too. A tumbler and nearly empty bottle of Scotch sat on the kitchen workbench, right next to a soup bowl.

"Damn it, Grant," she muttered, grabbing the dog's collar and lead, and turned to the sliding door to the patio. She jerked her coat from a hook inside the laundry, toed off black satin shoes, and yanked on fleece-lined snow boots. Mae found a small torch and went out on the patio, leaving the sliding door half open, in case the dog came back on his own.

Bryce's instructions had been to keep the dog close, but *keep the dog close* didn't mean *get close to the dog.*

The lackey had left an open bottle of champagne on the table, light from the house and overhead patio fixture reached to the edge of the terracotta patio tiles. The outdoor speakers blared a Perry Como song about catching a falling star. Torch switched on, she stepped from the covered patio into the lightly falling snow and skidded a few steps across a patch of ice. Equilibrium regained, she swept the torch across the ground and walked on, looking for icy patches to avoid and signs of Felix. Paw prints appeared in the blanket of bluish white. Clouds moved overhead, flurries drifted, the bright, peekaboo moon illuminated Felix's trail alongside tracks made earlier by deer.

She shoved a hand into one pocket and felt the dog's ragged ball there. Snow and ice crunched softly beneath her feet. Mae crossed the back garden and headed toward the barn where the dog loved to run in mad circles. The moon poked through the clouds again, making patchy shadows, turning twisted piñon trees into squat monsters that creaked in cold gusts of wind. Felix's trail led south, into the trees and brush.

A rush of dim movement, near ponderosa pines close to Evelyn Taittinger's studio, caught her eye. Mae switched off the torch and let her eyes adjust to the moon's light, watching for a moment. A shape shifted near the trees. "Holy Jaysus, don't be a coyote cornerin' Felix," she muttered and hurried forward, remembering things she'd once read about chasing off coyotes: wave and shout, maintain eye contact, throw things.

Throw things. She halted. Her hand closed around the tennis ball in her pocket.

Kitt, barefoot and wearing grey pyjama bottoms, crossed his arms. "I don't think coyotes play fetch."

Despite her prevailing idiocy and auditory illusions of a dead man, she made her way to the pine trees beside the old stable turned art studio. Moonlight appeared and vanished. The clouds shifted. Snow wafted down. The wind gusted and fell, music from the house fading in and out, and over it all the sound of snuffling became distinct. As she got closer, eyes glinted in the kaleidoscopic moonlight. A single coyote nosed something at the front of the studio.

That was it. There was nothing she could do. The dog had become coyote food. She'd lost Caspar, lost Kitt, and now she'd lost Felix. Snow began to fall heavily. Her throat tightened. What was the bloody sodding point of loving anything—man or beast—if it was simply going to die in some horrible way? She made a strangled little sound of self-pity and threw the ball. The coyote took off and grief exploded. She wept sloppily, noisily, sobbing helplessly until she'd become a whimpering, snotty mess.

"Hush now, Mae," Kitt murmured. "It's just a dog."

Out of nowhere, Felix appeared, ball in his mouth. He spun, rushed off into the dark, without a sound, and rocketed back, leaping at her, landing with his front paws splayed, bowing down, ready to play. The ball fell from his mouth and rolled to her feet.

Mae snatched the fuzzy toy and Felix sat. Gasping, swallowing, and sniffling, she grabbed him around the middle and slipped the collar down his long neck, hugging him hard. Half-weeping, half-laughing, heart in her throat, eyes hot with tears, the dog licked her and she froze, staring at a bulky shape at the front of the studio, snuffling.

Nose running, she moved toward the lumpy contour, dog on his lead. The torch shone over paw prints and shoe prints in pristine white that gave way to speckles of crimson, clumps of pink and red, and a dark ruby pond spread beneath a man's head. The wind kicked up a gust of snow, whipping hair into her face. The slap of biting cold didn't take her breath away, but Mr Grant did.

He lay on his side, a layer of snow over his hip and thigh.

"Jaysus Mother Mary!" She rushed to the crumpled form half-hidden by shadow and crouched. "Mr Grant... Russell," she said, giving him a shake before she tugged his coat and rolled him sideways.

Grant flopped over. The torch lit what remained of a face; one eye open, the socket of the other awash in dark blood, a flap of skin blown upwards, a hole ripped above his beaky nose. Mouth gaping, part of his top lip had warped, as had his chin. His ponytail had unfurled, his dark hair fanned out, flecked by dandruffy flakes of snow, bits of teeth, and globs of pinkish-grey brain matter.

A rolling whine filled her ears. Heat streaked through her, neck sweaty. She'd seen blood mixed with brain last July, when Kitt had crumpled on dark stone, his face battered, his nose bloodied, hands cuffed behind his back, the dead Sicilian slumped atop him. She'd stood over them both, vacuum cleaner in her hands *whining, whining, whining* in her ears. Fragments of the Sicilian's brain, blobby and grey, scattered amid bright red and pink, and the sickly scent of rose perfumed hand-soap drifted up from the floor and the dead man. The fragrance filled her nose, and she stared at torch-lit brain matter and lifeless men and bloodied snow until a dog came into view.

Felix sniffed and pawed at the butler who had gone to bed with a miserable cold and now lay dead in the snow.

"Breathe." Kitt knelt beside her. She felt his hand on her back.

"Think," she muttered. "Panic later, think now. Think and breathe." Everything smelled of iron and snow, and she breathed, taking in short, sharp, rapid breaths she couldn't get under control. Mae clamped a hand over her mouth and nose. She counted to five, dropped her palm, took the longest, slowest breath she could, and exhaled even slower.

"Get up," Kitt said calmly, hand moving to her elbow. "Get up, get out of here."

"Oh," she said. "Oh."

"Mrs Valentine. *Run.*"

Mae gathered Felix and sprinted to the house, Taittinger's music growing louder and louder. At the edge of the patio, she set the dog on his feet. He darted through the open sliding door, into the laundry, into the apartment. Herb Alpert's *Tijuana Taxi* battled the noise of blood rushing in her ears as her feet hit the patio slate. God only knew what easy listening hell would play next and her fingers had begun to spike with pins and needles. Dizzy, deaf but not deaf, breathing but not breathing, she leaned against the side of the table and patted coat pockets for her mobile. The feckin' thing was inside the apartment, charging.

With a mumbled curse, she took a deep breath, gripped the table's edge and shuddered again with heat, with cold, with dread, with lingering horror.

"You're going to pass out if you don't slow down," Kitt said, a towel around his neck. "Breathe, Mae."

She took another deep breath and pulled her coat around her. The whining rush in her ears began to subside. She looked at the open bottle of champagne someone had left on the table. Dry-mouthed, hands shaking, she grabbed the bottle, and closed her lips over the mouth and drank deeply. The champagne was flat.

"Something wrong?" A voice that wasn't a phantom of Kitt said above the music.

Mae choked on the liquid, coughing and sputtering. Ice-cold flat Brut poured over her neck and chest. She turned and the flame from a lighter illuminated David Case's face as he lit a cigar and stepped away from the wall, where he'd been half-hidden by shadows and empty champagne boxes. "Sorry," he said, thumping her on the back, cigar between his teeth. "Didn't mean to give you a start."

"Mr Case," she said hoarsely, moving away from his heavy-handed assistance, bashing into something hard with her toe. The hard wedge of *Parmigiano Reggiano* the dog had stolen from the kitchen spun at the tip of her right boot. Mae tossed the bottle of champagne out into the darkness beyond the patio's dim light and shook off the champagne's wetness. She picked up the cheese and straightened. "I need to use your phone, Mr Case."

Case puff-puffed his cigar. It was an expensive one. The smoke gave off an earthy, woody smell. "I know I can smoke at the front of the house, where you showed me earlier, but I wanted a little quiet, except there isn't any quiet. There's no escape from Taittinger's shit-house taste in music. You right, possum? You look like you saw a ghost."

"You're not far off the mark. Mr Grant... I found..." she swallowed, tongue drier than before she'd drunk the champagne.

"Breathe, Mae," Kitt said.

"I need to use your phone, Mr Case. Something's happened to Grant."

"I thought the dog was Felix." Case's brow furrowed, cigar between his teeth again. "Who's Grant?" Case moved closer, tapping ash from the cigar.

Mae leaned her bottom against the table, took a deep, steadying breath and blew it out slowly. The rushing noise in her ears surged, one, two heartbeats, and then receded. "Mr Basil's man."

"Oh, yeah, the butler." Case drew in smoke. "Pretty sick, isn't he?"

"He's more than sick, he's dead. I think he killed himself."

Smoke rushed from his mouth. "Did you just say he's dead?"

"Yes, I found him out there." She pointed into the darkness. "May I use your phone? I need to ring the police."

"I left it in my room. Maybe you better take me to him. I have medical training. He might still be alive."

"Trust me, he's dead. I'll go inside. I just...need a minute."

"Okay, yeah. Okay. Shit. Take a minute. Catch your breath." Case leaned on the table, half-sitting beside her. "We'll both take a minute." He smelled of cigar and red wine when he sighed. "Listen, I won't say anything to Jools, but how much have you had to drink, Valentine?" He set his cigar on the edge of the table.

"Oh, balls." Mae mumbled and slid off the edge of the table. He was drunk and she'd done enough breathing and calming and regaining her composure.

A faint buzz came from a mobile on vibrate. Case patted his chest and pockets. "Huh. I guess I do have my phone." He pulled the mobile from his jacket, lifted it to his ear. "Well, you were right. Housekeeper found him."

The bottom dropped out of Mae's stomach, the world shrunk to a pinpoint, and exploded in slow motion.

CHAPTER FIVE

Mae shoved David Case hard, but his stumble from the table's edge was as lethargic as a leaf floating on water. His phone drifted to the ground and bounced like a drowsy balloon. Her feet took an eternity to move across the tiles to the half-open sliding door. Case snagged the back of her coat and she spun in a dawdling circle. In a graceful ballet arc, she slid an arm out of a sleeve and left him with a handful of wool.

With a sluggish Tai Chi lunge, he caught the chain around her neck and twisted it along with the front of her damp dress, drawing her forward, his nose to her chin. "*Sssssstop! Waaaaaait!*"

Mae swung the fat wedge of *Parmigiano*, slamming it into Case's head. Time snapped back to speed. Her brain and Kitt shouted, "Run!"

Her coat slipped off, her glasses flew from the chain, and she shot for the door, for the safety of the crowd inside, her fingers barely brushing the edge of the metal doorframe. Case clamped her wrist and yanked, twisted, wrenching her arm behind her back, dragging it up high. She lost the cheese and hit the table face down, the force drove the wind from her, she watched the cigar roll off the edge.

Mae couldn't scream—not that anyone inside would hear her over the honeyed voice of Bobby Darrin playing indoors and outdoors. Case's weight bore down, the hard edge of the table dug into her diaphragm, making it difficult to catch her breath or even breathe. Heavy, he was so heavy and she was immobilised, right hand wedged beneath her throat, her left arm twisted behind her back, pinned to his chest. She kicked back and he leaned on her harder, forced her legs apart with a knee, the heft of his body and gravity pressing down. Vintage Dior taffeta and netting tickled as he dragged up fabric. His blood dripped beside her nose. Breath sweetened by wine, his hand touched the back of her right thigh, slid around to the front, slowly, hesitating, as if a devil argued with a drunken angel on his shoulder and the devil was more seductive with his promise, but only just. His hand ran up the inside of her thigh.

"Do it," she panted, amorphous white splotches of fury and inadequate oxygen blighting her vision as she rasped, "Don't... fanny around. Just go ahead... and feckin' do it. Ya miserable... manky...ginger-nutted lush."

"*Ginger-nutted*?" Case said, his words hot on her sweaty, cold neck. "Jesus Christ!" he hissed.

In an instant, the warmth of wine-scented breath was gone, his weight gone too. He jerked her upright and let go.

Her knees, soft as warm wax, rebuffed their weight-bearing role and function. Mae stumbled sideways, sucking in air, and tripped over the block of cheese, landing on her arse. She scrambled across the tiles, trying to get her uncooperative knees to coordinate with her uncoordinated feet. With a roll, she snatched up the cheese and wobbled upright. She'd once killed a man with a toilet brush and she could kill this man with a chunk of Italian cheese because killing was easier than most people knew. Her brother had been a hooligan and boxer and he'd taught her the targets to hit: throat, eyes, nose, ears, neck, groin, balls, knees, and legs. Killing was easy and she was going to kill this man with a brick made of cheese.

Bobby Darrin told them 'Macky was back', and Mae launched herself at Case, cheese swinging. He stepped sideways and momentum kept her going, right off the edge of the patio onto the same patch of ice she'd slid on earlier.

Slipping, spinning, she caught a glimpse of Case, something black in his hands. He snarled through his teeth, "Stop, listen to me! *Just stop!*"

The world a twirling strobe of dark and white, she went down hard on the edge of the terracotta tiles. Cheese wedge popped from her grip, breath shunted from her lungs, the rushing blood in her erupted into bursting stars that were soon eclipsed by heavy wool smelling of her own perfume. In a heartbeat, she was upside down and breathless, a shoulder pressed into her spasming diaphragm. Trapped, wrapped in the coat she'd shrugged out of moments before, she became a bundle of dirty washing, Case's stream of profanities drowned out by Tom Jones belting *It's Not Unusual*.

Heat caressed her legs. A door slammed. The music loud, Case tossed her from his shoulder, and she sank into yielding cushions. Soft weight fell upon her and she twisted, gasping, tearing from the snare of her coat, yanking the wool from her head until she realised she was facing the backrest of the sofa she'd been sleeping on for two months.

Mae rolled over, kicked off blankets and pillow that had toppled upon her, and found Felix and Case beside the sofa.

Tom *whoa-ho-hoed*. The TV flickered from beneath Grant's bedroom door. She sat up. The dog licked her elbow. Case stared down at her, a trickle of blood curved around his eye. He reached into the pocket of his jacket, pulled out something black. Mae heaved hot and sour champagne all over his outstretched hand.

"Oh, for fuck's sake!" Case bellowed over music, shaking off vomit and a dog vigorously humping his leg.

Ten seconds later, Felix had lost interest and Mae held a spew-sticky wallet at arm's length, squinting. Her reading glasses were somewhere outside. French, Spanish, English, and Arabic printed on the smartcard popped into focus behind a window of plastic in the bi-fold leather. "Simon Reed?" She looked at the man poking the wall pad music control, killing off Tom Jones. "Your name is Simon Reed?"

He looked back and nod-shrugged.

"And you work for," Mae glanced back at the ID, "*Interpol? Are you feckin' with me?*"

Simon Reed shrugged again.

Mae threw the wallet as hard as she could. The ID bounced against him and fell to his feet. Felix sniffed the leather then hopped on the sofa beside her.

Reed picked up his soiled wallet and pitched it into the sink behind him. "Look, I'm sorry about where I put my hands. I'm really very sorry. An apology doesn't make it okay, and I'm not trying to make an excuse so I feel better about making you think I was a rapist, but I had to make certain you didn't have any weapons."

She shifted her position on the sofa, the dog rested his head on her thigh, "Do ya really think I would have hit ya with cheese if I'd had a pistol or knife hidden somewhere on my body?"

"I don't know. There's blood on your face and hands. I thought it best to be cautious."

Mae looked down at knuckles and fingernails that were clean and pink, and palms blotched with Grant's blood. "Oh Jaysus," she gasped.

"You're Irish?" he moved around to the other side of the kitchen bench and began to wash his hands.

"Yes," she said, rubbing her palms on her champagne-sodden dress, glancing at the end table, where her phone sat beside the TV remote. "Why didn't you bloody say you worked with Interpol at the start?"

"You hit me with cheese before I could." He touched the cut in his hairline and the darkening, thin line of dried blood that curved from the inside of his eye, over his cheek, and down his chin. "Do you feel better now?"

"I always feel better after being sick all over a man who assaulted me. Why did you kill Grant?"

Case—*Reed* pulled apart his bow tie. "I didn't kill him, petal."

"Right. Interpol doesn't do undercover work or kill."

"No, they don't. The ICPO facilitate communication between agencies, don't carry weapons, and we don't make arrests. Interpol supports national law enforcement and stands aside while the locals do the actual police work, the arresting. The method may be unorthodox, but I came here to facilitate communication with a contact." Reed reached for the wallet. "It went a little skewiff."

Mae yanked off a boot. "His being dead, is that what you mean by *skewiff*?"

"Yes."

She pulled off the other boot. "Did you kill him?"

"No."

"Then who did?"

"Maybe you did."

"Feck off." The boot hit the floor.

"I'm kidding. You thought he killed himself."

"Is that what you think?"

"No. We came here to talk to Grant, but someone else talked to him first."

"You already knew he was dead before I went outside, didn't you?"

"Yeah. We found him just before you went to look for the dog. Sorry he got out. We didn't know he was in here. Towel?"

"Second drawer beside the sink." She watched Reed open the drawer, dry his hands with one towel and wallet with another. "*We?*" she said. "That's the second or third time you said *we*. The man in the cowboy hat, the one I saw you kiss, is he your fiancé or Interpol partner?"

The light above the sink shone on his red hair, highlighting silver amid the ginger as he dabbed drying blood from his face. "You got a problem with my kissing him?"

"Who you kiss is not my concern."

"What is then?" He grinned suddenly.

More or less barefoot in stockings, she exhaled, frowning, got up and began folding blankets. "Does this have something to do with the Lab in Los Alamos? Was Grant involved in espionage at the Lab or is this something drug-related? Is Somerset with the FBI, ATF, or local law enforcement?"

"Yes, no, since that TV series about the teacher turned-meth-maker everyone thinks New Mexico is the drug centre of the universe, and you ask a lot of questions." Reed left a heap of damp linen on the worktop, and returned to the sitting room. He removed his jacket, undid shirt buttons below his collar, and sat on the arm of the sofa. "When Somerset gets here ask him the same questions."

"What's he going to tell me?"

"He'll tell you exactly fuck-all, which is what he knows about wine."

The dog settled on top of the folded blankets. Mae pressed her lips together, went to the kitchen to wash her hands, the tumbler, and remnants of Grant's bowl of chicken soup. She placed the glass and bowl in the basin, turned on the faucet, then shut it off without washing anything. "Is the Jefferson bottle real?" She grabbed the damp hand towel and took it to the sticky spot on the carpet in front of the sofa.

"That depends on what you mean by *real*."

She blotted remnants of sick on wool pile. "You're pretending to be a private equity investor and wine collector and you brought a bottle of fake wine to sell at a private auction. Why?"

"I told you, I was here to facilitate communication with a contact."

"You mean facilitate communication with a contact while committing fraud, right?"

"I did say it was unorthodox. Why do you think this has something to do with the wine? And why do you care?"

"You came here with a bottle you were going to try to sell to my employer."

"Maybe I did. Maybe I didn't."

"*Maybe I did, maybe I didn't,*" she mimicked his slightly nasal Australian intonation and stared down at the sick-yellowed tea-towel. "What about the provenance, the documentation you said you had, is that fake too?"

Reed chuckled softly. "I see. I see where you're going. To talk to Grant, I had to walk the walk, to get my foot in the door and not look suspicious. The papers are authentic. Well, copies of authentic documents from Monticello. They wouldn't give me originals."

"Why should I believe you're with Interpol?" She looked at the redhead and contemplated launching the dirty towel at his handsome face.

"Would you like to see my identification again?"

"The Jefferson is fake. How do I know your ID isn't too?"

"You don't." He glanced down at the cuff of his shirt, seeing the speckles of blood and vomit he'd overlooked before.

"I ought to ring the police." She glanced at her mobile still plugged into the charger on the end table.

"I'd prefer you didn't."

"I don't care what you prefer." She got to her feet and moved for the phone.

Reed stepped in front of her. "Nah, leave it there."

"And if I don't, you'll hit me?"

"I'm more concerned you might try to hit me with it. You're a bit of a pistol. I'm asking you to have a seat and wait for Somerset."

"What for?"

"You're asking so many questions, petal." He made a face and yanked his shirt over his head.

"Because you're telling me nothing." She went back to the kitchen sink with the limp tea-towel. "Why are you here?"

"Why are *you* here?"

"I'm the bloody butler, ya mingin' eejit." She swore in Italian under her breath and her fingers balled up the smelly cloth before she changed her mind about hurling the lank thing at him. "What did Grant know or do? Was he really a butler?"

Reed clomped to the sink, dress shirt in hand, and rather gently moved her from the front of the sink. "I can tell you this much. You split my head with a block of cheese and then you spewed all over me. Somerset can tell you the rest." Freckles speckled his bared shoulders. Dark ginger hair sprayed his chest. He was quite fit for a middle-aged man, like Kitt had been, but Reed was older, handsomer, and had a weariness about him. "Here," he held out his shirt to her, "maybe you can get out the stains."

Mae looked at the shirt, looked at him, and headed for the bedroom.

He grabbed her elbow. "What do you think you're doing, possum?"

"I'm bloodied, cold, and wet, and I'm not about to undress in front of *you* and expect you to wash my clothes." She jerked away and left Reed to deal with his fetid sleeve and went into the bedroom she never used.

In the dark, she made her way to the walk-in wardrobe, switched on the light inside, found the red silk dress and matching shoes, and took the things into the bathroom. She flicked on the recessed overhead lights and caught sight of herself in the mirror. Blood marred not just her palms; there were smears beside her mouth and up her cheek as well.

With a shudder, she washed away Grant's blood, cleaned her teeth, brushed her hair, fixed what little make-up she wore, and dragged off a champagne-stained, blood-sticky black taffeta dress.

Mae sat on the edge of the bathtub, red dress in her lap. There were a few possibilities pertaining to this...situation. First, if Case —*Reed* worked for Interpol, having Bryce verify that would be straightforward. Second, if Reed's being here had anything to do with why she was here, then Bryce already knew and that information hadn't been part of her 'need to know' package. Odds were Grant had died because someone here was dealing in counterfeit wine. However, third, if Bryce didn't know Reed, then Reed or Case —or whoever he was—was full of shite, she was in this arse-deep, and trying to climb out of the window in the bathroom was probably a good idea.

Hands trembling, she adjusted the chain around her neck, rolling Kitt's ring through quivering fingers. There was nothing like seeing a dead man and running for one's own life to get the adrenaline going. She looked at sullied taffeta she'd tossed on the edge of the washbasin and snorted. What the hell was she doing here? And what the hell was she going to do now?

Kitt would have told her to put on boots and a warm coat and climb out the window, but she had to be contrary, she had to look at all the options: get the boots and warm coat from the wardrobe and leave via the bathroom window in the boots and warm coat, or be contrary and stay and finish the job she started. She decided being sensible was a better option than being angry and contrary, it was a *safer* option. Then she remembered Felix.

Right, she'd leave, but not without the dog. The dog was coming with her. She'd lost Caspar. She'd lost Kitt. There was no way she was losing Felix too, feck the fact he didn't belong to her and dognapping was a crime.

Mae put on the dress and red shoes, trying to figure out how to get Felix and leave without Reed's interference. What was the first thing in the sitting room that she could smash over the man's head —the bowl of apples? Maybe the lamp on the bedside table had a better heft? She went into the bedroom.

"Have you learned nothing?" Kitt said from the edge of the bed. This time, he wore a dinner suit, arms crossed, bow tie perfect, his ugly handsome features an amalgam of her imagination and how she'd seen him over the years.

"Oh, sodding Jaysus," she coughed.

"Didn't being mugged, didn't being nearly murdered in my kitchen last year teach you anything about being alone with strange men?"

Mae shut her eyes.

"You should have run," Kitt exhaled. "You should have gone inside the minute you got back to the house, gone inside to the safety of a crowd of people instead of chatting with Reed. What are you doing here? What the hell are you doing here?"

Yes, what was she doing here? Why had she taken the position and done a favour for a man who had accused her of crimes? Had it really been to avoid going mad, to avoid falling into the same abyss there'd been after Caspar had died? Or was there something more to it? "Being productive." She rubbed her temples for a moment. "I'm being productive."

Kitt laughed. "Of course. Of course. Productive. How do you know Reed isn't lying?"

"I saw his credentials."

"How do you know they're real?"

"I don't. I don't know what's... Oh, God. Stop," she said, opening her eyes, dropping her hands. "Stop."

"You've cut your hair," he said, very softly.

Mae swallowed, and felt a smile waver on her lips as she studied a delusion thrust upon her by trauma and grief. "You've grown a beard again."

"Do you like it? It's quite ginger—and a little grey."

She looked away, down at her feet. "It's very distinguished."

"Ah, distinguished. You think I look old."

"Do you feel old, sir?"

"No, I feel stale, over-boiled, and deep-fried. It's been an eternity since I've had a decent cup of coffee and your scrambled eggs."

"Don't they serve breakfast in hell?"

"American coffee, Mrs Valentine. That has been my hell. I have been in hell since I left you."

"Yes. You left me." She looked at him again, longer this time. "The spy in a dinner suit is a cliché, yet the clothes have always suited you. But your nose? The broken nose is an interesting touch. Is it prosthetic, a standard part of a spy's disguise kit, or just your skill with applying make-up?"

"I'd like to say it's the spy-kit Stephen Fry model, but it's all mine."

"And shearing your hair so short?"

"Concussion. Stitches. Had to make sure I hadn't gone soft in the head."

"Evidently, I'm the one soft in the head."

"With you being here, I'm inclined to agree. You're very thin."

"I was getting a little doughy in the middle."

"I liked you a little doughy in the middle. Do you still find me unconventionally handsome, Mae, or is Reed more your style now?"

"Reed is a cowboy-snogging pretty-boy."

He chuckled.

Mae saw Kitt with that grin of expectation, the one that said he was waiting for a quip, for her dry wit, waiting for that delicious banter they'd shared to spark to full life. God how she missed that, how she missed him, how she missed the spark to the life they'd had, the spark to the life they might have continued to have, and she strangled the cry rising in her throat. "No. I'm not doing this. You're *not* here," she said. "You're not, and I've crossed over into madness. This never happened with Caspar. I thought about what he might say, I saw him sometimes, I heard him like I heard you outside, like I hear you now, but I never carried on a conversation with his bloody feckin' ghost, and I'm not going to stand here and chit-chat with yours."

"Mae."

She rose, her breath ragged, impatient, angry. PTSD, she'd developed PTSD, like her brother, and it was turning chronic. Was there a family predisposition for PTSD? "No, God damn you." Shaking, she clutched at the chain around her neck, squeezing the ring hanging from the slim, twisted gold, and walked away. She threw open the bedroom door and stomped into the sitting room, gritting her teeth, clutching a ring that belonged to another dead man. "*Eejit. Fool,*" she muttered and the other eejit in the sitting room looked at her.

Reed buttoned the damp cuffs of his shirt, his eyes travelled over her, up and down, and he smiled faintly, like Kitt.

"Do that again and I'll give you a black eye."

"Do what, petal?"

"Look at me that way, call me *possum* or *petal* again."

"Sorry. It's a nice dress. It suits you better than the last one."

"Yes it does," Kitt said, behind her.

Felix trotted over, nosing her, licking her knee. Mae flexed her hands. "Shut up," she said. "I don't want to hear any more shite!"

Reed laughed.

Felix huffed and so did Mae. The dog wandered off to the sofa and blankets. Mae crossed her arms and glared at Reed. "You're an arse."

Behind her, Kitt laughed. "I think arse is putting it mildly."

"Would you shut up?" Mae ground the words between her mint toothpaste-flavoured teeth.

Reed adjusted the other sleeve, and smiled broadly, the way Kitt had when he was amused. "She doesn't like you very much, does she? And who could blame her? I don't like you either, Hamish."

Mae stared at Reed, his eyes vivid blue-green. "What did you say?" she whispered.

"I don't like Hamish either. Never have. The little shit."

Mae turned and the room expanded and contracted at once, colours magnified and garish. Cold blue-grey eyes of a living apparition regarded her dispassionately. The softened wax quality returned to her knees, flowing down and up into her chest, spreading, melting through her. "Away with ya," she whispered.

CHAPTER SIX

R eed hurried over and grasped her elbow. "You know, Kitty, I think Valentine's about to pass out."

"I'm not going to pass out," she said, and the man's grip barely registered, the words she'd spoken a far-off hum.

"Hello," Kitt said, concerned by the two feverish splotches of vivid pink standing out on her cheeks. He dragged a wooden chair from the dining table, placing it beside her. "Sit down, Mae."

"I don't want to sit down," she murmured.

"Well, isn't this glorious," Reed snorted and led her hands to the back of the chair. "Loelia in Singapore, the nurse in Athens, and this one. I think you take the whole playboy spy thing a little too seriously, don't you? So, how do you know her?"

"She's my butler."

"I don't work for you anymore," Mae mumbled.

Reed looked Mae up and down and laughed. "You're absolutely shameless, Kitty."

"Give us a minute, *Reedy*." Kitt didn't know what to do, didn't know how to proceed. Mae was overloaded by shock, the shock of his presence compounded by the shock that had come from finding Grant dead, and the shock that had come from Reed's bungling intervention outside. Kitt made a fist, fingers curling peculiarly into his palm.

Mae stared at him, hands shaking on the padded top edge of the chair, her facial expressions a free-form jazz tune of emotions. As much as she was staggered by seeing him, her presence had him reeling. He'd bungled it a few minutes ago, let anger and fear and shock get the better of him. He wouldn't do that again. "Give us a minute, Reed," Kitt said.

Reed exhaled. "Yeah, nah. I've done that already. I gave you more than a minute and she hit me with a wedge of cheese."

"Be glad it wasn't a toilet brush. She killed a man with a toilet brush once."

Mae inhaled deeply and took a step toward him, frowning, blinking, her breathing shallow, staccato, her eyes shifting to Reed. She shook her head, pointing at Kitt, "But he knows nothing about wine."

"Simon," Kitt gave Reed a hard look. "A minute. Please."

"See? Good manners make all the difference." Reed turned and went into the kitchen.

Mae lifted a trembling, tentative hand to her forehead. "Major Kitt?"

"Hello, Mrs Valentine."

Mae took a rattling breath, moved another step closer, the moment silent and slack, her mind blank. The tips of her fingers poked his sternum. "You're here."

Kitt reached out, pulled her close, held her tightly. She stood stiff in his arms. "I'm here."

"You're not dead."

"I'm not dead." His eyes stung and her fingertips began to probe across his middle, digging into his side the way Saint Thomas would have dug his fingers into the wounds suffered by Jesus Christ before believing his resurrection. Or maybe that was how he felt, resurrected. There had been that moment, when he'd been convinced that he was dead and he'd never see her again, and yet here she was, where she wasn't supposed to be. He shook and her rigid body trembled against him. He didn't know which one of them shuddered more. "It's all right," he said, perhaps more for himself than for her. "It's all right," he said again, even though it was anything but all right.

Mae laughed thinly and pulled back, eyes running from the curve of his bent nose, over his bottom lip and the whiskers covering his chin. For a half-second, as if she were about to kiss him, her lips parted, but her gaze shot to Reed, to the black cowboy hat on the kitchen worktop, and back again. "You're working?"

"Yes."

Mae stared at him. What she had witnessed and borne in the last twenty minutes had been frightening, disturbing, enough to disorient anyone, but Kitt recognised the shock shifting in her eyes as she stared at him, the room quiet except for the dog licking his nether regions. He watched it happen. The first bubble of emotion that her mind seized upon wasn't relief or joy or excitement. Her shock kicked over into unmistakable, unreserved fury. "Oh, you sodding *liar*!" She tore from his arms, and swore, louder, more Irish intoned, and more coarsely than he had ever heard her swear before. The noise startled the dog and drew amused Reed into the sitting room.

Christ, she was angry. He knew she'd be angry, but she didn't corner the market on the fervent emotion. He'd been running on spleen and bile for the last two months and was simply far better practised holding his rage in check than she was. Calmly, with a slight chin jerk, Kitt sent Reed back to the kitchen. "Mae."

"Why?" she said, brushing away moisture that had crept

beneath her eyes. "Why?"

"We'll discuss this later."

"Is it because I said *no*?"

"You didn't say *no*, you agreed to a very long engagement, and this is about safety. Mine...yours. Always yours."

"My safety? This is about my safety? Yes, how could I forget that? How could I be so stupid? Why didn't I ever stop and think it through, like Bryce told me to? How'd I forget I was dealin' with a feckin' professional liar." She looked over at Reed. He watched them from the other side of the kitchen worktop. "Are ya workin' with that one over there, just using him, or is he a liar too? Oh, I hate ya. I hate ya so much."

"No, you love me." Kitt glanced at the diamond ring dangling from the chain she wore. "I know you love me."

"Oh, dear God!" Reed gave a short burst of a laugh.

Kitt ignored the man's ongoing amusement. "Why are you here, Mae?"

She inhaled, very slowly. By the time she exhaled, Kitt realised he was wrong about being better-practised at holding anger in check than she was. Mae jerked back the reins on rage and eased into professional, slipping into cultivated English dialect, which made her sound very much like Princess Anne. "You said we'd discuss this later. What an excellent idea." She smiled, and there was something saccharine, something calculated in the way she did it.

The hair on the back of Kitt's neck prickled. "I know you're angry about Christmas," he said. "And about this too."

"Excuse me, sir, I have work to do."

"No, Mae," he said. "You're leaving. Right now."

"Oh, there it is, that façade, that cloak of detached nothingness you wear so well." Her smile remained, hands clasped behind her back.

"Indeed. You're still leaving." Kitt smiled back.

She watched the dog hop off the couch and trot over to Reed. "My leaving would not be professional. I have a contract. And I don't work for you anymore, sir."

"Write a letter of resignation. You're leaving."

"I'm working."

"You're going."

"I'm staying. You've killed a man. Your job is done. Mine isn't. You leave."

"Is this serious, mate?" Reed crouched to scratch Felix under the chin.

Kitt ignored Reed and lifted a hand to touch Mae's shoulder before he thought better of it. Yes, she was going to leave, he'd see to it, he'd knock her out if he had to, he'd... A flickering notion skimmed the periphery of his mind, skipping across his resolve. Her being here instead of London was every kind of wrong there was and it threw him, made him sloppy, inept, slow. The flickering notion, a matchstick of thought tried to strike, sparks skipped up his spine. "Why are you here?"

She moved, heels tapping on the kitchen tiles. "You and that silly Christmas tree. I needed *something* to do for Christmas."

"You couldn't have gone to see your brother in Dublin, like you always have?"

Mae laughed, high and bright, and began washing a soup bowl. "I had to deal with how you left me. I had to get away from all those things, those memories of you, and the promise of a future I'd never have. Sean praying for your soul would been not have been a comfort."

"You made an actual promise of a future, Hamish?" Reed straightened, brow arching.

"Simon." Kitt smiled up through his lashes, at the redhead pushing at the dog trying to hump his leg. "I'm not asking."

"Yes. You made a promise of a future." Chuckling to himself, Reed went into Grant's bedroom and left the door open.

Mae reached for a towel, mirroring the angle of Kitt's head. "You are such a bully."

"I am, Mrs Valentine." He crossed into the kitchen and this time Kitt took hold of her shoulder, turning her from the sink. Despite his so-called detached coolness, a round of nausea and alarm rose in his gullet, the moment of queasiness more sour, sweatier, and heart-pounding than when he walked into the party and saw her standing on the other side of the room, kissing Russell Grant. How he hadn't knocked everyone out of the way to get to her still amazed him. Sparks skittered up his spine again. "All right. You're here because you needed 'something to do' for Christmas."

"I'm here because you left me with a Christmas tree and weren't coming home."

"I told you I'd always come home to you."

Mae gave Kitt another sickly-sweet smile and dried the bowl. "You died in a shipping container in Singapore. How could you come home if you were dead?"

"I had postcards sent to let you know otherwise. I'd thought you'd work it out." As soon as he'd said it he recognised the asinine futility of what he'd thought and what he'd done.

"Postcards." She went on smiling, the brightness flashing on incredulous for a half-second. "You thought that would... Yes. Yes, you did."

The sweat on the back of Kitt's neck turned both cold and fiery. His grip on her shoulder slackened. Her laugh a small sniff, Mae flicked his hand off as if his fingers were bits of lint, and he had the sensation he was nothing more than a bit of lint drifting to the floor. The injuries he'd sustained had made him stupid and desperate to think that sending her postcards would refute the news of his death. Amazed by his level of irrationality, he looked from her to the dog nuzzling its nose into her hand and drew a fat red circle around one more option. The match flared.

This was not a bizarre coincidence. This, all of it, from Geneva to the hell in that shipping container in Singapore, to standing here staring at Mae, had been a God almighty set-up. He'd heard it and missed it. *Do you like dogs, Mrs Valentine?* Llewelyn, in his stage actor's voice, had asked for a Christmas favour. The dog was the bloody favour, the goddamned skinny little ginger dog.

Kitt knew there had been a rat. While he had an idea who the rodent was, realising there were two was nearly as nauseating as finding Mae here at this house. An unstable swell of incredulity, confusion, rage, and nausea rushed into his gut. He swore, his words crude and strident. Mae's being here dog-minding had *everything* to do with him. How in hell had Bryce let her take the position?

She smoothed silk over her hips, the same way she often did when she wore an apron. "Postcards," she sniffed. "Of course, you'll explain this later, but I know this is what you do. Bryce enlightened me some time ago. I know how this works. It's a 'need to know' thing I didn't need to know. You needn't worry. I'll keep my mouth shut. I'll play along. You had to kill Grant. It's your job. Now, I'll tend to mine."

Kitt stared at her. "What exactly is your job here, Mrs Valentine?"

With a swish of red silk, she turned on her heel and headed for the door.

"Mae, what are you do—"

"When you finish here, Major Kitt, I never want to see you again. You may consider the lease on your flat terminated. Now, please let yourself out, and this time, be sure the dog stays in. Oh, and since you and *Mr Reed* are done killing, sir," she grasped the doorknob, "I'll assume you'll *not* be staying for breakfast."

Kitt swallowed the clammy nausea that had crept in and stared at a door that had just closed. After ten seconds or so, he crossed the sitting room, going into the bedroom Reed claimed he'd already searched. The dog followed, nosing into the back of his knee for a moment before trotting over to sniff and paw a pair of Grant's socks. The TV was on, the sound low. On screen, cheering, happy people revelled in Times Square to welcome the New Year. Kitt elbowed switch the light switch.

"So..." Reed said from the bathroom doorway.

Kitt held up a hand. "Don't. Don't say a bloody word."

"You always expect the worst. Maybe I was going to ask if you were okay."

"You weren't."

"Okay, maybe I wasn't. Is she going to be a problem?"

"She's a goddamned nuisance, but I can handle her."

"Yeah, you were doing a bang-up job of handling her." Reed leaned against the doorframe, arms crossed. "Your butler? Really? The help, Kitty? You slept with your help, the help you said was an older woman?"

"She's older than me."

"She's middle-aged."

"So am I. So are you."

"You love her?"

"Yes."

"Idiot."

"Yes."

Reed exhaled noisily. "I suppose you want me to get her out of here?"

"Yes. But not yet. Keep an eye on her. Her presence isn't an incredible coincidence. She's here because of me and I need to know why."

"You don't think there's a logical explanation?"

"No, do you?"

Reed exhaled again. "I don't know, but you sending her post-cards was fuckwitted."

Kitt ignored Reed and the nausea somersaulting through his gut. He reached for the messenger bag and picked it up with a handkerchief. "Did you look through this?"

"Yeah. Did you see anyone in or near the art studio?"

"Only Mae."

"Hasn't this has gone to shit. With Grant dead, I'm going to have to pull the plug."

"Give me twenty-four hours."

"You've had a month."

Coolly, Kitt tipped his chin ever so slightly and smiled faintly at the redhead.

"Shit." Reed made a gruff noise in the back of his throat, head shaking. "The things we do for love."

Kitt unzipped the middle section of the bag. "Where was his passport?"

"In the pocket on the side of that bag. Why are you going through it again?"

"In case you weren't thorough enough."

"I was thorough enough."

Kitt dumped the bag's contents onto the bed, turning the bag inside out. He pulled a little penknife from his pocket, opened it, and sliced along a seam, cutting cloth from leather and a flat strip of lightweight, padded balsa wood. He slipped the wood from the new pocket he'd made. The centre of the wood strip was fitted with a passport, opened and flattened to resemble the padding. Kitt began to prise it up with the little knife, careful not to damage the document with the razor-edged blade no longer than the dull little knife Molony had in the shipping container. "I see your idea of thorough enough," he said and the bedroom bleached from sight, and Kitt stood neck deep in handbags, scarves and sunglasses, the torn plastic on a crate spattered with vomit and blood, mosaic-tiled eyes peeking out.

"*What time is it*?" Dalton asked.

It was suddenly preposterously muggy, the stench of corpse-filled shipping container filled Kitt's nostrils. "*Chichiltic*," Popo laughed and dead eyes swarmed with flies *buzzing, buzzing, buzzing.* The balsa wood, handkerchief, and passport fell from Kitt's grip.

He barely made it to the toilet.

Violently retching, he emptied his stomach, the rotting smell and buzzing replaced by the stink of his own vomit and sound of his own gasping.

"You're cactus," Reed said from the doorway, open passport in his grip. "When was the last time you slept, mate?"

"You weren't thorough enough, I'll sleep when this is over, and I'm not your mate." Kitt heaved one last, fruitless time and shifted from his knees, leaning back against the cool, tiled wall.

Whether it was Mae's presence or the little blade, one of them set had off vivid memories that were disjointed and out of step. That's how it was; his memory triggered by tiny things: a pocketknife, a handbag, and he tried to knit together more, beyond the handbags, scarves, sunglasses, and face made of mosaic tiles, beyond Dalton asking the time. Checking his watch—a watch he no longer had—began a chain of stinking, blood-soaked, cock-up of events that Kitt could not remember in a manner that made sense.

The dog wandered into the bathroom, nails tippy-tapping across tiles. The animal eyed Reed, turned in a circle one way, the other, and plopped down, head on Kitt's thigh.

"What do you know, someone here actually likes you," Reed snorted.

ELATED, unnerved, furious, dazed, a veritable whirlwind concoction of emotions, her mind hummed and Mae stood at the edge of the party, eyes on the crowd and Kitt's preposterous cowboy hat. He laughed, shook hands with Nash, and snagged a glass of red wine. Kitt found tea abhorrent and he despised wine, the stuff gave him a headache, yet five minutes after he'd finished a Burgundy, he quaffed a Merlot then he moved on to bourbon, bourbon, and more bourbon. Over the next forty minutes, she watched Kitt chat with guests, with Basil, the couple with the Georgia O'Keeffe collection, flashing a charming smile. Then Reed stepped in, slipping an arm around Kitt's shoulder, saying something into his ear, which led to another charming smile. Schmoozing, Kitt moved through the crowd with easy grace, with confidence. He danced with five different women and two men.

That he was here and alive, dancing, wearing a dinner jacket, bow tie—and cowboy hat—was more difficult to believe than when Bryce had told her Kitt was dead. Bryce. Did he know Kitt was alive, was the fecker just doing his job when he lied to her, or had he been duped as well? Had things been engineered, had she been manipulated into a position to look after a dog and a keep an eye on the habits of a man who drank and collected expensive wine? It was all such shite. *Remains*, Bryce had gotten her with *remains* and the tears that had trickled out of his grim, green eyes. Bryce and Kitt, they were both feckin' spies; deception, manipulation, political strategies, murder made up their profession.

Eyes on Kitt leading human Christmas tree Emmy Foley in a waltz or foxtrot or whatever dance it was, Mae swore under her breath and crossed the room, telling wait staff to collect plates and glasses. When she glanced back, Emmy's pine-green dress swished about her, breasts bobbing like flesh ornaments as she smiled up at Kitt.

Mae spun on her heel, her own dress swishing across the back of her knees. Man. Bully. Hero. Saviour. Five months ago, he'd been those things to her, and now he was simply a real, very much alive, *liar*. And here she was, a liar like Kitt, playing another game of deception and manipulation with a touch of murder, and there was nothing she could believe about anything, or anyone, including herself. *I never want to see you again.* What rot. She wanted to go to him, to wrap herself around him, press her face to his chest, crush against him until they melted and their bodies fused and he could go nowhere without her.

Months ago, in trying to understand, to dig down to the core of what led a man to risk his life to do intelligence work, she undertook a little research. Risk-takers, she learned, had a higher level of dopamine, which drove them to seek out new experiences. Risk-takers had a lower level of serotonin, which quelled impulsive behaviour. Without needing to dig too far, she knew that she wasn't here because she simply wanted to be productive and get over Kitt's death. She was here because she'd discovered, five months ago in Sicily, that she liked taking a risk, liked the rush that intrigue gave her. Her life, her career had been of such careful order, and she had enjoyed the symmetry of that life, she had excelled at the skill it took to put order and tranquillity in place when chaos endeavoured to reign. However, having a role in bringing down an international money laundering ring, one with ties to people smuggling and the Mafia, had been inexplicably invigorating. More inexplicable was how killing two men during that action felt so...satisfying, and the rush that came from finding a dead man in the snow outside was oddly similar. There was some part of her that wanted to put order to the chaos.

Eejit, she was a self-deceiving eejit believing she needed to be productive when the productivity, when all of it, was about taking risks, about becoming addicted to adrenaline, about the seductive hunt for it, the tantalising possibility of finding a hit of something other than anger or nothingness. She liked the possibility that Taittinger could be a wine conman. She liked the thrill of clandestine observation, liked the deception of playing a dual role. She liked pretending, liked living the lie, liked being a liar.

But she didn't like being lied to.

Kitt caught her watching and smiled, cold blue-grey eyes seething like liquid nitrogen. With a nod, he tipped his hat, a feckin' bloody Old West cowboy saying *'ma'am'*. He turned, leaned close to speak Reed and the redhead took his hand, twining their fingers together. Then her sightline was eclipsed by an older couple dancing to Sinatra's *Somethin' Stupid*.

Everything inside her head told her to be sensible, to leave, to get out, to walk away. Mae shut her eyes. Yes, she was somethin' stupid, this was somethin' stupid—this was unwise, undeniable, and inescapable.

Milton Foley's *haw-haw-haw* dragged her from stupidity to reality. When she opened her eyes, she saw Reed scowl, snag a tumbler from a tray and lean even closer to the man who had lied to her about never lying to her again.

Out of all of them, Mae knew she was the biggest liar of all.

"Valentine," Taittinger said, suddenly beside her.

Mae jerked her attention to her current employer. "Dr Jools."

Taittinger stroked his goatee. "You changed your dress."

"There was a spill."

"Oh, yeah. Felix and the kitchen disaster. You okay?"

"May I be candid, Dr Jools?"

"Sure."

"I'm a wee bit tired."

"Hope you're not getting whatever it is Mr Grant has."

Mae's laugh came out a little higher pitched than she liked. "As do I."

"You've been awesome with everything. I appreciate it."

"Thank you, Dr Jools. Again, I apologise for not being present to settle Mr Somerset."

"Not a problem. I did see the mess Felix made. And we still have a spare room if an idiot," Taittinger looked over at the laughing photographer with the handlebar moustache, "like if Derek over there gets too plastered to drive." Derek coughed a mouthful of cake and creamy white icing all over a pretty brunette, narrowly missing the hot pink silk of Miss Bleuville's Alexander McQueen gown, crumbs spilling over the digital camera around his neck. "He came recommended, but that guy's a bit of a drunken disaster, isn't he?"

"It's not my place to say, Dr Jools."

"No. Of course not."

Mae cast her gaze back to Kitt and the scowling Interpol agent. "But I believe he's neck and neck with Mr Somerset."

Taittinger's laugh was a low, rumbled huh-huh-huh. "You notice Somerset has something of an equal-opportunity roving eye, like right in front of his fiancé?"

Play along. Mae inhaled, wearily, a touch of devious fit well with 'play along'. She gave a soft chuckle.

"What? Go on. Tell me."

"Forgive me, Dr Jools. It's not appropriate."

"Oh, come on."

She leaned close. "I overheard Mr Case accuse Mr Somerset of trying to get Dr Brennan's friend, the woman with the white hair, into bed for a ménage à trois."

"Bella? That old winosaur's gotta be over fifty." He glanced at her sideways and grimaced. "I know, I know. Sorry. Age utterly is irrelevant—unless you happen to be a bottle of wine." He laughed, raising his glass to the man he knew as Mr Case.

CHAPTER SEVEN

Reed returned the toast his host made from across the room and made an impatient sound. "Well, he's very amused. What do you suppose she's saying to him?"

"She's not going to give us away." Kitt took the tumbler from his hand. "Stop glowering. It's unbecoming for a man as handsome as you." He had a swallow of bourbon, ice chunk *clink-clinking* in the crystal.

"You and your damned ego." Reed reclaimed the tumbler and poked the hat back with a finger, tilting it on his head.

Kitt licked a burning drop of liquid from his bottom lip. "I told you I can deal with it."

"Is that what you call spewing, dealing with it?" Reed had a small sip of the Old Grand-Dad and made a face.

"Vomiting is not a sign of weakness."

"No, but your housekeeper sure as hell is." Reed glanced in Mae's direction again.

"Butler." Kitt watched Mae as well. She'd moved away from Taittinger to speak with Nash. The man had an appalling dress sense. "I told you, she won't say anything."

"You trust her?"

"More than I trust you. Change the subject, Simon." Kitt took back the cowboy hat and set it on his own crown.

"Just tell me something. Did you really gi—"

"I said change the subject, Simon." Kitt reached for the glass and had another swallow.

"Did I mention that besides being interested in wine, Nash and Basil were stoked to see one of Taittinger's cars, an old Sunbeam he's restoring?"

"No, you didn't mention. I didn't see a Sunbeam in the garage."

"It's in the barn. Have you been to the barn yet?"

"It's locked up tight." Kitt swirled the glass, sliding the chunk of ice around in the amber liquid.

"What are you going to do now?"

Kitt was rather fond of bourbon, but not this one. The Old Grand-Dad sweet corn mash tasted hot on his lips, had a hint of vanilla, and a metallic finish, like blood in his mouth. "We are going to improvise."

"We? No, no. I'm done making shit up as you go. I got you this far."

"And look what happened to your plan. Have you got another one?"

Reed's smiled dryly. "I'm thinking we all jump in my hire car, head south, and retire to an island in the Caribbean."

"I'd prefer Sicily."

"Fine." Reed exhaled. "Sicily then."

"Or?"

"Or we keep talking to these lovers of fine wine and find out what my mate Grant was up to before somebody here killed him." Reed looked out into the room of guests. "And then I leave."

Kitt tipped back the cowboy hat and followed Reed's gaze to a woman with striking white hair. She raised her glass, tipped her chin, and gave them a nod. Then a couple dancing to Nat King Cole singing *L-O-V-E* eclipsed her. "Pretty, isn't she? Ask her to dance, Simon."

Reed scowled. "My feet hurt."

"You always wondered what it is I do. It's gather information in any way that fits the occasion. Mingling, *dancing* with other guests, her for example, fits the occasion."

"You want to fit the occasion, it makes sense to dance with me."

"Why would I torture you when your feet hurt?"

"Yeah, yeah. It's not what I know, it's what you know and won't tell me. What do you think that passport means? What did you find outside, before your butler spoiled it all?"

"Are you envious of her?"

Reed's smile held more than a tinge of rancour. "Why did I ever pay attention to your bloody text?"

"Because you love me almost as much as she does."

"You're a prick."

"You only have yourself to blame for that."

"Of that I am painfully aware."

"Here. Take this." Kitt shoved the drink into Reed's hand. "I'm going to dance and mingle and ask questions to gather information."

"Wait." Reed put a hand on Kitt's shoulder. Then he had a slug of alcohol.

Kitt sighed, the sound somewhat exaggerated. "All right, one dance, but I'm leading."

"No. What are we going to do about the body?"

"Nothing."

"Nothing?" Reed's mouth drooped open for a moment before he snapped it shut, teeth clicking.

"Whoever killed him would probably wonder how he wandered off. You're not thinking clearly. How much have you had to drink?"

"Not as much as you, and of course I'm not thinking clearly. This sort of thing is your gig, not mine." He pressed the tumbler to Kitt's chest. "I got you here and now I'm done. I'm back to following protocol, doing things by the book."

"You're not going anywhere until I say so." Kitt knocked back the last of the Old Grand-Dad.

Reed laughed. "Are you threatening me?"

"While I'll never outgrow the desire to throttle you, Simon, we're improvising, remember?" He glanced at their approaching host, at Mae taking a position near the wall a few feet away. "She's going to play along, just like you." Kitt turned side on and smiled at Taittinger. "Great party, Tatts," he said, exhaling the scent of sweet bourbon, his words deliberately sloppy, his accent Australian. "I appreciate the hospitality."

Taittinger chuckled. "*Tatts*. I like that. Well, you two seem to be enjoying yourselves."

"We are." Reed smiled broadly.

"You feeling okay, Somerset? You look queasy like a Sunday morning." Taittinger pulled a face, teeth showing.

"Delayed flight, overbooked flight, bumpy flight, and I'm not the best at air travel."

Reed heaved a snorted chuckle. "You get motion sick on an escalator, Ian."

"I should have stock in Dramamine." Kitt shook the tumbler. Ice inside tinkled against the glass as he waved it a one of the wait staff. "Oi, I'm gonna need another!"

Reed set a hand on Kitt's shoulder. "That's an impressive collection of vintage English sports cars you've restored. Ian does that too."

"Restoring anything now?" Kitt swallowed dregs of bourbon.

"A Sunbeam."

"Nice." Kitt nodded. "My father had one. It was a real pearler."

"A what?"

Reed translated. "Pearler, as in your vintage car is a pearl."

Taittinger chuckled. "Okay. Pearler. The pearler needs new paint, a transmission rebuild, and a total brake overhaul. Would you like to see it?"

"That'd be sweet." Kitt burped and smiled.

"Maybe you've had enough, Ian."

Kitt shrugged off Reed's hand. "Nah. The night's still young." He popped an ice cube into his mouth and began to suck it, slurping and hissing liquid through his teeth.

"Earlier today, Dave," Taittinger faced Reed, "you mentioned Australian collectors were putting down whites."

"Mm." Reed nodded. "Char—"

"What series, Tatts?" Kitt crunched an ice cube.

"—Chardonnay is proving t—"

"Is it a Tiger or an Alpine?" Kitt pushed the cowboy hat back a bit and scratched his temple.

Reed glanced at him with appropriate irritation and mouthed sorry to their host.

Taittinger cleared his throat. "Sunbeam Alpine, Series II. How about I take you to see it now?"

Kitt shook his head. "Tomorrow, tomorrow, when I can get behind the wheel. I'd have to be a bloody idiot to drink and drive. D'you wanna dance, Tatts? Dave-o's feet hurt."

"Dave-o?"

"Him." Kitt waved the tumbler at Reed. "David, Dave, Dave-o."

Taittinger chuckled. "If you don't mind, I'd rather dance with Ruby."

"Well, that's sad." Kitt's mouth pursed.

"Oh, hey." Taittinger's grinning geniality twisted into a furrowed brow. "I didn't mean any offen—"

"Mate, I mean your wallflower housekeeper, all alone on New Year's Eve." Kitt looked at his watch. "And it's nearly midnight."

Reed snorted. "It's eleven-fifteen, Ian, but why not thrill the old bird and work off some of that grog in your veins." He glanced at Taittinger. "Women love him. Maybe not as much as I do, but they find him...irresistible."

"They do, Dave-o." Kitt shoved the empty tumbler into Taittinger's hand and wobbled the few steps to Mae.

"Hello," he said over a swinging duet of Johnny Mercer's *Baby It's Cold Outside*. "Would you like to dance, Mrs Valentine?"

Mae glanced at him. "Thank you, sir, but I'm working."

"Ah, yes, ever the professional. Always on the job. You are dedicated—and dancing." He tugged her away from the wall and into the small group dancing, drawing her into his arms, smiling. "I need a little help."

"You need more than a *little* help."

Kitt leaned in closer, her palm pressed to his chest. He caught her *L'Air du Temps*. The scent of carnation, bergamot and rosewood mixed with her body chemistry and released as her body temperature rose. Or perhaps it was his body temperature that had elevated and his warmth transferred to her, fragrance rising as his heart rate did. It was a peculiar instant of pleasure and dismay because he'd tried to remember the way her perfume had smelled, when he'd been in that stinking container. Bizarre that he'd recall how he'd tried to conjure up any part of her he could as he lay at the edge of death. He hated that the exquisite fragrance of the woman he had tried to imagine was now attached to a memory he wanted to forget and needed to remember. Rationally, he knew that was then, this was now, and now he was nervous instead of dying.

Nervous. He was nervous and nervous was new. Mae agitated

him in every way there was to agitate a man, turned his brain into a miasma of queasy fear, desperate longing, smouldering anger, and undiluted love. He wanted to dip his head and kiss her softly, and resented that he couldn't, but what he resented more was her presence here. He hated that she had joined him in a situation teeming with menace, with treachery. At the same time, he had never been more thankful for anything in his life. She was succour amid his life's hostility. Perhaps he was getting old or was old already because he had never known he could want, or need, such a thing as succour. He smiled down at her, at the face she held impassive, at hazel-green eyes bright with walled-off ire.

What a fool he was. How often had he seen it happen? Men in his profession went soft in the head as they went soft in the heart. Hard-hearted as he was, as he had been, he'd always believed that one day he'd be brought to his knees by a serious injury, or die by his own hand, not succumb to a woman. Yet in spite of cynicism and darkened scrap of a soul, he'd learned there was something rather delicious in surrendering to Mae, the woman who would be the death of him—if he didn't get her killed first.

Mae studied the flat brimmed-hat black above Kitt's forehead. "Gentlemen remove their hats indoors."

"Yes, gentlemen do."

"Really," she said, "a cowboy hat? You're a cowboy now, not a spy?"

"It's not a cowboy hat, it's an Akubra, the hat worn by Australian jackaroos."

"A jackaroo rounds up cattle, like a cowboy. It's a bloody cowboy hat. And you're Australian now, are you, calling everyone *mate*, wearing that ridiculous hat? Not sure your accent's as good as Reed's."

"Reed is Australian born. What did you say to Taittinger that he found so amusing?" he said, stepping her to the left.

The tip of her shoe grazed his ankle. "I told him you and Mr Case had a lover's spat."

"Ah, quick thinking."

"Yes, it was."

He spun her out, pulled her back in, and wasn't certain if he'd lost rhythm or if she'd gouged her heel into his foot on purpose. "That, Mrs Valentine, was my toe. I know you've never been much of a dancer, so odds favour that you're simply dancing and not trying to hurt me." He looked down at her again, one eyebrow arched. "Do you want to hurt me?"

"Hurting people is your speciality." Mae smiled and glanced at Reed over her shoulder. "If anyone wants to give you a belting, I'd say it's Mr Case—I mean *Mr Reed*. I think that man really loves you."

"That's the only reason he's here."

She met his gaze, solidly. "You do have a history. Now nice. Another little morsel of your past, of your mysterious youth. You're very much like an onion, sir."

"Yes, my life has had many layers."

"I meant how you make people cry." Mae looked over at Reed again. "Is he a good kisser? He looks like he'd be a good kisser. He has a sweet smile. Do you think he'd kiss me at midnight if I asked?"

"He is not a sweet man and you're not his type."

"But you are."

"And you're mine."

She glanced at Reed once more. "Is there anyone you don't use?"

"Are you even trying to keep time with the music?"

"I'm helping you. I am dancing with a drunk party guest. Butlers are known for being professional regarding appropriate etiquette, while drunks are known for being unsteady on their feet."

"Unsteady. Yes. I am. Christ, you rattle me."

"I don't rattle you at all. Nothing rattles you."

She stumbled when he changed direction. He did too. "You know," he said, "I think this is quite an aptly-titled song."

"I'm not cold, I'm angry."

"Yes, I gather. About the postcards."

"As if they matter," Mae said.

"They matter very much. The postcards matter because you're here instead of home, and since you won't leave I need to know if you'll work with me."

"What on earth do you think I've been doing, dancing?"

"No. You're irrefutably not dancing."

"And you're not leading."

"I'm drunk. I have an excuse." He watched her swallow and felt himself do the same. His hand pressed to the small of her back, bringing her a little closer to feel more than simply the warmth of her hand in his, or her palm pressed to his chest. The smell of her perfume drifted over him again. Sweating, he was sweating, the heat from his neck trapped beneath the collar of his shirt and bow tie, and he hissed through his teeth in exasperation. "Forward-side-together, back-side-together, forward-side-together, it's a simple box step," he said and she bumped into his chin and mashed his other foot. "Oh, you are hopeless. One day, I'll teach you to dance."

She tipped her chin, head angled. "But not tonight."

"Yes, not tonight. One of us has a headache."

"I hope it's you."

The left side of his mouth briefly quirked then flattened into something aloof.

Mae's pale smile resembled a faint grimace of pain. "When I found out what you do, what you are, I should have walked away."

"I should have let you go."

"I should have given notice and walked away, gone to live in Ireland to look after Sean, but I couldn't help myself then any more than I can now. What do you want me to do?"

"Stick to your usual routine. Basil's going to wonder where his butler is. Reed said Grant had the flu. That's useful. Keep it simple. Be professional."

"I am always professional, sir."

"Yes. You are. Stop calling me sir."

"What shall I call you then, Mr Somerset? Ian? Major? *Liar*?"

Those words rattled his bones. "Before the auction tomorrow, find Grant outside. Ring the police. His death will look like suicide."

"How do you know?"

He moved her in the simple box step, his timing perfect, his head slanted slightly.

"Set up many of those scenes, have you?"

Kitt glanced at Reed sifting past people, with Taittinger in tow. "Oh, goody. I'll come to you later and explain what I can then, but now, I need a reason to excuse myself so I can have a better look around outside."

"So, you're going to ham up playing drunk even more?"

"I am drunk."

"Ha! You never stumble or slur when you're hammered."

"Well, no one here knows that." He frowned suddenly, his hold of her loosening. "You really think I'm a ham?"

"No. You're the entire pig, sir."

The corner of his mouth twitched again. "I have missed your honesty. Would you like to be a side of bacon or a pork chop along with me? Play up the hostility you feel a little?"

Her eyes narrowed. "Are you suggesting I hit you?"

"Yes."

She snorted. "And you tell me I watch too many spy films."

"I grant you it is unoriginal. However, it's useful and... Yes. It would be unprofessional of you. You would never behave in such a manner, particularly at a social event such as this."

"Oink-oink," she muttered and Kitt moved back, taking her

along in the box step and her foot slid between his, hooked his heel, the hand she'd rested at his shoulder gave a shove. He stumbled in reverse, she tripped with him, and he landed on his arse, his back hitting the wall. Mae came down across his lap, her knee grazing close to his balls. His head hit the wall. His hat came off. The little bronze sun god statue on display in a wall *nicho* above him teetered and fell, knocking his cheek. There was a sting to the blow, a burning on his cheekbone.

Kitt touched the spot. His fingers came away with a smear of red. He smiled and Mae scrambled to her feet, looking properly aghast, left hand to her mouth. He smiled again, broadly, genuinely. How had he not noticed that she'd removed the Edwardian diamond ring from her chain and put on the third finger of her left hand?

Music continued to play. Nearby guests fell silent for a moment, others laughed, some went on dancing and conversing.

"You're smashed, full as a goog." Reed helped Kitt to his feet.

Kitt kept on smiling at Mae. She straightened the neckline of her dress, and fell back to her usual butler's calm, if not somewhat weary expression. Taittinger picked up the cowboy hat and adjusted his glasses, trying to hide his amusement. "Are you okay, Valentine?"

"Yes, I'm fine, Dr Jools. If you'll excuse me." She glanced at Kitt, slipped past chuckling, chin-rubbing Reed, and headed in the direction of the kitchen.

Taittinger handed Kitt the cowboy hat. "I don't think she likes you," he said with a chuckle.

"Jesus, Ian." Reed shook his head.

"What? You said give her a thrill." Kitt grinned and settled the hat on his head, pulling the brim low.

"I said dance with her, not fall down drunk with her. Bourbon on top of red wine and Dramamine is not a good idea." Reed exhaled.

Taittinger put his hand on Kitt's shoulder, shot Reed a sympathetic smile, and leaned in closer to Kitt, "Maybe in this case, drinking any kind of booze was a pour choice."

"*A pour choice*? You're hilarious, Tatts, but," Kitt moved nearer, "nah." He pulled the flute from Taittinger's hand and downed the remains of the man's champagne.

With a sigh, Reed took the glass from Kitt and handed it back to Taittinger. "I think I'd better take him to bed."

SOMETIME AFTER THREE A.M., he opened the door with barely a whisper. A nightlight in the kitchen cast his shadow eight-feet tall on the cabinets and wall. His socks shush-shushed over tile and carpet, moving toward the bedrooms before his shadow turned about, and he shushed into the sitting room, stopping in front of the sofa.

A dog's head popped up, narrow snout poking through a skin of blankets. There came a huff of impatient breath. "You would get here the minute I finally nod off."

Kitt pulled off a knit cap and unzipped his thermal jacket. "Why can't you sleep in a bed large enough for two adults, Mae?"

"You know why."

"Yes, you hate to sleep alone. Except you're not alone. A dog? Really?"

"One word from me and he'll bite off your broken nose."

Kitt looked at the slip of a dog beside the bed linen-shrouded slip of a woman. "Goodness me, he is terrifying."

"I never thought to get a dog before," she said. "Dogs are lovely. They're loyal, trusting, and live without pretence. They are honest in what they want from you."

"You think I'm not honest?"

"You played dead. Felix doesn't know that trick."

"I believed I was a dead man, Mae, and when I realised I was alive, I had postcards sent so you'd know too. You didn't get my postcards, did you?" He removed his socks, twisted them into a ball and tossed them in the direction of where he'd left his joggers. Kitt looked at her in the half-light, suddenly remembering when she'd whispered, *come home* in rank, semi-darkness. He switched on the brass lamp that sat on the end table beside the sofa. "Do you know, as I lay dying my last thoughts were of you?"

Mae put an arm over her eyes. "Go away."

"I told you we'd discuss this later. It's later. And I know what you want."

"You know what I want? You're a cracker."

"Well, am I wrong? You're here on this couch, sleeping with a dog because you hate sleeping alone in anything larger than a peapod."

Mae said nothing, her arm still across her eyes.

"You're not going to give me an inch, are you?"

Her breathing remained soft and even.

"No. No, you're not. Sod it." Kitt scooped her up, linens and all, and set her on her feet. He stood there, holding her and the blankets tightly, and it came upon him without any precursor. His first sob came out in a hiccup, the second full of tears, the third as snotty and wet and undone as a frightened little boy waking from a nightmare.

Uncovered, Felix hopped off the couch and nudged his thigh, and Kitt went on weeping, as months of tension broke apart. Mae pressed her face to his chest, trapped, half-mummified by the bedclothes wrapped around her. "Oh, what a baby ya are," she sighed.

"I know," he sniffled. "I know."

"Hush now. Hush now, Hamish."

Kitt lifted her, carried her across the sitting room and toed open her bedroom door. Dim light spilled into the dark room. He crossed the distance to the bed, laid her on the mattress, and settled in beside her, tucking loose bedcovers around them both, wiping his face and nose. He held her close, her head on his chest. "Go to sleep, Mrs Valentine," he said, voice gravelly with dissipating tears and a cool nose poked into his neck. Half a second later, the dog dropped down at his ankles, chin on his calf. "Don't even think about it, Sport."

"Felix. His name is Felix and he has a better a chance of staying here in this bed than you do, Kitt." She shut her eyes.

"Reed said he's something of a humper."

"Felix likes to try exert his dominance."

"Who's top dog in this bed right now?"

"I am, of course, ya crybaby. And he knows it."

"As do I." Kitt settled his arms about her again.

Silence stretched out. Mae thought he'd drifted off. She opened her eyes and glanced up at his trim beard, at his cheek where shadowy light turned the thin, scabbing, slice the little statue had made on his cheek almost black. He was here, trying to repair, to reconnect, and she was...she didn't know what she was. "I'm sorry I knocked you down," she whispered.

"No, you're not. You enjoyed it," he said, in a wide-awake voice.

Yes, Mae had enjoyed knocking him on his arse, it had been cathartic in a way, but it was disconcerting to find pleasure in his fall. How far had she slid into the depth of soullessness? "I'm tired, shirty, and I don't have the energy to do this or to have you try and seduce me."

"I couldn't seduce you if I tried."

"Are you going to try?"

"Do you want me to try?"

Mae said nothing.

He turned her slightly, his mouth at her ear, his lips brushing the shell, and he ran fingers down her throat, into the open neckline of her nightgown and between her breasts, skimming across the edge of her nipple. "Would you like me to try?" He kissed the little hollow behind her ear and trailed his hand to the hem of her nightdress, fingers running beneath the elastic of her knickers. "Shall I touch you?"

She pushed his touch away. "That I can do myself."

Kitt went still. "What is it you want then?"

"I want to sleep soundly, in a bed with you holding me, so that when I wake up in the morning I'll be fresh and ready to figure out how angry I have to be. And I want...I want..." Mae exhaled. "Oh, feck."

"What do you want, Mae?"

She twisted in his arms and sat up, yanking her nightgown over her head. "To feckin' make love with you one last time."

"With the dog watching? Wait. One *last* time?"

"Go to bed, Felix," she said. There was a quiet *thump* as paws landed on the carpet.

Mae looked at Kitt for a moment and he held her gaze, yet her hands moved tentatively. She took hold of his black tee, bunching it up his chest to bare his flesh, and moved no further. He tugged the shirt off. The garment joined the nightdress on the floor, followed by his track bottoms and boxer briefs. Still hesitating, she pushed him into the mattress, pressed the weight of her naked skin to his, and kissed him carefully, as if he were a bubble she could burst. Her hands moved the same way as her mouth, her touch delicate on something fragile. A love found and lost and found again, *this man* found and lost and found again, it was so fleeting, so easy to break.

Kitt began to touch her the same delicate way until her caution altered to something more solid, her fingers firm, groping, grasping, pressing him close, closer, and he understood why she'd hesitated, why she went slow, why she dug her fingers into him now. The new urgency wasn't about satisfying desire. This was about permanence. She wanted to ensure that he wasn't a ghost, that he was here. Once she had established his intransience, she began to kiss him the way he should have kissed her when he'd arrived home from Geneva, the way he should have before he'd left her home alone with a spindly Christmas tree and fallen into a hellhole, the way he should have when she'd come out of the bathroom and found him sitting on this bed hours ago.

She kissed him long and slow and deep, and he would have laughed at himself because a woman, this woman, was his home, his life, and it made his heart ache, his head hurt, *he* hurt with startling emotion that merged with pent-up desire, and the grisly images he saw when he closed his eyes—and sometimes when he left them open. With a half-sob, half-groan his mouth opened under hers. Their tongues tangled and his hands went to her breasts, fingers tracing around them. The sound of his breathing began to match hers. Mae bit his neck and stroked the length of his spine, palming his arse, pushing him as near as she could.

She was warm and soft, and he realised he was just as warm and soft—frustratingly warm and soft. His passion intensified, his hunger for her an open maw he was eager to feed, and yet, despite how he touched or kissed her, or how she'd darted her tongue in his ear and rubbed against him, that soft frustration continued. Rather than focus on the malleability, he trailed his fingers down her torso, skimming between her thighs.

With an impatient huff, Mae dragged his hand away. Kitt kissed her breasts, her ribs, her belly, kissing until his mouth met the softest, warmest part of her—and found himself just as soft and warm as before. For half a second, her breath caught, she quivered beneath his lips, and his pliable state didn't seem to matter, but her hands moved to either side of his head and she drew him back up the path he'd taken. She didn't want his mouth, hands, or fingers.

Kitt lifted his head. "Mae, I can't," he said, shifting to rest on his hip beside her, a few centimetres of space between them. "I ca—"

"I don't want to talk." She nudged him sideways, slid a leg over his hips and straddled him, hair spilling over one eye. "I don't want to talk, I want to—" she reached back and grasped yielding, flaccid, warm flesh. "Oh."

"Oh? Not, 'what a blow to manhood, what a betrayal to virile spies everywhere'?"

"Do you really think I would mock you for being the Spy Who Can't Get It Up?"

"Ouch."

Frowning she released his unstiffened flesh. "I can do better."

"No, no. That one was fine. I know you're angry, but I am happy to find your sense of humour is still intact."

"I'm not angry with you about this." She sniffled. "I'm confused, hurt, exhilarated, and shattered. I'm all over the place with you. I could laugh, cry, cut you into pieces and feed you to Felix."

"Well, that's gruesome. And angry." He reached up and pulled her hand, kissing the heel of her palm. "I've drunk too much. The altitude takes a little getting used to and I'm tired. I'm perplexed and frightened, very frightened. You frighten me. You being here scares the living daylights from me. My manhood notwithstanding, it's a matter o—"

"*Notwithstanding?* Aren't you clever." She sniffled, slipping her hand from his, savagely wiping her running nose with the back of a fist. "How are you hurt, exactly?"

"I cannot tell you how pleased I am to know you still want me, inoperative as I am."

"You're so bleedin' arrogant."

"It's part of my charm."

"You know what I would find charming? If you would shut up, hold me, let me fall asleep, and feck off in the morning."

"And that sort of honesty is part of your charm." Gently, he drew her down to his chest and she tucked her head against his shoulder, sniffling, slipping alongside his body.

"Why are you at a private wine tasting? Where did Reed get the Jefferson bottle?"

"He borrowed it to get us in. I thought you wanted to go to sleep."

"I'm too awake now. Tell me a story."

"I'm not sure where to start."

Mae lifted her head and squinted. "Start with when you left me with a Christmas tree."

CHAPTER EIGHT

Kitt reached over Mae and switched on the bedside table lamp. He needed light in the room to tell her what had happened. He slipped beside her again and played with her hair. "The Foreign and Commonwealth Office asked us to assist in a matter of antiquities that went astray from the Government Art Collection. Not our usual fare, but one goes where one is assigned, particularly when the curator of the collection goes missing."

"You were investigating theft, kidnapping, or both?" Mae nestled her head into the pillow.

"Both and more. Dr Vida Zora went to visit family in Beirut and never arrived. A portion of the antiquities she oversaw were not stored in the museum vaults, rather the items were kept in what was considered a secure location in Geneva. Normally, art crime squads collaborate with local authorities over theft of this sort, but this involved British Government assets—one of which was a Byzantine Maronite icon. Museums and private collectors often consulted Dr Zora for conservation advice. My colleague and I went to meet with her former associate, an expert on Aramaic and Hebrew artefacts, Sir Walter Molony. You may have heard of him."

"He's a professor or something with a position at the British Museum?"

"Yes. I've worked with him before. This time we met him in Singapore, went on to Beirut, the Syrian border, and back to Singapore, trying to find Dr Zora—"

Her head came up from the pillow. "You went to Syria in the middle of a civil war?"

"Just the other side of the border for a very brief stretch. And you know it's not the first time I've been to a country engaged in civil war. Didn't you ever think about where I went or where I'd been after I came home banged-up from a trip abroad? Didn't you want to ask what happened or where I'd been?"

"Yes, but I knew that you wouldn't tell me. And once I knew what you were, what you are, I didn't want to think about it. What can you tell me?"

Kitt was quiet for a moment. "Once upon a time, bad people stole things and no one lived happily ever after. The end. What do you know about freeports?"

Mae yawned and snuggled her cheek to his chest. "They're secure places fine art services like Christies, museums, and wealthy people store valuables, art, wine, cars, and such. Some people use them to avoid paying tax on very expensive things or hide assets from spouses they're about to divorce."

"Exactly. About five years ago, a man named Mikhail was accused of hiding hundreds of millions of pounds worth of paintings and antiquities at the Luxembourg Freeport, to conceal them from the executors of his deceased partner, Freudenstein. It was all over the news. Do you remember that?"

"Vaguely. Mikhail was cleared, wasn't he?"

"Yes, but that case led to an audit of donated pieces to the

Government Art Collection and the discovery that certain pieces of art and antiquities from the collection recorded as housed in the secure freeport, were in fact not housed in the secure freeport. For example, last year, customs agents outside Paris recovered the missing Maronite icon on a tour bus. No one on the bus claimed the piece. After that, the audit continued. Other items were found to be missing. Then goods one usually doesn't expect to be stored in a freeport turned up. Do you know much about smuggling?"

"People move goods in and out of countries illegally, drugs and such."

"The merchandise smugglers move varies. Every network is different, but an arms smuggler isn't going to also deal in Dutch master paintings unless something goes awry. Something goes awry once, it's an accident, three times is a pattern. The goods, schemes, and agents shift, but cash still changes hands, cash is still king, and cash is hard to trace. Merchandise, however, can leave a trail, one that's often easier to follow."

"And that's where you come in."

His fingers stroked through her hair. "I'm more interested in where you come in. And why."

"You said you wanted to have a happy Christmas, asked me to marry you, and then died, remember?"

Kitt gave a small, dry laugh. "I began working on this case last year, just after the audit on the storage units in Geneva began."

"You were in Geneva last February."

"I was pulled off the Geneva posting in May."

"You went to Turkey in May."

"I was reposted, but the assignment was the same. I came home in July, just before Sal Tornatore tried to kill you in my kitchen, and you exposed corrupt bankers and an international money laundering ring."

"Did I interrupt your little investigation?"

"Not exactly. I had to update and file the bloody paperwork. At the end of September, Swiss Customs contacted Special Operations Division. Llewelyn put me back on task. I went back to Geneva and you knocked out a wall in the flat downstairs." Kitt paused. The path of this investigation was convoluted and so was his explanation. "Are you following this?"

"Go on," Mae said in a voice anything but sleepy.

"Customs carry out checks at Freeports. It varies from site to site and it's based on risk analysis and resources. The Freeport companies and fine art storage services, like Christies, have their own employees, their own security measures. Security is tight at freeports, there's a customs office entrance at the front, turnstiles, keypads, locks, safes, bunkers. Places are temperature controlled."

"Yes, for the works of art and wine."

"Precisely. Delivery vans come and go from these facilities. The curious thing is that yes, some pieces went missing, while others were left behind, or replaced with items that didn't match what owners claimed to be part of their storage inventory."

"Somebody was picking and choosing what they wanted?" Her fingers trailed across his chest.

"Possibly. Stranger still, found within one of the Geneva Freeport units was a crate full of handicrafts, decorator tile samples, reproduction Persian rugs and knockoff Omega watches packed inside knockoff Chanel handbags. Knockoff handbags and watches contravene intellectual property laws, but the focus was on Swiss authorities uncovering evidence of theft of the artefacts, on looking for corruption in freeport companies, FreeSuissePort in particular and their supposedly airtight security. We wanted to find Dr Zora. The Swiss team believed there was some kind of criminal syndicate at work, a very well organised syndicate, and the British and Swiss Governments were inclined to agree. There was speculation that Dr

Zora might be the head of the group. That seemed a logical hypothesis, until more handbags turned up."

Mae's fingers circled the lumpy scar on his shoulder, the one she'd made with a broken broom handle last July. "These things are always about money, aren't they?"

Kitt glanced at her. "Why aren't you asleep?"

"Why haven't you bored me?"

"It's impossible to bore you when you find me so fascinating."

"And frustrating."

"I do love you. Very much."

She stopped tracing the scar, her words brittle. "What does all this have to do with you dying in Singapore?"

"I don't exactly know. You're multilingual. Have you ever heard the word *chichiltic*?"

"No. It sounds Hungarian, and I don't speak Hungarian."

"It's not Hungarian, it's Nahuatl, an Uto-Aztec language. It means *red*." Kitt slid his fingers from her hair, tucked his hands beneath his head, and stared up at the squared moulding around the ceiling light. He shifted his gaze to the head on his chest. "Are you sleeping?"

"No. Tell me the rest."

"Do I have to?"

"Yes."

He went back to staring at the ceiling. "As in Geneva, an inspection of units at the FreeSingaport in Singapore revealed further missing fine art, paintings, jewellery, antiques. Singapore's CAD—Commercial Affairs Department—had a different theory. They believed legitimate and undisclosed assets were being moved from place to place as a matter of tax avoidance or insurance fraud. Paperwork for one unit led us to shipping containers in the Port of Singapore, where, instead of turning up priceless goods taken from freeport units, we found moth-eaten Persian carpets, cheap artwork, and decorating samples of mosaic wall tiles. There were boxes of handicrafts and crates of knockoff Louis Vuitton, Prada, and Chanel handbags, sunglasses, watches. Reproduction luxury goods are a violation of intellectual property law and big corporations like their money. Usually, for a haul that size, Singapore Customs would contact Interpol, but this case was driven by Singapore's CAD cracking down on ill-gotten gains. The matter was kicked to Singapore Customs who traced the shipments back to the Port of Beirut's container terminal."

"Did Dr Zora turn up in Beirut or Syria?"

"Neither. Unsurprisingly, Beirut discovered a missing painting, some jewellery, pieces from a unit in Switzerland hidden in a load of junk ready for shipment to Singapore, however Lebanese Customs were rather alarmed by what they found in one container, all mixed in with birdbaths and garden statues."

"Let me guess, knockoff Gucci shoes and drugs?"

"No, late Soviet-era weapons."

"Define late Soviet-era weapons," she said, and her fingers tickled through the hair on his chest.

Kitt watched the absent movement of her fingers. "Lebanese Customs Administration believed they'd found missing nuclear weapons, stolen by an Afghani Mujahedin commander in the late eighties, buried in Syria, smuggled out and into Lebanon. It looked a lot like one, was very detailed, but again, most smugglers don't mix merchandise; they don't mix drugs with pirated sunglasses, or trade merchandise for weapons. Weapons smugglers want cash, not a swap for handbags, and crates of weapons make people nervous."

Her fingers stopped tickling. "Nuclear weapons, you went to recover nuclear weapons?"

"Well, I am a spy and it *is* the stuff of spy stories."

"It's the stuff of a clichéd spy story where one man saves the world."

"I couldn't be that one man?"

She gave a little laugh of disdain, fingertips resuming tickling strands of hair. "How many bombs were there?"

"I think you've hurt my feelings."

"So, you're not going to tell me?"

"Are you ever going to nod off?"

"Nuclear bombs, it's a nice try, but I don't believe you."

Kitt chuckled. "You didn't believe I had a ring either and—what is that you're wearing on your left hand?"

"I'm still waiting on the sister and the brother."

"You don't believe me?"

"About the sister, the brother, or the bombs?"

"Yes."

"I don't know what to believe. You're the spy who came back from the dead."

"We do it all the time in film and fiction."

"Yes, my only frame of reference. Is this fiction, Kitt, or fact?"

Kitt stuffed his hands beneath the pillow and laughed again, the sound hollow and cheerless. "I've told you what I can. The bomb was a prop from a film set that a collector in Kuala Lumpur had purchased at auction. Once we ascertained it was a prop, we let the shipment go and followed it back to the Port of Singapore. My colleague Dalton, Professor Molony, and local Singaporean port and customs workers opened shipping containers. The last two containers made it plain that we were looking at something more than tax avoidance, insurance fraud, and hidden luxury assets, more than theft of works of art and historic artefacts. This was, this *is* about corruption, inadequate safeguards, weak inspections, the counterfeiting and piracy of intellectual property, money laundering, and terrorist financing. The first thing I did was notify a contact at Interpol. Two minutes later it became obvious that the two dock workers assisting us in Singapore weren't really dock workers and all hell exploded." He breathed in softly, deeply and exhaled without a sound. "I'm afraid can't tell you anything more than that."

She huffed. "Jaysus, you and Bryce and your whole gobshite feckin' spy 'need to know' mantra."

"You have no idea."

"Then give me an idea."

"I have no idea. There are things I can't tell you because I can't quite remember. I have a little...memory issue."

She snorted. "First it was back from the dead, then nuclear bombs, now it's a spy with amnesia."

"James Bond and Jason Bourne had amnesia."

"Then you're playing true to type after all."

"I'm not playing anything."

"You expect me to believe this?" She lifted her head, rising on an elbow.

"It's not exactly amnesia. I had a blow to the head, lost a lot of blood, and nearly died of heatstroke. It put Swiss cheese holes in my memory. I remember, but I don't remember how it all unfolded, who did what exactly, but there are two things I can tell you for certain."

She inhaled and exhaled with a shudder. "So, tell me," she said through her teeth.

"I love you."

Mae sat up, blinking back angry tears, scowling, bedclothes tucked under her arms. "And?"

"Reed."

She huffed again and sniffled, wiping away wetness beneath her eyes. "He loves you and you're using him."

Kitt sat and considered his words. "Yes. Reed and I have a history. He's a twat, the most trustworthy twat I know next to Bryce, and he's keen to ferret out rot. IP, intellectual property, that's his speciality within Interpol's Trafficking in Illicit Goods and Counterfeiting Unit, but he's currently seconded to an international consulting and investigative firm specialising in IP. He's helping me follow up on a lead, an old informant who had a girlfriend from a family of smugglers in Malaysia."

Her frown faded into a peculiar little smirk as she adjusted the blankets around her. "Grant. Grant told me he'd worked for a family in Malaysia."

"Yes."

"Who killed him?"

"I don't know yet. I was just getting started, Mae. Meeting Grant was only the beginning and he didn't seem like much of a beginning. Until Grant died, Reed thought I was grasping at straws. I arrived here late because it wasn't certain if Grant would be here with Basil or in Canada with Mrs Basil. Once it became clear, Reed made arrangements to meet Grant on the rear patio, except someone else led or sent him to Lady Evelyn's art studio. Did you see anyone inside the studio when you found the body, Mae?"

"No, I was preoccupied with his being dead and—Lady Evelyn? I had no idea Taittinger's mother was titled." Mae gave a groan. "Over Christmas I addressed her as Mrs Taittinger. How embarrassingly unprofessional of me."

"Yes, you ought to be ashamed. Shall I continue?"

"Go on."

Kitt grabbed the pillow and shoved it behind his back and the headboard. "What I need you to understand is that I had to be, and I have to be, careful. It may seem like a worn-out spy film plot, but after being ambushed, my being dead became a means of self-protection. I had to be certain everyone believed I was dead, so I could finish this."

"Because you don't quit anything."

"Neither do you. I thought there was a rat inside. Well, that rat has made its way here. I tried to let you know, the best way that I could, that I was alive, despite what you were told. I thought you'd work it out. Truly, Mae, I haven't used you, I haven't lied to you, and I didn't plan this in advance. Someone else did."

"Who?"

"I have a thin little notion, a feeling my colleague Dalton is the rat and absolutely no proof, but I'm now seriously considering it might also be Llewelyn."

"Why would you think any of this has to do with Llewelyn?"

Anger streaked into his chest. His voice softened to a near whisper. "You're here. And it's not a coincidence, there's no such thing as coincidence in this kind of work. Before I left, I overheard Llewelyn ask you about dogs, if you liked them. He has two bloody dogs."

"Bambi and Thumper."

"Yes. At the time, I believed he wanted a new butler, that he was setting up a plan to try to lure you away from me."

"Lure me away?"

"Not like that. I know the man. I know how he thinks. He phrased it like he wanted you to do him a favour. You held your own with the old codger, put him in his place, yet here you are. Imagine my shock when I arrived at this house, you were across the room, kissing Russell Grant, the man I travelled here to meet."

Mae issued a short, nasal huff of exasperation.

"Were you threatened, is that what happened? Did Llewelyn mention prosecution for your unwitting involvement in money laundering and the Suisse Global debacle, some kind of trumped-up criminal activity related to the events last July?"

"No."

His expression turned as cold and hard as the diamond on her left hand. "You *volunteered* to do Llewelyn a bloody favour?"

"I was not about to sit at home and pine for a dead man."

"It's what you did for Caspar for sixteen years."

"It is not. I was productive. I worked."

"You worked and pined. It's all my fault then?"

Her expression remained as hard as the diamond on her left hand.

"Yes, it's all my fault. Now you're looking after Taittinger's dog."

"No, I'm Taittinger's butler. Looking after Felix comes with the position."

"And?"

"You think there's an *and*?"

Kitt rubbed at the whiskers sprouting on his neck. "Mae. Llewelyn wanted you somewhere where he could keep an eye on you, there's an *and*. The work isn't simply butlering and dog minding, is it?"

"Why does he want to keep an eye on me?"

"Because he's been keeping an eye on me."

Sitting, she rearranged the blankets, tidying the only mess she had control of. "That's ridiculous."

"That's this business. The *and*, Mae."

Mae straightened thick cotton. "I'm observing Taittinger."

Kitt mulled this over for a moment. "Observing him for what?"

"He's suspected of counterfeiting wine."

"Ah."

"Why does that 'ah' sound as if you already knew?"

"Early last year, wines suddenly started appearing at auction, bottles of Bordeaux not seen since WWII, bottles listed on ship manifests before WWI. There was talk of wine fraud amid some wine investment firms in the UK. I wasn't aware the theory had crossed the Atlantic. Have you found anything to implicate Taittinger?"

She shrugged. "Nothing that indicates he's committing fraud. I've seen him drink and buy a lot of wine, collect bottles and glass for his mother's sculptures, and tinker with the sports car he's restoring in the barn. Does that settle your mind about Llewelyn being nefarious?"

"No. How long are you supposed to be observing Taittinger?"

"A year."

"A year? Is that how long you thought it would take to get over me?"

Her snigger was as insipid as her smile. "You expected me to mourn forever and waste away to nothing over you."

His gazed travelled over her naked flesh. "You are rather thin. There is so little of you left. Yet I rather like what remains."

She pulled the covers to her shoulder. Her lifeless smile faded. "Bryce said your remains were found in a shipping container in Singapore."

This time, Kitt exhaled. "Things unfolded in a way that offered me an opportunity to move about with a little more freedom than usual, with no one to answer to except myself. I let myself be declared dead." Kitt shifted his left hand. "That container was nightmarish. We went back to the port in Singapore ready to find more phony weapons and copies of Chagall prints. Customs led us to containers that had been held up in port, or more likely intended to go astray. Inside those last containers were rolled-up carpets, crated decorator samples of tiles, reproduction artwork, fake handbags, and the bodies of Dr Zora and others who I suspect lost their lives trying to migrate with the help of cold-blooded human-traffickers. We were led back to Singapore and that container on purpose. Eleven innocent people died in a ghastly, sickening way. And I didn't."

Mae looked at him. His ugly-handsome features relaxed, mouth flat, eyes cool and steady, as if he were unaffected by the story he told, by the events he'd survived. "Do you feel guilty about that, Kitt?"

"Guilty, no. Angry, yes." He curled his hand into an awkward fist. "They died because I missed something. My mind was not on the work, it was on you. My mind is always on you. So, this really is my fault. I bear the weight of it entirely, my funny Mrs Valentine. I was arrogant and daft enough to think it was necessary to complete an assignment, daft to believe finishing what I started was necessary. Only now it is necessary. My following protocol had the very real potential of endangering lives. I had no choice but to improvise. Improvisation is often part of this work, but sometimes improvisation backfires. I didn't plan to leave you at home with the Christmas tree. I had every intention of coming home to you for Christmas. I had a service send you postcards so you'd know I was coming home, so you know I wasn't dead, no matter what you were told. *Quando, Quando, Quando*, I thought you'd work it out."

Mae's sniff of disdain was milder than Kitt expected. "A phone call would have been better."

"It's a cock-up. I admit it." He let out a quiet breath. "The less you know about me, the better it is for you, the safer you are. But the less you know about me, the worse it is for us. Bryce didn't lie about finding remains." Kitt held up his left hand. "I left something of myself behind in that container, more than blood."

Mae stared at the lopsided remnants of his ring finger and pinkie. "Oh, feck."

"A bit dramatic of me, I know."

"Does it hurt?" She touched two truncated fingers.

"Not anymore. At one point, it was it was badly infected, swollen like a balloon. I was a mess, Mrs Valentine. Battered, bruised, and out of my mind."

She exhaled, with more than a little exasperation. "I want to hate you. I don't want to care. I must be out of my mind to care."

"Goodness me, you care."

"Why do you get all the good lines here? Why do I have to be the straight man?"

"It's much more difficult to be the straight man."

She pressed her lips together for a moment and huffed peevishly. "Don't think losing a knuckle's worth of finger means I've gone all soft and mushy and forgiven you for you dying."

"Fingers. I lost knuckles' worth of *fingers*. Intelligence officers avoid drawing attention to themselves. Distinctive marks, like scars or missing fingertips, draw attention."

"Oh, that's what the cowboy hat's for, to distract from missing finger bits."

"Did you say you're thinking about forgiving me?"

"I haven't decided yet. It depends on how well you hold me while I sleep."

He gave her a soft smile, and pulled her into his arms, settling with her onto the mattress. "As much as you want me here to hold you while you sleep, I want to wake up in the morning and open my eyes to find you beside me instead of the phantom of fetid, rotting corpses."

"God in heaven." She rose up, hand going to his cheek. "Right, now I feel sorry for ya."

The glint in her eyes pacified the demonic images that slithered at the back of his mind. "I believe you do." Kitt kissed the inside her palm, below her left thumb.

"Do you want to tell me about it?"

"I just did." He drew her down again.

She snuggled into his neck, saying, "Impotence, missing fingers, a waking nightmare. Not exactly spy material anymore, are you? Maybe you should retire."

"Oh, so you do know the plan? Why do I need to tell you anything more?"

Mae groped for the bed linens. "There's something else I want to know."

"What?" A heavy blanket fell down over his naked skin.

"How did you end up here?"

"Reed. It's the second time the old twat's saved my life. When I didn't respond to his messages, he sent his mate, Cureo, to the port in Singapore. I'd be dead if he hadn't."

CHAPTER NINE

"What time is it?" Dalton whispered.

Kitt looked at his watch. "Nine-fifteen," he said, his voice thick, as if his mouth was full of pasty, lumpy porridge he couldn't swallow. Everything around him, the air, the walls, his own skin were all as thick and pasty and sweaty as porridge in a pot.

The lock fell, the container doors swung open, and the dockers, who could have been from the Philippines, South or Central America, elbowed each other, arguing, pointing, *Chichiltic*.

A rotten stench assaulted his senses.

The NCB officer backpedalled and vomited. Bodies, four of them lay in between open crates of counterfeit handbags and reproduction artwork. A knockoff Prada handbag hanging from his wrist, Molony floated in over the dead, his words warbling as he cast aside a Persian rug, "Excellent craftsmanship, but what we have here are higher quality knockoffs." His hand passed through a mosaic, fingers ghostly caressing a garland of grapes.

"To-long! To-long!"

The shorter docker flicked his long plait over a shoulder and smiled. "*Chichiltic.*"

"What time is it?" Dalton whispered.

Someone screamed in Malay, "*Teedak! Teedak!*"

A rocket of blood shot from the thin NCB officer's throat and turned to a ruby fountain that flooded the container. Kitt began to drown in the bloody, soupy heat. Corpses floated around him.

Laughing, knee deep in a sea of crimson, the Malay customs broker patted her barely out-of-his-teens Chinese assistant. "*He's stone, lah.*" Her long locks fanned out as she spun around and hit the crate. Eyes peered out through a cascade of grapes and leaves.

"What time is it?" Dalton murmured.

"No! *Amo, am—*" words became a gurgle, a shaft of sunlight glinted off the stainless-steel shaft of a slashing blade, and Molony stumbled, fumbling uselessly with a tiny Swiss Army knife.

Dalton, teeth blood-smeared, raised his arms in a defensive move. "*What time is it?*" he hissed, Rolex strapped on his wrist.

The ocean of blood drained away, Kitt snagged the edge of the wire with two fingers before it bit into his neck. The metal twine sliced into flesh and bone, forcing the heel of his hand to his throat. He was asphyxiating himself and laughter spun in circles around him, the docker's plait swayed like a pendulum. "*Chichiltic.*"

The woman screamed and screamed and screamed.

"What time is it?" Dalton laughed. The boy, nineteen at most, fell without a sound and Kitt basted in his own blood, the heat stole his breath, and the universe closed in until there was black, starless nothing.

Kitt opened his eyes, heart pounding, mouth dry.

The stink of death vanished. Mae's soft slumbering body welcomed him. He'd dreamt of stifling heat, yet it was freezing in the bedroom. He'd kicked off the bedclothes.

Shivering with a chill, with lingering, obstinate apprehension, he reached for the blankets and Mae, gathering her close. His heart slowed. Incrementally, dismay and horror sloughed off as he held her. Sleep was a necessity, a restorative requirement of body and brain. Nightmares were his mind's attempt to process past and present stress and trauma, and he wasn't afraid of them, but he did resent them robbing him of the rest he needed. It had been idiotic to hope that sleeping beside Mae would settle or reveal the provocation of his nightmares, and it had been wrong to think they could ever be together in a customary way afforded to other couples. The green-glowing bedside clock indicated he'd slept a little less than two hours.

What the hell was it, what principles had driven him to lead the life he had and spurn a tradition he'd never known he'd want? He looked at the woman asleep in his arms, a truthful melancholy enveloping him as he enveloped her. How hard would it be? How hard would it be to give up the ethics he'd lived by and quit without finishing a job that had nearly finished him? How hard would it be to wake Mae and simply vanish together? They could go to Sicily, to Australia, Belize or someplace where it was always summer...

A few minutes fantasising about a different life was enough. Kitt didn't try to fool himself into believing quitting or disappearing would miraculously alter reality. However appealing the idea of quitting, of vanishing, there were reasons, responsibilities, promises he'd made that prevented that being an option.

Reluctantly he shifted from the bed, leaving Mae to sleep. He crept into the sitting room and found his shoes. He sat and tied on his joggers. The dog on the sofa lifted his head and slid off the couch, wandering over with a prancing step, plopping his chin on Kitt's knee, gaze expectant. "All right. All right." For a moment, Kitt ran a hand over sleek fur, stroking the dog's soft ears. Then he jerked his chin toward the bedroom. "Go on." The slim-bodied animal went into the room with Mae.

Kitt let himself out of the apartment, exiting through the laundry, onto the patio. He zipped his dark, thermal running jacket to the neck, drew on a knit cap, pulling it down over his ears to keep out the chill of early morning air. Sunrise was more than an hour away.

He retraced the same path he'd taken earlier in the night, following the perimeter of the house to search the garage again. He left footprints, as he had last night, but wind and drifting snow would cover them the way it would have covered Grant in front of Lady Evelyn's studio. He dug under the seats of a Jeep and old British convertibles, rummaged through car boots, and found nothing more than an empty packet of chewing gum. In an instant, Kitt's mind flashed upon a dead man's mangled face. He smelled violets that turned into a nightmare of fetid flesh, the stench clawing at him again, harder and more viciously than when he'd been asleep.

He went outside, breathing in frigid air. There was one way and only one way to dig down to find the things he needed, and that was to accept everything and anything his brain threw at him, however chaotic, and try to see something he'd overlooked.

Dalton asked the time and Kitt glanced down at his watch. "Nine-fifteen," he murmured and breathed in an icy phantom odour, letting it wash over his mind, acknowledging the sensation.

In seconds, splintered images skittered across his line of sight and Kitt tried to look beyond recalling the spraying blood, to look past the glint of flashing blade. He saw Molony falling backwards, Dalton's bloodied teeth, the customs broker's fingers clutching at a torn throat, long, dark hair fanned out against tattered bubble wrapping that flapped over tiles. The corpses at the front of the crate, the woman, the shiny handbags, coloured decorator sample mosaic tiles of a face, of cascading grapes framed by wooden slats, Kitt drew his eyes through the memory, searching the moving picture inside the container laid out in his mind. *Chichiltic*, he heard the word over and over, but what couldn't he see?

He'd been through war zones, the aftermath of natural disasters, had been exposed to appalling instances of finding and recovering the dead, but this had been the first time a traumatic event had altered his ability to clearly recall an incident.

"God damn it," he muttered beneath the early-morning stars. He took a deep breath and began to run. Frigid air stung his nostrils, burned his eyes. Tears streamed down his cheeks as he took off toward the front of the house. It would be easy to tell himself the icy nature of a light wind caused his tears, but there was no wind, and he didn't believe in self-deception. It was relief, it was fear, it was frustration, it was the need to make sense when he knew there was no sense to be made. In the dark, Kitt sprinted for the driveway, running down the long length to the gate at the main road, and out, following the twisting, hilly topography. He ran and ran and ran until the mechanical muscle memory of running took over and his mind went blank and then he simply ran and ran and ran, until his clothes were soaked with sweat and his throat and lungs burned.

The setting bright moon drooped towards the mountains to the west, the sky a star-dotted deep purple scattered with darker clouds. In the quasi-dark, Kitt walked back up the long driveway to Taittinger's home. He took his time, catching his breath, letting his body cool down in the winter chill. His unhurried pace took him along high mounds of snow, aspen trees bare of leaves, the old barn where Taittinger's head bobbed past small, bar-covered rectangular windows.

Kitt moved by the double-garage door and around to the side entrance, where a security touchpad glowed on the wall. The touchpad was very much like the one he had at home. Despite the bars and the security system, the lights burning inside made it easy for Kitt to watch the activity indoors. He moved closer to a window, skirting the exterior, staying in shadow. Inside sat a tractor, a car covered by a cloth, and gardening paraphernalia. Along one wall, beneath the windows at the rear, sat firewood and a row of rectangular, hip-high wooden crates, the sort often used inside shipping containers. Taittinger ferried bottles from one wooden crate to another. He sorted the bottles by colour or size, held them up to a lamp to inspect them, and tossed them into a third wooden crate lined with heavy canvas.

When he'd searched the house, garage, and guest rooms last night he'd found nothing unusual, and he witnessed nothing unusual as he observed Taittinger through the window. Nothing odd or illegal took place, but why would a barn filled with firewood, crates full of bottles, a tractor, and an old car under restoration need security? Taittinger's guests were collectors. Collectors often had an interest in more than one thing. Interest in a vintage car was not uncommon. It was possible Taittinger was counterfeiting wine, but in the ten minutes Kitt watched, as his sweat evaporated in the dry, bitter air, his host did nothing but sort bottles. Then the man paused. He lit up a joint and began to smoke it, never going near the shrouded car.

Winter's frostiness began to prickle Kitt's hands. The remaining knuckles of the third finger and pinkie on his left hand ached dully. He flexed his fingers, stuffed his hands into the pockets of his jogging bottoms, and moved off to the curving house. What a foolish arse he was to have climbed out of a warm bed leaving behind a woman he loved. Why—*how* had he ever left Mae behind in the last few months?

Kitt went inside, shut the door, leaving the cold and his foolishness outside where it belonged. He went to his room and showered, the water as hot as he could stand. Then he dressed and went downstairs, cowboy hat in place. Basil met him at the bottom of the staircase.

"Good morning, Somerset," Basil said, hands on the sash of his navy-blue dressing gown, dark circles under dark eyes. "You seem to have recovered, better than Miss Bleuville. Better than Jools. I expected you'd still have a sore head, like many of us do."

"I do." Left hand in his pocket, eyes hooded, Kitt said, "But I had a walk and a breath of fresh air. That helped. A little."

"Well, hope you rugged up, else you'll come down with what Grant's got."

Kitt went for a hackneyed line he knew Mae would appreciate. "Yes, he certainly looked dead last night," he said, observing Basil for physiological changes; rapid eye blinking, a pursed mouth, nervous laughter, signs that might indicate a lie, a cover-up, or guilt, but there was nothing. "How is Grant this morning?" He adjusted the cuffs of his pale blue cashmere pullover.

"I thought it best to let him be. I'm certain Valentine can look after anything I might need while he rests."

"You're a very kind employer." Kitt pinched the bridge of his nose and screwed his face.

Basil chuckled. "I find a good fry-up for breakfast helps."

Breakfast. What a magical word. Kitt felt himself grin half-heartedly. "Is breakfast being served?"

"Yes, and you'd better hurry if you want any. Mr Nash is something of a bottomless pit. Valentine's refilled trays twice already. I know you...you..." Basil half-turned, sneezing three times. "Blast! The last thing I need is the flu. I know you got in late yesterday evening. We all had a good look at the cellar. Have you had a chance to see it?"

"I have. Thank you. What did you think of the Sunbeam?"

Basil's brows arched in surprise. "You're interested? I had no idea. Jools never said anything. Well, that's wonderful, makes it all a bit more exciting when there's more interest. See you back in the dining room. Left my phone upstairs."

In the background, Rosemary Clooney's warm voice musically murmured *Hey There* and Kitt lingered on Basil's mention of breakfast. A tingle that had nothing to do with warming toes and limbs struck him as he went to the dining room. He paused at the edge of the space. Ruby, Nash, Reed, Taittinger, and Basil's temporarily vacant seat, the guests had all made it to breakfast. One of them, all of them, none of them could have killed Grant.

"Do you ever not wear that hat, Somerset?" Nash slopped butter on a slice of toast. Half a second later, he dropped the knife, fumbled to pick it up, and lost it again. The knife *clanged* against the edge of his china plate, the toast fell into his lap, buttered-side down.

"Uhhh," Ruby groaned and adjusted dark sunglasses, a green beverage clutched to her bosom. She mumbled a scratchy, "Mornin'," and sucked green sludge through a straw.

"Yeah, g'morning." Taittinger, eyes half closed and red from smoking dope in the barn, reached for the cup Mae had placed by his plate. "Help yourself."

Reed looked up from his tablet. "It took you all this time to smell the coffee, Ian?"

Kitt gripped the back of the chair across from him. "There's coffee?" The room held the aroma of bacon, maple syrup, and eggs —Mae's scrambled eggs. A rush of salivating joy nearly made Kitt shout. He moved to the sideboard. He lifted a white plate with a yellow and black Art Deco design he identified as an old Aynsley pattern, and proceeded to inspect each covered dish, rolling back the opaque lid of everything on offer until he found the eggs.

His moment of drooling elation faded.

The equivalent of a demitasse teaspoon of scrambled eggs remained in the tray.

He stared at the dish, the leftover scrap of his black soul utterly destroyed. "Is this last of the eggs?" he said.

"Ask Mr *Nosh* there." Taittinger rubbed his temple.

A substantial mound of mouth-watering scrambled eggs sat on Nash's plate, toast crumbs down the front of his orange jumper. "You should have gotten here a little earlier, Somerset."

"Clearly." Kitt's eyes shifted from the eggs Nash crammed into his mouth to the empty sideboard dishes. Weeks of stewed diner coffee and abysmal fast-food breakfasts in airports had changed him. Never in his life had he wanted to kill a man over something so trivial. A solid clout to Nash's temple, with the pot of tea Mae had just brought in would suffice, but Kitt preferred to avoid violence before breakfast, and he didn't want to break vintage china. "Might there any more scrambled eggs, Mrs Valentine?"

"Early bird gets the worm, Somerset." Nash shook his head, making something of a show of his lack of hangover. Mae poured tea into his cup.

"I'll leave the worms to you, Bob." Kitt lifted his eyes to Mae. "Eggs, Mrs Valentine?"

"I'm afraid not, sir."

His grin smug, Nash dumped milk into his tea, teaspoon stirred *ding-ding* against the china cup. "Chin up, people, the ski slopes await."

"You're serious about skiing?" Basil returned to the table.

"Y'all mind talkin' soft like church mice?" Ruby winced.

Reed lifted his mug of tea. "Are we too loud for you, Ruby?" He had a swallow.

"Everything is too loud for me this morning."

Kitt half-whispered, "The eggs, Mrs Valentine?"

She glanced in Kitt's direction. "Unfortunately, sir, there was a kitchen mishap last night that left me short on eggs this morning. However, there is plenty of bacon, pancakes, French toast, and a lovely regional dish; a breakfast burrito of spinach, mushrooms, black beans, cheese, and green chile." She gave him a bland smile and placed the teapot beside Nash. "Shall I fix your plate, sir?"

Kitt knew the expression on his face was one of quizzical disbelief. *Bacon? Mushrooms?* Mushrooms in a dish was the same as having clumps of dirt in food. He loathed mushrooms. And she knew it. "I'll look after myself."

"As you wish." Still smiling blandly, she watched him slap a pancake on his plate and try to drag a scrape of egg from the chafing dish.

He took his seat at the table, across from Reed again and glanced at Taittinger's mug. "Is there more coffee, Mrs Valentine?"

"Of course, sir,' she said, "I'll get you a cup," and went to the kitchen.

"God help anyone who stands between you and coffee," Reed muttered, without looking up from the news he read on his tablet.

For an eternity, Kitt stared at his pancake and three hundred years later, Mae placed a steaming mug beside him. He reached for the yellow-and-black-edged china cup, inhaled the delectable aroma of what he believed was a small lot Tanzanian-grown bean, and almost wept with delight. Kitt brought the cup to his mouth, drank deeply, and immediately coughed. The coffee was horrifically sweet, so sweet it burned his throat.

Mae's smile was as sickeningly sugary as the coffee. "May I get you anything else, sir?"

Kitt looked down at his coffee and back at Mae. She had turned and proceeded to collect the chafing dish that had once held precious scrambled eggs, taking it to the kitchen.

Was poisoning his coffee her way of trying to tell him something? Or was she still angry? She had every right to be angry with him, but maliciously vengeful was a side of her he had never seen before and he looked into the cup, annoyed, dismayed.

Nash snorted. "If you're going to be sick, the loo's down the hall."

Rather than launch himself across the table to strangle the egg glutton on the other side, Kitt lowered his head, gazed through his lashes, and smiled broadly.

"Vegemite on toast." Reed didn't look up from his tablet. "You need Vegemite on toast, Ian."

"Is that what you ate, Dave?" Taittinger coughed. "That why you're all bright-eyed?"

"M-m. Brought my own." Reed pushed a small, bright yellow and red tube across the table. "Two slices of toast with a thin smear of this. Would you like me to pop some bread in the toaster for you, Ian?" he said, his gaze warm and adoring.

"Yes, thank you, darling." Kitt gave Reed a smile as treacly as Mae's had been.

Nash eyed them both, his laugh prissy and nasal. "Rather than eat that sludge, "perhaps *y'all*," he said glancing at Ruby and Taittinger, "might refrain from drinking if you can't hold your alcohol."

Kitt kept on smiling, reached for the Vegemite and knocked the sugary cup of coffee from the edge. The aromatic brew splashed across his abdomen and right thigh. The liquid, not quite hot enough to really burn, slopped down upon his lap, darkening his pale blue cashmere jumper. He bolted upright, swearing.

With Nash laughing, Ruby holding her head, and Reed's brows arched, Kitt set his hat on the table and started for the kitchen, shaking drops of coffee from his hands. "Mrs Valentine," he called out, yanking off the pullover, pushing through the swinging door, "I need you!"

The door flapped behind him. In the centre of the room stood a large table laden with a basket of fresh fruit, a pitcher of orange juice, a box of mixed mushrooms—and a shallow bowl of eggs.

Eggs.

There it was, what he had always endeavoured to avoid in his relationships with women; the murky with emotions and expectation, where feelings were hurt and bitter tears shed. Only this time it was his emotions, his expectations, and his feelings that were hurt. How astonishing that it came down to eggs. He shuffled his feet with more than a little impatience.

Mae, her head inside a large stainless-steel refrigerator, said, "I'll be with you in a moment."

"How long are you going to punish me?" He threw the pullover on the table beside the bowl and rubbed his thumb over the lumpy tips of two shortened fingers.

Mae straightened and turned, a bunch of celery in one hand. She looked him up and down, at the wet patch on his thigh, at the jumper in his hand. "I'm not punishing you."

"Yes. You are." Kitt leaned against the edge of the table and let his eyes shift to the bowl of beautiful brown eggs he knew Mae would insist on being free range. "You are surprisingly petty."

She crossed the tiles, tossed the celery on the table, and took the pullover. "They're hard boiled. Where's your cowboy hat?"

Kitt lifted an egg. It was room temperature. He set it on its side on the tabletop, watching it as he gave it a spin. The damned egg kept spinning and spinning.

Without a trace of a smug smile, raised eyebrow, or sarcastic tilt of her head, Mae carried the cashmere to the sink and began to rinse it, her back to him.

An arse. He was an arse. "I apologise. I am sorry, but seeing these eggs, the coffee, and all the sugar in it. What would you have me think?"

"I put sugar in your coffee?"

"A sand bucket's worth."

"Taittinger takes his coffee with sugar, five teaspoons. You two are the only ones who drink coffee. I wonder if the cup I gave him had any sugar in it at all." Her shoulders slumped slightly, as if she were appalled by the unprofessionalism of her indiscriminate sugaring.

"If I had to point the finger at anyone here, I'd go with Bob Nash, but I've found nothing to implicate him in anything criminal aside from his fashion choices and selfish discourteousness. I've found nothing on anyone. I need to get into the barn. Can you help me with that?"

She stopped rinsing cashmere and faced him this time. This time she lifted a brow. "Yes. Was there something else?"

His chin jutted forward. "Are you wearing my watch?"

Brow furrowing deeply, she went to the refrigerator, pulled something from the door, and came to stand beside him at the table. "I've only ever witnessed you this way once before, hungover, hungry, and cranky as a wee babe in wet pants," she said, handing him a bottle of cold water. "What a frightful combination."

Without a word, he unscrewed the top and guzzled the entire litre of spring water. When he was finished, he held the bottle in his left hand, most of his fingers wrapping around the plastic. Eyes on the floor, he said, "I feel cheated. I haven't had your scrambled eggs since September, since before I went to Geneva." He lifted his gaze to hers. "Cheated. Four months without your eggs, Mae. Four months. Through no fault of our own, we've been cheated of four months. Except in a way is my fault. I have myself to blame, and I'm sorry. I'm sorry I hurt you. I'm sorry I made you grieve again. It was not my intention and I regret, very much, that I put you through hell."

She undid the leather strap at her wrist and traded his watch for the empty water bottle. "I'll make you coffee before I go," she said softly.

Kitt paused, the watch half-secured on his wrist. "You're leaving? Thank Christ."

She left his side and put a kettle to boil. "Have you forgotten? I have duties to perform, dogs to exercise, guests to ferry to ski slopes, dead men to lie about finding."

"Yes. There is that."

Mae reached for a packet of coffee beans. "What? No instructions, no..." she lowered her voice an octave and mimicked him precisely, "...remember to breathe, Mrs Valentine?"

"Since you asked, look after Taittinger and Basil if necessary, do whatever butler things Grant would have done for him, because that's the sort of butler you are. Sort out whatever you need to for the lunch this afternoon. After that, you're leaving."

"I'm doing nothing of the sort," she said, a little louder than she'd meant to, and moved across the tiles until she stood in front of him and the coffee beans perfumed the air between them. "My leaving would look suspicious. With a murder in a cosy mystery such as this, on a country estate such as this, suspicion always falls on the domestic help, such as the butler."

"This is not a cosy mystery. It's a somewhat gritty cosy romantic spy thriller that tries hard to be amusing. Like you are now."

"Whatever the genre, have you considered that maybe you need me here?"

"I don't. After you 'find Grant' and get me into the barn, you're leaving. This is not negotiable."

"You're right." Mae set the coffee on the table. "We are not negotiating anything."

Head cocked slightly to one side, Kitt stared at her. "You are the most stubborn, contrary woman."

"Because I don't let you dictate what I do or make decisions for me? Or because I want to finish what I started, like you?" She grabbed the back of his neck, jerked him down, kissed him hard, then let him go. Abruptly.

Off balance, Kitt bumped into the table and reached back to

steady himself. The tips of his fingers upended the bowl of eggs. Amid a crash of blue crockery and the insipid bounce of cracking hard-boiled shells, two bright orange yolks exploded upon white tiles.

He looked down at the gooey, sticky mess that had spattered his shoes, and back at Mae.

CHAPTER TEN

She had expected last night's paw and boot prints to be covered by fallen snow. She'd expected the bits of Grant's flesh to speckle the slate patio at the front of the stable-turned-art-studio. She'd expected a dark crimson pool to shine bright against white snow that was somehow whiter in the morning sunshine. Mae was prepared for blood spatter on the sand-toned wall beside fold-back glass doors to make a fleshy, macabre piece of modern art. She was ready for blood on the windowpanes and the stuccoed front, things she hadn't been able to see in the dark of last night, and she stared at the stippled red, thinking about how one removed blood from painted stucco.

Cleaning vomit was easy, a few towels, a dish soap or laundry detergent, but blood, like spray paint, could be tricky to remove. Blood needed a cleaner with an enzyme in it to dissolve the protein without damaging the surface beneath the stain. Not the bleaching agent in denture cleaner, but perhaps peroxide and white vinegar. She'd have to look in the laundry or the barn to see what was on hand to—

What strange priority her mind made of stain removal over the death of a man. She couldn't help how her brain viewed the scene automatically, professionally, despite there being no need to be professional because this was not a 'real' job; the position was pretend, as pretend as Kitt's cowboy hat and Australian accent. She knew her reaction was shock, not callousness.

Felix pulled on his lead, wanting to get closer to the body, and she looked at the site of Grant's death, less than three metres from where she and the dog stood, half-shrouded by a clump of bushy piñon trees. It was chilling, grotesque, and Mae stared with sick fascination, with morbid curiosity, with a strange rush of excitement, the same rush of excitement as when she'd found two dead men last summer. There was just one thing, one very bizarre, unexpected issue with this winter death scene. Mr Grant wasn't part of it. Instead, Mae stared at a deer.

Its neck had been ripped open.

"LOOKS like we're all going to stay here and recover, but Valentine will take you up to the ski run, Bob," Taittinger massaged his eyelids, fingers beneath his glasses.

"Well, hell, I'm not going alone." Nash, decked in out shamrock-covered ski bottoms, leaned his snowboard against the side of the display case full of old tin toys. He glared at the others who were in no condition to cross-country ski, snowboard down the Pajarito slopes above Los Alamos or skate the town's little ice rink. He left the room to change and Mel Tormé crooned *Heart and Soul* to the hungover audience drooping about the great room.

Felix trotted in, prancing past the wide chair Taittinger shared with Ruby. Suddenly, the dog rocketed around the great room, spun in circles, and bit the rug under his paws. Head bowed to play, he barked and shot off around the room again until he leapt upon the ottoman in front of Reed and Kitt. Half a second later, Felix hopped back to the floor and began sniffing a trail of something. Hunched low, legs spread, Kitt pretended to doze. Head tipped against the little couch, brim of the cowboy hat screening his eyes, he watched the skinny animal for a moment, then set his attention on the others.

The Chungs, the newlywed couple from Hong Kong, wouldn't arrive until lunch. Kitt hated that he was mildly curious about them solely, as racist and culturally insensitive it was, because they were Asian and might, with the faintest possibility, have a connection to what had occurred in Singapore. Instead of focusing on his shameful thoughts, and desperation and the iniquity of racial profiling, he set his attention on the present, on the people in the room.

Basil stood at the fireplace, warming himself. Slumped, Ruby's sunglasses remained in place as they had during breakfast. Forehead in her hand, she shaded her eyes from the glare coming through the windows, or perhaps from returning Mr Nash and his trousers, which were turquoise and dotted with tiny white stars.

"You still hungover, Ruby?" Nash plopped into a white armchair that made his trousers look even brighter. He had a book in his hand.

"Are you sure that green slime you drank at breakfast was supposed to cure a hangover?" Reed said, brushing the dog aside, phone in hand.

"It's not a hangover, it's a grape depression," Still cannabis-mellowed, Taittinger laughed, perched on the arm of Ruby's chair, rubbing her shoulders. "Is there anything I can get you, Ruby?"

"More aspirin." Ruby groaned. "I think I may die."

From the right, Mae entered the great room. Kitt watched her and she looked at him, dour-faced, back stiff. She gave him a solid stare. He lifted his head slightly and scratched his nose, finger pointing toward Taittinger. The dog scampered to her side, licking her hand, and she kept staring, eyes widening slightly, subtly. With a small pulse of her jaw, she approached Taittinger and leaned close to the bespectacled man.

Taittinger's ever-present smile faded and his mouth formed a clear, single word, 'What?' He rose from the sofa's arm, adjusted his glasses, rubbed his goateed chin, and left his spot beside Ruby, following Mae.

She halted near the ottoman. Kitt listened to their quiet exchange. "There's blood everywhere," she said.

Taittinger chewed his bottom lip for a second. "Are you okay?"

"I'm a little shaken. All the blood and gore. It's rather gruesome."

"Yeah. Yeah, you would be. Probably coyotes. They go for the weakling."

Weakling? Kitt listened intently.

"You don't think it could have been..." Mae turned slightly to cough, eyes squinting then flashing wide at Kitt, "...a bear?"

Kitt stayed in his slumped, sprawled-leg position, listening, watching. *Weakling. Coyotes. Bear.* Yes, something had gone arseways and balls up.

Taittinger rubbed his chin again. "There's that much of a...mess?"

"Perhaps I ought to ring animal control?"

"That and," a deep groove dug into Taittinger's brow, fingers pinching the end of his chin whiskers, "I guess I'll call Hector. Have him send one of his men over to... Right in front of the studio?"

"Yes."

"Valentine, sugar," Ruby cupped a hand to the edge of her dark, oversized sunglasses, sheltering from the snow-bright outdoor glare. "Could you pull down the shades in here, maybe turn off the grandma music?"

"Of course." Mae crossed the room, dog on her heels, and tapped the touchpad on the wall. Music stopped, grey shades rolled down, filtering out the brightness of the late morning sun.

Taittinger licked his lips and began to clear his throat.

"You're not coming down with Grant's bug, are you, Jools?" Reed tucked his phone away.

Arm on the stone fireplace mantel, Basil chuckled. "I think Jools and Ruby are still feeling the effects of a New Year's Eve well spent."

Ruby smiled, albeit wanly. "You have such a nice way of putting things, Baz, but I've got whistle-belly thumps and skull cramps. I'm thinkin' I may go back to bed for a bit—like 'til the Chungs get here this afternoon."

"I have to be honest," Nash straightened, book in hand. "I thought ten-thirty was too early a start for you people. Look at Somerset over there. So much for the healing power of Vegemite."

Basil chuckled. "How anyone can eat that salty muck I'll never know."

Ruby sighed. She made a half-arsed attempt to get up but sank back into the chair.

"Hey, uh, everyone..." Taittinger began, voice a little croaky with tension. "I need to excuse myself. I've got a small situation to tend to."

"You mean how your dog needs to go to canine obedience?" Basil pushed Felix away from his knee.

Felix trotted to Ruby's wide chair, hopped up, and plopped down between her and the cushions, head on her lap. For a moment or two she scratched his chin. "Oh Lord, dog. You're sweet, but not now, I can't. I just can't." She prodded him off the chair.

Undaunted, Felix moved on.

"Don't even think about it, mate." Reed shifted and waved his arms, preventing the dog from latching on to his leg. Instead, Felix hopped onto the sofa, walked over Kitt, and squished into the small space between his thigh and armrest.

For two seconds, Kitt lifted his head, had a look about, crossed his arms, and slouched into his pre-jostled position.

Taittinger, frog gone from his throat, stretched out his hands like a referee at a sports match. "I know you might want to get some fresh air, or have a cigar, maybe you might even change your mind and go for a ski, but if you do, stick close to the house. Looks like we may have a cougar or black bear roaming around on the property." He adjusted his glasses and licked his lips again.

"A bear?" Basil's eyebrows undulated, arching from left to right, his dark moustache twitching. "How do you know?"

"There's a...carcass."

"What kind of carcass?" Reed asked.

Nash glanced up from his book. "Don't bears hibernate in winter?"

"They come out now and again, but yeah, this time of year it could have been a cougar. They're active year-round. A cougar's more likely." Face pinching, Taittinger gave a helpless shrug. "And this one took down the deer Valentine found."

"You know," Nash balanced the open book on his yellow-clad thigh, "a set of antlers above your fireplace would look quite rustic, manly."

"Right, Bob." Ruby chuckled softly. "Nothin' says masculine like a set of antlers. Was it a doe or buck, Valentine?"

Faces turned in her direction. Mae pressed both hands over her mouth. Her shoulders sagged. She knew exactly, exactly what to do. Her actions were artful, flawless, and, for a brief moment, it gave Kitt a sense of pride that immediately turned to regret. She was here because of him, play-acting because of him, in the centre of danger because of him. "Forgive me. Blood makes me a little..." She swallowed. "What did you say, Ms Bleuville?"

"Oh, shit, Valentine." Taittinger led Mae to the ottoman in front of Kitt and Reed. "Sit down."

"Aw, dang, yes, sit." Ruby nodded. "You ought to be restin' peaceful, sugar, not here."

"So, were there antlers?"

Mae's briefly eyes shot to Nash. "No antlers." Stiffly, she sat and began to fidget with the strings tied at the front of her apron. "It's out there, outside in the snow, right in front of the old stable and the—"

"You have a stable, Jools?" Nash snapped his book shut. "I like horses."

"No, no." Taittinger shook his head. "It used to be a stable, now it's my mother's summer art studio."

Mae shuddered. "There's so much blood." Slyly, with skill that made Kitt inexplicably proud and horrified, she rose, gave another shudder and plopped back onto the ottoman. "I beg your pardon, Dr Jools. I believe I'm a little light-headed."

Kitt sat upright, shoved his hat back, a groove of sleepy irritation on his face as he looked about the room.

"If you'll all excuse me." Taittinger exhaled unhappily and left his guests.

Nash tossed his book aside and hopped to his feet, looking at everyone "Well, isn't *anybody* going to give Jools a hand? Aren't any of you going to help?"

Kitt yawned and counted. He got as far as seven before Nash headed out of the great room. "What's going on?"

"Don't concern yourself. Just go back to sleep, Ian," Reed leaned over, kissed Kitt on the mouth, shoved the cowboy hat back over his eyes, and exited in the direction Taittinger and Nash had gone.

Ruby looked at Basil, Basil glanced at Kitt, and Kitt yawned, and began counting again. He knew human nature well. *Help?* Nonsense. Long ago, it had ceased to surprise him how people were drawn to gape at car accidents, house fires, disaster zones of any sort. *Helping* Taittinger had nothing to do with it. Kitt got all the way to six before Basil pulled Ruby to her feet. The pair went after the Nash, Reed, and their host.

A long moment of silence filled the room. Finally, Mae sighed. "Russell Grant's body is missing." She stood, went to the window, and watched the snow fall. "He was replaced with a dead deer."

"So I gathered."

Snowflakes meandered to the cold, white ground. The last fifteen minutes had been surreal and absurd, right down to that smacking kiss Reed planted on Kitt. Mae crossed her arms, snorted, and muttered, "Anything for Queen and country, use whomever you must, lie back and think of England."

"I didn't quite get that, Mae."

"Sorry. I said, anything for Queen and country, use whomever you must, lie back and think of England."

"Actually, it's lie back and think of you," he said, directly behind her.

Mae turned and looked at him, one eye squinting. He'd taken off the hat.

He wore a faint, somewhat mocking smile as he removed his brown jacket and slid it onto her shoulders. "Is that an additional thing you'll have to come to terms with about me and my work?"

"No. But I wonder what it makes you?"

"A professional."

"Well, I never thought of a spy as a whore, but you are getting paid. I hope you enjoyed it. Reed is rather attractive."

Ever so ridiculously nonchalant, he slid his left hand into a trouser pocket. The navy-blue polo neck he wore turned his eyes a deeper blue. "He likes to irritate me."

"You don't look irritated." She pulled the jacket close.

"Christ, he's a terrible kisser."

"Perhaps he thinks the same thing about you."

"I don't give a damn what he thinks. He ate onions. They were in that mushroom burrito thing you made. Whoever taught him to kiss should be put up against a wall and shot."

She snorted and mumbled something again.

"What was that?" Kitt left her by the window and moved to the sofa.

"Everyone thinks they're a good kisser even when they are not."

He leaned on the arm of the sofa and regarded her. "I am a very skilled kisser."

Mae smiled again, softly, but the softness had pointed edges. She came toward him. "Who taught you to kiss?"

Kitt bit his back teeth together for a half second. "A pretty Greek girl named Vassiliki. I was fifteen."

"And what did you learn from her?"

"A little tongue goes a long way. Who taught you to kiss?"

"A pretty American girl named Lisa Patton. Is that what Reed did, slip you a little too much tongue?"

The left corner of his mouth lifted. "No, no. Let's go back to Lisa Patton."

"You are curious about the strangest things."

"The point is I'm curious."

"And I'm pissed off."

"I hadn't noticed. Lisa Patton?"

Mae crossed her arms. "We were eleven and were acting out something we'd read in a romance novel."

"I like romance novels," he said.

"Read many, have you?" Mae gave him that look, the one that told him he was full of shite.

He'd missed that look. "You think *Jane Eyre* is the only romance

I've ever read? A man can learn a lot from the much-maligned, humble romance novel. Everything, from the agency of women, power dynamics in relationships, communications skills, to kissing and how to have sex, it's all there between the pages."

"If you learned so much, where did you go wrong?"

"I've had a little trouble with the ending. And, I suspect, so have you. There was, a very long time ago, a woman—a girl, really. I thought I loved her, but she very nearly killed me. She stabbed me in the back, literally. That scar, the one at the top of my shoulder blade, the one you like to run your fingers over, she did that."

Mae gave him another reminder that he was full of shite. "What was her name?"

"Honor, which was something she did not possess. With the benefit of hindsight, I know that whatever I felt for her wasn't love. It was infatuation; immature feelings of passionate tenderness, or whatever passes for what you think is love when you're twenty and stupid. The point is you are new ground for me. I don't know what I'm doing, or really how to do it. I'm improvising. I'm usually quite good at improvising."

Again, she squinted an eye.

"Right. I'm terrible at improvising anything with you. You, on the other hand...I must be honest and admit I was impressed how well you improvised."

"I was good, wasn't I?"

"Quite."

"Then why don't you trust me, Kitt?"

"Oh, but I do," he said, aware the pause before his reply was a fraction longer than it ought to have been.

She crooked her head slightly, a pale smile on her lips. "I am not going to stab you in the back."

"Perhaps not intentionally," he said, and knew how positively ridiculous and childish it made him look, but sometimes being ridiculous and childish opened one's eyes to what one failed to see. "That's why you said *no* isn't it?"

"When we first met," she moved closer, "when you were laid up with a detached retina and I brought you Chelsea buns and coffee, you were convinced I wanted something in return for my kindness. Because of your work, you are so accustomed to not trusting anyone that you fail to understand you can trust me, really trust me."

"I'm a fool."

"Romance novels. Communications skills." With a *pfft*, she uncrossed her arms and shook her head, muttering under her breath.

"I'd apologise to you again, but I know that won't make any difference. Some things are out of my hands. One cannot control the variables in intelligence work. I forget that sometimes, particularly when it comes to matters that involve you when those matters shouldn't involve you at all."

Her muttering ceased. "Did you find anything else, anything when you searched rooms and the house last night?"

"No. There was nothing in Lady Taittinger's art studio either, except two crates of glass and a metal supply cupboard. There's nothing in the garage but cars. The barn, I haven't been in there yet and I'd prefer to get in without breaking in. Do you know the key code?"

"Yes, but you won't find anything in the barn besides a tractor, gardening stuff, crates of glass, and the car Taittinger's restoring. I've already searched. More than once. I was very thorough."

"You and Reed need to leave thorough to the professionals."

"I *was* thorough. I even searched the car."

"How splendid." Kitt rose from the arm of the sofa.

Mae looked at him, at the way he stood so casually, so relaxed, left hand at his side, the natural curl of his fingers hiding two missing knuckles. "Don't tell me you're angry."

"I sodding well am."

"Are you angry that I *thoroughly* investigated the barn or is this about the eggs?"

Kitt stared at her woodenly, controlled in that way he knew frustrated the hell out of her. He really did not want to frustrate the hell out of her, yet if he let loose his own frustration his expression would turn him even more petulantly childish than he'd already been. What was it about her that reduced him to behaving like a sulky five-year-old deprived of his favourite toy?

"Really?" She sniffed. "The eggs? You still think I did it on purpose, you think I denied you breakfast, that I was exacting revenge?"

"Revenge is a very human need." He glanced at the dog asleep on the sofa.

"Oh, yes, you trust me." Mae exhaled a scornful laugh. "Power dynamics. Of course. That's what this is about: control and domination. You try to control the people so that the dominant player wins. You once said the work you do was a game."

"It *is* a game."

Her mouth curved into an anorexic smile. "We're all sixes and sevens with each other, aren't we? Up and down. I can't quite get my head around it. I saw you everywhere when I thought you were dead. I heard you. Every man was you. Is that happening now? *Are you alive?*"

"Pinch me."

Mae snagged him by the waistband of his trousers and shoved her hand down the front.

"Perhaps pinch was a poor word choice." Her hand slid along the length of him, back and forth. Kitt drew in a sharp breath. "Mrs Valentine, what are you doing?"

"Just checking." She pushed him backwards and he bumped

into the sofa's arm. Her fingers moved, delightfully, and kept moving.

"Last night," he swallowed, "you thought I didn't want you, didn't you?"

"And now?" She gripped his flesh, stroking.

"Control and domination. You may have the winning hand."

"That," she paused her movements, "was terrible."

"I'm only trying to meet your fictional spy expectations."

"I am not a spy." She withdrew from his trousers.

"No. You're not." The little quirk of his mouth had revealed his amusement. His eyes had grown warm for a while, but his mouth twisted, matching the curve of his recently broken nose. "This is how it's going to go. Grant's murder and the disappearance of his body is on me, not you. Llewelyn putting you here to watch Taittinger, that's over. You are done." Kitt sat on the arm of the sofa and took a breath. "Please. Please, Mae. I can't focus on what I have to do with you being a nuisance to worry about. You know I can't see beyond you. I am sloppy, blind to anything but you, which is going to get you, or me, killed, genuinely this time. Can you understand why I am asking?"

Mae began to rub the heel of one hand into her forehead mumbling, cursing in Italian under her breath.

"Yes, you understand. And you're not going anywhere without me, are you?"

She looked at him and ceased trying to grind a hole in her skull, head shaking, slowly. "I nearly left last night. I was going to smash Reed over the head with a fruit bowl, grab the dog, and go, but then you came back from the dead. Do you understand why I won't leave?"

"You are, at times, a maddeningly wilful woman, Mae."

"A *yes* would have been sufficient. If I were a man, you'd call me stubborn, determined, tenacious, strong-minded, but because I'm female I'm *wilful*."

"If I were trying to be sexist I would have said you're a *headstrong girl*, Mae. This is not your profession. And I said please."

"You think saying 'please' and 'I love you' is enough?"

"Will you ever cease to be angry with me?"

"No. And I shall stay here until I complete what I was asked to do, just like you. My work is contingent upon wine and what I find out about these people. You're going to help me and I'm going to help you find out who killed Grant. Maybe by then I'll be done bei —" With a huff, she ground her forehead again. "These people. I have no idea what I am going to tell Bryce about Reed or you, particularly since the information he had on you two was false, which I suppose is standard misinformation spy shite."

Ice burst into Kitt's bloodstream. Cold sweat prickled the back of his neck. "Bryce is your handler?"

"Yes."

Kitt cocked his head, one eyebrow arched. "Just how is Bryce handling you?"

She dropped her grinding hand and mirrored his expression. "And you believed I was petty?"

"Yes. That was quite uncalled for. I apologise."

"I don't want an apology."

"What do you want?"

"You."

"You have me."

"But I didn't. You died. What I feared came to fruition. You died and I was alone again." She looked at him, eyes bright with ire and frustrated tears. "But Bryce, Bryce has been a very good friend."

"I do believe I'm going to kill your very good friend."

"Enough. He didn't talk me into anything, if that's what making you spout homicidal hyperbole. He was simply a prompt to remember that I could save myself, as I had when Caspar died. I couldn't look at your clothes, your toiletries, your insanely enormous bed. I couldn't have those reminders of you about me. I had to rid myself of them, yet clearing out your things, clearing away reminders of you wasn't enough until I remembered I could bury myself in work, like you did for years to ignore your feelings for me. With work, I could ignore you the same way; only you were still everywhere. I could not escape you." She let out a quivering breath and swallowed.

"You're going to be angry about this, angry with me, for years."

"Yes. No. I don't know, but I can't really blame you for this," she sniffled, a tear dribbling. "I knew you'd be a heartache. I can't blame you when I knew that. You lie for a living. It was my choice to not ignore what I felt for you, to act on it." Jaw set, Mae inhaled through her teeth and exhaled raggedly. She turned in a circle and sank down onto the sofa, waking Felix. The skinny dog took that as his cue to move into her lap. "I loved you and then, Jaysus, Bryce told me you were dead. You were gone and I'd only just found you."

Kitt watched her become somehow smaller. "I'm here now," he said.

"But you weren't. I believed you were dead." Furious tears trickled out fast. "And don't you *bloody* say anything about your bleedin' postcards. You were dead, and work was my way to process what I had lost, so I wouldn't fall into a pit of PTSD like my brother. The work Llewelyn asked me to do held a strange connection to you, to the life you led. I think that's why I agreed to do the favour he asked. I wanted to know why, why you do what you do. The only way I can explain is that I was angry you died, and I wanted to understand you."

"You understand me."

"No. I don't understand you, or myself." It wasn't the way she curled over the dog and stroked the animal that made her look so tiny, it was something different; it was a surrender, a collapse, an utter and unmistakable defeat. A guttural sob worked from her throat. *"Oh Jaysus. Jaysus,"* she muttered, and what remained of her tenacity crumbled.

She was correct. They were all sixes and sevens with each other. The shock had worn off for them both. Kitt had known her decompensation would happen eventually, but he was completely unprepared, and anything he thought to do seemed anaemic. When she began to weep in a way he'd once seen her cry for her dead husband, Kitt had no clue, no useful thing to say, no idea how to comfort her, or if it was wise to try, but he had to try.

Ready for her fists, for her anger, for her snotty nose to wet his neck, Kitt sat beside her. "I'm sorry," he said, the words feeble, his eyes burning. Had he really believed sending her postcards would be enough of a sign, enough proof of life? Yes. Yes, he had, and his action had been anaemic, he was anaemic and far feebler than the consolation he tried to give her, than the regret he tried to express. "I'm sorry," was all he could say, pathetically. "I'm here. I'm sorry. I'm here now."

She looked at him, her face awash with tears that blamed, screamed, hated, and loved him, muttering obscene words and phrases at him as she cried and cried and cried, her hand running along the dog's soft fur over and over. Breath staccato, sniffling, she hiccupped and shuddered. "Who's the crybaby now?"

Kitt laid a hand on her shoulder. "Hush, now, Mrs Valentine," he said tenderly.

Mae sat up. She let the dog go, rose, and tugged off her apron, wiping her nose with it. "Let's get on with it then. The others are occupied. You wanted an opportunity to see the barn. Now's your chance." She shrugged off his jacket and jerked on her steadfast mantle of professionalism.

CHAPTER ELEVEN

A blend of weedkiller, grease, motor oil, and milled wood scented the air. While Mae had turned off the music in the great room, Wayne Newton's *Danke Schoen* filtered in through the garage barn's hidden speakers. Immediately, Kitt found the touchpad and shut off the bloody music. "That's better," he said, poking up the brim of the cowboy hat, scanning the barn's interior.

Divided into two areas, one side was laid out like a garden supply shop, with bottles of weed killer, liquid fertiliser, insecticide in tidy rows on two shelves. Bags of potting mix and rock salt sat stacked on pallets near the front of a small tractor. He crossed to the other side, past various tractor attachments and implements, and went to Mae. She stood with Felix beside a car, its curves visible beneath a blue cloth.

The shrouded front end of the vehicle sat close to metal ramps, the kind mechanics used. The ramps, set atop one another, almost touched stacked planks that had once been pallets and shipping crates. Three intact shipping crates used as storage containers, lay beneath the windows at the rear of the barn, one full of packing material, the second and third brimming with empty wine bottles. Large garage doors, the sort that rolled up, closed off the front of the barn. The entire space was warm, heated by the solar system on the roof.

"What are you looking for?" Mae unhooked the dog's lead.

"I haven't a clue. What have you been looking for?"

"Evidence of bottle tampering. Boxes of paper labels. Stamps. Wax. Blending codes. Come on, let's get to this. I don't have a lot of time. I have to greet the Chungs when they arrive and sort out nibbles and dinner."

"All these people need is bread and wine." Kitt began to lift bottles out of one of the crates, stacking them to the side.

"I did that last week. There's nothing at the bottom but a few dead bugs and there's no false bottom either."

He replaced the bottles and crouched, inspecting the base where cobwebs and messy spiderwebs trapped bits of bark and the odd leaf, but nothing else. He rose, turned, and looked at the cloaked car, thumb running back and forth over the tips of his two shortened fingers.

What was so interesting about this car that three guests had asked to see it? The other restored sports cars in the garage held nothing secret. No one had any interest in seeing the Morgan Plus 4, MG-A, Austin Healy Sprite or Triumph Herald, but the Sunbeam...

Mae watched Felix sniff about. "I've been here two months and I've searched the whole house. I've looked up in the loft and down in here too. I've found nothing. Taittinger likes it tidy in here the way he likes his home clean."

"What's in the loft?" Kitt pointed above her head. A pulley suspending a hardtop for the car and an overhead crane with a remote hand-control hung down.

"Old car parts, rims, seats, a broken engine," she said. "I arrived the week Taittinger and Hector pulled out stuff from this car."

"Hector?"

"Hector Rodriguez. He's a jack-of-all-trades, a landscaper, a mechanic. He was the distinguished-looking Native American at the party, but he may have left before you arrived."

"Have you seen Taittinger and Hector work on the car?"

"Yes."

Beyond the wheel marks on the concrete below where the tractor sat, the barn was neat, organised, shop-like. It reminded Kitt more of a display in a catalogue rather than a functioning workspace. Taittinger might have been fastidiously clean, but to Kitt the lack of dirt and typical garage detritus was an anomalous red flag, even more anomalous than the security system and bars on the windows. He pointed. "Any idea what came in those disassembled wooden crates?"

"Some hand-painted tiles for the terrace Taittinger's having Hector build in the spring. It could have been things purchased at auction, rugs, wine, pieces of art, antiques that are in the house, or hoses and brakes for this little sports car."

"Have items usually come in wood crates like these?"

"Sometimes cardboard boxes. Depends on the size. A good number of things have been delivered since I arrived. The only peculiar thing that arrived was a freeze-dried dead rat from an irate wine merchant ex-girlfriend. That sort of thing ever happen to you?"

"Discretion is the sign of a well-trained spy."

"'A gentleman never discusses past relationships' also would have been acceptable." Mae chuckled softly.

"We both know I'm not really a gentleman." He tipped his chin toward the bottle-laden crates. "What size were most of the deliveries?"

"Well, Goldilocks, some were big, some were medium, some were small."

"Did you unpack any of the larger crates?"

"No. Taittinger likes to do that. If needs help, he calls Hector. I unpacked the star-shaped red rug on the wall in the great room, the ugly sundial in the upstairs hallway, and a full set of Penfolds Grange from 1951 to 2012, but I was there when Taittinger opened the rat."

"What happens to the wood from the crates?"

"Some of it is used for fireplace kindling. The rest is left outside for landscaping. Hector feeds it into a wood chipper for mulch. I do believe last week's large crates are now the chips lining the driveway."

"Very convenient." Kitt pressed his lips together, hands on his hips. He looked about the space, eyes settling on the blue tarpaulin.

"Oh, the car." Mae crossed the space, grabbed the edge of the dark blue fabric and whipped it off. "*This* is what you should drive."

His brow arched. "Oh, yes. A hot pink 1962 Sunbeam Alpine. Indeed. You say my Bentley is far too girly a sports car and yet you suggest I drive Barbie's convertible?"

"James Bond drove one in *Dr No*." She began to fold the cover.

"I am not James Bond, and his car wasn't pink." Kitt tossed his cowboy hat on the car's dash, took off his jacket, draped it over the driver's seat, and crouched low, looking at the fall of the concrete beneath their feet, at the non-skid rubber mat that lay like a large run under the car. At first, the mat appeared to have an unusual shape, but it lay crooked on the concrete, despite the fact the area it covered looked square.

"Maxwell Smart drove one in the American TV series *Get Smart*."

"Why all the sudden knowledge about the cars driven by fictional spies, Mae?" Kitt went around to the right side of the garish car and examined the mat under the right front tyre. On his knees, he ran his fingertips along the edge of the rubber mat.

Mae moved and sat on the bonnet, car cover on her lap. She watched him poke and prod the dirty black rubber. "I've been conducting research into spies and the lives they lead. I thought it best to start at the lower end of the spectrum."

"I recognise a thinly-veiled insult when it's aimed in my direction."

Mae grinned. "It's not aimed at you as much as it is your car."

"Love me, love my Bentley GT." It was slight, very slight, and if he hadn't been flattened on his stomach he wouldn't have noticed. One corner of the mat had a faint crease, as if it had been folded back. "What do we have here?"

"A dirty rubber mat."

"No. The mat is clean. I think the real dirt's underneath." He tugged up the corner and looked beneath it.

"What do you mean?"

"Get in the car, Mae."

"Why don't you get in it?"

"It would be easier if you got in and I pushed."

"I know it runs. Or used to. I've seen Taittinger take it down the driveway drive and back. You'd look better in it than he does."

"Nice try, but I'm not getting in. I need to roll it off the mat."

"Why do you need to roll i—you think the car and mat are hiding something."

Kitt tipped his head.

"Why don't I get in and pop it in neutral." Mae tossed the car cover on the passenger seat and climbed into the convertible. The seat hissed as she slid onto the stitched, slightly dusty leather. She put the window down, Felix hopped in, scurrying over her lap and settled on top of the cloth. Mae engaged the clutch and nudged the gear knob into neutral. "Go on," she said and Kitt began to push.

"Brake and put it in a gear." Kitt moved around to where the right fender had been, bent, and lifted the mat, flopping it back on itself until it touched the front tyres. "Hm." He looked left and right, straightened, and reached for the crane control overhead. Half a second later the barn was filled with a low hum and metallic clang. "Ah, indeed, you were very thorough." With a grin, he rose and looked at Mae behind the wheel, brushing light dust from his dark blue shirt and charcoal trousers. "This is why you leave things to the professionals."

"If you found a hidey hole beneath this gorgeous little car, I shall be very annoyed." She climbed out of the car, leaving the door open, and looked down at a metal platform lift that led to a dark space beneath the barn. "Well, shit."

"My love, I cannot tell you how very happy I am that you're angry at something else other than me." He peeked through metal mesh. "The light from here is reflecting on things below. Shall we take the lift and have a look?" He held out his hand.

Mae gave a two-toned whistle, took Kitt's hand, and stepped onto the non-skid platform. The dog appeared and plopped down beside their feet. Again, Kitt reached for the crane control suspended above, examined the four buttons, and pressed one. The platform began to sink, humming softly. When it stopped, Kitt figured they were three and a half metres below ground. The space beyond faded into darkness, but light from above glinted off glass not far from the lift. He felt around outside the lift, found a switch and toggled it. Lights flickered on. To the right and left, two metres high, sat row after row of racks filled with bottles of wine.

Brick-walled, the wine cellar stretched the entire length of the barn. Aisles ran from end to end. The room was dry and cool, the temperature, according to the large digital thermometer hanging on the nearest row, 55°F. Kitt looked out over the wine cellar and grinned.

"You are smiling like a little boy on Christmas."

"Am I?"

"Yes, and it makes me wonder. What *did* you do for Christmas?"

Kitt lifted her hand and kissed the middle of her palm. "I spent the day at a casino, playing poker with a very unlucky one-eyed Frenchman who lost everything he had."

"You beat him?"

"Yes, I thrashed him and took every penny he had."

"So much for Christmas cheer and charity."

"I was very charitable, Mae."

"You mean you didn't touch his good eye?"

"Did I already tell you this story?" He folded her hand to his chest and glanced at the wine again. "What did you do for Christmas?"

"I roasted a turkey."

"Did you pretend it was me?"

"Why would I do that when I knew you were already roasting in hell?"

"You are not that far off the mark. Let's have a look, shall we?" He tugged her off the freight lift. The skinny dog followed and then went to have a sniff around.

Mae squeezed Kitt's hand. It was warm, calloused, the fact parts of two fingers were missing not even noticeable. The only perceptible differences that came with this handholding were that Kitt was alive, truly alive, he'd ferreted out a secret wine cellar, and wasn't smug about it. She'd anticipated smugness, or at least a comment about how she had no business being in the spy business, and she must have been looking at him with some kind of expectant expression.

"This," he said casting his eyes to all the wine, "is why you are here."

"And it proves nothing except Taittinger has two wine cellars. He is a wine collector and this is a wine collection."

"Perhaps this is where he keeps the fakes."

Mae looked at him, sucking in her cheeks, pursing her mouth for a moment. "Would you know how to spot a counterfeit wine? Would you even know what to look for?"

"No. But you do."

"No, I don't."

"I thought you were a trained sommelier, a knowledgeable professional, an expert specialising in all aspects of wines?"

"I thought you were a dashing, daring, wine-quaffing, save-the-world spy, but you don't know a Merlot from a Pinot Noir. When I think about it, you really let down the spy brotherhood, don't you?"

He smiled again, head tipped, one brow arching. "At least I'm dashing."

Her hand in his, Mae went along with him down the first row of shelves. "You do know how to wear a dinner suit, but that's beside the point. I'm not a sommelier, I'm merely a well-trained butler. I told Llewelyn what I know about wine comes down to what to serve with what meal, something every decent butler and the wine steward in any fine restaurant would know. This is a bottle of Petrus, worth about two thousand US dollars, and it looks like every bottle of Petrus I have seen before. There are," she stood on her toes and counted from top to bottom, "eight of them." She let go of his hand and moved a little further along the row, pulling out bottles to examine along the way. "Here are six Henschke Hill of Grace shiraz, all 2006 vintage, usually around $600 a pop. These ten are Giaconda Nebbiolo from the Piedmonte region of Italy, $100 maybe. All different grapes, all different values. Would you like to know what food to pair with these wines?"

"Red goes with meat, white goes with fish, and bourbon tastes better with both. What more do I need to know?"

"How about, there are bottles of bourbon, scotch, and whisky on these shelves too."

Kitt hurried to her side and looked where she pointed. "A

Gordon & MacPhail Generations Mortlach seventy-five-year-old single malt whisky, The Macallan Lalique sixty-two-year-old single Malt scotch whisky, and Old Rip Van Winkle twenty-five-year-old Kentucky straight bourbon." He whistled, impressed.

She laughed. "So, I report this cellar to Bryce, you try to sneak a taste of the Macallan Lalique when my back is turned, and...then what?"

"What were your instructions, what were you told to look for to ascertain if Taittinger was blending his own wine and passing it off as something else?" Kitt turned and went back toward the lift.

Mae watched him move around the portion of the cellar hidden by the folded freight platform. "Anomalies; old bottles and very, very old bottles. Old paper, ink, stamps, corks, handwritten labels on very old bottles. A pattern to the bottles he's collected, bottles in tubs of water to soak off labels, a kitchen set up with tubes and chemistry glass carafes for measuring and mixing, anything that might be used for blending wines, the way Kurniawan did with Burgundies in 2012."

"Kurniawan was Malaysian, wasn't he?

"Indonesian." She headed down another row and kept talking. "The capsules all appear to be original, the labels legitimate. I've never found old paper, ink, stamps, glue or wax, or aged corks, and no formulas scribbled anywhere. Llewelyn seemed to think that engaging a master sommelier wasn't necessary, that my knowledge base and years in service were enough." The slight muffled sound of rumpling plastic travelled down the rows. "I don't see anything I was told to be mindful of down here, and I certainly haven't found anything in the other cellar in the house, or anyplace else on the property."

Mae went on looking at expensive wines mixed with extraordinarily expensive wines. She counted three bottles of 1945 Domaine de la Romanee-Conti Grand Cru, four bottles of 2008 Le Pin, two 1975 Egon

Müller zu Scharzhof-Scharzhofberger Riesling Trockenbeerenauslese Goldkapsel and nine bottles of a 1921 Schloss Vollrads German Riesling. "This may be something," she said, "or it may be nothing at all. Every so often there are printed sticky labels, fixed to the top of the rack, with some kind of letter and number code. For example, RN3 dash F16 or BRB12 dash M09. They could be cataloguing or blending codes."

"At this point, who knows?" Kitt ran his hand over the rear side of a half-folded heavy carpet atop a shipping crate that sat to the left of the freight lift. The rug was stained and dusty, the dirtiest thing he'd come across on Taittinger's estate, and it made his mouth go dry.

The front of the very old, hand-knotted Sarouk Persian rug had an intricate pattern in shades of deep red, dark blue, and cream. "When did Taittinger's new Persian rug arrive, the one you hung in the foyer?" he said, the hair on his neck prickling. There were rugs like this in the containers in Singapore, but they were polyester reproductions. The rug over the crate was wool and silk, threadbare and moth-eaten in places. It wouldn't be worth much in this state.

"Just before Christmas," she called out. "Well, this is different."

Kitt turned around, shrugging off the prickling and the prod it failed to give to nightmarish memories. He travelled back in Mae's direction, glancing at Felix with his nose shoved in between bottles. "Have you found a secret passage?"

"No," she snorted, voice slightly muffled. "There's no more wine, but there is art. Lots of it."

"What kind of art?" Kitt looked down one row of wine bottles and then another. He paused. "Where are you?"

"Back here. Go to the end and turn right."

He followed her directions and repeated his question, "What kind of artwork?"

"Art that doesn't quite match Taittinger's taste for the cosmos."

When Kitt found her, she stood beside an open shelf full of sculptures and carvings of various sizes, looking at a figurine that resembled a woman with enormous breasts, but turned out to be a woman holding a child. "That's a fertility goddess."

Mae looked up at him through her lashes. "Naturally you'd know about fertility goddess statues."

"Technically, it's not a statue, but a figurine from the early Bronze Age. That round one there, I believe," he pointed, "is Aztec, while the gent performing fellatio is Peruvian."

"You know nothing about wine, but everything about bourbon, Minton china patterns, pornographic Peruvian and Bronze Age fertility figurines."

"You can eat off china."

"And the fertility figurines?"

"I'll leave that to your very active imagination."

"Men are such little boys sometimes." Mae gave a little laugh. "The day before yesterday—when you hadn't yet arrived—there was a discussion about Venus figurines and phalluses."

"The phalluses are on the shelf above you." His gaze flicked above her head.

She poked a thumb over a shoulder. "This place goes on and on. There's more down this way, little boy. Bigger things."

"Bigger isn't always better."

"Oh, stop." She turned and headed toward the rear wall where various sized boxes and wooden crates sat. The dog appeared and shadowed her.

Kitt laughed and shadowed the dog, rubber-soled boots softly *ss-ssing* on the slate tiled floor. The room did go on and on. "Why does it matter if these pieces down here don't match Taittinger's taste? Tastes change."

"I get the feeling that question is rhetorical, Kitt."

"I'm thinking out loud. And you're here looking for patterns, aren't you?"

"Perhaps he's embarrassed by his little collection of knobs and diddies and that's why he keeps them down here with the wine."

"*Knobs and diddies?*"

"My point is, phalluses might not match his pattern, but those boxes over there are hand-painted tiles for the terrace he wants Hector to build, and these things here fit his taste." Mae stopped in front of a slab of a fresco framed in by wood and sheeted with plastic, and waved her hands over zodiac images of warped, yet still distinct, Aquarius and Pisces. "He collects work with a 'celestial' theme."

The rows of wine ended. This vast side of the cellar held nothing but wooden crates, some unopened. Various boxes had the front removed and had been half-unpacked, like the fresco. Small boxes sat on shelves, other things stuck out or peeked through polystyrene bits. Bronze bowls and vessels were swathed in bubble wrap, round carved stone slabs rested against the frame of a crate bubbling over with straw-like wood shavings. Other crates and boxes contained various large automotive parts, windscreens, exhaust pipes, and chrome bumpers that had lost their lustre.

Mae pulled out her mobile. "Those three long boxes arrived the same day as the rug in the foyer. And the stuff over there with the carpet half-covering a Greek, Roman, or," she snorted, "a *Bronze Age* fresco, is similar to the one in the house." She turned and began to take pictures of the wine and cellar.

Kitt crossed to the two crates, both of equal size. A crowbar rested near the bottom of the one that had been partially opened. He began to slip away another rug. "It's a mosaic, not a fresco. Frescoes are paintings on plaster." The rug dropped to the clean, tiled floor below and his eyes ran across thick, clear plastic torn apart in several places. Behind the tattered plastic sheet, shit-brown smudges and rusty fingerprints smeared across a tiled, not painted, surface. Cascading grapes and a face peeked out from the mosaic, tile eyes looking at him. The grapes dangled down to a woman's shoulders.

The air turned rank with the sudden stench of decay.

Mae's phone clicked like an old-fashioned camera, the noise an unnecessary throwback to the days when cameras had shutters and actual film. The dog snuffled his nose into the rug and plopped down on top of it, front paws crossing. "*What time is it?*" Dalton said.

Nausea unwound, the snake of it slithering through his stomach, curling along his spine. Kitt pushed it away, shoved it down. "Christ," he muttered, swallowing hard, battling the nausea. "Oh, Christ."

"Oh, Christ what?" Mae said from someplace very far away. Kitt looked at her and back at the dried smear of shit that was a dried smear of blood.

"What time is it?" Dalton asked.

Queasiness undulated, rippling the fear that kicked up his pulse. The rug gone, Kitt's hands shook when he ripped off more plastic and yanked a wooden cross-brace from the frame. The action revealed a face set in mosaic tiles, a woman wearing a vine-woven garland, bunches of grapes hanging above her shoulder. He stared at the tiny tile portrait, and the world around him putrefied and distorted like the faces of the dead in the container.

Dalton bleated about his goddamned broken watch, and, in a climate-controlled wine cellar, Kitt stared at a mosaic tiled face framed by grapes and let the deluge of horror crash over him.

CHAPTER TWELVE

What a thing it was to relive a moment, to physically be half a world away, yet mentally exist in another place with time vividly recreated right down to the stench. Handkerchief to his nose and mouth, Kitt rose from the fetid corpse and moved away from the crate that held the same contraband handbags and scarves as the last container, which unlike this one, had not also served as a tomb for Dr Vida Zora and three others. Bloody hell, amid bodies, counterfeit goods, and the presence of the Malay customs broker representative, her young Chinese assistant, Dalton whined about his broken Rolex, and what idiot wore an expensive dress timepiece to such a filthy job, anyway? Bill Dalton, that's who.

Not that he was any better, thinking about Mae and the Christmas tree and his proposal and how he hadn't considered she'd ever say anything except *yes*. Since that was the case, it was time to get out, to make a move in another direction, to retire without keeping his hand in anything related to intelligence work.

The green-faced NCB officer had sunk to his knees outside, downwind, opposite where he had vomited. The Chinese assistant harbourmaster splashed his face with bottled water. The Indian-Malay, or possibly Nepali, dockers Molony had roped into service to open the containers shook their heads and shrugged, Tzin securing his plait, thickset Popo snapping chewing gum that, before the doors had swung open, smelled of violets.

The Malay customs broker patted her young assistant's back. "*He's stone, lah.*"

"Get him out of here," Molony pinched his nose. "Her too."

"What time is it?" Dalton asked.

Jaw tight with annoyance at himself, at Dalton, Kitt sent a text to follow up the call he'd made to Reed—*As per your suggestion. Shithouse, henhouse, sweatshop*—and glanced at his own watch, a practical Citizen. "Nine-fifteen," he grumbled.

"*No! No!*" Molony shouted from the open doorway.

Kitt looked up and the Professor, tiny knife in his hand, fell through the door of the container, face down behind the NCB officer shrieking, "*Teedak! Teedak!*"

The assistant harbourmaster tumbled inside the space, arms stretched out to the screaming customs broker, his arterial spray spattering her face. "*To-long! To-long!*" she cried for help in Malay.

"Christ!" Kitt hissed, dropped his phone and hurtled himself clear of a pallet plank Popo swung at his head. He rolled to his feet as Tzin, the thinner brother, slashed out at the NCB officer. The still-green-faced man stumbled and staggered as blood erupted from the gash across his throat.

Dalton fumbled for the palm pistol strapped to his ankle and the length of pallet wood struck his back, splintering, knocking him out of the container, the *pop-pop* of two bullets ricocheted off metal.

Tzin moved for the boy. Kitt ducked another blow and tried to reach him, tried to drive forward and shove the kid out of the container, shouting at him to run. Then a length of wire passed in front of his eyes and caught the fingers he'd raised in defence. In an instant, jerked in reverse, the floral scent of Popo's violet chewing gum gusting into his face.

Wire digging into his throat, Kitt witnessed the woman's desperate try to intervene and save her petrified young assistant. Tzin gutted her with a single slash. Screaming, entrails spilling, she spun and slid down the front of the wood frame of a box, dark hair fanned out, clawing at the plastic and rug wrapping, exposing the patterned tile beneath.

Kitt dropped to a knee and dragged Popo down with him. Tzin's knife flashed again and the young man fell next to the woman without a sound, and Kitt rammed upwards. The thin metal wire bit deeply into his neck, into his flesh, slicing through bone, and his skull met nose. Blood exploded into his hair. Popo's grip on the twisting wire garrotte slackened. He slumped and staggered away.

Kitt tottered, saw Dalton lurch sideways, his expression a chilling rictus of missing teeth and bloodied, frothing spittle. He fell over the twitching bare legs of the NCB officer in the doorway and landed on Molony. With a thin gasp of breath and then another, Kitt tripped across a corpse and dug at the wire eating into his throat. The top knuckles of two fingers dangled, bone exposed. He heard the faint whistle of swinging wood before it cracked his occipital bone. He dropped chest-first on the side of the crate, smashing his face, bouncing, and crumpling, landing on a rotting corpse, torn, trapped fingers stuck between his throat and the wire, lights, colours, shapes bursting in his blood-sodden vision.

Dazed, half-strangled, half-blind, no part of his body functioned normally. Breathing was a chore. Sound warbled in and out, he heard groaning, laughter, a repeated word—*chichiltic*—a language that wasn't Chinese, Malay, or Singlish, a language his addled mind knew was out of place in this part of the world. What were they saying?

Jostled and lifted, he floated for a moment then crashed onto the bones of a body. *Chichiltic*, the splintering and crackling of wood and plastic, the stomping of feet, laughter, *chichiltic* it all wavered softer and louder over the noisy thrum in his ears. Through blurry, blood-muddied eyes that wouldn't close Kitt stared at Tzin's bloody face, at Popo's open laughing mouth, at long black hair stuck to ripped plastic, at a bunched-up multicoloured rug, at a distorted old painting of a woman wearing a garland of grapes that hung to her shoulders. He stared until the grapes withered and died and everything around him rotted and stank and day became night and night blistered beneath an absent sun and Kitt began to roast in his own skin.

Christ. Oh, Christ. At fault and yet faultless, he had been trapped by his inattention, by thoughts of a Christmas tree and a woman he loved, by his own self-preservation. He had been made powerless by a goddamned length of metal packing wire digging into his throat and could do nothing more than fight for his own life, watch a young man die, and long for a woman he loved. *"Come home,"* a voice said, from very far away, over the screaming woman, over the deafening silence of the boy who would never grow to be a man, over his own congested panting for breath. *"Just come home."*

The visions flickered, shifted, and spun along from beginning to the end, where he'd believed he'd met his end, when the last thought he'd had was of Mae, and Mae was there, really there, shaking her head at the ancient mosaic depiction of the Four Seasons. Kitt had to move, had to exit the grisly, decaying, depraved horror before it started again.

He found Mae's hand, and through a veil blotted by illusory, blood-drenched gore, he turned, squeezing her hand, compressing down the nightmare and queasiness that wanted to liquefy his guts.

He pulled her to the front of the other still-wrapped crate. He took a breath and tore at the plastic sheeting, uncovering another old mosaic depicting the Four Seasons; an urn filled with blossoms, a winged man crowned with wheat, a heavy-lidded woman wearing a garland of grapes that hung to her shoulders. "God damn it," he said quietly, through his teeth. "There are two of them."

"Two of what?" Mae stuffed her mobile back into a pocket beneath her apron.

No part of this mosaic was marred by dried blood. It would have been so easy to be unhinged, to grab the crowbar and swing it, but Kitt dug in and clawed his way back. Barely, just barely held on to the antipathy that urged him to kick and tear and smash the sodding mosaic. Softly, evenly, he drew in a long, deep breath, and swallowed down his whirling cyclone of hostility. "It's not the wine," he glanced back over Mae's head to the other side of the cellar, "it's the artefacts."

"What do you mean?"

Kitt gave an arid smile. "You're here looking for counterfeit wine, but Taittinger's not counterfeiting wine. He's smuggling artefacts. I thought we'd uncovered a contraband ring, peddling phoney handbags, but this is directly connected to Switzerland, to missing pieces from freeport storage units. The bloody art and antiquities down here. This stuff, Mae, those tiles aren't for the terrace Taittinger wants built. It's a mosaic, an artefact stolen from a freeport or smuggled out of Syria, Iraq, or Afghanistan." He pointed. "That piece was in the container where I almost died. Those brown smears on the plastic torn off the mosaic, that's blood. Someone was, someone is willing to kill to ensure no one finds out where this artefact came from, or where it's going."

"You think Grant knew where it was going?"

"Possibly. How often does Taittinger send large parcels?"

"Every now and again. Crates of bottles to his mother in Florida, two or three bottles of wine, or a set of six we've packed and sent. It's picked up by a service. He receives deliveries of larger things—the rugs and car parts, mostly. I don't really understand." Mae's brow furrowed.

"Neither do I. But I have some ideas."

"Such as?"

What could he say, how could he explain when he couldn't explain to himself, or prove it? "This isn't going to make any sense, but I don't know quite yet. I have a box of puzzle pieces, some of which fit the puzzle, some that might fit, and some that change shape. I haven't a theory. I'm merely grabbing at whatever I can."

"You're improvising."

"Yes."

"You're also sweating." Her eyes traversed his forehead and hair as damp as the small of his back and underarms. "How can you be sweating when it's thirteen degrees down here?"

"Un-pretty things occurred the last time I saw this mosaic." Kitt went on breathing evenly. "I died, Mae. Except I didn't. 'Come home,' you said. I heard you. You heard me, I heard you. *Come home.* I think that's why I sent you postcards, so you'd know. So I'd know."

Mae fell silent, watching him. He was certain she was considering ways she might ease his clammy discomfort. Her hand moved to touch him before she reconsidered. Instead, she sucked her bottom lip and half-smiled, half-grimaced, flesh between her teeth. "You remembered everything that happened?"

"Yes."

"You don't want to tell me about it, do you?"

"Not at all."

"I'm sorry I asked. I'm sorry I suggested you think about it again."

Kitt blinked, slowly, drinking in the woman who stood apologising for something she'd had no control over any more than he had. "I want to think about something pleasant," he said, and reached for her, taking her wrist, letting the feel of her cool skin fill his clammy palm. He pulled her forward, grasping the chain with the glasses hanging around her neck and dropping it over her shoulder. "I want to think about how you smell." He drew her very close, nose nestling into her neck so that he could breathe in the scent of her and drive out the lingering malodorous, hellish phantasm of that container. Softly, mindfully, listening to the way her breath caught, he nuzzled his lips into the tiny spot behind her ear, and pressed his hands to her back. "I want to think about how you smell, and how you feel. You feel real, whole, here, and I don't want you here, except I want you here." He lifted his head and found her mouth.

She gave a small, muffled laugh of disbelief, made a tiny noise of satisfaction, and sank into him, into the kiss, and his chilly clamminess quickly dissolved into a soft, shared heat. "What have I gotten you into?" he murmured and kissed and kissed and kissed her.

Mae pulled the tail of his shirt from his trousers and slid her palms up his back, her touch warming his cool, damp skin, delight giving him a chill of a pleasurable nature. The remnants of the depravity he'd borne witness to evaporated. He kissed her, she kissed him, and *buzz-buzz* intermingled with the sound of their breathing. *Buzz-buzz. Buzz-buzz.*

Mae drew back and reached beneath her apron, into the side pocket of her dress. She read the mobile's screen as Kitt unbuttoned the top of her dress. He leaned in and kissed her throat as she swallowed. "Taittinger wants me."

"As do I."

"You're not having me here."

"No, I'm not having you here. I'm kissing you here." His head moved. "And here. And here." Her skin prickled beneath his lips.

Mae shivered. "All right, you win. You are quite skilled when it comes to kissing."

"As I said," Kitt stepped away from her, "Vassiliki taught me well."

Mae buttoned her dress. "I have no wish to hear of your former girlfriends, even the one you had when you were a skinny, hormonal teenager. Taittinger knows I'm in the barn showing you the car. He's on his way here." She gave a whistle for the dog.

"Actually, I was a bit podgy." Kitt tucked in his shirt tails and offered his elbow. When she looped her arm through his, he led her to the freight lift, waited for the dog to get on board, and switched off the lights. Mae pressed the wall control and the lift rose to the barn above.

The platform stopped. For a moment, he held her close and absorbed her heat, her presence, her fingertips stroking the stubble of his shaved hairline until the dog grew jealous, rose up to paw at the back of his thighs. Kitt let Mae go, grabbed the overhead control box, pushing a button. Felix trotted off the platform and cowered behind Mae when the perforated metal platform closed with a light *clunk.*

Kitt flopped the rubber mat back into position, moved behind the convertible to roll it back into place, and waited for Mae—and the dog—to get into the car. The convertible in its original place, Mae got out of the pink disaster and stood in-between the open door. The dog curled up on the passenger seat. Kitt took his jacket from the seat and smiled.

"I don't think I like that you're so smug and cheerful and handsome all of a sudden," she said.

"Since we've found something on Taittinger, you can report to Bryce via a nice text message."

"Shouldn't I meet with him in the morning, as arranged?"

"No. You can leave and I can get on with my bloody work without worrying about you."

"All right," she said faintly, one hand on the doorframe.

Kitt nearly choked on his surprise and half froze as he put on his jacket, arm pausing in a sleeve. "Thank you." He pulled on the jacket.

"You're feckin' welcome." Mae exhaled. "Since you found what I was looking for, I'm done. Where do you want me to go? May I go home?"

Where did he want her to go? "No. I'd send you to Sicily, to your friend Fiorella's, but Bryce knows where that is and if Bryce knows, Llewelyn knows. I don't want anyone to find you. This means I'm going to have to ask Reed to help me again, which is going to expose him even more than it already has." He grinned, suddenly amused, phone in his hand. *Mae leaving. Arrange safe house. Now*, he tapped the message to Reed. "On the bright side, it's going to piss him off."

Mae put both hands on the searing pink car. The skinny dog scampered across the seat and made his way to her, nosing his snout into her elbow. She reached back and rubbed his ears. "I don't understand that sort of amusement," she said. "I don't understand why you think it's hilarious to piss off a man whose help you need."

Kitt's smile grew wider. He turned, watching through a window for movement outside. "Didn't you ever do things to piss off your brother because it was fun?" He looked back at Mae. "No. No, you didn't, but I'm sure it was the other way around."

"It was. Sean used to tease me mercilessly, poke me, pinch me, do things just to get a reaction, and I never understood that. My mam used to say it was how he expressed how much he loved me without being all girly. Years later, I found out later that was absolute shite. Sean told me he did it because it was fun but couldn't explain why. And then he apologised for tormenting me."

"You have a very kind brother." Kitt said, reading Reed's *Right. I'll just pull something out of my arse* reply.

"My brother's a priest who believes confession is good for the soul. When I go, I'm taking the dog with me, Kitt."

You've 1 hour to be a colorectal magician, he wrote, and looked up from the screen. "Sorry?"

"Felix. He's coming with me." She turned and gazed at the pretty little face of the animal. "Yes, you are coming with me, little man," she murmured as if the dog were a baby.

"He's not yours, Mae." Kitt sent the message.

"I have to take him with me."

"But he's not your dog."

Mae sighed. Felix rested his head in her hand as she massaged his ears. "If I leave, and you die for real this time, what will I have left? I'm taking the dog."

"I'm not going to die."

She watched Felix hop back into the passenger seat and curl up once more before she set her eyes on Kitt. "The belief you have in yourself is astonishing."

His mouth quirked. "Someone has to believe in me." He opened the car door a little wider between them. "Come around this side and kiss me again."

"No."

"You denied me scrambled eggs, don't deny me a kiss too."

"I did not *deny* you scrambled eggs."

"You let that gluttonous Irishman with the atrocious dress sense and ghastly hair eat them all. That is the same as denying me scrambled eggs. Come here." He tucked his mobile in his jacket pocket and put on the cowboy hat.

"I think you have an ulterior motive."

"Yes."

She stayed where she was.

"Here's my ulterior motive." He had a quick glance out the barred glass that framed the curving house. "Give or take thirty seconds Taittinger will be at the door, and you're buttoned up all wrong."

She looked down at herself. "Right. You were worried my new employer might see my diddies. How gallant of you."

"Have you another employer see your...assets, Mrs Valentine?"

"*Assets?*" Mae slanted her head, one eye squinting.

"*Diddies?*"

"Besides you, no."

"Well, which of us do you prefer?"

She re-did the buttons. "You mean which one of you I'd rather have see my breasts?"

"I meant which one of us do you prefer as an employer, me or Taittinger?"

"Well..." she pretended to think about it, "...Taittinger's never feigned death."

"I bet he never proposed marriage either."

"You're quite proud of that, aren't you?"

"I have an idea," his eyes wandered over her breasts. "Unbutton that again."

"You are joking."

Kitt inclined his head. "You see it all the time in spy films, a henchman distracted by pretty diddies. I'm clearly distracted by them."

"You told me spy films were full of shite. Taittinger's not a henchman, he's the villain—Jaysus, just look at his house."

"Yes. I suppose you are correct. Honesty is the best policy." The mobile buzzed in his pocket.

Mae sat on the edge of the driver's seat, sideways, legs crossed. She blew out a puff air as a blast of wintry air rushed in.

"Valentine?" Taittinger called out.

"Over here, Dr Jools."

Taittinger's boots shuffled across the concrete and around the tractor. "Oh, hey, Somerset." He removed his glasses and polished off the fog that coated them when he'd come indoors.

"Glad to see you've made yourself at home. Know you're welcome."

"Very kind of you, Tatts. Thank you." Kitt touched the brim of his cowboy hat.

Taittinger glanced at Mae. "You doing all right, Valentine?"

"I'm coping, Dr Jools."

"Good. Good." Taittinger laughed weakly and pushed his glasses up his nose. "That deer was rough stuff. Hector's sending some boys over to take care of it all. You right to see to whatever they need, Valentine?"

"Of course," she said, eyes flicking to Kitt. "That's my job, sir."

"Thank you." With a sigh, he leaned against a hot-pink side panel and gave the convertible an affectionate pat. "Well, Somerset, what do you think of her?"

"Mate, I love her." Kitt said, eyes on Mae. She had one hand on the wheel and one on the dog.

Taittinger replaced his spectacles and ignored his dog the same way the dog ignored him. "I know the colour sucks, but the rest of her is pretty sweet."

Mae turned and gave Felix a scratch under the chin. "You're such a good boy," she cooed.

Kitt refrained from rolling his eyes and shifted to stand across from Taittinger. "Yes, the car is sweet, but I'm more interested in what's beneath it."

"She was once powder blue and, the pink aside, she's about as original as they come. Dash is original, the upholstery is original, the chrome is original, hell, even the engine is original. When I found the car, there were a couple of dried-out dead snakes in the cowl, the things could have been *windshield vipers*." Taittinger began to open the bonnet. "Have a look."

"I'm more interested in what's beneath the car."

"Yeah, but, it's original." Taittinger scratched his chin, eyes travelling over the car. "The exhaust is shitty, but the V8's in decent shape... Oh." His brow furrowed. "You moved the Sunbeam." He fumbled into the pocket of his quilted winter vest and pulled out something shiny and made of metal.

"Goodness me." Kitt regarded the small, semi-automatic pistol pointed squarely at his chest.

Mae got out of the car, hands on her hips as if she were an unamused Irish nanny, and everything went arsewise.

She stepped in front of the naughty boy with the lethal device in his hand, and Kitt uttered filthy words under his breath.

CHAPTER THIRTEEN

"Dr Jools," Mae said evenly, "what are ya doin'?"

"I'm protecting myself from a thief." Taittinger coughed.

"Don't be ridiculous."

"A man can be as ridiculous as he wants when he has a gun, Mrs Valentine." Kitt said, voice full of warning and irritation, every trace of the Australian accent he'd employed gone. "I suggest you get out of the way before he does something as ridiculous as you standing in front of a handgun pointing at your chest."

With a huff, Mae squinted and turned to glare at Kitt. While the expression he returned remained unperturbed, his eyes were cold and hard, tinged with a note of astonishment and a very clear question asking what the feck she thought she was doing. She swivelled back to Taittinger and huffed again. "The man may be a drunk, but he's not about to steal your car. Now, put that thing down."

Taittinger went very still for a second. Then his jaw worked back and forth as he sawed his bottom teeth across his top lip.

With a shrug, Kitt smiled broadly, a lethal gleam in his stony blue eyes.

"A standoff. Really." Mae exhaled and faced Taittinger. Improvise, she had to improvise because it was that or Kitt would wind up with a bullet lodged in his flesh. Or she would. "This is all a bit stupid, but it doesn't mean *you* do something stupid," she said, emphasising that key pronoun so that Kitt knew she meant him.

If she'd had access to a toilet brush, a vacuum cleaner, or a wedge of cheese, Mae would have used them, but the only thing in her pocket was a mobile and the keys to a hot-pink car. She drew forth the phone and held it in her outstretched hand. "Dr Jools, be reasonable. Be the smart man I know you are. Let the authorities handle this. Put down the gun. Better still. Give it to me. Let's trade. The phone for the gun. You ring the police."

Taittinger shook his head. Self-loathing mixed with hostility on his face. "Idiot! Idiot! I should have known better. It happened at a party Ziffler gave ten years ago, right under his nose. All the wine in one place. Judith said I was being foolish not having better secur—Judith. Shit, *Judith*."

Kitt crossed his arms. "I'll be honest, Tatts. I don't like wine; it gives me a ferocious headache, but we both know your wine tasting isn't why we're in this quandary, don't we?" Air stirred around Mae's legs as he took a step sideways.

"*Ah-ah-ah*." Taittinger straightened the gun that had begun to sag in his quivering grip, training it on Kitt.

"Would you like to talk about Judith?"

The younger man's face twisted into an ugly snarl. "That soulless bitch doesn't get that she can't just have whatever bottle she wants as a reward for being philanthropic. That's not how this works. You're her client, aren't you? The Jefferson. Yeah, I should have known. The three of you played me."

Elbows out, hands still on hips, Mae stepped back in front of Kitt. "Put down the gun and take the phone, Dr Jools," she said. Sweating, Taittinger was sweating. Perspiration gleamed on his forehead. In a second or two, beads would drip down his face. She had him. "Here." She thrust the phone forward. "I'll dial *nine-one-one* for you." She tapped the screen, two beeps audible, and suddenly she stumbled sideways. The phone hit the rubber mat, her arse hit the open car door, slamming it, startling Felix. The dog sat up and let out a sharp bark.

"I apologise for the roughness, Mrs Valentine." Mae glared at Kitt and he, standing no less than sixty centimetres from Taittinger, ignored her.

"You picked a hell of a time to play chicken." Taittinger adjusted his grip and raised the weapon to Kitt's face. "Do you want to die?"

"No, do you?"

After a swallow, Taittinger gave a thin, wavering laugh. "You've got some big balls." He lowered the pistol to chest height and held it, both hands shaking.

Arms crossed, Kitt closed the gap, the semi-automatic pistol pressed over his heart. "Go on. Shoot me. Then shoot Mrs Valentine and your dog while you're at it."

"*Shoot the dog?* What the feck's the matter with you?" Mae shouted.

Kitt's smiled widened. "You know something? My hangover's finally gone."

"Shut up," Taittinger hissed through his teeth, sweat trickled from behind an ear and he ground the nose of the weapon into Kitt's chest, muttering, "Shut up, shut up, shut up!"

Kitt's hand flashed. Metal *klunked* against the side of Taittinger's skull, his glasses flying off. He let out a whoop of pain, clutched his head, and fell to his knees, blood flowing between his fingers.

Amid Taittinger's swearing and moaning, Mae's hammering heart passed down her gullet and back into her chest. She glowered at Kitt, shouting, "You feckin' mad bastard!"

He gave her a flat, calm look, a maddening, detached look she'd loathed but had come to miss, only now the look was loathsome and maddening again, and he strode toward her, ever so coolly settling a hand on her shoulder. Mae knew blistering anger lived beneath that layer of frigid dispassion, and he leaned in close, lips brushing her ear as he enunciated every word, "Never. Stand. In. Front. Of. A. Weapon." He straightened and let her go, one eyebrow arched when he stepped back. "Am I clear?"

Mae went on glowering. "He could have killed you."

"Don't you know that statistics show that more individuals are injured or killed by their own firearms, Mrs Valentine?"

"*Pfft.*" Mae narrowed her eyes. "Statistics. You do know how to comfort a woman. You're really a hell of a poker player, aren't you?"

"No, I'm just an exceptional liar." Kitt twisted to the right, pointed the weapon at Taittinger, and fired, *snap-snap-snap*!

Mae leapt back, the dog scurried around inside the car, barking, Taittinger moaned, and Kitt went on being calm and detached. "It's not real, Mrs Valentine. Real pistols don't have the word *Detective* embossed on a die-cast barrel." He tossed aside the vintage toy cap-gun, grabbed Taittinger by the back of the collar and dragged him across the concrete, depositing him against the car.

Felix sniffed the air, shook himself, and plopped back into the passenger seat.

Adrenaline still coursing through her system, Mae bent and picked up Taittinger's spectacles. He sat, knees up, hunched, holding his head, swearing. She tapped his shoulder and held out his glasses. Feck, it was surprising how much she wanted to stab them into his eyeballs. The urge to make him bleed was savage, shocking, and nearly as distressing as how little remorse she knew she'd feel if she did. Mae took a breath.

Taittinger looked up at her, his pupils larger than normal in the soft light of the barn. His fingers quivered more than hers did as he took his glasses, mumbling a stuttering, "Th-thank you."

"Did you have a little smoke of something, Dr Jools?" she said.

"Yeah. T-the, th-the deer, you know. I needed to relax. Y-you want some?"

Mae untied her apron, and Taittinger winced when she pressed it against a little trickle of blood near his ear. "You deserved that. You deserve more. You seemed like a pleasant man, I was convinced you were, and I liked working here, but Jaysus, the two of ya are feckin' eejits. You both need a good belting." She glanced back at Kitt for a moment. "I'm giving you notice, Dr Jools. My contract stipulates an obligation for the next two weeks, but one of us has to be sensible and professional."

Cool, unruffled, Kitt leaned against the car, hand in a trouser pocket, eyes on Taittinger. "Ah, professional. Does that mean you'll give us a moment, Mrs Valentine?"

"And leave you two to belt each other?"

"I appreciate loyalty to an employer, but be honest, wouldn't you like to give him a box about the ears?"

"I've more a mind to ring the police and have you both charged with idiocy."

Head angled slightly, and a faint amused curve to the left corner of his mouth, Kitt went on watching Taittinger. "What for? Idiocy isn't a crime, and there's no reason to bring the police into this. I don't want to press charges."

Mae clenched her teeth. "I don't care if you want to press charges or not. It's for my own safety and the safety of others. Did you forget my dope-smoking employer wanted to kill you?"

The corner of his mouth rose higher. "Yes, why is that, Tatts, why did you feel the need to be so murderous when I merely wanted to chat about your extra wine cellar?"

Taittinger dragged the apron from his head. "What do you really want, Somerset?"

"I told you. I'm very interested in the cellar below. Please, tell me about it."

"Get fucked." Taittinger crossed his arms and looked away, jaw tight with thin defiance.

"That's not very punny. And I asked politely." Hand came out of his pocket. Kitt straightened.

Taittinger flinched, whacking the back of his head on the car. "Okay, I get it. You'll knock me around until I tell you what you want to know."

Mae exhaled with noisy irritation. "I don't think that's going to happen, is it, Mr Somerset?

"No. Not with you here." Kitt offered Taittinger a cold smile before his gaze flicked to Mae. "No one is in danger of losing his life, limb," his attention fixed back on Taittinger, "or fingers. Unless he puts a hand back into a pocket."

"Okay! Okay!" Taittinger held up both hands.

"Let's go back to the cellar under the car. And place your palms on your knees."

Frustration and nervousness plain, Taittinger did as he was told, hunched over and grabbed his kneecaps. "Would you just take the wine already? Tell soulless Judith I hope it makes her happy."

"My hole." Mae gave a snarl of exasperation, rolling her eyes. "This has nothing to do with your ex-girlfriend, Judith. He wants to know to whom all this belongs."

Confusion made Taittinger's dark eyes look larger and owlish behind his glasses as his gaze bounced from Mae to Kitt a few times. "M-me and p-private individuals," he stammered. "I keep their very expensive wines in a climate-controlled location until they are ready to collect it. He sat up, spine straightening with newfound confidence. "I'm storing the wines. If you take it you're not robbing me, you're robb—"

"Yes, yes. You buy, sell, and trade wines. Mrs Valentine

explained it to me. You're a cosmologist, an oenophile, a wine merchant, and a something of freeport all in one, aren't you?"

"So, Judith didn't send you? You're not here to rob me and take whatever it is she wants?"

"Heavens no. I'll leave the robbery, and the wine, to you. Tell me, is any of the wine in the cellar below, counterfeit?"

"Why the hell would I have anything to do with counterfeit wine?" Taittinger screwed up his face.

Kitt jingled the change in his pocket. "That's why Case is here. Counterfeiting is his speciality. And he's why I'm here."

"What the fu—" Taittinger's mouth dropped open and his tongue tried to form words while his face flared pink with outrage and shock.

Mae snorted. It was amusing to watch him squirm.

Again, his gaze sprang back and forth between them a few times. "Count-count-counterfeit?" his voice cracked and went up an octave on the end, as if he were going through puberty.

"That's right." Kitt nodded, his smile showing bottom teeth. "You're suspected of buying, selling, and manufacturing counterfeit wine. You're on an Interpol watch list of suspected counterfeiters."

"*Wh-what*?" For the third time, Taittinger's wide, owlish eyes darted from Kitt to Mae. "I'm on a what?"

"He said you're on an Interpol watch list of suspected counter-feiters."

Taittinger swallowed and stared at Mae. "Did you...did you know about this, Valentine?"

Mae crossed her arms. "I found out last night."

"And you're helping him?"

"Yes." She looked over at Kitt. When he gave a very faint nod, she continued making up shite to go along with his improvisation. "I had no choice. What he said was quite sensible and I did not wish anyone else to come to harm."

It might have been the light, but Taittinger's complexion took on a slight green tinge.

"You're quite fortunate to have a butler as thoughtful and professional as Mrs Valentine, Tatts. She talked me out of dealing with you last night, wanted to spare you the embarrassment, but she is cooperating. I do hope you'll do the same."

"The Jefferson. I should have known. I should have fucking known!" Taittinger stared at Kitt. "You and David, are you guys even engaged?"

Kitt said nothing.

"Oh, God. You've forced him to cooperate too. You're using him."

Kitt gave a faint sigh. "The world is based on give and take. You do something for me and you have an expectation of reciprocity. In a sense, to have our needs met, we all use the people we know. Interpol works with all sorts of organisations and uses all sorts of resources. Think of me as a resource."

"For counterfeiting wine?"

"No, for so much more. Case will discover what Mrs Valentine and I know; this has nothing to do with wine, not in a way that matters significantly, because you're not concocting a phoney vintage. Those numbers above the bottles, they aren't wine-blending codes, are they? It's a notation for who owns what, isn't it?"

"That's not a crime."

"No, it isn't, but that's not all you're doing."

The colour drained from Taittinger's face and stopped at his neck, his throat a mottled rash of green-tinged pink.

Kitt glanced at Mae, her mouth pursing to cover her amusement. "You know, Tatts, we did have a very good look around the cellar," he said. A low chuckle rumbled in his throat. "All your money and talk of philanthropy, social justice, supporting the less-fortunate, the forgotten, the unwanted, rescuing those who need rescuing most. Mrs Valentine mentioned even your dog is a rescue.

Very admirable of you. Wouldn't you say that's admirable, Mrs Valentine?"

"I might, sir." Mae moved around to the other side of the car. Felix lifted his head and she began to rub his ears.

"It's sad." Kitt exhaled softly. "That admirable trait is nothing more than pretence. You use your friends to raise money to give to charities so you can satisfy your social conscience when you're nothing more than a thief."

Suddenly, Taittinger blinked his owlish eyes, his expression took on a hue of outrage. "I haven't stolen anything. I've *never* stolen anything in my life."

"And next you're going to tell me you're just a cog in a wheel and you didn't invent the wheel. Come now, you've been sprung. Tell me about the zodiac mosaic in the cellar below. I know the piece is Roman but tell me more about it."

Mae watched Taittinger squeeze his kneecaps. His laugh dry and short. "You know your art."

"Not really. I had a colleague who knew a great deal more. I learned a lot from him. For instance, I know the other mosaic of the Four Seasons is Syrian. Where did the two mosaic pieces in the cellar originate? A museum? A family home? A village in a war zone? A looted World Heritage site? Or perhaps a freeport?"

He swallowed a few times before he peered up at Kitt, the green tinge fading. "Oh!" Taittinger let go of his knees, rubbed the back of his neck, and shook his head. "You think...I see. I see what you think. Those pieces are art samples."

"Samples?"

"Yeah, like the shipping labels say. Did you read the shipping labels?"

"If you mean did I read the false declarations you deliberately used to bring the property into the United States clandestinely, then yes, I did. Would you like to try again?"

Taittinger adjusted his glasses, his mouth flattening as he looked over at Mae.

"My brother is a priest, Dr Jools. He's devoted to St Jude. He likes to tell people that St Jude's not just the patron saint of lost causes, but a vegetarian as well. He also says shite like, '*confession is good for the soul.*'"

"You don't believe me, Valentine?"

She smiled very softly.

Taittinger ran his tongue around his lips, as if they'd gone dry and stuck together, and he looked from Mae to Kitt, and shook his head again. "Those of us who collect antiquities can help. We can save a cultural heritage by supporting those who work to preserve. If we support the curators and museum employees, and university professors who risk their lives to protect the treasures terrorist factions like ISIS, ISIL, Daesh, whatever you want to call them, destroy, we can save the cultural heritage."

"Surely you are not that guileless." Kitt laughed. "Yes. Yes, I can see you are. Are you familiar with the conservation work of Dr Vida Zora?"

"Who?"

Nonchalantly, Kitt brushed dust from his sleeve. "Sometimes the same social forces involved in the illicit trade of antiquities are also involved in arms looting and terrorism, which is exactly what you're participating in. And you know that. And what of the ordinary people, the desperate ones living in desperate situations? They loot or collect pieces and sell them so they can feed their families. The merchants they sell to pay a pittance and then they sell the things they bought to dealers at local gold and antique markets for a larger fee. Those dealers sell them for an even great sum to western collectors like you. But that's the small end of the market. Pornographic pieces and the mosaics in the cellar have often passed along a chain of corruption that extends around the world, and it spreads through all levels of society. You are, whether you want to accept it or not, involved in financing terrorism."

More colour returned to Taittinger's face, his neck dusky pink. "I am *not*. I'm preserving history. The wholesale looting of a country's treasures is a matter of international importance. I know the facts. This sort of smuggling has gone on forever. The bad guys just change names. Twenty years ago, pieces like mine travelled through Afghanistan, former Soviet republics, and out from Russia to Western capitals like London. Look, maybe I can't do anything about terrorism and arms trading, but I can do something about unscrupulous buyers and dealers like Basil, Nash, and...others."

Kitt's left eyebrow quirked. "Basil and Nash are interested in the pieces you have?"

Taittinger gave a huffing grumble of frustration. "Yeah, well, not everyone is here for the wine like Ruby, Foley, and David."

"What about the yet-to-arrive Chungs?"

Taittinger half shrugged.

"You said you had something they wanted, Dr Jools." Mae stopped rubbing the dog's ears. "Now I know why Mr Nash and Mr Basil asked about the Sunbeam."

"Interesting." Kitt ran a finger around the edge of his chin whiskers.

Taittinger's lips spread into a weak, yet proud little smirk. "You really believe I'm in this for the sake of money, but I'm not. Didn't you hear what I said last night? We're dealing with a human crisis. This is about preserving culture and human history."

A small smile twitched on Kitt's mouth. "I believe you believe you're on some kind of crusade."

"I keep the antiquities that have been stolen safe for cultures on the verge of having their history destroyed. Don't you see what I'm trying to do?"

"Yes. Who's working with you?"

Mae watched Taittinger squirm, as if the seat of his trousers suddenly filled with ants. "I work alone," he said.

Kitt smiled again. "It's clear you don't play poker. How do these things get to you?"

"Delivery companies—Universal Deliveries, Delivery Express, whaddya think?"

Mae gave a small cough. "Hector Rodriguez has ferried deliveries from Santa Fe, Albuquerque, and Las Cruces for you, Dr Jools."

"Come on, Valentine, can't you be on my side?"

With a soft smile, Mae resumed stroking the dog.

"What's he got on you, Valentine?"

She lifted the dog from the seat, set him on his feet, and looked at Kitt. "Are we almost finished here, sir? The other guests will be getting hungry and Felix needs exercise."

"Almost, Mrs Valentine. Hector would be?"

"Hector is an old friend, a landscaper and mechanic," Mae said. "He was at the party last night. Rather attractive Native American, looks a bit like Cary Grant, has a dent in his chin and long hair. Perhaps you danced with him?"

Kitt gave her a sidelong glance. "I must have missed the chance. How does Hector get the pieces get into the country, Tatts?"

Pale pink and dry, Taittinger's tongue ran across his lips. "I don't know." He shrugged. "That's not my end, or Hector's. He just picks things up when I ask him."

"All right, then what is your end? How do they get to your home?"

"I told you, they're delivered."

"By UniDel, DelEx, and sometimes Hector. What's the point of entry into the country? Do they start with Judith?"

"No, not with Judith."

"Then with whom? The Chungs?"

Taittinger's nose began to run. He pressed his palms to his face, fingers shoved under the lenses of his glasses, frames bunching up to his forehead, and he moaned and muttered beneath his hands.

"You actually want to do this the hard way, don't you?"

Hands came away but glasses stayed stuck to Taittinger's forehead. He went still. Tears trickled. The silence broken by Felix licking where testicles had once been. His spectacles dropped down. "Who the hell are you? *What* the hell are you?" he said, eyes wet and wide.

"Impatient."

"A username," Taittinger sniffled, "that's all I have. "It's all social media, online art forums, instant messaging."

"Instant messaging, a terrorist favourite, or the Dark Web. The username?"

Taittinger squirmed and fidgeted as ants returned to burrow in hard. "*Chichiltic*," he whimpered, and swiped at his snotty nose.

The saliva dried in Kit's mouth, as if he'd taken a spoonful of the red volcanic soil used to make New Mexico's snowy roads drivable. He looked at Mae, back at Taittinger, and smiled, head down, eyes peering through lashes.

"Oh, feck," Mae muttered.

"Oh, fuck," Taittinger snivelled, "I'm fucked. I'm fucked, aren't I, Valentine?"

Mae shivered at the murderous gleam in Kitt's eyes. "If you're involved with terrorists, Dr Jools, yes, you are, as Italians say, *fregato*."

"Your funding terrorism through philanthropic means aside," Kitt moved forward, "the thing that sticks with me here, Tatts, is that you're suspected of counterfeiting. Now why is that? Where would Interpol get that idea? Who would accuse you of such a thing?"

"*Fucking Judith*," he blubbered and snuffled. "Sending me a dead rat wasn't enough? I'd never, never counterfeit wine. That's a crime against nature worse than dating a woman who's more than five years older than you."

"Dumped you, did she?" Kitt smiled softly.

Taittinger blinked, mouth drooping.

"Older women know what they want and Judith didn't want you. Smart woman." Kitt set his gaze on Mae, watching her rub the dog's furry chin. He looked back at Taittinger. "How does Russell Grant fit?"

"What do you mean how does Russell Grant fit?" he said, twitching and rocking with imaginary bugs excavating an uncomfortable rectal fistula. "Jesus. What do you mean, how does he fit? What does he mean, Valentine?"

Mae tilted her head. "I believe he means Mr Grant knew about your antiquities preservation and that's why he's dead."

Taittinger stiffened. "Grant's in bed with the flu in the servant's quarters."

"No, he's not." Kitt's cold smile didn't wane. "There was no cougar or bear. You've been threatened, haven't you? Yes, you have. After all, you did come to the barn after smoking a little cannabis, and you had a gun in your pocket—a toy gun, but a gun nonetheless. That dead rat Judith sent you. Mrs Valentine told me about it. You really think it was from Judith?" He moved and stood beside Taittinger, towering down from above. "You aggravated someone and you thought the deer was that someone sending you a message," his head tilted to one side, "the sort that says *time to stop*. But Mrs Valentine found Grant last night in front of the studio, before he was replaced by the deer. I saw him too. He had a bullet in his face. So maybe the message is actually a warning. A rat, a deer, a threat, or a warning, you never know with terrorists. Either way, you're quite fortunate I'm here."

Mouth open, Taittinger froze, snot running over his moustache.

Mae burst out laughing. The two men turned to look at her. She shrugged. "A lavish party at a country estate, men in dinner suits, women in finery, fine wine, fine art, fine music, fine murder, and a little dog—it all feels so very Agatha Christie."

"Indeed, it does, Mrs Valentine. We must be cautious. Other guests may begin to die."

Wet, owlish eyes blinked slowly. "What do you want me to do, man?" Taittinger said, his voice tight and raspy. "What do you want?"

A sudden lightness loosened his shoulders. Kitt looked at Taittinger, the man shot a twitchy, pleading glare at Mae. Kitt turned his gaze on her too, and the momentary weight that had lifted tumbled back down, a bag of snakes and rocks and lead, hitting hard. He grunted and returned his attention to Taittinger. "What do I want?" Kitt crouched, set forearms on his thighs, and smiled broadly. "I want to flay you. However, there's what I want, what I'm going to do, and what you're going to do. Fortunately for you, you enjoy recreational drugs from time to time."

CHAPTER FOURTEEN

The light shifted, sunlight shrouded in a haze of falling snow. Kitt watched fat flakes meander down to meld with the pristine white on the other side of the glass. The mountains and canyons, the glimpses of blue sky, the pop of green brush and pinkish rock peeking from the snow were very beautiful. Some time ago, Mae had suggested he visit a spa in New Mexico, and he understood why she'd made the suggestion. The landscape was—if one set aside snow-hidden murder and the theft of cultural artefacts—bewitching, and if he remembered his geography, the spa wasn't too far from here.

Pity it was too late to grab her and go there.

Music filtered into the room again. The Ink Spots harmonised about loving the *Java Jive* and Kitt looked at his watch. He'd been nothing but too late for the last five months. He had never been more aware of time or more irritated by waiting for something to begin—or end—as he was now.

He rubbed his thumb over the odd, smooth tips of pruned fingers.

Wineglass in hand, Reed crossed into the great room, and joined Kitt at the windows.

"How'd the working bee go?" Kitt said quietly.

"It turned into Nash discussing the removal of antlers with a couple of Latino gentlemen who are excited by the prospect of eating venison." Apprehension bracketed Reed's mouth. He looked out at the north-falling snow, the moving distant clouds, the afternoon sun shining on the valley and mountains to the east. He sighed. "Fuck. I cleaned up a crime scene without reporting a crime. I destroyed evidence of a murder. What's the worst that'll happen? I'll lose my job or be jailed. Either way, my career is in the toilet."

"Ah, but think of where your career will be if this next part goes off right, and if it does work, you can leave in the morning."

Reed lifted a sceptical eyebrow and glanced at Taittinger guzzling a glass of wine as he arranged bottles of wine brought up from the cellar. "He's already pissed."

Kitt looked at Taittinger too. "Perhaps I don't need you anymore."

"*Shithouse, henhouse, sweatshop*, you passed along information, and I was doing my job. Maybe I still need you. Ever think of that?"

"Shut it, Simon."

"And what about," he sniffed, "Valentine?"

Kitt cut his eyes sideways. "She's a fortress of unmovable loyalty and professionalism, and I love her." He watched a dark bird circle high in the sky and flexed phantom stiffness from missing knuckles and fingertips. He turned, eyes still on the bird, smiling faintly. "I've cocked it up. I'm about to cock it up even more."

Reed shook his head. "You think giving her that ring made it all real?"

"No, her wearing that ring made it real." He watched Felix shadow Mae. She set out spittoons, bread and nibbles, pausing to run a hand down the dog's slender neck, murmuring nonsense at him.

"You could say 'thank you,' you know."

He faced Reed and all his freckles. The man was in his fifties and had boyish freckles. "You're right." Kitt nodded once. "Thank you."

"You're welcome, you little shit."

Kitt laughed softly.

"Now what?"

"Once everyone goes down, collect the wines that were brought here for sale, your Jefferson included. Put them in the garage, in the boot of Taittinger's Jeep. It will look like Mae's stolen them. Then check out each and every person who was at the party, including the catering staff. Mae will have all the contact details."

"You nearly died in a container full of counterfeit luxury goods, Grant, a man whose former girlfriend came from a family known for exporting counterfeit luxury goods, was the most promising lead, our host is an antiquities smuggler, and now 'party guests' is the best you've got. Can you remember anything else Molony mentioned, any associates or links to the Yeoh family, anyone with a grudge, anything at all besides *chichiltic*?"

"Grant's the only common factor. You know what I know."

Reed grabbed the end of Kitt's bearded chin between two fingers and gave it an affectionate shake, cowboy hat jiggling. "Kitty, you know fuck-all and can't even prove the fuck-all you know."

Over the next twenty minutes, guests began to gather in the great room. Dean Martin sang *Memories Are Made of This*. Newly-weds Ernie and Anna Chung arrived. The thirty-something couple canoodled on the loveseat, swirling and sniffing wine, listening to Basil paint a picture of a deer torn apart by a bear.

Ruby shuddered. "I've been huntin' with my daddy, but heck,

that deer was grisly. I had nightmares in the middle of a morning nap."

"I've seen worse," Nash sipped a 2007 Gaja Barbaresco.

"Of course you have," Reed muttered.

Basil chuckled. "To be honest, that was tidy compared to when wolves massacred our sheep."

"Oh, domestic livestock has no chance with wolves." Nash had another sip, made a face, and spat it back into his glass instead of the spittoon. "Who chose this sour raspberry soaked in dirty jocks?"

"I did." Anna Chung raised her chin, dark hair gleaming. "And I taste perfumed berry, rose, tilled earth, baking spice, and a hint of new leather."

Nash sniffed his spit-spoiled glass. "Sorry, yes, you're right, Anna. It has hints of leather—arse-smeared leather."

"You're a dick, Bob," Ernie took his wife's hand, "but you're right, that bottle's corked. I haven't liked the last two. Maybe that's why the cowboy's gone with bourbon."

Steely-eyed, Mae poured amber liquid into Kitt's tumbler. An exceptionally well-trained butler skilled at remaining unobtrusive and inexpressive, Kitt understood the intention of the tiny almost-sneer that tilted the left side of her mouth. Infinitesimal, the tilt conveyed how much she wanted to smash the bottle of bourbon over a skull, yet whose head did she want to bring the twenty-year-old bottle of Mitcher's Single Barrel down upon, his, Nash's or Taittinger's?

The dog lay across the wine-collecting antiquities-smuggling cosmologist's lap. Neck blotchy and red like his eyes, Taittinger massaged Felix's ears, slowly, methodically, the movement hypnotic, soothing his fear, masking his level of inebriation.

The left edge of Mae's mouth rose a fraction.

Kitt smiled to himself. Her near-smirk had nothing to do with him at all. Her derision was focused on Taittinger, not because of the artefacts in his wine cellar, but because of the dog. Kitt had a sip from the glass she'd filled. "Do whatever you need to keep up appearances," he said, "but you are leaving in fifteen minutes. Pack light."

"Yes, sir." Mae nodded without protest, without a contrary squint of her eyes, the ideal professional butler, her attention on the job, on the needs of the other guests, on Nash who had moved to the fireplace, on Ruby perusing wines on the other side of the room.

The inflection of the *sir* gave him an indication of her irritation beyond Taittinger and the dog, and something about her lack of objection raised his hackles, a thin filament of alarm fluttered in his stomach. "What is it?"

She met his gaze, and there it was, the squint he'd expected. She glanced at the brim of his hat and then her eyes flashed angry. "I know what you're planning to do."

"Oh, goody. I'm glad you know. I haven't quite figured it out yet."

Mae's stomach ached with the plan he said he hadn't figured out. Eventually, that ache would move to her heart and she wanted to shout at him, except she'd been the eejit who'd thought his coming back to life would mean an end to heartache, and shouting wouldn't save anyone. "Why can't you leave too? I'll send Bryce a message about what I found, without mentioning anything about you, and then you and I leave together."

"You want me to quit?"

"Yes."

"That would hardly be professional of *me*." His gazed to the left and he squinted, as if trying to remember something, "Haven't we heard someone say that before?" His eyes turned to her. "Goodness, the look on your face says, 'Oh, do shut up, Kitt.' I apologise for my cheek."

"Thank you, your contrition makes it all better." She cast a glance at Taittinger absently scratching Felix's long neck. "I see your bloody point. I don't like it. And I don't like Taittinger's sudden interest in the dog either. How did I not see what a phoney he was when his behaviour with the dog said it all?"

"Perhaps he's finding comfort in the dog, like you did."

"Finding comfort?" She sniffed. "No, you scared the be-jaysus out of him. He's using Felix as a shield should real bullets start flying his way. The feckin' phoney."

"Isn't that what Felix was for you?"

"A shield?"

"A comfort to you."

"You could pick a subtler way to say I told you so."

"I would never say, *I told you so*."

One hazel eye squinted more than the other.

"Yes, I would say, *I told you so*."

Ruby moved to sit beside Taittinger. Mae poured another splash of amber liquid over ice in the tumbler in Kitt's hand, three fingers and two shorter stubs wrapped around cut crystal. "Do you trust Taittinger to do what you told him to?"

"He's scared, in fear for his life and no, I don't trust him, but there's not much of a choice, for us. He's already slipped something relaxing into the bottles the guests chose from the cellar. He'll sit there, with the dog on his lap, and everyone will nod off, with Reed supervising."

"Is the 'something relaxing' chloral hydrate?"

"Chloral hydrate. Just how much research did you do into trade-craft, Mae?"

"Tradecraft, is that what the intelligence world calls the knockout drugs?"

Kitt brought the tumbler to his lips, hiding the quirk of his lips.

"What happens if people decide to leave?"

"No one is going anywhere. These are responsible oenophiles and they drink responsibly. However, if anyone tries to leave, they'll find they have car trouble." Kitt glanced at Reed. "Cold weather can wreak havoc on a car's battery, and so can Reed."

"Yes, you have it all sorted out and a back-up plan in Reed."

"That's why he's still here." Kitt had a swallow of the Mitcher's. "I am sorry about the dog, Mae," he said and smiled at Ruby as she moved to perch on the arm of the sofa, beside Taittinger.

Mae muttered something uncharitable.

"Fifteen minutes. Pack. Leave your bag in the laundry. I'll put it in the car. If Taittinger asks, you're going out to buy more eggs for breakfast."

"You've thought of everything."

"Yes, I have." His mobile rang. Kitt knocked back the bourbon, stuffed the glass into her hand, and left her at the window, answering the call. "Happy New Year, Mum!" He crossed the room. "I can barely hear you... David, Mum says Happy New Year!" he said loudly. "Yes, reception is dreadful. Hang on, it's better upstairs."

Mae watched him head for the foyer, phone at his ear. She opened a bottle of already drug-spiked red, a vintage so old it looked as appetising as brown water. She poured the rusty vintage into Ruby's waiting glass. "I'll be needing to tend to a few errands before dinner, Dr Jools."

"What's that, Valentine?" Taittinger smiled daftly, eyes glassy, bloodstream saturated with weed and wine already.

"Dinner for this evening and lunch tomorrow are well in hand, but owing to a mishap in the kitchen last night, I'll need to fetch a few things, eggs and such for breakfast."

"Oh, yeah, li'l Felix was a bad boy last night." He stroked the dog's ears, running them through his fingers. "You were bad, bad boy, wern'cha, Felix? Ruined a hunnert-dollar cheese. What's for dinner?"

"Moroccan chicken with honey, and Loubia stew for Mr Nash." The hand she held behind her back became a fist, fingernails in need of a trim dug into her palm. "Would you like to try this bottle before I go?"

"Nah, I'm enjoying this Gippsland Bass Phillip Reserve Pinot Noir—nothing wussy about it, punchy and a li'l loud, like strawberry pie made'a meat. Goo' call, Ian," he *huh-huh-huh* laughed, words becoming sloppier.

Mae stepped back and patted the side of her thigh. "Come, Felix."

The dog began to sit up, to move off Taittinger's lap, but the man lay a hand on the dog's back. "No, no, no, fine, he's fine, Valentine. See? See?" He ran his hand down the animal's spine. "See? He's not humping. No more *humping*." He laughed suddenly, drunkenly, with just a touch of on-the-verge-of unhinged.

Half a bottle. She held a half bottle of an $800 wine in her hand, a 1967 Grange Hermitage that connoisseurs said was sweet, complex, perfumed with apricot, violet and fig. Science had proven that human beings were fooled by labels and could not tell the difference between a cheap or expensive wine when tasting it. No one would be able to tell the difference if she'd hit Taittinger with a cheap or expensive bottle, and God help her she wanted to hit him with the bottle of Grange, she wanted to knock him out, snatch his dog, grab Kitt, and leave.

Her mouth went dry, eyes beginning to burn, throat tightening. "Very good, Dr Jools," she said.

Twelve minutes later, she was in the beige Volvo, with a suitcase, no dog, and only herself to blame for how she'd spend the rest of her life alone. It was a very strange thing to be resigned to knowing, and she held the steering wheel loosely, the control she had over her life just as slack.

Kitt didn't care much for the way Mae disregarded the reddish icy patches on the bitumen or the distance between the car, the guardrail, and its proximity to the edge of the mesa. Mute and fuming, she had driven halfway to Los Alamos, up along the curving road that skirted a rock face and sheer drop, before he broke the silence. "I am sorry about the dog, Mae."

"I don't want to talk about the dog. I've accepted my future solitude."

"Melodrama doesn't suit you, Mrs Valentine."

"I think I'm entitled."

"I suppose you are."

"Where am I going?"

"To a car that's waiting for you to drive out of here."

"Of course you're not taking me," she snorted.

"Directions are already set in the GPS. Just follow the little map."

"I can't get you to change your mind about my staying or you coming with me, can I? You've got it all planned and I'm no longer part of it."

Kitt said nothing, unable to look at her, watching instead the impending doom of her driving them both over the edge of a cliff. Focusing on impending doom that was never going to eventuate made it very clear he couldn't look at her because the real impending doom would come in a short while. If he looked at her now he'd have to be honest, the honesty would bring the doom. She would see right through him. It was easier to bear her irritation as she fell quiet again and kept on driving.

The silence between them stretched as the incline of the road flattened and they reached the top of the mesa. With the winter sun low above the Jemez Mountains, the route straightened onto the Pajarito Plateau, leading them past the Historic Los Alamos Project Main Gate and brick tower, toward the tiny town that ushered in the age of the nuclear bomb.

During World War II, the US had commandeered Los Alamos and land around it for the secret Manhattan Project that developed the atomic weapons dropped on Hiroshima and Nagasaki. After the War, Los Alamos had continued on as a base for ongoing nuclear research, much of it secret, and the town and residential areas grew out atop surrounding mesas stretching out like crooked fingers. Kitt gazed out at the picturesque setting, the town still hiding secrets much the same way he did.

At the edge of town, just past the municipal airport, the road forked. "Stay to the right," he said. "Take Canyon Road all the way to the United Church."

She pointed. "The way straight through town and left, is a better route. It misses the twists and bends and is less likely to be icy."

"You know your way around here."

She heaved a noisy sigh of resignation. "I've spent the last two and a half months in the area and it's a small place. Hard to get lost, but I feel a little lost now, Kitt. How did you figure it out? How did you tie what you saw in the wine cellar together with what you saw in the container?"

With a small laugh, he scratched the chin of his itchy beard. "I guessed."

"You guessed?"

"The work I do is all about supposition."

"I thought it was about improvisation."

"It's guessing, improvisation, connecting dots, and moments of utter tosh. When you were a child did you ever play the game where you have a sentence with a word missing here and there and you fill in the blanks? Hamish jumped in his *blank* Bentley and *blank* to *blank* for a *blank* of scrambled eggs. I gave Taittinger the sentence, he filled in the missing bits. I have something to work with, something to go on. Isn't that lovely? No counterfeit wine means you're done. Done and, nearly, gone." Kitt turned to her as the car halted at a set of traffic lights beside a science museum. "Now," he said, and waited.

Mae looked at him, the sun through the windscreen lighting up his eyes with a scorching blue flame. Calm, detached, his substantial fury held in beneath a practised façade, fifteen degrees below zero. He'd maintained that veneer since they'd left the barn. "Now?"

"Now, let's talk about what you did."

Mae reached out and angled the vent to blow warm air on her chest. "I wondered if we'd revisit that, if you'd feel some need to scold me again, and I want to know why. Why is it acceptable for someone to point a gun at you but not at me? Why can you protect me and keep me safe, but I can't protect you and keep you safe?"

"As professional as you are, you are not the right kind of professional. You have no business being here, being part of this world, being part of my world."

The light changed and Mae accelerated through the intersection, passing a hardware shop and post office. As they approached the Fuller Lodge, the building left behind from the old Boys Ranch School, she turned left and then left again into a carpark.

"What are you doing? Where are you going?"

"I want a coffee."

"And I want you to leave town, before sundown."

"Well, Sheriff," she said, mimicking Ruby's Texan drawl perfectly, "this is how it is." She pulled into a car space in front of a stationer, restaurant, and chain coffee shop. "You can run me out of town after I get coffee."

"I think you're stalling."

"I think I'm gettin' coffee. May I get you somethin', sir?"

"No, thank you. And you've got ten minutes."

Mae left the engine running, undid her seatbelt, and got out of the Volvo. Eight and a half minutes later, she climbed back in, an iced coffee topped with whipped cream and a domed lid in hand.

"When did you start drinking iced coffee?"

"Bryce has them. I wanted to try it."

"Bryce," Kitt muttered.

Mae put the cup in the car's cup holder, pulled out into traffic and drove along a heavily wooded stretch of road. She made a left just past the Jewish Center with its A-line red roof and went down a laneway half-hidden by thick pine boughs. Mounds of snow lined the sides of the pot-holed bitumen and gave way to ice and tyre tracks in a good ten centimetres of snow. The trail dog-legged around an ochre garden shed and came to an end at a breeze-block carport shadowed by pine trees.

"Which one?" she said, pointing at the three cars under the carport.

"The white Toyota Camry. The boot's unlocked. The key's inside the first-aid kit. Push button start. Follow the GPS to your destination."

Mae put the car in neutral. "Here we are again, right where we were before, back at the start of October when you brought home a Christmas tree, and left me."

"And now you're leaving me."

"Because that's what you want."

"Because it's the only choice there is."

"No, it's the only choice you've given me. If I hadn't agreed, you would have drugged me with whatever you put in Taittinger's wine." She tore paper from a straw and shoved it into the plastic cup of coffee.

"I am sorry about Felix. Truly. Where you're going isn't a place for a dog, and this is not how I want us to part, with you still so angry with me."

"It doesn't matter about Felix. He's microchipped."

Kitt bit his molars together. If the dog was chipped, then odds were everything that had happened had been deliberately orchestrated, right down to Mae's presence, and he could guess why, but *why* didn't matter right now. He disconnected from the rage he could not act upon, prioritising instead what he could control. And so did Mae.

With an absurd, breathy laugh, she lifted the coffee and returned it to the holder without taking a sip. "I have no real right to be angry with you. This is your life. This is what you do, what you are. I'm angry with myself for thinking that there...that I... I shall get over it. It's one more thing about you and my life with you I'll write in my journal."

"I'm not going to die," he said softly before he tipped his head. "You keep a journal?"

"Remember, you suggested it might help me process the things that have happened over the last year? And you're right. It helps; more than I thought ever it could." Mae stared out the tinted window at the three vehicles beneath the five-space breezeblock carport for a long, long moment. The car's heating system whirred, blowing out heated air. "Kiss me and feck off, Kitt."

"Do you want me to kiss you goodbye?"

"I want you to kiss me and go on with your bloody plan."

"You really think I have a plan?"

Her head came around. "As good as you are at obfuscating your thoughts behind a wall of maddening calm, right now you are so transparent." She sniffed a small laugh. "Not how you want us to part. You're going to kiss me, make sure I get in that car, and I'll never see you again."

"Well, you did say you never wanted to see me again."

Her expression told him just how full of shite she thought he was.

"I'm not going to die, Mae."

Soft and bizarrely sympathetic, her smile was the sort a headmistress gave to a little boy who'd been denied permission to go on an excursion with the other schoolchildren. "Even if, by some miracle, you don't die, I really won't see ever you again."

"Mae, y—"

"I can tell by your great, unimpressed face of stone you wonder why I would think that. Well, you said it yourself. Your work is nothing but guessing, improvisation, connecting dots, and moments of utter tosh. I guessed. Don't tell me I'm wrong."

The whirring of the heater grew loud in the silence that fell between them, and the ticking of his watch joined in with the low hum of the running engine.

At last, eyes burning, he said, "I was a fool to ever believe I could do this, that we could have something. I cannot put you in a position or have you put in a position where your life is in danger because of me, because of the work I chose to do, the work I have to finish. I don't want to see you come to harm by trying to keep me from harm. So you're right, I'm going to kiss you and you're going to walk away."

"When did you decide this for me?"

"The second you stepped in front of Taittinger's gun."

"Which you knew was a toy."

"I didn't know that until I got a little closer."

"Maybe you're right. Maybe you're wrong. Maybe things between us will never be the same. I was scared. I am scared, but I agreed to a very long engagement."

"Yes, you did, which brings us back to I'm going to kiss you and you're going to walk away."

"Coward."

"Yes. Oh, yes." In one move, Kitt twisted, leaned across the gear shift, pulling her over, hand at the back of her neck, his mouth on hers. The kiss was warm, firm, and tinged with the taste of his tears. He let her go, sniffling. "Get out of the car, my love. Please."

Dry-eyed, exhaling softly, Mae pulled the diamond from her finger. She lay the ring on his thigh, turned, lifted the coffee from the holder, and swung out of the car.

Kitt expected her to slam the door, but she shut it normally. She opened the right rear passenger door, grabbed her handbag and suitcase from the seat, closed the door, and walked away in a way he hadn't anticipated. Like so many men, he bought into the sexist, stereotyped expectation of high drama, high emotion, shrill, raised voice, a slammed door. Her display was simple, matter-of-fact quiet disappointment. With him.

He would have preferred the stereotype.

Without looking at the bloody thing, he pocketed the ring, climbed over into the driver's seat and, for a moment, sat behind the wheel watching her through the darkly tinted side window, as she said he would. He put on the cowboy hat. While he sniffled and swept away tears, she moved from the carport to a rubbish skip at the far end of the brick structure. She lifted the skip's lid, changed her mind about tossing the coffee into it, went back to the Toyota, opened the boot, and deposited her bags. Then Mae got in the car, drink in hand, and started the engine.

Kitt wiped his nose, sobbed, swore, put the Volvo in gear, and went out the way they'd come in, passing an old green VW Beetle driven by a man with a handlebar moustache. Despite the various physical injuries he'd sustained in his life, and coming so close to dying, he had never known true agony before. He sobbed again and his stomach squeezed up into his oesophagus alongside his ragged, raw, aching heart.

Mae watched the Volvo in the mirror until a VW came into view and stalled behind the Toyota before it could reverse into in the car space beside her. She watched the man at the Beetle's wheel swear and try to start the car. The engine made a noisy *rrr-rrr-rrr* and kicked over into that unmistakable Volkswagen hummingbird-like sound—and died out. The second and third attempt proceeded in the same manner. For a moment, in exasperation, the man's head drooped against the steering wheel.

Mae cut the motor and climbed out of the car, coffee in hand. The man threw open his door and climbed out. "Sorry! Sorry!" He waved an apologetic hand, slammed the door. Snow from the Beetle's roof fell on his three-piece tweed suit. He brushed it away from his jacket, a sparkle of white fell on shoes not meant for winter. He slipped on a patch of ice as he moved to the front end of the car. Mae assumed he'd start pushing. Instead, he opened the bonnet, which in the case of the old Beetle was the boot. After a second or two, he swore and his head popped around the side of the boot's lid. "You don't have jumper-cables, do you?" he called out to her, handlebar moustache bouncing on his top lip.

"I don't." Mae gave an apologetic shrug and moved to the end of the Toyota. "You want a hand to a push?"

"Unless you're in a rush, I can wait. My girlfriend will be here soon. She has cables. Hey, I know you from somewhere, don't I?" He began moving toward her car. "We met—" he slipped and slid and fell on his arse.

Mae went to help him up, but he gave a laugh and got to his feet, found his balance and took a few careful steps until he stood about a metre away, under the half-brick carport behind the Toyota, hands in tweedy pockets. "Yeah," he said. "We met. The party. I took your picture last night. You're the butler. Never met a lady butler before." Now sober, the moustachioed dapper-dressing photographer came closer, hands going into his pockets as a snow-dusted figure moved around the rear of the VW.

"Car trouble?" Kitt's words came out in little clouds. The front of his jacket dappled with white, the brim of his cowboy hat and his beard sparkled with ice, as if he'd fallen into a snow bank.

The photographer exhaled and turned, hands coming out of his pockets, a tiny gun gleaming in his grip. "You picked the wrong day to play good Samaritan, cowboy."

The weapon levelled with Kitt's nose.

CHAPTER FIFTEEN

Mae hurled the iced latte. The domed, plastic lid blew off on impact, coffee, ice exploded against the man's shoulder, a sharp thunderclap hurt her ears. Kitt rushed sideways, his body a blur. The cowboy hat flew, and the crown of her skull met breeze-block wall. The breath exploded from her lungs when she was crushed between the bricks, the man's broad back, and the full force of Kitt bearing forward.

Whipped cream and coffee droplets hung in a handlebar moustache, the scent of vanilla latte mingled with the peppermint-infused breath blasting into Kitt's face. He slammed the manicured hand clutching the tiny Derringer 9mm Cobra against thick brick, again and again. The damned thing would not dislodge, one round left in the pistol.

Mae grunted and gasped for a full breath. Kitt knew she was safer where she was, compressed by two bodies and hard, flat surface, than in a position where a bullet could hit her. The goon jammed upwards with a knee, missing the intended target of testicles, delivering instead a jolt to the groin that would leave a lump and colourful bruise for a few weeks to come.

Against the block wall, two circus strong-men engaged in a battle of brute strength, and crushed Mae, stomping her feet, kicking ice cubes across the concrete slab. Trapped by their combined bulk, she strained to move, to breathe, to help Kitt. She grunted and pounded her free hand into the dandy's tweed-covered side while he hammered into Kitt's left kidney. Rapid-fire, the blows continued.

Kitt's grip on the man faltered for a millisecond. The balance of weight began to shift, the pistol twisting toward his temple, hammer cocking, but the crushing mass of their bodies altered enough to give Mae minute space. Her breath came in a sharp, noisy gasp, she jerked her trapped arm free, and boxed the chap's ear, something dark clutched in her fist.

The seconds slowed in the manner that Kitt had long ago grown accustomed to. The man's eyes widened. The petite 9mm curved, the muzzle flashed with a near-deafening *crack*! The bullet hit brick, masonry falling, striking and scraping Mae's cheek. The Cobra bounced off the not-quite-a-gentleman's two-toned saddled bucks. His body sagged back against Mae and Kitt drove knuckles into his nose, a spray of scarlet dappling her cheek.

Time resumed its normal course. Jaw clenched, electric pain flowed into Kitt's guts.

"Ya gammy lout!" Mae shouted, pushed at their assailant, shoving him, knocking off his horn-rimmed glasses. Blood flowed over his lips and down his chin, his bow tie crooked.

Kitt's eyes watered from the acidic sting, his kidney charred from the thrashing, but he kept moving. He kicked the spent pistol aside and hit the man in the throat and stomach. Clutching at his throat, the natty dresser struck the Toyota, slid down the car and crumpled in a gagging, coughing heap.

Then Mae swore like an old Irish sailor. She rushed to him and Kitt wanted to fold into her, to hold her close, but he fixed his attention on the hacking un-gentlemanly gentleman and bore her inspection, knowing, as she looked him up and down and searched for blood or an injury of any sort, her expression would be a mix of concern, fear, and fury.

"Are you hurt?" she said, her breathing rapid and shallow with fright.

"I'm fine, if not a little deaf. Thank you for your quick thinking. Sorry about treading on your feet." He said, aware how much his ears were ringing. He realised how much his heart was pounding, how slow he'd become, and how foolish he was to believe getting her out of here would fix anything. "Deep breath, Mae," he said and took one himself, tamping down his fear and anger, but not the unexpected theory that had taken off in his mind. His theory soared like a kite.

She rubbed the crown of her head, fingers coming away with a small streak of blood. "Jaysus, why it is someone always has a gun when you don't? What's the bleedin' point of having weapon skills when you *never* have a weapon when it matters?" Mae swallowed, inhaled and exhaled slowly, and squinted at Kitt. "I don't think I've ever been so happy to be pissed off that you trust me so little you'd come back to make sure I'd left."

"I recognised him from someplace, but seeing Grant stuffed inside the Beetle's boot really set me off." Kitt groaned, partly because of the shooting pain in his back, partly because he'd learned nothing from past experience when he'd left Mae 'safely behind,' and partly because this was one more twist he never saw coming. He looked at her. "Your face. You're bleeding." He drew a small flick knife from a pocket.

She peered around him, looking at Russell Grant's shiny black shoe poking out of the VW's open boot. Then she touched a stinging spot on her cheek, fingertips smearing through tiny dots of blood. "It's a scratch. I'm not really hurt, but I am mad." She gave an absurd little laugh and glanced at the blade he flipped open. "You gonna kill the rat-arsed feckin' hipster?"

"It depends." Without looking, Kitt grabbed her hand and kissed it. "You," he said to the still-sputtering, wheezing man. "On your knees. Lock your fingers behind your head, cross your ankles."

Hacking, watering brown eyes on Kitt, the man did as he was told, the green straw once in Mae's coffee now protruding from his ear.

"He was the photographer last night." Mae gave Kitt's hand a squeeze and released it.

"Yes, that's it." With an amused puff, Kitt settled his focus onto the man's face. "What's your name?"

"De—*cough-cough-cough*—Der—"

"When you're ready."

For a moment or two, the man hacked, cleared his throat, and spat. "Derek," he said, hoarsely.

"How old are you, Derek?

"Twenty-two." He cleared his throat again.

"Been at this long?"

"About eighteen months."

"You have a great deal to learn here, Derek, especially about women. You wouldn't know it to look at her, but she's quite bloodthirsty until she's had coffee, and you spoiled her coffee. Explain this," Kitt held up the tiny Cobra 9mm two-shot.

Derek exhaled, swiped his bleeding nose on his bicep, and winced when the straw in his ear knocked into his elbow. "Okay, you got me," he said, voice raspy. "I was told to hurt her, to scare the hell out of her, not kill her. You, well, I didn't count on you being with her; thought you were a random, but I figured it would be easy. I'd bring you down and then take care of her. Guess you showed me, huh? I wasn't going to kill you. I don't do that sort of thing. I don't rape either. There's a commandment about killing, you know, and I don't kill. You gotta have a code to live by. You want someone dead, you call somebody else. Everybody knows I don't rape and I don't kill. I intimidate. I break legs and kneecaps, and dislocate shoulders, that sort of thing."

"You're the very model of Christianity." Mae crossed her arms.

"Look, I sin. I'm a sinner. We're all sinners, but I don't kill."

Mae squinted. "Well, I do."

"Yeah, uh-huh, right." Derek snorted and spat out blood. "Damn, I think you broke my nose, bro."

"That I did," Kitt said.

Grimacing, Derek shifted his top lip from side to side, and cast his eyes to his right, in the direction of the green plastic sticking out of his ear. "Yeah. You busted it clean, but I gotta say the thing she shoved in my ear hurts even more. I'm supposed to leave it right? That's what you do with stuff like this, right?"

"Yes, it's always best to let professionals handle these situations, rather than amateurs, and really, truth be told, she does kill," Kitt tapped the end of the straw with the point of the knife he'd flicked open. "And so do I."

Derek's yelp of pain died abruptly. His brown eyes darted back to Kitt and his gleaming, sharp blade. "Okay. I see. You intimidate. You're pretty good at it too. You want my attention? I'm paying attention. You want the money he paid me already? It's in the inside pocket of my jacket."

"I don't want your money, or any other things you may have in your pocket, but I do want you to pay attention. Are you really paying attention?"

"I'm all ear."

"Oh, he's funny, Kitt."

"She thinks you're amusing, Derek. You know, I can kill you and it won't hurt a bit. Would you like me to tell you how I'd do that?"

Mae exhaled. "I don't think I like where you're going with this, Kitt."

"This is utterly the wrong time to tell me your question about killing the rat-arsed hipster was rhetorical. This is the wrong moment to say we should leave him here and run because you've had enough violence and death in your life."

"I don't think it's necess—"

"Christ, Mae, the 'we're all sinners' bit is absolute rot. He nearly shot me in the face. He was going to kill you. He was going to kill us both. Isn't that right, Derek?"

Derek grinned, blood all over his teeth. "Forgive me, Father, for I have, you know, sinned." He ran his tongue over his crimson-stained incisors, around his lips, licking at one corner as if chocolate were there instead of blood. "How'd you lose your fingers?"

Mae gaped at the young man, briefly, and shook her head. "He's high, Kitt. You're high, aren't you, Derek?"

"Maybe just a tad." Derek chuckled. "You two are spoiling it all for me. I should have been out of here by now. I'm getting all mellow and you're fucking up my slide into joyous. Can we hurry it along?"

"In a minute. Who wanted you to kill us?"

"Honesty time? There was no us, just a..." Derek looked at Mae "...her. I don't know you, bro, like I said, you were random, but you're not random at all. I get you, brah."

"So you killed Grant? Where'd you'd get the deer?"

"A guy I know. You lost your fingers working, didn't you? I bet you've got some awesome stories to tell."

Kitt let loose a muttered string of obscene phrases before he smiled, brilliantly. It made his eyes crinkle. "Honesty time. You made a mistake, didn't you?" he said, smile dazzling and vicious.

"Yeah, I didn't count on you coming back."

"Yes, there's that." Kitt nodded.

Derek sighed. "Last time I do something that boneheaded."

"I mean your earlier mistake."

Derek gave a shrug. "So, sue me for being sexist. I thought she was the housekeeper. It was 'do the butler.' Women usually aren't butlers." He chuckled lightly. "First guy dressed the part, made it easy. I followed him outside. Didn't know I'd fucked up 'til after."

Nausea wriggled in Mae's stomach, wriggled and flopped like a gasping fish on the sand. She stared at Kitt, feeling dry lips part.

"Anyhow, I believe in being thorough and rectifying my errors so here I am." Derek's voice turned soft, sleepy until he hawked up a glob of blood and spat again. "Come on. Let's get on with it."

"Give me a name. Who wants her dead?"

"Who...what?" Nausea fell away into a deep hum in her ears and thrum in her chest, and Mae moved closer to Kitt. A muscle pulsed in his jaw.

"Some guy named Lou." Derek exhaled, licked his lips, and ran his tongue around his teeth.

Kitt went on smiling coolly. "Could you be a little more specific?"

"Lou something that sounds like a girl's name."

"Llewelyn?" Mae muttered what Kitt already believed.

"Yeah. Lou Ellen. That's it. So, can we get this over with now, bro? I wanna die feelin' this buzz."

Knife in hand, Kitt cocked his head and levelled his cold, grinning gaze on the tweed-clad, piss-poor, would-be assassin. "Well, you know, you can't always get what you want."

"HE WAS GOING to kill me and stuff me in the boot with Grant, wasn't he?"

"Yes." Kitt exhaled softly, Derek's digital camera on his lap. "A nuisance, Mae, you're a sodding nuisance." He turned and stared out the windscreen.

Mae stared at him. What was the word? Compartmentalise? Yes, that was it. Cowboy hat on his head, he looked out the window, at the beautiful view of mountain and sky, unmoved by the recent violence and she was jacked up, excited, over-caffeinated—and hadn't even had coffee. At the same time, she was mortified by what had to be bloodlust. "How do you not let this affect you?" she said.

"I'm not unaffected. I merely choose to focus on now rather than before."

"Meaning you choose to examine your actions later?"

"Only when they involve you. Especially when they involve you." He went on looking out at the sun and shadow play on mesas and the valley. "I know what I do is abhorrent, yet it is seldom without purpose."

"For Queen and country." Mae sniffed.

"You don't believe in serving your country, protecting those you hold dear?"

"I believe in protecting those you love and protecting a common humanity."

"Not so different really, is it?"

She mulled over his statement or suggestion and ran a finger across the stinging scratch on her cheek. It had scabbed over. "I suddenly feel as though I need to go to confession."

"You do know a priest."

Despite his soft, controlled breathing, Mae noticed he gripped the steering wheel tightly, squeezing the life from something lifeless. The whiteness of his knuckles showed through smears of blood and the beginning of bruising.

Looking at the shortened knuckles of his stubby fingers set off a tingle that was primal, bloodthirsty, and strangely triumphant. The concoction and surge of adrenaline brought on by events in the last hour would fade, Mae knew that, but she was thinking clearly, and his knuckles, the whiteness... Even the best poker players had a tell; the whiteness was his, and she knew his detachment was tenuous. "You can't do this, can you?"

"Do what?" His fingers loosened on the steering wheel, set the camera in the centre console, took off the hat and shoved it on the dashboard. Then he turned at last and looked at her instead of at the rocky view.

"You can't do this without me, can you?"

Stone-faced, Kitt got out of the SUV, almost, but not quite slamming the door.

Mae watched him move around the bonnet, head along the footpath, and pause at the low wall. Sunrays turned his hair dark ginger. He stood in a scenic tourist overlook park, casually taking in the breathtaking vista of the mountains, mesas, the Rio Grande, all bathed in oranges, pinks, and soft mauve of the late afternoon sun. Then he bent forward and vomited. Twice.

When he straightened, he wiped his mouth with the back of his fist. Hands in trouser pockets, he continued along the path, as if he hadn't been sick.

Mae sighed, rummaged in her handbag, and climbed out of the Volvo.

From this height, the river in the valley below sat in violet shadow that reminded Kitt of a bruise, the sort that he'd find on his ribs and back later. The valley around the river stretched out wide, filled by reddish-pink, orange and painted mesas, deep green piñon trees, the Sangre de Cristos Mountains a hazy, black-and-blue as the rising moon peeked over snowy caps. The temperature was dropping. In half an hour, it would be colder and dark.

Kitt turned away from glowering at nature's splendour and took the tissue Mae had thrust beside his ear.

"You have a bit of sick on your chin."

He wiped his chin, balled up the tissue in his fist, and turned his face from side to side. "Did I miss anything?"

Mae shook her head, licked her bottom lip, smiled, and began laughing.

"You think it's funny I had sick all over my chin?"

"I think it's funny that I make you sick."

"You get a thrill from my vomiting?"

"Yes."

"No, you don't." He looked at her. "Ah, yes, you do." With a shrug, he shoved the tissue into a pocket. "Why?"

"It's weirdly...flattering and somewhat endearing because it means I know how much you love me. I also know how scared you are, and that's funny be—"

"My fear is amusing?"

"I'm amused because I never would have survived that business with Caspar's trust and the Mafia. I couldn't have done it without you. And now, you can't do this without me."

"There are times, Mrs Valentine, when you have the strangest sense of humour." He shut his eyes for a moment, opened them, settled what he knew was a peevish gaze on her, and said, peevishly, "No, I can't do this without you because somehow you're part of it."

Mae's smile was positively sunny.

"Are you enjoying this?"

All sense Mae had of triumph evaporated. Tingle gone, her strange reality crashed into place. "Oh, yes. Finding Grant dead made me feel alive. Killing two people last summer made me feel alive, the same way hearing you break Derek's nose and neck made me feel alive. Is that what it is, is that why you do it, the lying, the killing? Because it's exhilarating, something that really lets you know how alive you are? However sick it may be, I'm enjoying it."

"No, you're not."

"Yes, I am, and see? This is what I meant when you proposed. I truly liked that you broke his nose and broke his neck. I enjoyed watching you shove him into the boot with a dead man, particularly when I was supposed to be dead in that boot with Grant, and that is why I said no. Well, part of why, but you knew I would turn you down. You knew what I was afraid of, and you counted on my refusing your proposal."

"Did I?"

"I think deep down you wanted me to say no, so that you could let me go and pretend it was my choice to walk away."

His cool detachment had returned. "You didn't say, *no*, Mae, you said you would consider a very long engagement. That's not *no*. And you do not enjoy those things any more than I do."

"You've never taken pleasure in your job, in say, stabbing a pen into a Mafia accountant's hand after he tried to have someone you love killed?"

"I think this may be your trouble. Enjoyment and satisfaction are not the same thing; a sense of gratification is different to enjoyment. Shoving a Montblanc pen through Ernst Largo's greedy little hand last summer was immensely gratifying."

"Thank you for the clarification."

"My pleasure."

She tucked back a wisp of hair that had come undone from her tidy French braid. "If you don't enjoy it, then why do you do it? Why do you do work that puts you in a position where you might have to kill? Or be killed if you don't kill first?"

Kitt regarded her for two seconds and smiled ever-so-faintly. "I come from a family with a highly developed social conscience, one that instilled the value of giving back, of community, of service, of social justice. Like Taittinger, only...genuine. When you're born into this world with more wealth and comforts than you could ever need you have a moral responsibility, an obligation to give to others less fortunate, to look after them, to share your wealth, and not merely in a financial philanthropic capacity."

"That was a lovely speech."

"I thought so too. You can blame my mother for my ideals or blame the Kennedy era. She was in the Peace Corps and *Médecins Sans Frontières*."

"Your mother was American?" Mae plopped down on the low wall, eyes scrunched up, head shaking at his revelation. "Jaysus, you certainly pick the oddest times to tell me about yourself. A philanthropic capacity. Janey Mack, you think you're Batman, don't you?"

"Well, I know I'm not James Bond or Julius Taittinger, Batman's parents were dead, and you simply assumed mine were."

"As you wanted me to." She looked at him, eyes still scrunched. "I'm not going to ask. I'm not going to be enticed by titbits about you. Rather than discuss your family, your grandiose ideas about saving the world, and having to think about what that really means, distract me, redirect my attention instead of contradicting me, instead of reminding me."

"You want a kiss and a cuddle? You do recall I was just sick in the bushes, don't you?"

"Do I look like I give a damn?"

He reached out and yanked her into his arms. For a long time, he held her, and she held him, propped him up, actually, and didn't even know. Crows *caw-cawed* and hopped about the great rocks on the other side of the wall they stood beside.

She sighed into his chest, fingers stroking the hair at the back of his head. "I don't give a damn. In fact, I don't seem to have any remorse about what just happened to us. Twice, I've watched you break a man's nose, and today I've watched you break a man's neck. I have no remorse in seeing you do it. I wanted you to do it. Is it easier breaking a nose or breaking a neck? Tell me."

"I didn't break his neck. I severed his spinal cord. He'll be a paraplegic for the rest of his miserable life—if he doesn't freeze to death in the Beetle's boot first."

"Was that easy to do? Sever his spinal cord, I mean." She pulled back and stared at him, awaiting a reply.

He let her go. "Mae." Kitt regarded her for a long, long moment as well, and cursed himself for being a quixotic, bloody, goddamned fool, for being a ruinous, bloody, goddamned professional fixated on finishing his goddamned bloody foolish job. Years ago, when he'd first rented the flat she owned, when he'd detached a retina and been confined to sit immobile on his arse all day, she'd arrived on his doorstep with coffee and a tray of Chelsea buns. That morning, he should have shut the door in her face, but he hadn't, which made him wholly responsible for her confusion, for her anguish, for her erroneous delight.

He smiled, very softly. "I'm sorry. I am sorry for all of this, for what you've been witness to. I never should have let it get this far." He touched her cheek with the back of his fingers. "I should have let you go."

She sat on the wall and smiled back, just as softly. "I should have walked away."

He had a seat beside her and took her hand. "You're half-frozen."

"Am I?"

Kitt took off his jacket and draped it over her shoulders. "You shouldn't be part of this. Any of it. Killing is an awful thing. It's much easier to vomit."

She laughed and then sighed, heavily, looking out over the valley, his jacket warm and damp with perspiration.

Kitt swung his legs up, and lay knees up, on top of the wall, cold stone a makeshift ice pack for the hot flame in his back, his head in Mae's lap.

Her fingers moved through his hair, brushing out tiny, sandy bits of mortar. "You live in another world. If I want to be with you I'd have to live in that beautiful, horrible, and fascinating world too. Do you see? I'm fascinated by you, by what you do, by the mechanics of it, by what it is that makes you do what you do, and I wonder what that says about me?" Her sigh had a tinge of remorse to it. "I think I took on the position to spite you. When you died, I was so angry, I took the position because had you been alive you would have told me—no, you would have *demanded* that I do no such thing."

"I fascinate you?"

"That's what you take away from what I've just said?"

"I fascinate you." Kitt pulled her fingers from his head. He kissed the centre of her palm and laid her hand on his chest, right over his heart, his hand on top of hers.

She heaved another sigh and gazed down at him. "You're the most fascinating man I've ever known."

"More fascinating than Caspar?"

"Is that important?" She pulled her hand from his chest, lifted his head from her lap, and rose, gently settling his skull on top of the wall. "Is that important, Kitt?"

"Trust is more important, and I've given you every reason to mistrust me." With a groan, Kitt got to his feet and followed her to the car.

She climbed behind the wheel and waited for him to get in the other side. "I trust you with my life," she said, once he'd slid into the passenger seat and shut the door.

"Which scares the living daylights from me."

Mae laughed, a dry, rasping noise. "I know what you are. I may not understand, but I know. The strangest thing is that I trust you more than I trust myself, and I scare myself more than you have ever frightened me. I keep telling you that." She lay a hand on his thigh.

He glanced at the fingers that leached cold warmth into his skin, and then into her face. That stray wisp of hair curved around her chin. "Is there something you have in mind, a suggestion about climbing into the back seat and steaming up windows?" He put his hand over the top of hers. "I'll disappoint you, like I did last night. My back feels as if it has a flaming poker slicing into it. A kidney jab will do that."

"A shag is the last thing on my mind."

"What is on your mind then?"

"Llewelyn, Taittinger's stolen artefacts, who wants me dead, who wanted you dead. Us." She turned her hand and closed her fingers around his. "If this is going to work, we can't have secrets, we can't keep things from each other, even if you think it's for my own safety."

There were a few things he hated to admit or face as true. For three years, he'd tried to ignore the feelings he had for Mae, tried to pretend he could keep them hidden, told himself that holding them at bay made so much more sense than all the trouble she would be, and yes, she was trouble. Most of the trouble came from those moments when she was right about something that had nothing to do with her. "You're right. You're right and I hate that you're right." Kitt squeezed her hand. "What you know about intelligence work comes from books and film. You think it's all guns, dirty bare-handed fighting, and killing. Mostly it's paperwork, handling and receiving information, delivering bribes, not one man saving the world from nuclear annihilation."

"So you've said."

He let go of her hand. "It's not sexy, it doesn't make for an exciting tale, but it's true. There are times an intelligence officer may be seconded to work with a team and do shadowy unpleasant things as part of that team. Because of my military background, I have often been seconded to a team, as I was in October, as I have been on numerous occasions over the last three years we have known each other. That is all I am willing and able to tell you about what I do. Some topics are—don't laugh—classified. Do you see where I am going with this?"

She ran her tongue over her teeth to keep from chuckling. "Not yet."

"I find it vexing that I won't be able to do this without you. I find it exasperating that, for you to go on trusting me, I have to tell you things I believe are better left unsaid. I find it irritating that you and Reed form part of a team, but all of this frustration is the reality. Part of me likes that you're here because I know where you are, and part of me hates that you're here because I know where you are. This reality means I will always put your safety and Reed's safety first, as I see fit, whether you like it or not. And you are correct. For this to move ahead there are things you need to know."

For a half second, she blinked, her lips parted, her brow rumpled repeatedly.

"Surprised you, didn't I?"

"What gave it away, my gob hanging open or my dumbfounded blinking?"

"Neither. It was your undulating eyebrows, which were, I must say, quite fetching."

"What do I need to know?"

"At the moment, the personal is less important than the...business side of things." His mouth tipped at one corner. "Listen to me carefully. This is the most important thing I will ever tell you."

"I know you love me."

"Yes, so then, this is the *other* most important thing you need to know, particularly should you again find yourself in a situation where someone has a gun and you don't. Or if there's a knife, or if there is a threat of violence of any sort. Are you listening?"

Mae snorted and started the car's engine. "I do not need another scolding from you."

"Bloody woman." Kitt reached across and twisted the key in the ignition, killing the engine. "Why is it you dislike taking instruction?"

"I take instruction fine. What I dislike is you speaking to me in a patriarchal tone."

"I'm serious."

"Of course you are. You're looking at me with your head down and eyes up, staring at me through your lashes. That's you at your most serious. I must say it's quite fetching."

Kitt lifted his head. "You are maddening, Mrs Valentine."

"It's part of my charm."

He exhaled, slowly. "Please, Mae."

"Good manners are always appreciated. What is it you want me to know about facing potential violence?"

"There is one word you need to remember. And I really like how you're leaning in to show me you are attentively listening."

"Thank you."

"*Run*, Mae. The word is *run*. Don't stand there, don't throw a punch, don't throw a cup of coffee, don't lash out with a block of cheese, don't strike with a toilet brush, and don't stand in between the muzzle of a gun and another man. *Run*. Do you understand?"

"Yes."

"Now promise me."

"I promise."

"What, you promise what?"

"To run, should the potential for gun violence arise." She

exhaled and ran her tongue over her front teeth. "There's just one thing."

"Christ. What?"

"What will you do in the same situation?"

"This isn't about me."

She dug her fingers into the seat upholstery. "Why not? Why doesn't the same direction apply to you? Why can't you run?"

Kitt gave her a faint smile. "We could sit here and talk in circles about this for the next hour, but there's something we need to think about."

"Such as?"

"Llewelyn and Bryce."

"You really think you're going to change the subject?"

"When were you supposed to meet Bryce?"

"Yes, you changed the subject." She looked heavenward for a moment. "Early tomorrow morning."

"How early?"

"Six-thirty."

"Where?"

"Ruby K's, a café in Los Alamos."

"Indoors. Thank God almighty. I look forward to seeing him."

"You look forward…" Mae fell quiet, except for the drumming of her fingers on the edge of her seat. After a moment, she stopped the drum beat, licked her bottom lip, and inhaled. "You think he's responsible?"

"I don't know."

"Does Bryce know you're alive?"

Kitt turned to her fully as he drew on his seatbelt. "Perhaps."

"What's that supposed to mean?"

"It means perhaps."

"Is that good or bad?"

"We'll find out tomorrow when you meet him."

Mae gave an incredulous shake of her head and started the car's engine again. "Now you want me to see him?"

"I want us to see him. I'm coming with you. I'd enjoy a bagel from Ruby K's."

"How did you know they sold bagels?

"It's not my first time in Los Alamos."

"Naturally. The last time you were here you dealt with actual espionage at the Los Alamos National Laboratory, didn't you?"

"That's classified."

"Feckin' balls."

Kitt's mouth quirked. "The Ruby K's has been there more than ten years, the Fuller Lodge even longer. Pretty place, the Lodge, wood panels and exposed beams, a log cabin on a grand scale. But first things first. Continuity is important, especially when improvising. Before we proceed with anything here's another matter to attend to. You need to buy eggs."

She gave him a sidelong glance and pulled away from the parking space. "After three years in your employ, I am only beginning to understand exactly how much you think with your stomach."

One supermarket stop and nine minutes later, Kitt got out of the SUV at the bottom of Taittinger's driveway. "I'll take my time getting back."

"Going to have another look at the wine cellar?"

"And the studio. There's something we missed." Kitt grimaced when he twisted and climbed out of the car and put his jacket on. "Find Reed. Stay with him. And for the love of all that's holy, Mae, keep those eggs safe."

Mae parked the Volvo in the garage, took the groceries across the patio and into the laundry where Felix met her, his long tail whipping back and forth. He'd been shut between the laundry and kitchen.

Happy to see him, giddiness overtook her and mixed with lingering adrenaline. She set aside the groceries, snatched up the animal, and gave him a cuddle. The dog poked his snout into her neck and she sniffled, going into the great room with Felix snuggled in her arms, and Shirley Bassey belting out a song about diamonds. Mae stopped dead.

Bodies, supine, loose and open-mouthed had wilted in chairs, crumpled on sofas, collapsed onto the floor. Crackers, bread, nuts, empty bottles of wine had turned the Persian rug into a relief map around Nash and his bright-orange runners.

Lifeless, Taittinger slumped sideways on the sofa, Ruby's strawberry head in his neck, a deck of cards scattered about near her feet, as if the pack had exploded.

Newlyweds Ernie and Anna Chung, together on a wide ottoman, lay locked in an embrace amidst the chaos, Anna's long black hair a veil over both of their faces.

Reed, head back, throat exposed, long legs spread, held an empty tumbler loose in one hand, wrist propped on the arm of his chair, a little pile of cashews on his chest.

CHAPTER SIXTEEN

The rolling *snnnaaarrrk* that burst from Basil's open mouth gave her a start. Her heart bounced to her feet and back into her chest. Mae put the dog on his feet and moved deeper into the den of unconscious, not dead, oenophiles, stepping over spent bottles and food scraps, and switched off the music.

"Before you say anything, Kitty," Reed said suddenly, "I wondered what sort of charge would be tacked on to my sentence, but I thought, since I'm already in this arse deep..." He sighed.

"Mr Reed," Mae's heart bounced again as Felix gobbled something near Nash's foot.

Reed's relaxed features twisted into a frown, his eyes popped open, and he sat up, cashews rolling down his chest. "Shit." He gave her a hard look. "Kitty fucked up. I'd ask if you killed him, but I think his fucking up is more likely."

She surveyed the unconscious. "What the bloody hell happened?

"Well, petal, alcohol increases the effect of whatever Taittinger and I put in the wine. I was surprised he drank it too, although he did have the look of a man who'd shit himself and was trying to hide it."

Mae took off her coat and tossed it on a vacant chair. She flicked her gaze about the comatose houseguests, the upended spittoons, the dog snacking on things that weren't healthy canine treats, at the untidiness and all those wine bottles, one of which was a 1945 Domaine de la Romanee-Conti Grand Cru she'd seen in Taittinger's hidden wine cellar. Despite understanding the necessity of *neutralising* guests, this was scandalous, inhospitable, and utterly unprofessional. This was akin to serving tainted food that sickened visitors. "This won't do. This won't do at all. You'll have to help me, Mr Reed."

"I thought that's what I was doing, possum." He rose, hands going into his pockets, cashews spilling onto the Persian carpet. "You're not supposed to be here. You're supposed to be on your way to a safe house, in the car I arranged for you to drive there. What happened to your cheek?"

"Someone followed us. There was trouble."

"What kind of trouble? Where's Kitt?"

"He'll be along soon. And I meant you'll have to help me put these people to bed."

"You want to put these people to bed?" He moved closer to her, stepping around the dog trying to sink small teeth into a crusty loaf of sourdough bread bigger than his head, and paused an arm's length away to look her up and down, his scrutiny cold, hard, and careful.

She looked back at him the same way.

"Yes, I see. He said you were, let me see if I get this right, *a fortress of unmovable loyalty and professionalism.* Hardly romantic, but Kitty loves you."

"I know."

"Do you love him?"

"Mm-hm. So do you."

"Sadly, I do. What happened to the ring he gave you?"

"You'll have to ask him." Mae started with Reed's brown leather shoes, and slid her eyes from there to his crotch, the flat stomach hidden behind a dark green polo-neck jumper, his chest, freckled face, and top of his ginger head, before reversing the path back to his shoes. Then she met his pretty blue eyes. "I believe Kitty said you were, and let me see if I get this right, *a twat*."

Reed burst out laughing. "Oh, I *like* you. It's a pity Kitty's fucked up things with you." He smiled handsomely, eyes crinkling. "Okay, who do we move first?

"Mr Nash. His trousers are giving me a headache."

The Irishman glowed in turquoise trousers and a red, black, and yellow Watford FC jersey, air puffed and popped from his bottom lip.

"Nash is a headache," Reed said and turned to the sleeping newlyweds. "What about those two?"

"The bedroom next to yo—"

"What part of 'be sensible' confused you, Simon?" Kitt stood at the edge of the great room, eyes cold, mouth curved in a smile without warmth.

Reed exhaled. "It seemed to be taking too long. Nash was not cooperating, spitting out everything. I had to help things move."

"So you put the backup phial in every bottle?"

"Look, mate, I may be adept at sleight of hand, but this sort of thing's not my gig, it's yours. I don't do covert ops. I'm doing the best I can, and all you do is whinge about it. Where were you?"

"Finding a passageway running from the barn cellar to the studio, where there's a freight lift hidden under a crate of glass. It's smeared with blood."

"Blood?" Reed clucked his tongue. "So much for your being thorough. How'd you miss blood, *Kitty*?"

"Every bottle, Reedy?"

"I told you you're getting too old for this work."

"*Every bottle*, Simon?"

Mae watched two men stare at each other coolly, their shared history suddenly palpable in a way it hadn't been before. Irritation, pain, respect, love, it was on icy-hot display and Jaysus, what an eejit she was not to have considered the significance of their past more carefully, with more attention. "Such an eejit," she muttered.

Kitt glanced at Mae as she muttered something under her breath. She looked tired. He would have traded his *fatigued* for her tired. He needed coffee, a shower, eight to ten hours of solid sleep. He ached all over. If Taittinger's taste in recreational drugs had run to cocaine, Kitt would have had a snort. "Why *every* bottle?" he said.

Reed scratched his neck. "It makes sense when you think about it. They were all drinking. They've been drinking all day and they all drink a lot. They all had hangovers this morning, except for Nash." He snorted. "Flunitrazepam can cause drowsiness, dizziness, loss of motor control, lack of coordination, slurred speech, confusion, sedation, gastrointestinal disturbances lasting twelve hours or more, and amnesia. Sounds like a bender and hell of a hangover to me. They'll all be crook in the morning, Nash included."

"Indeed." Kitt studied the room for a moment, his thumb tapping pared-down fingers. Then he scooped up Ruby. "When we're done here, coffee, Mae. Please."

Reed grabbed Nash under the armpits. Mae grabbed his ankles. They lifted the man together.

"No, no." Ruby's strawberry head lolled against Kitt's shoulder. "Put him on the sofa. Turn him on his side. Grab that book over there and put it under his hand."

"Why does he stay here?" Reed said as the man's deadweight plopped onto sofa cushions.

Mae smoothed an apron that wasn't there. "Because this is

about plausibility. Nash boasts about not getting drunk, so he fell asleep reading."

"Are you thinking about switching professions, petal?"

"THE PACK IS in the side pocket of my duffel, in the walk-in." Reed finished tying his shoe and rose from the bedroom's love seat, his frown deep. "Why would he do that? Why would Timothy Bryce have any part in this, Hamish?"

Kitt looked at Mae. She sat in the charcoal armchair near the door, Felix on her lap, her mind elsewhere, fingers absently stroking the dog, ruminating, he supposed, on the last two days or few hours. "I'm not saying he does." Weary and heading towards exhausted, Kitt turned his attention to Reed. "He might. He could. I thought there was a rat, but maybe it's *rats*. Bryce could be as much as Llewelyn could be part of this. I have to contemplate that prospect, but at the moment I'm leaning more toward Dalton and Llewelyn playing major roles in this."

"Based on what, an assassin's mention?"

"Wouldn't that make you consider the possibility?"

"No. Not that alone, but what you suggest about her," Reed glanced at Mae, "being in a position that has a connection to you, whatever it is, means somebody wanted her out of the way, or wanted her where they could keep an eye on her." Reed ran a hand through his hair. "You've considered that, haven't you?"

"You know I have. Have there been rumblings in your world?"

"No. The handbags and other counterfeit intellectual property you found in those containers are a link in the supply chain we've been following. Lyon passed along our initial heads up to your lot, and you all went about business. You rang, then you sent me notification from Singapore; *Shithouse, henhouse, sweatshop.* Routes and methods are shifting, and I can justify my presence here for that reason, without any connection to you, if I need to, and I will need to, but I'm safe, Hamish." For a moment, Reed was quiet. Then he jerked his chin at Mae. "Who knows about her, departmentally speaking?"

"Only Bryce. Departmentally speaking, she's seen as a loyal employee, one harbouring feelings for me, but she's not considered to be..." Kitt glanced at Mae petting Felix, "...my type."

"She's certainly not twenty-three."

"Careful, Reedy."

Head shaking, Reed stared at Kitt, irritated. "I thought you were supposed to be good at your job, commendations and such, and you never imagined she might—"

"I make him sloppy," Mae cuddled the dog close, "careless, unfocused."

Kitt watched her drop a kiss on the animal's snout, but her eyes were fixed on them. "Yes, you do," he said.

"Touching." Reed frowned. "What does she know about me?"

"Exactly what you wanted her to know, Simon."

Mae set Felix on the carpet and squinted at them both. "Why don't you ask me what I know?"

Kitt scratched his neck. He needed to shave. "This is not the time for speculation about who knows what about whom."

The dog sniffed at Reed, paws clasping around his knee for a second before Reed swore and gently pushed him away. With a soft, contemptuous snort, he went to the door, opened it and paused. "Is there anything to eat, petal? Have you made dinner?"

"Mae. Her name is Mae, and find your own dinner, Simon, she's not your butler."

"She's not yours either." Reed's jaw shifted from side to side, eyes hard on Kitt.

"*Simon.*" Mae got up, stretched her arms overhead. "You'll find leftover risotto, a quiche, cold roast beef, and mustard potato salad in the kitchen fridge. I'll be down soon to clean up and prepare for tomorrow's breakfast and lunch."

"Thank you, *Mae*." Reed jerked open the door and left the room.

Mae shut the door Reed had left gaping wide. Felix trotted across the carpet, hopped up onto the bed and snuggled down between the throw pillows. "If you really want Reed's help," she said, "you'll catch more flies with honey than vinegar."

"That's your strategy, not mine. You're honey, I'm bully."

"You shut all it out and shut it off, but not everyone is you. I don't care if you had a relationship with him any more than I care about all those women you were involved with before me, but not everyone can let go of feelings or turn them on or off."

"I really don't give a damn what Reed needs or wants."

Kitt heard a faint, 'Liar,' as he went into the walk-in wardrobe. He grabbed Reed's duffel and found the zippered case he wanted. Slightly larger than his hand, he took the case to the chest of drawers, opened it, and began to sift through the objects inside; a pen, a stickpin, a pair of reading glasses, a small blue pouch, a tie clasp, a stainless-steel watch, a key fob for a BMW, and a yellow lighter, placing everything on top of the chest of drawers before he reached for the pouch.

Mae watched him begin to unknot the strings of a little blue bag. "What do you want me to say to Bryce tomorrow?"

"Keep the bits of truth. You've found a second wine cellar and no evidence of counterfeit wine."

"Then what."

"Then I'll talk to him."

"You're coming with me?"

"If anyone wakes and wonders, we've taken Reed's car to the landscaper's drunken bunny lecture. Meanwhile, we'll begin gently, in a non-threatening manner. With you speaking to Bryce first, for a few minutes."

"Because in your current mood you can't speak to him in a non-threatening manner?"

"Yes, that and call it a gut feeling—one I assure you has nothing to do with me thinking with my stomach."

"I didn't say anything about your stomach."

"No, but it crossed your mind." Kitt found what he'd been looking for and held out the tiny, pale pinkish-coloured object to her. "This one ought to fit. Here, have a look."

"What is it?"

"Genuine spy-craft equipment. Go on, take it."

She slipped on her glasses, drew the item from his hand, and inspected it. It was the size of a small peanut, slightly pointed at one end. Warily, Mae eyed him over the top of her reading lenses.

"Goodness, I didn't expect a frown. I thought you'd be thrilled to finally see a stock prop from the world of espionage and spy thrillers."

One eye squinted. "Exactly where am I supposed to... Is this inserted or do I swallow it?"

Kitt chuckled. "It goes in my ear, not yours. This bit is yours." He held out a piece of jewellery.

"Oh. Yes, of course." Mae gave the little stickpin a cursory once-over and looked at the earpiece a little closer. There was a tiny, clear stalk barely visible, an antenna she guessed.

"Did you think it was a suppository?" Kitt took the earpiece from her hand.

Her laugh was a minute pop of air. "No, I wondered if it might be inserted subcutaneously, like the microchip a technician put in Felix."

Kitt glanced at the dog. "I already know I'm under your skin as much as you're beneath mine, but in the morning," he pushed back a curving swathe of hair from her chin, and touched the shell of her ear, "I'll be listening." Kitt moved closer, his fingers inserting the stickpin into the lapel of her dark dress. "With this, like so, in plain sight, yet out of sight, but never, ever out of mind." His thumb ran down her jaw. She'd washed her face, removed traces of dust and Derek's blood, a slice, a purple bruise all that remained of those violent moments.

"Yes, to your detriment." She smiled faintly.

"And yours."

"You're tickling me."

"Do forgive my clumsiness." He let his fingers drop away and leaned against the chest of drawers. "There are benefits of not needing to cooperate with others to complete an operation. No one to answer to, no toes to worry about stepping on, no international treaties to mind. And this time, it's not necessary to tape anything to your breasts, as when you insisted on joining the Largo action last July. I didn't want you there then, any more than I want you here now, but at least now there's no tape." His mouth flattened and he shook his head with annoyance. "Christ, that tape left *such* a rash on your poor diddies."

"You remember the oddest things."

"I think the fact we should focus on here is I remember."

"Yes." Mae rolled the earpiece between her fingers, staring at the motion. "I'm sorry you remember. I've wondered how you live with the things you've done, how they affect you, if they affect you at all, and I can see that they do. You're not heartless or ruthless as one might assume. As, I admit, I thought you would have to be. You could have killed Derek. I expected you to kill Derek. I wanted you to kill Derek, but you actually have some kind of moral code." She met his steady, passive gaze, her brows arched. "You don't like killing, do you?"

"Let's keep that quiet, shall we?" He straightened.

Mae took off her glasses and licked the scar at the corner of her mouth. "It's not about nationalism or conceit or regret. You actually believe you're doing good."

"Perhaps I do."

"Oh, you do. You buy into the one man can make a difference, one spy can save the world from itself mentality. You believe the fictitious film spy codswallop as much as the rest of us. Perhaps you do? *Perhaps*, my hole. You *do*."

"You have such delightful a way of putting things."

She held up the earpiece, grinning wryly. "I bet you really like the gadgets too."

Kitt's mouth may or may not have fleetingly quirked.

Mae went on smirking. "So I'll be in your ear?"

He pulled the stickpin from her dress. "Yes, you'll be the devilish little voice and conscience on my shoulder, as you have been since the day you put me in my place with a tray of home-made Chelsea buns and told me you didn't suffer fools. We already know Taittinger is a fool." Kitt turned to the items on the chest of drawers and lifted the stickpin. "Let's hope he's not also a prick."

"You know, I think this story has had enough puns from Taittinger."

"Why does he get all the fun?" Kitt pulled his shirt over his head, his movement careful, cloth covering his grimace, but not his grunt of pain. "Please, check if Reed has an Oxford or some kind of button-down shirt in the wardrobe." He left Mae in the bedroom, went into the bathroom and washed his hands and face. The wide mirror above the marble vanity showed livid bruising, red, blue, and purple, spread down his right side. He turned slightly and caught the bloom of colour on his right flank and the mottled skin above his kidney. He draped the towel over a shoulder and prodded the tender rainbow.

Mae lay a rather ugly blue and white Oxford shirt on the vanity. "All in a day's work," she muttered, eyes meeting his in the mirror.

His grimace faded into a dry grin, his head cocking ever so slightly to one side. "My love, bruises are just temporary tattoos."

"No, no. A bruise is a badge of honour." She matched his wry smirk. "And you've been honoured worse than that."

"Indeed." He turned about, reached out, and touched the little scar at the corner of her mouth. "This is just a scratch."

"Yes, a mere flesh wound." Her eyes travelled over his variegated ribs before she met his gaze again.

"Actually, it's not a flesh wound, it's a soft tissue wound."

"You had to go and get technical."

"No, I had to go and get punched."

"The silly things you've borne for my safety."

"Silly? Not gallant, not chivalrous, not *heroic*?"

"As I said, all in a day's work." She clasped the two shortened fingers tickling her chin and ran her hand down his discoloured ribs, her touch delicate.

Kitt's breath caught.

"I see what a nuisance I can be."

He gave her a faint smile and drew her hand from his torso. "You'd be less of a nuisance if you'd fetch me some ice."

"Of course," she said, let his fingers go, slid another towel from a rack, and left him in the bathroom.

Kitt grabbed the toothpaste and flipped open the top. Instead of finding his toothbrush, he wound up standing there, looking at bruised skin and bare feet, Colgate in hand, hating the sudden feeling of being left alone.

He'd come so close. Alone. God almighty, alone, it was a startling sensation he'd never had before, even when he was the only one left alive in an oven-like shipping container, even when he'd been dying in that oven-like shipping container. His own company had been enough, always been enough, but alone meant something else entirely now, and the idea of his own company being enough had become unfathomable. What he'd tried to do had been a practical necessity, wrong, even if it was right. Mae had to understand that. He wanted her to understand.

Idiotically, Kitt glanced at himself in the mirror again, at the tube of toothpaste in his hand. Minty blue gel hung from the white mouth, bright blobs on the grey-white tiles. He'd strangled the life from the tube. He threw the Colgate in the basin and went into the bedroom.

Crouched by the chest of drawers, the door to a bar refrigerator open, Mae had upended an ice tray in the towel she'd taken from the bathroom. "It's not what I wanted, Mae," he said.

"I'm sorry. I didn't think. You'd prefer something more pliable." She rose, handed him the ice. "Peas. Frozen peas would be better."

He pressed the cold compress to his ribs. "It's not what I wanted. What I said, what we were doing before Derek, you getting in that car, you walking away, it was the right thing to do. It was the right thing, it's the right thing now, even if it's wrong, but it's not what I want."

"Oh, that." Mae sighed, a thin, acquiescent *mmn*, and shut the fridge. "I'll get you the peas," she said, and went to the door. She paused, hand on the knob and turned, mouth pursed for a moment. "What do you want?"

Kitt crossed the room in a few strides until there was a ruler's length of distance between them, the space so minuscule and so vast. He looked down into her face, at the thin, red scabbed scratch on her cheek, at green-flecked hazel eyes staring back. "You. Any way you will have me. You don't really want to marry me and I don't want a very long engagement. Still, I'd have you any way you'd have me, except that's not practical, not safe, and I understand your trepidation. Finally. I see exactly what you mean. The potential of losing you in two ways and being responsible for that in more ways than one, it's not what I want, and that was not what I wanted. I thought it was better to live with a lonely heart rather than a broken one, yet neither option is right."

Another *mmn* hummed in her throat. "Maybe it's right."

"You think it's right?"

"Maybe it's right. Maybe it's wrong. Maybe we can talk about this when we are both home again."

"Whose home, mine? Yours?"

Her lips parted slightly and something in her eyes flickered. It wasn't defiance, acceptance of the truth, or sadness for what they both knew was best, but whatever that flicker was Kitt saw it as she held his gaze. "Does that matter?"

"Mae."

This time her sigh was noisy. She dropped her eyes and rubbed the back of her head. "We're both eejits, you know. Look at what we have. Who has that? We're feckin' eejits. Does it hurt very much?"

"It's mauling my guts."

"I mean all that bruising. Does the bruising hurt?"

"It throbs, like my heart does for you."

She groaned. "That's terrible."

"I know." Kitt moved aside and sat on the arm of the chair beside the door, pulling the hand towel from his shoulder, setting the cloth on the seat back. "I had a dream. We were driving, you and I, a leisurely drive, like the weekend we went to the Cotswolds and had that ghastly ploughman's lunch in Burford. But in my dream, we weren't in England. I don't know where we were. We took our time and drove, going along a twisting road that seemed to go on forever. The trees were changing colour. The sky was so blue. You set your hand on my thigh. You smiled at me and made a lovely suggestion. It was so simple, so straightforward. How could I say no?"

"Oh, it was *that* sort of dream."

"No, it wasn't *that* sort of dream. We drove that twisting road together, drove and drove until we found a little house with a small garden, a stone fence and lots of trees, apple trees I think. Christ, we were happy, so happy I didn't want to wake up. We kept driving that long, winding road, your hand on my thigh, you smiling at me, and we kept coming back to the same little house with the garden, the stone fence, and apple trees. Finally, finally we stopped there. We got out of the car and went into the garden. There was a dog waiting there for us. It was a very nice dream."

She said nothing for a long moment, simply gazed past him and out the window at the blackness outside. When she turned, and looked him, a faint smile tipped the corners of her mouth. "Is that what you think I want?"

"No, I think it's what I want, a home. With you. And I don't know how to convince you, you are my home. Do you know I never believed I had a soul? Except I've come to realise something very strange. You are my home. You are my soul."

She drew a breath, her exhale a half sigh. "You know, you had me. Almost. I was right with you, even with the bit about the dog and being your home."

"I liked the bit about the dog."

"Yes, I pictured Felix."

"Where did I go wrong?"

Head shaking, *tsk-tsking*, she said, "You mixed up your Brontës. We are not Emily Brontë, we are Charlotte. 'You are my soul' is too 'I am Heathcliff.' You know it is." She shook her head. "Mr Rochester and Mrs Fairfax, or yes, even Jane, yes, *Jane Eyre*, that's a fair comparison to make of us, given your brooding moodiness and my high and mighty moral principles, however crumbling they may be, but Cathy and Heathcliff in *Wuthering Heights*?" Mae rolled her eyes. "He's a psycho and she's not much different... Then again, perhaps you're correct. Perhaps you have the right Brontë after all."

His eyes narrowed slightly. "If one considers the depiction of debauchery and alcoholism in *The Tenant of Wildfell Hall*, I've always thought Anne Brontë a better fit, yet that was before I met you, my sweet, sweet Jane Valentine. And my very awkward, unoriginal, yet fanciful point is simple. Life is what you make it, and this is what I've made it. This is what I've known. Until you. Now I want a different life, a life with you. I have to keep you safe. When this is over, when we're home again, we'll pick up where we were, we'll go on as we were."

"You mean as we were before or after you proposed a very long engagement?"

"Both. Together, but separate, to keep it as The Consortium sees it."

"I don't want that. I don't want a very long engagement."

He looked at her, gaze steady, unblinking. "Is that why you returned my ring so easily?"

"Easily?" Mae laughed faintly. "I returned your ring when you made it clear you were leaving me. Again."

"Technically, you were leaving me."

"Semantics." Mae rubbed the back of her head again. "Semantics, Kitt."

"*Hamish.* How's your head?"

"I've quite an egg." She moved her hand and met his eyes and leaned toward him, bending forward a little. "Feel it."

Kitt slid fingers into her hair and traced over the lump she'd sustained when he'd slammed her into a brick wall and squashed her, an assassin sent to kill her sandwiched between them. "Oh, you have. A little bit of a scab too. You need some ice. Good thing I have some." He shifted the freezing compress from his ribs, ready to lay it against her skull, but she touched his chin, fingernails scuffing through his beard and down his throat.

Kitt dropped the cold towel, ice cubes dislodged, hitting his bare feet as he stood, and his mouth was on hers, hands in her hair.

He bumped her into the door, and kissed her slowly, with immeasurable tenderness that she matched until she laughed, the sound buzzing his lips.

"What?" He lifted his mouth a fraction.

"Your timing is terrible," her words puffed beneath his nose. "Reed's coming back."

Kitt drew away slightly and took his hand from her hair. He reached behind her, poked the centre button-lock on the doorknob, and every scrap of tenderness fell away.

Eyes locked on his, she tugged the cloth of his fitted boxers, fabric slipping down his arse and growing erection while his impatient, overeager fingers pushed and pulled and jerked until her dress parted. His pants dropped to his ankles. He grasped the waistband of her blue tights and ridiculously sensible, waist-high cotton knickers, shoving the combined elastic and cloth down with his right hand, as his left slid between her thighs.

His fingers slipped into hot and slick and wet, and he gasped, laughed at himself, and watched delight widen her eyes.

"I thought about what your stubby little fingerlings might feel like." Mae smiled and bit her bottom lip as his shortened fingers moved.

His breath caught. "Did you?"

"Yes."

Kitt watched her. He loved watching her pleasure build. She pushed forward, scooting their combined weight from the door twisting sideways, trying to walk him backwards to the bed, where the curious dog eyed them, but her gait was hindered by his hands and the tights around her knees. His fingers dislodged, they half-tripped sideways over the towel full of ice cubes and found the chair beside the door. She back fell onto the cushion and Kitt went to his knees. He yanked her knickers and tights, leaving them to trail from one foot like a streamer, grasped her legs and dragged her forward, down the seat. He pushed her knees apart and, without pause, grace, or dignity, thrust into her as their mouths came together.

Mae wrapped a calf around his battered middle and Kitt grunted at the pain that streaked up his spine before it was replaced by grunts of hedonistic carnality. Her breaths, short and sharp, were a counter-melody to his low, animal groans and rapid, unrestrained thrusts. He leaned over her and she sucked on his tongue, fingers in his hair, fingers in his beard. He plunged deep, deeper, and she drew him as close as she could, their rhythm quick-quick-quick until she arched up slightly, altering the friction. She went still for a split second and cried out into his open mouth before he made the same sound of release and clutched her to his chest. Then they melted into the chair, Kitt boneless upon her.

"I'm sorry," he said, out of breath, which he preferred to blame on the high-altitude location, rather than the fact he'd sprinted in what was essentially a sexual one-hundred-metre race. "I wanted to take my time."

"Did you...hear me...telling you to slow down?" she said, as breathless as he was, and her fingers tickled around the back of his neck.

"No."

"That's because..." she swallowed, "...I didn't."

"I wanted to take my time. Time is so precious. You are precious," he said, cheek resting on her breast.

She gave a soft laugh.

"You think my declaration is trite, or is it that you love mocking me?"

"Maybe I do. Maybe I'm cynical and I don't need that sort of reassurance, or perhaps I do find it trite. Perhaps it's experience, perhaps I know time is precious and life is short, and life is precious and time is short. Perhaps, I'll take what I can get, when I can get it. I realise that now."

"Did this realisation happen after last night's unfinished business?"

"We will always have unfinished business, Kitt."

"I like it so much better when you call me Hamish." He kissed her exposed nipple.

"Would you miss calling me Mrs Valentine?"

"You'll always be my Valentine."

"You're getting very good at the corny lines." She laughed and his knees began to sting from rubbing the patterned rug beneath them. He shifted and the weight of Mae's leg upon his back began to make his bruising flare with pain. He lifted his head. "Mae, your leg, could you move it, please."

Her calf slid away. "*Stay,*" she said, her tone authoritative.

"As much as I'd like to, I need the ice, and my knees are on fire."

"I didn't mean you, I meant Felix."

Kitt glanced over a shoulder. "He watched us the entire time, didn't he?"

"I have no idea, I was rather occupied by you and..."

"And what?" Kitt lifted his weight from her torso, leaving her sprawled inelegantly in the chair, legs akimbo with a full view of the little Southern Cross freckle constellation inside her left thigh, knickers-tights around an ankle, dress spread open, bra shoved up just below her throat. She looked positively glorious—and serious. "Oh, that face. What's on your mind?"

"What if we've gone about this wrong?"

Kitt straightened. The splendid, pain-killing endorphins of sex faded and his battered body began to ache again. He winced. "I'm sorry. I know that wasn't the most comfortable position. I'm paying for it now, bu—"

"No, no, I mean, what if we're thinking of this in the wrong way. Downstairs, Taittinger opened a bottle of Bordeaux, 1945 Domaine de la Romanee-Conti Grand Cru. I hadn't noticed the wine he'd chosen before we left and ran into Derek."

"How utterly romantic of you to bring up Derek and Taittinger's wine."

"You need to run, or eat, or vomit to be able to think clearly after a traumatic event. It appears I need a good shag."

"Despite the duration, it was rather good, wasn't it?" He chuckled and picked up the hand towel. "Right then, about the wine."

Mae sat up. "The Conti was one of the wines in the barn cellar. It started me wondering why Taittinger was so convinced that you were going to steal the wine for Judith."

"The soulless wine merchant, rat-sending ex-girlfriend in Florida."

"Yes. Her. Why would Taittinger think she wanted to take his wine as some sort of reward for being philanthropic when he said he was storing the wine for others? I wouldn't call storing wine for wealthy friends philanthropic, would you?"

"Where are you going with this? Do you think the wine is fake after all?"

"No. it's all real. There's more prestige in owning rare wine than there is in drinking rare wine. Taittinger's not storing those bottles for others. They're all his. Bryce told me there wasn't a money trail to follow. I think that's because no money is changing hands. Taittinger's fee for the artefacts is wine."

CHAPTER SEVENTEEN

A lack of sleep and no breakfast stung Kitt more than the bitter cold and thickly falling snow. Mae parked Reed's hired Ford between a Mercedes sedan and battered old American pickup truck across the street from Ruby K's, a bagel café. It was early, still dark, but the establishment was open, a few patrons inside, none of them Bryce.

"You've been in that place before?" Kitt said from the back seat, watching through a veil of white flakes for his colleague to arrive.

"Mm-hm."

"Where's the lavatory?"

She gave a puffy little laugh. "Didn't you think to do that before we left Taittinger's place?"

His gaze was flat and ruthless. "Where's the lav, Mrs Valentine? Is it still in the back?"

"Yes. Where is your sense of humour this morning?"

"We spent the night documenting items in the barn cellar. Then I got a thimbleful of sleep because Reed cuddles like a needy, frightened child, and he snores too."

"You could have slept with me on the sofa."

"There was barely enough room on the sofa for you and the dog. Why didn't you sleep in the bed and let Reed take the sofa?"

Mae crossed her arms. "I'm practical. Neither Reed nor you would fit on that sofa. You refused to let me sleep in my quarters and I wasn't keen on sharing a bed with three boys."

"Three boys?"

"Felix."

"The darling little dog isn't yours."

"What a foul mood you're in, Kitt, and you're not even hungover." Her head tipped to one side. "Are you jealous of Felix?"

"Yes. He slept curled behind your knees while I had a snoring Australian wrapped around me." He looked at the café again. "Bryce will go to the back, near the lav."

"How do you know?"

"Humourless intelligence officers, even the Moneypenny types like Bryce, are trained to be aware of their surroundings and know their exit routes. It's basic safety. You choose a position where you can see all the exits. There's often an exit close to the lav."

"It's all about checking your six and keeping your back to the wall, right?"

"Checking your six. Chloral hydrate. Just how many spy thrillers have you watched, Mae?"

"Enough to know Jason Bourne is a far better spy than James Bond and you. You don't see Bourne getting cheesed off because he didn't have coffee and scrambled eggs for his breakfast."

"Oh, you make me want to be a better spy." Kitt watched Bryce walk into the snow-filled car park. "You think missing breakfast is why I'm cheesed off?"

"I know that's why you're cheesed off. I'm beginning to suspect you went into intelligence work because you needed some way to work out the murderous rage you feel when you don't have a good breakfast."

"I am quite calm."

"You are detached and yet, under all that cool detachment simmers murderous rage."

"Perhaps." Kitt watched Bryce cross the lot, enter the café, and shake off snow from his coat.

"So, you do feel murderous rage?" Mae turned and looked in the backseat.

Kitt smiled sweetly, his eyes colder than blistering nitrogen. "My love, I could snap a neck."

"I'll get you a coffee in the café and pretend it's mine. I'll also pretend you didn't say that bit about snapping my neck."

"I said I could snap *a* neck, not your neck."

"Yes, but you looked right at me when you said it." Her eyes flicked to the black, low-crowned rabbit felt thing on his head. "Are you really going to wear that stupid hat?"

"Yes. It keeps my cold heart and cold blood warm."

Mae twisted, opened the door, and got out, paused for a moment and exhaled. She pulled something from the middle of her handbag and tossed it on the backseat. "It might be time to further your education." She shut the door and headed across the street.

Kitt watched her go into the café and adjusted the volume of the device in his left ear, glancing at a book she'd tossed on the seat beside him. It was a dog-eared romance novel, *Flowers from the Storm*.

He'd read it before.

BRYCE'S MOMENT of surprise lasted only a heartbeat or two. The Welshman swiped a hand over his chin and shook his head. "Kitty."

"Bryce." Kitt smiled.

"Nice hat."

"Palms down," he said.

Bryce flattened his hands on the table. "You broke protocol."

"Thank you. Yes, I broke protocol. Here, I know how much you like the sickly-sweet ones." Kitt set an iced drink on the round table-top. He pulled out the wooden chair beside Bryce, placed the cowboy hat on the other seat, and took a moment to run a cautious hand over his colleague's chest, ribs, and pockets. When he found nothing, Kitt sat. "Mae, coffee, please," he said.

Mae pushed her black ceramic cup of coffee across the table to Kitt. "One of you is a better liar than the other." She glanced at Kitt, at the iced coffee he'd ordered, and back at Bryce. She didn't want to believe Reed's supposition that Kitt's colleague, Kitt's *friend*, had betrayed him. Bryce still looked like a superhero in disguise, but was it possible he was a villain? "I need to reconsider the sort of men I whose company I keep. Why did you lie to me, Sergeant?"

"I'm sorry, Mae. Like you, I thought he was dead, until you showed me the postcards you left behind." Bryce unzipped a side pocket on his khaki green jacket. "I was a little surprised when I saw your postcards, Kitty, but it seems Mrs Valentine isn't very senti-mental and I have to say that truly astounded me." Bryce slipped a hand into the flat, square pocket. He withdrew an item and placed it on the table.

Kitt recognised the yellow postcard with the two fried eggs holding hands he'd sent to Mae. Inexplicably affronted when he had no right to be, Kitt slid his eyes to Mae. "You kept so little of Caspar. It makes me wonder what I'll find missing when I get home."

Mae bit her top lip for a moment. "You can replace clothes and such."

"You gave away my postcards and my clothes?"

She shrugged. "I didn't need to keep postcards or clothes as a reminder of you. You haunted me well enough without them."

"How long did you keep Caspar's clothes before you gave them away?"

Mae's mouth flattened and she inhaled. "You are not Caspar."

"No, I bloody well am not Caspar. You got rid of his things, except his ring and a photo of him in a silver frame."

"I don't wear his ring anymore and have no pictures of you."

"No, but you had postcards from me. You could have kept one of those in a silver frame."

Mae nodded, her smile treacly. "I'm unreasonably angry about you faking your own death and you're pissed off about my not keeping bleedin' postcards. Yes, that's comparable."

"I didn't fake my death," he said softly.

"I am not hallucinating your presence. I may have before, but not now."

Bryce gave a small laugh. "She has a point, Kitty. This looks very bad for you, professionally and personally. In fact, I'd say you're fucked."

Head down, eyes bright and cold looking up through his lashes, Kitt set his gaze on Bryce and smiled, rather demonically, Mae decided. "Don't you think he does the death stare well?" she said.

Bryce didn't laugh again. Kitt's expression didn't waver.

"Oh, not this testosterone showdown shite again," Mae muttered.

"Yes, Bryce, I broke protocol. It leads me to ask what that means for me now."

The Welshman sat back. "I said nothing about your postcards. You could have sent them before you died. There was no point in speculating, not when DNA testing," he glanced at Mae, "indicated we had your remains. I'm not exactly displeased to see you, Kitty, but you do realise I informed Reed of your demise, just as I informed Mae."

"M-hm. You know poor, devastated Simon's thrown himself into work." Kitt glanced at Mae.

"How did you get into Taittinger's?"

"Reed. He arranged a meeting with a now dead informant, got us invited to Taittinger's party. All we need was a bottle of the right wine."

Bryce sat back, hand still flat on the table. "I see." He drummed his fingers. "Who'd you use?"

"Somerset and Case Private Capital."

"Should have guessed by the cowboy hat. That cover's ancient."

"Yes. Like you."

"And my ancient arse is now bent over a table with my trousers down. You see my dilemma."

Kitt stopped smiling. "One of us being buggered is quite enough. Reed can verify the recent acts of buggery I endured."

"Who's buggered you, Kitty?"

"That is what I am trying to establish. I have an idea, but there's something I want to know first, Sergeant Bryce," he said.

"Sir." Bryce lifted an eyebrow.

Kitt looked at Mae. "Why is she sitting here?"

She shook her head. "You know why I'm sitting here."

"Let's stop this right now." Bryce held up a hand. "I can abide duplicity and covert operations gone rogue, but not domestic quarrels." He lowered his hand. "I had no choice in the matter of where this woman sits."

"You had orders," Kitt said through his teeth. "Christ, you were in the room when Llewelyn broached the subject of whether she 'liked dogs.' You could have stopped her from taking the damned job with Taittinger."

Bryce drummed his fingers again. "She has a mind of her own. And you were dead."

Mae sat back and crossed her legs and arms. "Thank you, Timothy."

"Timothy?" Kitt shot a terse look at Mae.

"Jaysus, you are prickly. Drink the damn coffee and I'll get you another." She began to rise.

"Don't you move."

Mae set her elbows on the edge of the table and leaned forward. "Don't you bully me."

Kitt bit his molars together and took a breath. "I apologise for my boorish words and actions. I am very, very tired and I haven't had breakfast."

"So that's where you two are now, the bickering stage." Bryce exhaled. "I looked after her the best she would allow. The best your circumstance would allow."

"She's very angry. And you've been looking after her?"

"All this time, as you ordered, Major."

"And you're her handler as well?"

Bryce's nod was slight. "As Llewelyn ordered. Two birds, one stone."

"I'm not a bird or stone," Mae mumbled.

"Who's monitoring?"

"A distant relative."

Kitt smiled again. "I could kill you, right here."

Bryce's eyes flicked to the iced mocha coffee sitting beside his iced-hazelnut-chai-latte-whatever-it-was.

"For feck's sake," Mae stabbed a finger on the tabletop. "No one is killing anyone here at this table."

"Mae," Kitt said, as if issuing a warning.

"Don't you look at me like you want to snap my neck." She

pushed her cup toward him. "Drink the damned coffee and get on with it."

Bryce laughed and shook his head. "Perhaps you'd better explain things."

Kitt wrapped shortened fingers around the mug and set his eyes on Mae. "I understand duty and so does Bryce. I know what he can risk and what he can't, and I understand his first duty does not lie with me." He shifted his attention to Bryce. "Are you put out?"

"No." Bryce folded his hands together. "I understand. Last year, you told me you had a feeling, an ongoing sense someone in Section SRR had a hand up a skirt. There have been inklings of corruption in several divisions. I know your instincts. Llewelyn has similar instincts. He believes someone has a hand up a skirt in Border Force and SBR. I know you well enough that you think anyone can be gotten to. Even me. Hence the iced mocha you brought me. I'd feel put out by that, but I don't think you really believe my hand is up anyone's skirt but Nari's." He lifted the mocha-latte and turned the plastic cup. "Flunitrazepam or sodium-pentobarbital?"

"Flunitrazepam."

Bryce set the cup down. "Thank you. My wife will be pleased to not be a widow." Bryce's green gaze flicked to Mae for a moment.

Mae knew her mouth hung open, and she stared at the mocha-latte, stared at Bryce, stared at Kitt, muttering, "Yer gits, the both of ya, feckin' gobshite gits."

"It's nothing personal, Mae," Bryce said, chuckling. "I'd have done the same."

For a second, Kitt's laugh harmonised with his colleague's and Mae went on muttering while the two eejits went on laughing. Her heart be damned, the rational part of her brain sent out the suggestion that it might be best to get up from the table and walk away from these two men, forever, to leave the life where colleagues who were also trusted friends thought trying to poison each other was nothing personal, except the curious part of her brain held her lashed to the chair.

Kitt reached for the black ceramic cup of coffee and had a gulp of lukewarm brew, which, thank Christ, wasn't bad. "Llewelyn's theory is someone got to me, that I'm a rat. Is that it then?"

"The theory was someone in the department—Gettler, Springer, or you—had a bit of dirt under their nails. You ticked a box, particularly after the matter with your butler last July." Bryce smiled at Mae. "If you recall, you broke with protocol then too. Then you and Dalton died. That threw a spanner in the works."

Kitt had another gulp. "Why didn't you come to me first, why didn't you ask me or outright accuse me?"

Bryce sat back. "There was thought you three might have been working together."

"Yes, I see how it looks bad, even if Reed authenticates." Kitt swallowed more coffee. "If I were you I'd haul me in and have me charged with treason."

"I am thinking about it."

"How does Mae fit?"

"Yes," Mae twisted in her seat, crossing her legs. "How do I fit?"

"Sir Ivar Hillary and Dr Julius Taittinger were among names that came up frequently on shipping logs that Molony flagged. Home Office had been tipped off that a handful of wine boffins might be dabbling in counterfeiting. Hillary and Taittinger were top of the list."

With a testy sniff, Mae leaned forward "Fakes and frauds and pretending, that's what you and this entire thing is about."

Bryce went on, "Rather than think it a coincidence, the theft of pieces, the freeport units in Geneva, the security force payoffs, the suspected corruption, the suspicion around you, Gettler, Springer

—we couldn't be sure, we had to rule out if the offences might somehow be..."

"Intertwined." Kitt found the word Bryce was searching for.

"Yes." Bryce's mouth pursed. "Intertwined or separate, which-ever, it was a remote possibility Llewelyn wanted covered, and it eventuated in Mae's recruitment."

"He wanted to keep an eye on her, thereby keeping an eye on me. A test of loyalty on both parts."

"Exactly. You know, Kitty, we could always share the iced mocha." Bryce tapped the plastic cup.

Kitt's grin was slight and short-lived. "There's a certain freedom in forgetting unpleasant things."

Without a word, Mae seized the sweating iced mocha, pushed back her chair, moved across the orange-red linoleum, and dumped the drug-tainted coffee in the rubbish.

When she sat down, Kitt said, "Flunitrazepam is Rohypnol; it alters memory, Mae. It's what Taittinger—and Reed—put in the wine yesterday. It would only knock Bryce out, not kill him."

"I'd have a shit of a hangover and a fuzzy memory, Mae." Bryce nodded reassuringly. "Of course, it's nothing like the impending hangover Kitty is facing."

Kitt smirked dryly. "Indeed, it looks dire for me, but let's move to something else, Bryce. Can you explain why Llewelyn decided to remove Mae?"

"He wanted to maintain surveillance on Taittinger, and he wanted to keep an eye on her. Originally, the plan was to place her with Sir Ivar Hillary and his house of hounds, when you and Dalton went off to Singapore, but she declined. Later, after you died, she changed her mind and she was placed with Taittinger. Her volunteering was a surprise, one that made you both look..."

"Involved in the crimes," Mae muttered.

"I was going to say guilty, but 'involved' is kinder. Anyhow, Kitty, I could not stop her from volunteering, I was not prepared to incapacitate her, and the assignment with Taittinger is merely observational, low-level risk." Bryce glanced at Mae. "I determined it harmless enough to render her static. I have to say you're a natural, Mae. Llewelyn was right. She's good at this, Kitty. She sticks to facts, doesn't waffle in her reports, takes clear pictures. Her paperwork is excellent."

"I fell for the crock of shite." Mae hunched forward, elbows on the table, heels of her palms grinding into her eyes.

"I did try to talk you out of it, Mae."

Kitt leaned forward slightly. "I don't mean static. I mean liquidate. When did Llewelyn decide she needed to be liquidated as an asset?"

"Remove. Incapacitate. Liquidate." Mae huffed dropped her hands. "Can't you intelligence types just say *murder*?"

A deep frown of astonishment darkened Bryce's face. "What?"

"The day before yesterday a bearded hipster hit one target before realising he had two. The dead man, Russell Grant, was a butler like Mae. Grant's former girlfriend was Stella Yeoh. The Yeoh family once had connections somewhere in the south-western part of the US. I never got the chance to find if those smuggling network connections had been re-established because the fancy little man killed Grant and then tried to kill Mae. Before I removed him from play, I—"

"*Removed him from play*? That's grand." Mae hissed air through her teeth. "Your entire profession is built on euphemisms, inconsequence, and worn-out stereotypes."

Bryce nodded and let out an absurd chuckle of agreement.

"Hipster-man mentioned Llewelyn, and she's here doing him a *favour*. Why does Llewelyn want her," Kitt glanced at Mae, mouth twitching once with faint amusement, "dead?"

Bryce exhaled and shrugged. "He doesn't as far as I know. Are you saying you think Llewelyn is your rotten apple?"

"No, I think *Dalton* is my rotten apple, but one never knows who's working with whom. He had to have help—Gettler or Springer...or maybe Roger Llewelyn."

"We have your rotten apple's DNA, remains, teeth, all pulled from a shipping container at the Port of Singapore. Dalton is dead."

"You had my remains and DNA too." Kitt drained the coffee from the mug and returned it to the table.

"Have you got proof Dalton isn't dead?"

"Not yet. The potential proof I had was killed on New Year's Eve. But then there's the art in the wine cellar, an assassin, and Llewelyn. Rats I haven't found. More proof I have yet to prove."

Bryce pinched the bridge of his nose. "This makes no sense, Kitty."

"Does this work ever make sense?"

"No, and that's half the fun."

"Fun? You think the work is fun, Timothy?" Mae's brow arched.

Bryce tipped his dented chin forward. "It does keep you sharp."

"Kitt," Mae set her eyes on him and tapped a finger over lips that curved into a peculiar smirk. "Timothy thinks the work is *fun*."

"Fun is relative."

Bryce reached for the postcard. "So it's suspect everyone, trust no one. You know I can't help you. You've dug a hole and both of you are now standing knee-deep in that hole. Is there anything you do know?"

"Did Mae brief you?"

Her smirk faded to a frown. "I thought you listened in."

Bryce looked at Kitt and then at the little stickpin on Mae's lapel. His mouth compressed for two seconds. "Well, I certainly missed that."

"Which is why you're a paper-pusher, not a field officer. Taittinger isn't a tiny wheel in a non-existent counterfeit wine ring. He's an antiquities conservationist and *smuggler*."

Bryce rubbed the dent in his chin and began to nod. "Right. Yes. I see where you take this. You think it links back to the Geneva Freeport."

"Yes. It won't take much digging to find he's also used several different freeports, Singapore in particular."

"Which proves nothing. A lot of collectors use freeports all over the world." Bryce set his green eyes on Mae. "You can prove he's not counterfeiting wine?"

Mae said, "I've found no evidence of fabrication. However, his friend Hector is opening a winery. Perhaps you should check him out."

"Then Taittinger's bottles are gen-u-wine?" Bryce's left eyebrow arched.

"Don't." Mae shook her head. "Don't do that. The wines in the barn cellar are real. I think the rare Bordeaux, Burgundies, and Rieslings are payment for the artefacts he's helped smuggle."

Kitt's mouth quirked for a moment. "I know artefacts in his wine cellar link back to Singapore."

"Can you prove any of this?"

Kitt let his gaze settle on the front window. "Prove. This is what I know. I lost part of my fingers and a good deal of blood. I was concussed. My nose was broken. I nearly died of heatstroke. It took me a little while, but I recall the disagreeable events. The mosaics hidden in Taittinger's barn," Kitt smiled, his cold eyes brightened as he looked at Bryce, "were in the container where Dalton, Molony, and the NCB officer, the harbourmaster, the customs broker and her assistant were murdered by the local dockers who weren't dockers or locals at all. The assistant was just a boy, nineteen at most, on an internship with customs, Bryce. Do you remember being that young?"

"Barely."

"There were nine containers. We opened seven. The first few containers were full of knockoff handbags, shoes, jackets and watches. The sixth was loaded with knock-offs, but other items were mixed in: furniture, decorator bathroom and kitchen tiles, bubble-wrapped artwork in protective wood-framed boxes, all to pad out the shipment. Those sorts of things aren't typically transported together, but Molony said the art and artefacts were reproductions, as phoney as the handbags. Fake with fakes. He said the same thing when we opened the seventh container, the one full of knock-off handbags. Raggedy Persian rugs were wrapped around mosaic tile samples, and corpses—Dr Vida Zora's and probably Nigerian migrants who paid to be smuggled out of Libya." Kitt scratched whiskers at his throat. "Then Molony screamed, Dalton was shot, and I was left for dead."

Bryce scratched his neck. "Molony's comment about the mosaics being reproductions is why you think Dalton is still alive and running all this?"

"It's more the fact how Dalton wasn't in the container when Reed's man found me."

"Reed's friend, Cureo, the Interpol local in Singapore. He sent the anonymous tip, and was there for the report. Did he set the container alight too? Not that it matters if he did, because we have Dalton's remains, Kitty."

"You had mine too. We're back where we started." Kitt folded his hands together, elbows on the table. Expressionless, his eyes moved between them for a moment, shifted to the front window, then to the empty coffee cup. "Who knows you're here, Bryce?"

"Head office, Station SWUS, and a distant relative. Do you suspect me?"

Kitt smiled, his chuckle all air. "Intelligence flows in two directions: information and misinformation. All that's needed is an opportunity, and I supplied one last July." His gaze slid to Mae. "You're right, Mae. I overlooked the obvious. I am a dreadful spy."

"I don't like the way you're looking at me." Mae frowned.

"I don't like the way he's looking at you either." Bryce leaned forward. "What are you getting at, Kitt?"

"You and Reed, I've dragged you into it. We've been set up, tarred with the same brush, Bryce. You're here to watch Mae while someone else has been watching you, keeping an eye on Llewelyn too, and here we all are, sitting together, watching each other."

"We're all sitting here except for Reed and Llewelyn," Mae reached for the napkin resting near the shortened fingers of Kitt's left hand.

Bryce sat back, jaw compressing. "Kitt, you don't think Simon…" he said softly.

Mae opened the napkin. "Reed said nearly the same thing about you." She dusted the tabletop, removing drops of condensation left behind by the tainted iced coffee. "All this suspicion. Do you three trust each other?"

"More than you know." Bryce crossed his arms. "You've got two hours. Get out. Run."

Quiet, calm, devoid of an expression of any sort, Kitt lay a hand on Mae's forearm, ending her fidgeting and needless tidying. "I didn't ask."

"That's why you've got two hours instead of one. Llewelyn, Kitty? Really? That's the theory you want me go with, Llewelyn and Dalton? Dalton is dead. Stone dead."

Kitt's chin rose slightly, his head cocked, the left corner of his mouth rose. "I never said it was going to be easy."

CHAPTER EIGHTEEN

The sun had begun to rise, turning the sky to the east soft pastel shades of blue and grey behind the cloud-heavy Sangre de Cristos Mountains. A fog of falling snow reflected the orange-toned lights still shining above the busy car park, the Fuller Lodge Art Center a rustic, giant log cabin glowing in the woods behind Mae. A steady stream of cars passed by, post-holiday employees returning to the Los Alamos National Lab. Bryce headed off on foot, moving down the snowy footpath on the opposite side of the street, his route taking him along half-frozen Ashley Pond, and trees wrapped with fairy lights.

Mae watched Bryce walk toward a hotel in the distance until a yellow hatchback slipped into a parking space on the street and blotted out his figure. She brushed snow from the driver's side door handle. "Now what, Kitt? Where do we go?"

"Let me think," he said, takeaway cup of coffee in hand, his eyes on her instead of scanning the car park, a task he'd carried out haphazardly when they'd exited the café. Yes, he was thinking, not about his curtailed time frame or what he could or couldn't prove, but about what was important, about if it mattered if he finished this job, about who he had been and who he had to be now, and his eyes remained fixed on Mae. He slid his thumb across the bumpy remains of two fingers. The motion had become a habit, one he had to break.

She opened the Ford's door and scraped snow from her boots. "What?"

"I have accounts. You can live quite comfortably for the rest of your life. All you need is the password. Antigua, Phoenix, pick a place. Go."

"I'm not running away. I'm not walking away. I'm not going anywhere without you."

"I've got to let you go." Kitt poked up the brim of his cowboy hat, shoving it back on his head.

Her boot scraping ceased. "You're exhausted. You're not thinking clearly. And don't even think about trying to drug me with that coffee once we get in the car." She straightened and shut the door so that a dual-cab pickup truck caked with reddish snow could park in the space beside them.

"I would never do that."

With a snort, Mae pulled the collar of her coat higher.

"I am a bully. I could force it down your throat."

She pretended not to hear him and set her attention squarely on the older Native American man who climbed out of the pickup.

The man wore a knitted cap with bear ears on top. "Ms Valentine," he said, smiling, delighted eyes beneath the teddy bear ears. The man reminded Kitt of an actor well-known for playing Zorba the Greek.

"Hello, Mr Hector."

Hector kept on smiling. "You came for my Sunrise Art talk at the Lodge? That's real nice of you." His dark eyes shifted to Kitt.

Mae turned to Kitt and pulled on her butler's veneer. "This is

Mr Somerset, a guest of Dr Jools'. He's intrigued by Native American culture. And wine."

Hector smiled. "My wife said nobody would come out in this weather, just the folks going back to work at the Lab, but you're made of tough stuff. I'm happy you made it." He took two steps forward, hand thrust out to Kitt. "Hiya. Hector Rodriguez."

Kitt shook the man's hand. "Somerset. Ian Somerset."

Mae let out a snorty chuckle, quickly turning it to a cough.

Kitt smiled genially. "I'm intrigued, Hector. Drunken Bunnies?"

"Rabbits, Drunken Rabbits. Is Jools coming, Valentine?"

Mae's smile was pleasant and diplomatic. "I believe Dr Jools and his guests enjoyed many different wines after a rather stressful day. I'm afraid Mr Somerset and I are the only ones awake this morning."

"Yeah, I get it. Finding a deer like that isn't pretty. That Nash guy seemed to enjoy it though." Hector's brow rumpled with disappointment he couldn't hide.

"So, it's Mr Somerset and myself." Mae glanced at Kitt, clasped and unclasped her hands.

Hector heaved an unhappy sigh. "This is why the Aztec people ferociously discouraged younger people from alcoholic intoxication. Of course, the elderly Aztec were allowed to drink *pulque* and get drunk because the *ueuetque* were held in high regard for their life experience, unlike the elderly today. Some people aren't interested, like Coyote and some of Jools' younger friends who only respect money," Hector sniffed. "Guess they're no different than I was at that age." Hector patted Mae's snow-dusted arm. "I am glad you're here. We start in five minutes, so you better hurry if you want a seat." He smiled and walked off over the ruts in the snowy car park.

Mae glanced at Kitt. He had no intention of staying to listen to a lecture. "Ten minutes," she said quietly. "We'll stay ten minutes."

IN SPITE of the cold and the early hour, the Fuller Lodge was packed, standing room only on the polished wood floor of the main hall that was once the dining room for the Boys Ranch School. Light gleamed down from traditional wagon wheel-like fixtures above. The massive room glowed with orange tones of old, hand-hewn pine. The head of a large buck sat above the massive fireplace, antlers still as vicious and lethal as they had been when the deer had been alive. Green Christmas garlands wrapped around the wooden beams and posts.

Kitt squeezed into a space beside a fat post and a woman wearing entirely too much patchouli, a scent where any amount constituted too much. Mae tucked herself to his left. He gritted his teeth and shuffled forward, a little closer to her. "Ten minutes," he whispered.

Hector, salt and pepper hair in a plait, stood at the front of the stone fireplace, a projection screen to his left, a podium and laptop to his right. He spoke with what some linguists referred to as a 'Rez accent,' a slight sing-song quality to his intonation. "My good friend Julius collects three things: classic British sports cars, art depicting the cosmos, and wine. Perhaps the most famous work of Aztec sculpture is *Sun Stone, the Stone of the Five Eras*, it's a late post-classic Mexica sculpture held at the National Anthropology Museum in Mexico City. My friend Julius would love to have this piece in his collection of Celestial art, but this piece weighs about twenty-four tons. Jools has a love of the past, of history. He says people are bound to repeat the past if they don't respect history." Hector paused and looked out into the audience. He waved his hand motioning with one finger. "You folks in the back see this okay, can you all hear me? Come on up closer, there's seats up here in the front. I don't bite, but I might spit a little."

The crowd laughed and patchouli woman moved through, giving Kitt a little distance from the wooden post. He glanced at Mae. "You look cold."

"How can I be cold when your radiating, seething anger is keeping me warm?"

A muscle in his jaw pulsed. "Ten minutes. We are staying ten minutes."

"You've made Hector very happy."

"Yes. Three cheers for grumpy me."

People settled into the front row, and Hector continued. "Okay. Okay. So, what's this giant calendar stone got to do with Drunken Rabbits and Oenology? History, art, and wine are all intertwined. You can make wine out of anything. Pueblo and Zuni tribes used fermented corn, aloe, *maguey*—that's agave—prickly pear and even grapes to make alcohol, but they didn't make art about wine the way the Aztec did. Now, the Aztec hold a special place in my heart."

Impatient in spite of his controlled breaths and years of training, Kitt shifted his feet, right hand swinging to his side. Mae turned slightly, her fingers brushing his once, twice, absolutely on purpose before her hand disappeared into the sleeve of her dark coat. Tiny ginger and white dog hairs stuck to the black wool.

Kitt crossed his arms, bumping into her absolutely on purpose. She transferred her weight, shuffling her feet, crossing her arms, too, tucking her right hand under her left elbow, the tip of her index finger circling around his. Despite his irritation, he caught her faint grin in the periphery of his vision and slid a fingertip to the vee between two of her fingers.

"My people, The Tewa," Hector moved to the next slide, a woman with a piece of pottery, "were not winemakers. The Drunken Rabbits Winery is very small and family run. We produce high-quality limited release Côt Noir or Malbec that rivals the Chateau Lagrezette Le Pigeonnier and Vina Cobos Marchiori Vineyard Malbec. My people are best known for their black polished and red polychrome pottery, but my family are sculptors and now winemakers."

Hector advanced to the next slide, a group photo of happy, smiling faces. He used a laser pointer. "This is my family," he said, and the green dot moved as he pointed. "My daughter, my nephew, my sister, my wife. My wife is Nahua, some say *Mēxihcati*, others still prefer Aztec. The pretty redhead beside her is her art dealer, Ruby, and the bald man with the Santa beard? That's one of our dear benefactors. We decided to name our first vintage after him. This is for you, my dear friend." The slide changed to a bottle of wine, the white label a stylised yellow Aztec Rabbit inside a red triangle, *Chichiltic* printed beneath.

A raucous *haw-haw-haw* lofted from the seated audience.

"Feck," Mae murmured.

Kitt's fingers closed around her elbow and he stared through the crowd, eyes halting on bearded Milton Foley's shiny bald pate and a heart-shaped port-wine birthmark.

"I'M TRYING to put this together, but I have no idea how any of it fits." Mae's elbow throbbed from where Kitt's thumb had dug in and led her out of the Fuller Lodge. She rubbed the smarting spot through her coat sleeve.

"Both hands on the wheel, Mae, especially in this weather."

Deliberately, she placed her hands at ten and two on the steering and checked the rear vision mirror. A battered, old, yellow Honda hatchback and jacked-up Dodge pickup travelled behind them. The heaviest traffic was going up the Hill, west to Los Alamos. Their route twisted down the plateau, the countryside snowy and picturesque, cars few and far between.

Kitt paid no mind to the beautiful and rugged landscape, his focus on the phone's screen and the information he found on Milton Foley.

"Did you meet Foley at the New Year's Eve party?" Mae said.

"Yes, and I danced with his wife."

"Is there anyone's wife you didn't dance with that night, Kitt?"

"Foley's a furniture retailer, owns a chain of stores across the American Southwest, and a museum of Biblical Art in Albuquerque."

Mae slowed. Snow had fallen more heavily southeast of Los Alamos. An icing of white stuck to the green and brown road sign. A dirty, orange plough cleared the road in front of them, pushing a white blanket to the pavement's edge, red soil spraying out from the sides and back end, sifting the dirt onto the snow. "Nash was a Premier League player, but he collects antiques. Is that the connection?" she said.

"I thought the same thing."

"What else have you thought?"

"Hector Rodriguez is a sculptor and Taittinger's passing fake artefacts as originals."

"Yes," Mae said slowly, staring at the road, mulling over the idea. "Makes sense why there's been an allegation of Taittinger's counterfeiting. You think Judith or Nash is the origin of the suspicion? Or maybe..." The plough and the Dodge veered off to the left, she veered right, the yellow car taking the same route. She turned and looked at Kitt. "When you were dancing with Mrs Foley, did she mention she and her husband ar—"

"The road, Mae."

Her eyes moved back to the windscreen. The wipers *tick-tocked*, sweeping away red-tinged wet spatter. "Hector's wife doesn't like Foley," she said.

Kitt pressed his mobile to his ear, eyes flicking from the road to the side mirror, to Mae, to the trimmed-down fingers on his left hand. "Get your things together, Reed. You're going to meet Bryce... Yes, everything..." The connection faded out and in. "I said every-thing...you're dropping out... About fifteen minutes... Who's awake... Yes, I know what it means. It means I could have had scrambled eggs."

Mae exhaled and shifted in her seat.

Kitt glanced at her and she dug into the pocket of her coat. "I found, *we* found Milton Foley...yes, the bald bloke with the birth-mark and laugh..." Paper rustled. Kitt looked at Mae again. She had one hand on the wheel and a small paper packet in the other, the rounded edge of a bagel poked out of the top. "Find what you can, anything you can. Grant had mentioned connections to a family somewhere in the southwestern part of the US. My guess is it's Foley..." The connection dropped, the call going dead. He shoved the phone in his jacket, reached out, took the bagel, and bit into cinnamon, orange, and cranberry-infused bread. Crumbs fell onto the crown of the cowboy hat on his lap.

A smug little grin tilted up Mae's mouth.

"You were holding out on me?"

"I forgot I had it in my pocket."

"Forgot like you forgot not all the eggs were hard boiled?"

She was quiet for a moment. A pickup truck laden with discarded Christmas trees ready for the dump rumbled past in the opposite direction and then Mae rumbled herself. "Jaysus, eat it already. I bought the damned thing when I got my coffee. I meant to give it to you, but the potential of you poisoning Bryce seemed a more pressing matter so I forgot about it."

Kitt had another bite, a savage one, and chewed the food as he chewed his anger and frustration and confusion, and she went on wearing that smirk, and he said it without thinking, "Do you love me, Mae?"

"Do I love you?" she snapped. "Whom else would I love, Reed? *Bryce*?"

"Caspar."

Mae exhaled, exasperated by his petty childishness and her inability to rein in her own petulance. Sixes and sevens, that's where they were again, that's where they were still, and that's where they would stay until this mess finished. She looked at him.

He looked back at her coolly.

Her eyes shifted back to the curve of the road ahead and she was struck by remorse and surprise. Those things he'd said about being more fascinating than Caspar, about the wedding ring and silver-framed photo... With the shock of his being alive, the anger over the necessary contrivance of his being dead, she'd never thought to consider a man as confident as Kitt could feel insecure, perhaps even a little jealous over a dead husband. Yet he was uneasy with the love she'd always carry for Caspar. Man. Bully. Hero. Saviour. Liar. Kitt was all those things. He was also *human*. He was a vulnerable man with human vulnerabilities and he needed... reassurance. Fear and anger had robbed her of compassion, blinded her to human frailty, to his frailty. She was still scared, still angry, yet now she saw how she had failed him.

Irritated, with him, with herself, she swallowed, her voice thick. "You believe I've held back because of a dead man."

"Mm-m."

"Caspar's not my ghost. He's yours. I told you, my holding back is because I've been so afraid. Not afraid of you or afraid of what you do, but afraid *for* you. Marriage is a promise, one I can make, but I don't think you can. It's grow old together, 'til death' we part, only your death may come sooner than later."

"You have that little faith in me?"

"However stupid, however irrational, I love you, Hamish. I'm in love with you, and you do what you do for those reasons you said you have. I haven't thought *what if*, I've thought *when*, and I need to change that, I nee—*what a feckin' tool!*" she shouted suddenly, and downshifted when the little yellow hatchback began to overtake them, another car in the oncoming lane. The Honda hatch fishtailed briefly, pulled ahead, and sped off, disappearing over a crest.

The wipers *tick-tocked*. The heater *whirred*. The tyres hummed along the wet pavement. Piñon dotting the undulating roadside landscape swish-swished by. The paper packet crumpled in Kitt's hand. He put it in the console between the seats, next to the romance novel.

Two minutes passed and expanded to three. Then to four.

"I apologise," he said finally. "I've been a jackass."

Mae's eyes burned as she watched the road. "I'm sorry I was short with you."

"I deserved it. I was a prick, and I like when you call me out for being a prick."

She dabbed at the trickle at her nose. "You do, don't you."

He turned to her. "Yes, I do. I always have. I love that you never let me get away with anything. Do go on with it."

"I'm sorry I haven't told you I love you," she said, eyes on the task of driving as she approached a rise in the roadway. Perhaps this was as simple as he'd said, and that, in spite of what he was, with the gratifying nature of what she'd done, with the way she struggled with the morality of her actions, with what she feared, 'I love you' was the only truth that mattered.

"I just wanted to hear you say it. These last months, with everything so uncertain I needed to hear something true." He bit into the bagel again, chewed and swallowed. The mobile vibrated in his pocket. "Why doesn't Hector's wife like Foley?" he said, digging about for the phone.

"Something about fundamentalist biblical literalism and an

ultra-right-wing take on Christianity. Or maybe it's how Foley laughs. Jaysus, that laugh."

Kitt read the link Reed had sent before the phone lost connectivity, eyes scanning the news article. "Perhaps it has something to do with Foley opening a second religious museum in Phoenix this Easter."

"You think he teamed up with Taittinger, Nash, Basil or all three of them?"

"Ah, I don't know. I had hoped you'd have figured it out so I could cease being—"

"A prick?'

"I was going to go with overtired, over-worked, sloppy, little crybaby."

She sighed. "I've come to realise that things like this always end in tears," she said, downshifting and slowing, suddenly, "or a car accident."

Kitt followed her line of sight. "Oh, goody."

Up ahead, the yellow hatchback that had passed them earlier had skidded sideways. stopping across the south-bound lane. A large Christmas tree, still wrapped with gold tinsel, lay split and scattered across the pavement. A piece of splintered trunk and branches lay atop the little car's bonnet. Pine boughs poked out from beneath the chassis. Motor still running, the door opened. A dark-haired man lurched out and sagged against the car, chin-length black locks blowing about his face.

"This is strangely reminiscent of my most recent Christmas tree experience."

"Yes, except you said there was a blonde in a little sports car, not a man who shit his pants and is cradling a broken arm, dislocated shoulder...or an infant. *Oh, my God.*" Mae pulled to the side of the road, stopped, cut the engine, and hit the hazard lights.

Kitt swore and handed Mae the half-eaten bagel. "Please, check for a first-aid kit. Hopefully, we won't need it, but..." He opened the door and swung out, a gust of chilling cold lifted his jacket as he shoved his useless phone back in a pocket.

The stocky man turned slightly, the rear of his bright blue jacket emblazoned with the white ES of the El Salvador National Football Team. Bagel in one hand, Mae felt around under the driver's seat and found nothing. She leaned across the console, fished beneath the passenger seat and her fingers knocked against a small box, pushing it back farther. She knelt and squeezed between the seats, arse in the air. Her hand closed around the box and the sound of tyres spun on wet pavement, the Honda's engine gunned. She straightened and Kitt slammed shoulder-first into the Ford's windscreen, blade of a hatchet turning the glass to a layer of spiderwebs beside his ear.

Swearing, Mae scuttled out of the car backwards. Kitt tumbled down and off the end of the bonnet, hatchet smashing a crease in sky blue metal. She dropped the first-aid box and snatched up a small Christmas tree branch trailing a gold foil garland. A frigid gust blew back the violent lumberjack's hair, revealing a mashed nose and colouring like an indigenous Native of Central America— or El Salvador, like his football shirt suggested.

Kitt rolled to his feet and stepped toward the man swinging back the hatchet. Mae shouted, and in an instant, everything moved at a crawl. Lethargic images winked from one to another, every slug-gish blink of her eye a new tableau.

Kitt caught the man's forearms.

Her feet pushed forward through thick marshmallow air, knees bending through marmalade.

Kitt had twisted the man's body and the hatchet behind his back.

The branch she hoisted to her shoulder moved like a spoon in cold honey.

Hands drifted to the back of the man's neck, and the crown of Kitt's head lazily ploughed into the Salvadoran's rosy-brown face.

A long-flowering, distorted scream of pain warbled and droned. Then time knocked back into place and the high sound pierced the air. The hatchet *thunked* to the pavement, shaggy black hair bounced and blew in the wind as the man sagged. When Kitt let him go, he reeled backwards, left and right, bumped into shin-high, reddish-tinged snow piled on the edge of the road's shoulder, and stumbled toward the roadway, his breath billowing out in steamy clouds.

Bagel still in hand, Mae dropped the short stick and puffed just as heavily. Kitt, unaffected, void of expression, as if nothing had happened at all, stood still, blood stippling his forehead, watching the man spin, lurch a few steps, and sink to his hands and knees, moaning.

"Kitt."

"Stay there. Mae. Stay there," he said, not looking at her. "Smart. Very smart set up. Ingenious actually, to use what was on hand. I got within four paces of him before I noticed it had all been staged, that the tree had been crushed by something bigger, and they'd just thrown the bits of trunk and branches around and under the car. This section of road beyond White Rock isn't heavily travelled at this time of year. Few people go to Bandelier National Park to see the kiva and homes of the Ancestral Puebloan people in this cold weather. That was lucky for you," he stared at the man, "and fortunate for us."

"Are you hurt, Kitt?"

"My pride is mortally wounded." Kitt took three steps, rammed his foot onto the man's back, driving him facedown to the ground. "I've dislocated a fingerling. And you promised you'd *run*."

"I would have..." she began. Mae's stomach lurched as Kitt gritted his teeth and yanked a twisted quarter of a finger back into place. "...except no one had a gun." She swallowed the sour taste in her mouth.

With a groan, the man tried to lift himself, snow, blood, and dirt mixing on his reddish-brown skin and wet black hair. He collapsed, moaning and whimpering.

Kitt glanced at her then back at the man. "Get in the car, Mae."

"I'm not going anywhere without you, and we can't leave him here."

"We're not going to leave him here." Kitt glanced at the Ford.

Mae followed his line of site. "Into the boot, like Derek?

"Not yet." His hand slipped into the pocket inside his jacket.

"Wait. What do you mean, *not yet*?"

"I need a minute to catch my breath, calculate my next move."

"You're going to be sick, aren't you?"

The man hunched onto his hands and knees and began to crawl, palms splashing through puddles.

Kitt let loose a string of obscenities. "You just have to be determined, don't you?"

Suddenly, the man was on his feet, shuffling toward the side of the road, looking back at them over his shoulder. The cold wind blew the hair from his face again.

Kitt's eyes narrowed.

"*What time is it?*" Dalton whispered.

Mae gasped. "Jaysus, I know him. He does landscaping work for Hector. His name is Coyote."

"*What time is it?*"

Coyote started running and shouting in a language that wasn't Malay, Chinese, Singlish, Nepali, or even bloody Spanish, and Kitt started after one of the two men who had butchered seven people in a shipping container in Singapore. Coyote ran up and over the bank of dirty, reddish snow and down the other side.

Mae sprinted toward the edge of the pavement and over the

snow mounded on the shoulder. She cleared the bank as the two men skidded across a frozen ditch. Kitt slammed into Coyote, threaded an arm around his neck and both men went down on the ice. Coyote's stocky weight gave him the advantage, he hunched up and twisted, fist walloping into the side of Kitt's chin.

Before he delivered another blow, Mae kicked out hard, the square rubber heel of her boot ramming Coyote just enough to set him off-kilter, and just enough to lose her footing. She slid, one sole split through thin ice into the water below, and she came down hard on her arse, jarring her spine.

Shock and confusion lasted two seconds. Icy liquid poured into the top of one boot, down her ankle to her toes. Then she was flung backwards, hard fingers digging into her windpipe, the El Salvador football fan upon her. She caught a glimpse of Kitt's motionless body and her head slammed against hard, cold ice. Ungodly pain rushed in, the pressure on her throat sharp, crushing. Stars, spots, and snowflakes danced before her, and she couldn't breathe.

Coyote laughed, a wad of purple-grey chewing gum in his blood-speckled mouth. She lashed out with the stick in her left hand, only it wasn't a lump of Christmas tree that she crammed into a laughing blood, spittle, and gum-filled mouth, it was a bagel. Bits of bread and cranberry spilled down upon her when Coyote straddled her, straightened his arm, his face instantly out of the reach of her hands and fingernails. Mae planted her feet on the slick ice, grabbed the fingers at her throat and bent them back, twisting, lifting a shoulder, gulping in air as she broke his hold.

All at once, he was gone.

Gagging, coughing, sucking in air, she rolled onto her side and saw Coyote on his knees, arching back. Kitt hammered his face with a wet sounding *sklitch-sklitch-sklitch*.

Blood arced and splattered across the icy ditch and pristine white. Scarlet, purple-grey gum, and teeth flew. Coyote fell sideways. Kitt rammed his face into the hole where Mae had broken through the ditch ice and pushed down hard.

The wind kicked up, blowing snow. Coyote began to buck and flail and Kitt strained to keep the heavier man down, knee in his back, arms locked. Thrashing wildly, hands and elbows swinging back, legs kicking, Coyote's head popped up out of the water, gulping air like Mae had a few moments before.

Hacking, she scuttled over the ice, and her hands and weight bore down with Kitt's.

The wind howled.

Snow blew into their faces.

Coyote's body smacked against the ice. Kitt bared his teeth, the air rushing in and out of his nose as hard and loud as the wind. "*No!*" he ground out. "*No!*" He shouldered her, shoving her hard. She toppled onto her hip and he forced Coyote's face deeper into the watery hole, ice cracking. The powerful man struggled, his fists landing blows blindly, hands grabbing, slapping. Kitt bore down. Mouth ruthless, jaw set, speckles of blood in his beard, his hard blue-grey eyes fixed on a point beyond Mae.

Mae clambered onto her knees. "*Oh, God. Oh, God.*" Blood moved in her head, the beat of her heart in the tips of her ears, in her lips, in her aching throat. Hot, she was hot all over, sweating despite the glacial cold, despite her frozen toes and red, raw hands, and she stared at Kitt pressing down, down, down, until he said, "*Enough,*" and shunted himself back across the ice, puffing out little clouds that mixed with wafting snow.

Then Mae looked down at her burning hands, long hair tangled in a black web about her fingers. She tugged and twisted and rubbed spidery, gluey locks. "*Get it off! Get it off!*"

Kitt slid over and jerked away the sticky black strands entwined round her thumb and pinkie. The hair wafted away in the wind and he cradled her between his legs, breathing hard, yet cool, maddeningly controlled. "Breathe," he said.

"I am breathing."

"You're rasping like you've sprinted a marathon. Slow down," he said gently, demonstrating.

"My throat hurts."

"I know it does. It hurts like hell to be grabbed like that. Breathe in slowly. Exhale slowly."

With a ragged inhale and then another, she twisted to look up at him. Blood oozed from a slice on his cheekbone. She looked back at Coyote. Silver and gold tinsel stuck in the man's black hair waved in the gusting, frosty breeze.

Kitt cupped her cheek and she turned back. "In and out. In and out. There. You've got it."

"Is he really dead?"

"Yes." The wind gusted and he tightened his arms around her.

She shuddered. "Why is it called cold blood when I'm hot all over?"

"That was not cold-blooded, Mae."

"I helped you kill him."

"You didn't."

"I would have if you'd let me."

"I know." His eyes strayed past her to the dead man and the half-smashed, quarter-circle lump of bread that lay near his toes. "You have the most interesting taste in choosing weapons," he said.

"Sean once told me anything can be a weapon,' she said, voice husky.

"And what sort of grievous harm did you think you were going do with a bagel?"

Mae shivered again and began to laugh. She looked at the spray of blood in Kitt's beard, at blood-speckles on his forehead, at the sliced bruise on his bleeding cheekbone, suddenly laughing, laughing, laughing, unable to stop because everything had turned into farcical, nightmarish nonsense. She laughed until Kitt helped her up and led her over the ice, across the snow, and back up to the road and the Ford.

"You said his name is Coyote. I know him as Popo," Kitt gabbed a handful of snow from the side panel and rubbed it between his hands until the blood was gone and his skin was bright pink. "I'll bet the driver who took off in the Honda is his brother, Tzin."

"You know the Coyote boys?" Mae shivered and snort-sniggered beside the SUV.

"Yes. They murdered seven people and left me for dead in Singapore." Kitt looked over to the snow banked at the side of the road.

Bryce had mentioned the need for proof and there, on the other side of the snow bank, proof was. Although proof of what exactly wasn't clear. Kitt had a basket full of proof with no solid connection to anything. He looked at Mae. She shivered and chewed her bottom lip, trying to stem her nervous chuckling, hands stuffed into the side pockets of her snow-dappled dark coat. She shivered again, with shock and cold, and he was concerned about her state of mind because he knew there was so much more to come.

The wind gusted, snow blew around them. His jaw ached from Popo's stupefying blow, but Kitt reached for her, pulled her close and kissed her hard and long and deep. Her nose was a nub of ice and it brushed his as she kissed him back with a desperately relieved edge, fingers pressing into his chest. A car went by, slowing to veer around the remains of a Christmas tree, honking its horn.

Mae pulled away. She touched the throbbing spot on his forehead and he got a good look at the purplish-blue thumbprint on her throat. "I'm so cold now," she said shivering again, "but we can't stay here like this."

"No, we can't." He dropped a kiss on her forehead and let her go, walking backwards toward the dirty snow bank. "Get in the car, start it up, get the heat going. When I come back, release the boot."

"Where are you going?"

He paused, diminishing snow drifting down softly. "I need to gather evidence and you need to get warm. You're in shock."

She gave him a flat look.

"You are. You're hot, you're cold, and you're standing here thinking you've developed a taste for violence, that you've become a sadist. You've got to process those thoughts, let them come, acknowledge them, let them go, and move on."

"Is that what you do?"

Rather than answer, he said, "Please, get in the car and get warm while I drag Popo up here."

"You're going to put him in the boot?"

"Would you prefer I strap him in the backseat?"

"Jaysus, the things people do to hire cars." She shook her head. "What if someone should drive along?"

"How many cars have come by in the last fifteen minutes?"

Mae got into the Ford. The engine turned over. For a moment, she watched Kitt climb over the piled-up ruddy snow. When his head disappeared, she leaned over and adjusted the dash air-vent, hands quivering. Rosy smears streaked her knuckles—dirt, blood or both she didn't know. She found her handbag and the antibacterial wipes inside, dragged out three and scrubbed the marks. She tilted the rear-vision mirror and checked the state of her face. Mascara pooled beneath her eyes. She dabbed the marks away and lifted her chin. Red and bluish blotches sat on her throat. She returned to her handbag, found the pink Hermès silk scarf Taittinger had given her for Christmas, and tied it around her neck. Her actions were a mundane activity to disguise what had happened, mentally and physically.

Kitt tapped the rear window.

The Ford's boot lid rose. Popo slung over his shoulder, Kitt stepped forward, bent his knees, prepared to shift the man's weight and dump him into the boot. Instead, he paused. "What the hell?"

Not quite as large as one might expect, the Ford's rear space was big enough for a set of golf clubs, or two suitcases, or a body, but not two bodies.

Kitt reached in and lifted away an overcoat shroud of camel-coloured cashmere. The blue eyes staring out were fixed and hazy. On his back, knees up, mouth open, a small calibre bullet hole in his heart, Walter Molony's fair English complexion had a greyish cast typical of a body dead for a few days, rather than a few months.

Kitt let the cashmere fall and two things clicked into place. The well-respected professor, expert and consultant who had assisted Special Operations Division and countless other intelligence agencies had fooled everyone, and Dalton had indeed died in the container.

"What in underfeck?" Mae suddenly stood there, staring into the boot. "I've seen this man. He brought Ruby to the house, he was her driver. Jaysus, what do you think this means?"

Kitt glanced at her. "It means Popo is riding in the back seat." He turned, dead man swinging on his shoulder.

CHAPTER NINETEEN

The car splashed and sped, travelling the curving and rolling five kilometres to Taittinger's estate, the road clear of snow and Christmas trees that had come adrift. Kitt drove, peering beyond the cracked web of windscreen.

"I can't reach Reed. There's no signal here, Kitt." Mae set the mobile in her lap.

"Try again when we clear this rock face." He glanced at the pock-marked stone walls on either side of the roadway. You were right when you said this was like an Agatha Christie mystery. Bodies disappear and show up in car boots. I think someone's been trying to clean up a mess they made."

Mae hugged herself, fingers tugging at the scarf she'd put on. "Where does this mess start?"

"With a man pretending to be something he wasn't."

A half-snorted laugh popped from Mae's nose and mouth. "I could say that about you and Reed, but do you mean Taittinger, Milton Foley, the man in the boot, or someone else?"

Kitt glanced at her sideways. "The man in the boot."

She was quiet for a moment or two, phone at her ear. Still no signal. "The dead man in the boot, do you—"

"Walter Molony. His name is Walter Molony."

"The professor, the art expert who died in the container?"

"Mm."

"Do you think he was working with Taittinger and Milton Foley?"

"It's looking likely." Kitt planted his foot on the accelerator.

"Aren't you driving a little fast for these conditions?"

"We need to get back as soon as possible, to make up for the ten minutes we lost at Hector's lecture, and the time we've lost back there. Reed's going to wonder where we are. Let's find him and get the hell out of here. I hear Belize is lovely this time of year." Kitt took the curve from the centre of the road.

Mae steadied herself. Popo flopped against the side window. "There's something I've wondered about. Before I came back into my quarters, the night of the party, I met Reed on the patio outside the laundry. Where were you?"

"In Grant's room. It's my fault Felix got out. I knew there was a dog, I just didn't know he'd be in your quarters."

The Ford rose up over a hillcrest and Mae's stomach moved along with it. "Reed got a call when we were on the patio. He said, 'You're right, I've run into some trouble with the housekeeper,' or something along those lines."

"You've nailed his accent, but what are you getting at, Mae?" Kitt barely slowed to turn into the estate's drive, side mirror coming close to one of the brick pillar lamp posts at the mouth of the drive-way. "What are you suggesting?"

"Only what you thought about Bryce and what Bryce asked you about Reed. Do you trust your brother?"

The Ford slid a few metres before Kitt regained control and accelerated, snow crunching beneath the tyres. "He told you."

"No. I guessed. When I first saw him, I was taken by how he moved like you, I imagined his smile was like yours when you really smile, but then I saw your ghost everywhere, even Taittinger reminded me of you. I didn't really put it together until yesterday. There's something about the way you glare at each other, how you speak to one another with an animosity that isn't animosity as much as it is the sort of antagonism siblings have. You said Reed kissed you to irritate you, and I said I never understood that teasing, that I hated when Sean goaded me."

The Ford rolled up and over the hilly drive. "I couldn't tell you."

"Yes. It's about safety, mine, his, yours. He didn't tell me because he respects your need for safety, but what if that sibling antagonism is actually animosity. Maybe he...perhaps he..."

"Hates me?" He smiled suddenly. It was a strange thing to smile about, to know Mae cared about his safety. Her concern was natural, but it was a kind of balm that soothed the ragged parts of the soul he'd accepted he had and come to value. "Reed understands. For years, self-preservation has been a priority. An intelligence officer never wants to be compromised or compromise those she, or he, cares for. What good would I be if someone I cared for was put in a dangerous position, if that person was used against me?" He brought the car to a halt at the front of Taittinger's home and cut the engine. Turning to her, he narrowed one eye, like she often did. "Oh, wait, that did happen. With you. It keeps happening with you. Up to now, I've never failed so miserably, or put Reed in the position where you are. I promised him, I promised our mother, I never would. Occasionally Reed finds my adherence to that promise frustrating and openly goads me."

She touched his chin. "I find mocking you works better than goading. So, do we leave Popo here to disappear or take him with us?"

THERE WAS a trail of vomit in the foyer.

Kitt glanced at the scratched but legible face of his watch. They had a little over an hour before Bryce notified Station SWUS and matters took their due course. The Rohypnol had been administered nearly fourteen hours ago. Depending on size and weight, the effects of the drug, combined with alcohol consumption, could last anywhere from twelve to fifteen hours. It was foolish of him to hope the time frame leaned more in the direction of fifteen hours.

"Mind where you step, Mae," he said, pushing up the cowboy hat to look at her over a shoulder. He watched her move around the smelly splatter and go past him instead of heading toward the staircase with him. "Where are you going?"

"To get Felix."

"It may be difficult to enter Belize with a dog, strict quarantine laws in place and such."

"Then you pay a live animal import fee or bribe an official. I know you've bribed officials before." She walked toward the great room and stopped dead at the edge of the large, open space. "All right. I suppose I've become used to this now."

Tongue pushing against a loosened molar, Kitt hurried ahead. "Used to what?"

"Finding bodies."

Kitt moved a little faster. "Whose?"

"Mr Nash is on the floor with a hole in his head. Felix is on the sofa, beside Dr Jools. Dr Jools has a gun in his hand, and I think this time his pistol is real."

Kitt swore. "Why aren't you running?"

"He's not pointing a gun at me, he's pointing it at himself, and... Hello, Felix...yes, you're a grand dog, a grand little man." She bent forward slightly. "Belize will never have seen a dog as gran—"

"And what, Mrs Valentine?"

"He's crying, sir."

"Goodness me." Carefully, Kitt moved around the edge of the room, parallel to where Mae stood looking down at the sofa and ottoman that faced the giant picture windows. The dog stretched up against her and licked her hands. Taittinger's hair stuck up on his head in wild tufts. He was barefoot, vomit on his chin.

She had a seat beside Taittinger. The dog settled between them. Kitt bit back an urge to snarl. Mae had given him an advantage by blocking the tearful man's line of sight. Sometimes she was too goddamned smart.

Softly, softly Kitt walked around to the side. Nash lay on the floor, a hole in his temple. Blood pooled on the carpet beneath his head. Crimson paw prints dappled the white chair, the ottoman, and sofa where Taittinger sprawled, clothes dishevelled, tiny pistol pressed to his head.

A wide-eyed shamefaced child, Taittinger sobbed. "Oh, I was only trying to help, to protect...to...make s-sure..."

She put a hand on his, the one he had resting on the dog. "There now," she said, as if she were an Irish nanny again and Taittinger her weepy young charge. "There now, hush. Hush and put that down. Tell me what happened."

"I-I-I..." Taittinger snivelled and looked at Nash. "No, no. I didn't do that. I didn't."

"Of course you didn't. You're an eejit, not a murderer."

He nodded furiously. "Yeah, yeah. I'm *stupid, stupid, stupid.*" He wailed and the hand holding the gun to his temple slumped into his lap.

Kitt stepped in, snatching the single shot Heizer PS1. Someone had a real taste for these palm-sized handguns. He checked it. It had been fired. Pointlessly, he shoved it into the waistband of his trousers and pulled it out again, the metal painful against his bruised abdomen. "Wine is out, but selling artefacts looted from war-torn regions of the world is in," he said quietly. "And you're passing off fakes as the originals, aren't you?"

Bawling, Taittinger looked up at him, mouth open, a string of spit stretched from his top to bottom teeth. He nodded.

Kitt took off the cowboy hat and flung it, his lips twisting with amusement.

Mae had always wondered about that grin, and the way it made Taittinger squirm made her wonder about it now. The Germans had a word for it: *schadenfreude*—taking pleasure in the misery, in the misfortune of others. Or was it something else? Was it more like a game? Kitt had once told her intelligence work was a game, and maybe it was. The player on the sofa blubbered about the game he'd just lost.

"I don't st-steal. T-they're..." sniffling, coughing, Taittinger pulled off his tear-spotted glasses, "re-re-reproductions." He began to hiccup and pant.

"Which makes you not just a thief, but a cheat as well. Would you say that's a fair description, Mrs Valentine?"

"Swindler, fraud, charlatan, con man, liar, those are all very fitting words to use, *Mr Somerset*."

"You don't steal the pieces, but you have copies made, yes?" Kitt bounced the little pistol in his hand. "Breathe, Tatts."

Taittinger swallowed. "Yeah, yeah, I-I have copies made, p-pieces I know have been looted from museums, villages, homes, archaeological locations, or h-historic places, I have them repro-duced in Ch-China. It's...it's to protect the originals."

"China, Dr Jools, really?"

Taittinger swiped at snot and streaming tears, nodding.

"You're a counterfeiter on a noble crusade, but you're full of shit." Kitt ran a thumb and forefinger around the end of his beard, from moustache to chin. The hairy thing itched, and he looked forward to taking a razor to it. "Foley steals the pieces and you have the original for a while, just long enough for a reproduction to be made by your good friend Hector; after all, the Rodriguez family are sculptors, but I doubt they know how you've used them. You've given them money for their vineyard, you've put them on the map with the vintage they've named after their friend and benefactor, Milton Foley. *Chichiltic*."

Taittinger's eye-squinting sobs dissolved into spittly, slack-mouthed surprise.

It was time to shave and time to end this sodding disaster. Kitt regarded the dribbling dolt. "You know, I believe you are shocked and you still think you're being philanthropic. I'd ask where you keep the originals," he chuckled at what was obvious, "but I already know. Everything is shuffled about from freeports to here, to the Rodriguez winery back here, then to Foley's museums."

"No," Taittinger slobbered, "*no, no!* You're wrong. You don't understand. Ruby... It's *not*. It's not wh—"

"Yes, it is." Mae sighed. "Did Mr Nash figure out you two had defrauded him out of bottles of very expensive wine? That's how they pay you for it, isn't it? Wine for artefacts. That's what Mr Grant knew, didn't he?"

Raw and desperate panic turned his voice to a squeal and Taittinger's gaze fell to Nash. "I thought I was protecting... This wasn't supposed to happen, this isn't what I wanted! I thought I was protect—"

Kitt cracked the tiny gun against Taittinger's skull, knocking him out. "Give me your phone, Mae." He stuffed the pistol into his pocket.

She shook her head, glancing heavenward, and handed over her mobile.

Kitt dialled Bryce and hoped the call connected. "Send a crew now. Locals are fine," he said when Bryce answered. "I'll cooperate."

"So much for Belize," Mae removed her coat and laid it over Nash. She turned back to Taittinger, slumped and drooling on the sofa, and picked up Felix.

Kitt slid a hand to the small of her back and led her to the foyer, the hallway and staircase. Without the usual easy listening music playing in the background, the house was eerily quiet. Upstairs, bright, morning sunlight poured in through high windows. They passed the room where the Chungs had been put to bed, and moved along, toward the bedroom Kitt had shared with Reed. Basil's door stood open wide. Inside, near the foot of the bed, Ari Basil lay face up, dark eyes staring at the ceiling, a hole in his forehead.

Turning, Kitt clamped a hand on Mae's shoulder. "Stay here," he whispered, eyes stern, commanding, "And if I say run, you bloody *run*. Do you understand?"

She nodded and stared beyond him into the room. All right, maybe she wasn't used to finding bodies. Blood had pooled beneath Basil's head. A man sporting a blue El Salvador football team jacket, lay across his legs, side of his head caved in by an astrolabe once displayed in one of the hallway's *nichos*, but he was still breathing.

Kitt pushed Mae and the dog away from the door. He drew the tiny, useless gun from his pocket, checked the space between the door hinges and frame, and went into the room.

Mae held Felix close. She had been here before, waiting for Kitt in a hallway. The previous time had been outside a kitchen in Sicily. A man had been sitting at a table listening to Cher, eating *spaghetti puttanesca* with his fingers while flipping through a girlie magazine. There'd been a struggle and gunfire, but she hadn't made a promise like she had this time. Fear began to twist its way into her good sense. As it had in Sicily, her pulse rate kicked up, fear, indignation, exasperation over being told what to do made her take a step toward the room. Then Reed appeared in the doorway, sunlight turning his hair bright red.

Mae froze and stared at Reed's hair, at his red head. Red. Red was...*chichiltic*. Bryce had haltingly inquired about trusting Reed. She'd asked Kitt the same question and his half-brother crooked a finger, motioning for her to come to the room, and she stood there, hugging the dog, unable to move, staring at a half-brother, at sun-brightened red hair, at blood smeared on his hands, the word *chichiltic* a whisper in her ears until Kitt's head poked out behind him.

"Oh feckin' hell," she muttered, and Kitt put a hushing finger to his lips.

Head cocking the same way Kitt's sometimes did, Reed came out into the hallway, frowning. He reached her in three strides, wiping his hands with a face cloth. "You okay, possum?"

Heart rate returning to normal, Mae took a deep breath. "What happened?"

"I was in the kitchen looking for breakfast when Nash was shot downstairs. Basil was dead by the time I got up here. I... I had to... act." Reed looked at his hands and the small towel he'd stained. "The Chungs are dead too. Jesus Christ," he murmured, head shaking. "I put this bullshit behind me when I left Europol for Interpol."

The door at the end of the hall opened. Ruby staggered out, groping for the wall to steady herself, pink chenille dressing gown flapping open, silky, figure-hugging nude nightdress beneath.

"Shit," Reed muttered, stuffing the face cloth into his pocket.

"Good morning, Miss Bleuville," Mae said.

Ruby squinted, "My God, Valentine, can you do anything about the sun out here?"

Quietly, Kitt shut the door.

Ruby wobbled along the hall. "Please say one of y'all has some aspirin or Tylenol," she groaned.

"Let me help you." Reed advanced and took her elbow.

"My Lord, Mr Case, I 'preciate you hurrying, but please, gently, gently." Ruby shuffled and Reed led her to his room, Mae a few steps behind. Ruby sank onto the edge of the mattress, strawberry hair spilling into her face as she groaned and groped into the pocket of her thick dressing gown.

Reed shut the door behind them and locked it. For a moment, he stood by the chair beside the door and looked at his hands, where blood had tainted his skin. He sighed harshly.

Felix moved in Mae's arms, she half smiled. "You're quite different from your brother, aren't you?"

Reed's head jerked up and he met her eyes.

"I guessed." Mae shrugged one shoulder.

"This here is the worst hangover I have ever had." Ruby moaned.

Reed exhaled. "The little bugger used to follow me around. He was a sweet kid, but now he's a cold-hearted prick—and I'm *still* looking out for him."

"Son of a bacon bit, what's a girl gotta do to get a little pain relief?" Together, Reed and Mae turned to Ruby. She stood beside the bed, a small handgun pointing at them.

For a split second, Mae thought she had another toy from Taittinger's collection, but Ruby's wry grin said otherwise. "Every woman knows you want somethin' done right you got t'do it yourself," she said.

The gun fired.

Reed blinked a few times, looked down at himself, and crumpled, bouncing against the chair near the door, hands clutching the wound in his thigh, incredulity on his face, dark red blooming on his jeans.

Terrified, dog squirming in her arms, ears ringing, Mae remembered her promise to Kitt, but shock reset her brain to a practicality different to running away. Reed's blood trickled onto the pale carpeting. The stain needed to be blotted up as soon as possible, before it spread farther, so that it wouldn't set. She put Felix on his feet, lifted the hand towel Kitt had left on the chair last night, and pressed it to Reed's leg.

Reed let loose a torrent of obscenities. Ruby winced, finger massaging her right ear, one eye squinting, mouth open. "Dang it," the strawberry-haired beauty said. "Sorry about that, David—I mean *Simon*. I'm usually a much better shot. I was aiming for your heart, but it's this hangover," she waved the weapon casually, "it hammers like a nutcracker, and it's got me shootin' sideways. 'Course, this ain't no *ordinary* hangover, now is it? I've got a big ol' black spot about what happened last night, and I'm not the only one feelin' that way. Poor Jools is beside himself. He thinks he killed Nash. What did you have him put in the wine, Valentine?" She sighed. "That photographer Wally hired and those idiot boys had every chance to take care of you, honey, but Milt's a honking fathead and if dumb was dirt those men would cover about an acre, because you're still here."

Mae's ears rang, a high *eeeeeee* dulling the sound of Reed's grunting.

"All righty now." Ruby took a black wallet from her dressing gown and tossed it in Reed's direction. It flopped open as it landed. "Since we're here in your room, Agent Simon Reed of Interpol, have you got any aspirin or a pain reliever of any sort? And don't lie, sugar, because who knows what part of you—or her—I'll hit next."

Reed sucked in air through his teeth. "*Shit, fuck, shit*. There," he jerked his head toward the bathroom, "in...*fuck, fuck*...in there with my toiletries."

"Good. Now, Valentine, you go into the bathroom and get me the aspirin. You might want to bring some for Simon here, although, to be honest, he won't need it for long."

Felix padded over to Ruby and rubbed his lean body against her legs the way a cat did. "Aw, sugar, you are a pretty little thing who needs lots of attention and lovin.' What the hell was Jools thinkin' when he got you?" She shoved him aside with a knee.

Fear turned to fury and Mae straightened. "Don't you feckin' hurt the dog."

"*Don't hurt the dog*?" Reed looked up at her, brows knit together in disbelief and pain.

"What kind of monster do you think I am?" Ruby made a face as Felix pranced over to Reed and lay down beside his outstretched legs, curling into a crescent, head on the man's shin. "I would never hurt an animal, especially one as beautiful as Felix. Maybe he's not the most obedient, and he's about as sharp as mashed potatoes, but he's sweet. No, no, I'd never deliberately cause one of God's creatures pain. I'd put a bullet in his brain and he wouldn't feel a thing. Can't say if Grant was as lucky as Felix and ya'll will be, seein' as that nitwit Milt hired shot him in the face."

Mae felt the air move into her lungs. Time neither sped up nor moved at a snail's pace. There was no roaring noise in her head, no deafness, no heart that tried to scrabble up her throat, no nausea. Emotion abandoned her and unexpected blankness settled in, as if she were already dead, and dead calm, she entered the en suite bathroom. When she found a blister packet of paracetamol in a toiletry bag, she reached for one of the two blue-tinted glasses on the vanity and knocked the toiletry bag to the tiled floor. Items spilled out noisily, bouncing and rolling. Leaving the glass on the vanity, Mae crouched, collecting dental floss, a deodorant stick, a tube of lip balm that had rolled across the tiles and stopped at the base of the toilet. She stretched for the tube and there, an arm's length away, in a larger, fatter stainless-steel cylinder, sat the toilet brush.

Five months ago, she'd killed a man with a toilet brush.

For three seconds, she looked at the bristly brush, at the strip of headache pills sitting beside the glass, and the blankness became a canvas full of a single, deliberate, necessary thought. Still crouched, she half turned, placed the lip balm and other things on the vanity. Then she opened the small cupboard beneath the washbasin, pushed aside hand towels and extra loo paper, and found the denture cleaning tablets, the ones she sometimes used to remove mineral deposits and make the toilet bowl sparkling white.

She rose, filled the glass with water, and walked into the bedroom, where Ruby held Reed and Felix at gunpoint. While they watched, Mae tore the little paper and foil packet and dropped two tablets into the water. The liquid effervesced, cheery and mint-scented. She held out the glass, hand shaking. "Ma'am," she said, a quaver in her voice.

Ruby eyed the liquid. "I haven't had Alka-Seltzer in years." She took the glass. "I can't remember, do you drink it while it's still bubblin' or when it's stopped?"

"As it's fizzing."

"Yeah, yeah, the bubbles make it work faster, like champagne." Eyes and weapon trained on Reed, Ruby downed the entire glass of fizzling water. Mae stepped in front of Felix and Reed, and the corrosive, partially-dissolved tablets began to burn, frothing Ruby's mouth. The water she had swallowed carried the caustic chemicals, torching her tongue, her gums, and oesophagus, and it came back up foaming and green-tinged.

Coughing, gagging, Ruby's lips began to swell and blister. The empty glass hit the rug, the handgun discharged. A thunderclap of noise, a sharp, powerful slap of angry, stinging wasps and jabbing needles mushroomed through Mae's shoulder, up along her neck.

Reed shouted, Felix raced about the room *bark-bark-bark*, and Mae stood rooted in one spot, torn foil packet in her fingers.

Ruby staggered across the rug, choking, gasping, hissing,

clawing at her throat as she lurched into the en suite, her actions desperate, frantic.

Mae wondered if what the woman felt was anything like when her own throat had been squeezed until it was about to burst.

The door exploded inward. Kitt shouted and Felix rocketed across the open threshold, skittering down the hall. Ruby collapsed back into the room, retching. Reed swore and Mae sank into the chair where she'd been shagged senseless the night before, the needles and wasp stings in her shoulder hot and wet.

CHAPTER TWENTY

Mae lay on a narrow bed in the Los Alamos County Medical Center. The painkiller she'd been given had resulted in a low-level sense of euphoria and a very dry mouth. She smiled at Kitt and her lips stuck to her teeth. "The bullet passed through muscle. I'll have a scar matching yours," she said, top lip glued to incisors.

"If I'd been faster you wouldn't have a scar at all."

She laughed. "You actually kicked open the door."

"Heroic of me, wasn't it?" Kitt moved to the side of her bed and set a plastic cup on the mattress. For a moment, he stared at her, eyes travelling over her, deadpan if not for the menacing fury that glowed like the hottest point of a flame.

"What?"

Kitt exhaled, a harsh rush of air from his nostrils. His head shook ever so minutely, before he touched her bruised throat and the hollow at the base. He kissed her then, mouth on hers solidly at first, then softening, remaining in place as his breath turned ragged. His tears trickled onto her cheek. She trembled, laughing or crying, he didn't know which. She never cried when he expected her to. Mae never did what he expected her to.

He pulled away and she touched his wet face, smiling. With a sniffle and a swipe at his eyes and nose, he reached for the plastic cup. It was full of ice chips. "These will help." He lifted to the cup to her lips and shook a few bits of ice into her mouth.

"How's Reed?" she said, sucking cold chips.

"Alive, pissed off, grumbling about a borrowed bottle of wine and how he's going to lose his job. You were both lucky Ruby was such a bad shot. He's going to limp for a while. He may lose his job. I'm not sure he'll ever forgive me for this."

"Yes, he will. Are you going to tell me off for breaking my promise?"

His head listed to one side. "Did you break your promise?"

Quickly, she shook more ice into her mouth.

"Thank you for not letting that woman kill my brother."

"You're welcome," she said, mouth full of cold.

He lifted her hand and kissed the middle of her palm.

"I scared the hell out of you, didn't I?"

"You did, yes."

"Have you vomited yet?"

"I don't always vomit."

Chuckling, she smiled, lips sticking to her teeth far less than before. "You know I find your vomiting endearing."

He looked at her, the cold blue of his eyes flickering with warmth and passion and fear and fury. "Christ, Mae," he said softly. "Christ."

"I'm sorry I frightened you," she said, just as softly, with just as much warmth, passion, fear, and fury.

"If I didn't understand your point of view before, I sure as hell do now." Kitt moved the tube connected to the cannula drip in her left hand and sat on the edge of the bed. The mattress made a crunching noise.

She rested her head on his shoulder. "I didn't do it on purpose. I didn't set out to prove anything to you."

"I know. I was dead. You needed to be productive." Kitt glanced at the glass wall and the door. Five minutes, he had five minutes—seven tops. That was probably all the time Reed and Bryce could stall for. "I'm sorry about the dog. I knew Taittinger would run when he came to. I just didn't think he'd take Felix with him."

Mae sighed and leaned back into the pillow. "Since he's microchipped, it should be easy for Bryce to find him and Taittinger. Then again, Taittinger could dump him somewhere." She went quiet for a few long seconds. "Do you think Ruby killed Molony?"

Kitt stroked her hair, a snarl of French braid. Despite fighting for her life, her hair had stayed in place all morning, the bed its undoing. "She did or Tzin did. With her connections in the world of auctions, art and wine, I think Ruby played everyone. Bryce and the locals may get more out of her, depending on the amount of damage done by the denture cleaner you got her to drink. You have quite the deadly knack with cleaning products, Mae."

"I didn't kill Ruby."

"No, you didn't."

"But I wanted to." Mae shook her head. "I tried to."

"You did what you needed to."

"I knew you'd say that." She laughed suddenly. "Ruby Bleuville and her strawberry hair. *Ruby—chichiltic*, right in front of us the entire time."

The left corner of Kitt's mouth twitched ever so faintly.

"Were you waiting for me to say something?"

"It was bloody obvious, Mae. How did you miss it?"

"How did *you* miss it?"

"I'm a terrible spy, remember? Plus Foley has that red birthmark on his head."

"Jaysus, I bet Taittinger thought he was protecting her from Tzin Coyote until she killed Nash. He tried to tell us that it was Ruby, not Foley, but we didn't listen. Has she said anything? Has Tzin?"

"Tzin is in a coma. Ruby has a tube down her throat. She did, however, give a written statement implicating Foley and the Coyote brothers."

Mae stared into the cup of ice chips, going quiet for a few moments.

"Mae?"

She exhaled uneasily. "How could what I did to Ruby feel so right and be so bloody wrong at the same time? How could I stand there and watch her choke and feel so smug about it? I feel so morally bankrupt."

"She shot you."

Mae lifted her eyes. "She shot me after she drank the poison I gave her."

"Don't you know? Life is not black and white or even shades of grey; it's a whole palette of colour, and some choices you make can't be shaded as good or evil, but as necessary forms of justice. Revenge is a human form of establishing social justice. Revenge activates the reward centre in your brain, and releases dopamine so you get a sense of pleasure from it. You asked me before and I admit it now," he said. "I get a sense of gratification from my work."

"You find killing gratifying?"

"Of course not. I once told you I have a very high sense of justice. I find aiding those who struggle with oppression, cruelty, a lack of justice, or autonomy gratifying. I live and have lived a life of privilege. This is how I choose to give back; this is how I choose to support a world so that others can...are you laughing?"

"Yes."

"It does seem rather ridiculous when I say it out loud. Listen to me now. You feel guilty when you have no cause to. You saved Reed's life, you've saved my life and your own life as well. There is no reason to feel guilt for that."

"Well, I was raised Catholic. I'm still Catholic."

"Perhaps you should talk to a priest."

"I have."

"You told your brother about me?"

"You told your brother about me."

"Point taken. What did Padre Sean say?"

Mae looked at the ice in the cup. "He told me to walk away."

"Smart man."

"Then he said love was precious and I'd be an arsehole to reject such a gift from God," she said, an ice chip between her front teeth.

Kitt chuckled softly. "The point I'm trying to make is what you struggle with, your moral ambiguity, it rests at my feet, but your actions, your assistance, however horrible, was necessary. It gave us a chance to make things right, to save lives. It gives us a chance."

"Is there still an us?" She slurped.

"Was last night really the last time?"

Her head turned slightly and Kitt thought he saw the flicker of a smile tug the corners of her mouth. "We agreed to talk about this when we're both home again," he said. "Except what that means is so uncertain."

"Because people in your line of work never really retire, Kitt."

"I wish you hadn't been right about that. I do apologise for it, and more, for what's to come. Circumstance means it's *go on as we were*, with our secret, very long engagement, what neither of us want. It's a compromise. Yet, even compromise might not be tenable." Shoes chirped across tiles outside the room, hospital staff moved quickly up the hallway. Kitt stepped away from the bed and took a breath.

"I don't want to be right. I want to be with you."

Kitt's smile lit up his eyes. "Bryce is married, but Bryce is not a field officer and marriage is not realistic for a field officer. It's not safe for you."

"Or you." Mae's lips twisted into a childish pout.

"It may not be what we want, but it's not rational for us to go on any other way than as we are, secretly engaged for a very long time."

"Because, departmentally speaking, I'm your trusted employee who knows how to keep your secrets, so it's stay as we are or walk away." She shook ice into her mouth.

"Not to heap on more gloom, but your walking away may not be necessary if I go to prison."

She snorted, crushing the ice she was supposed to be sucking. "Why would you go to prison?"

Kitt inclined his head. "Aside from how I threatened hospital staff if they didn't see you and Reed straightaway, I'm in this country illegally and I've killed two men."

"One. You killed one man..." Her mouth popped open for a moment, bits of ice melting on her tongue. "Derek. You...you... Oh."

"Yes. Into the Volkswagen boot he went with Grant. I wanted to spare you another struggle with your morals." He paused, until the hurried footfalls of hospital staff and others subsided. "I am sorry. I said I would never lie to you and yet...I did."

Mae swallowed.

Kitt leaned forward and kissed her. "Now then, don't be alarmed. Don't try to fight. Don't argue with them or with me. When they ask, tell them anything they want to know. Bryce will be here soon, and that may help, but first we'll have to deal with the locals."

She glanced at the door as it creaked. "You should have let me go."

"I should have walked away." Head slanted, he smiled, watching her eyes widen as the door hinge hissed.

"*Run*," Mae said, but Kitt didn't run. Instead, he got to his knees, put his hands behind his head, fingers laced together, and the door swung open, and then Mae looked beyond him, at a man clad in black tactical gear, at a woman holding identification.

The woman lifted her badge, a gold eagle at the top, the man snapped handcuffs on Kitt. "Mrs Valentine, I'm Agent Isabel Tanner," she said. "Homeland Security Investigations. You and Major Kitt are both in a fuck-ton of trouble." Attractive, middle-aged, her tailored suit smart, Tanner had a full head of white hair, exactly like the woman who had wanted to kiss Australian Reed at Taittinger's New Year's Eve party.

"Jaysus, Mary, Joseph, and all his carpenter friends!" Mae flung the cup of ice to the floor. "Is anything or *anyone* here not a feckin' phoney?"

ON THE FOURTEENTH OF FEBRUARY, Kitt walked passed the satellite TV installation van parked at the kerb and went up the front steps. He climbed the interior staircase to his flat and let himself inside, tossing his bag on the chair beside the coat rack. His bag hit polished wood with a *thump*.

There was no chair.

There was no coat rack.

There was no...

He gazed around his home, finding it lacked the certain qualities that made it his home. The fringed Persian rug in shades of green similar to the green of Mae's hazel eyes did not lie upon the floor. The button-backed Chesterfield sofa, the dining table near the big bay window, the Minton pieces on the bookshelf, the books, the lamps, the framed antique maps, everything, right down to the pillows in the window seat, it was all gone. The flat smelled of fresh paint, cleaning products and wood varnish.

His shoes squeaked on the gleaming polished wood when he stalked toward his bedroom. He hesitated for a moment then shoved open the door. His bed and wardrobe missing, the white timber plantation shutters closed.

Kitt went into the en suite bathroom, the space pristine, stark white and gleaming, void of towels, toiletries, toilet rolls, and toilet brush. An absent toilet brush was an odd thing to turn a man's happy homecoming into gaping, befuddled astonishment.

He turned in the doorway and faced the bedroom. Nothing. There was nothing left in the flat. No stick of furniture, not a stitch of clothing, not even a bloody ball of dust.

Dry-mouthed, he returned to the vacant sitting room. Water. He wanted water to dispel the dryness of his tongue and wash down the goddamn lump growing thick and hard in his throat.

The kitchen's swinging door, usually open into the sitting room, sat shut. Kitt kicked it, one booted foot smashing into the centre of the white-painted surface. The door flapped into the kitchen and returned, a pendulum on an oversized grandfather clock. He watched the motion, his mood swinging empty, wretched, empty... wretched...empty...wretched. A lump in his throat became a fist that reached down into his chest to squeeze the foolish, quixotic heart he never wanted to have. Yet there that heart was, aching with wretchedness, and self-pity, desolate, contemptible self-pity.

Mae had done the smartest thing. She'd left him, walked away and embraced the certainty of safety. His personal items had been moved out, the lease on his flat had been terminated. Permanently.

Eyes on his boots, the only footwear it seemed he had left, Kitt laid the flat of his hand on the kitchen door and pushed, gently. A toolbox lay open near the butler's pantry entrance. A lone stool topped with a small stack of books stood at the end of the worktop where he'd eaten Mae's scrambled eggs, drunk her coffee and swallowed the aspirin she'd left out when he'd been abysmally hungover. This sort of hangover was new.

Woefully, pathetically, he moved into the kitchen, looking at scuff marks on his shoes. He pulled out the stool, glancing at the book at the top of the pile: *Butlers and Household Managers, 21st Century Professionals*. What a lovely reminder of a love lost. He chastised his silly, yearning, already lonely heart and set the books on the worktop. The butler's pantry door squeaked and swung open.

"Oh!" With a start, Mae halted, soiled white bath towels in her arms, the door bumping softly into her backside.

In seconds, the lump in Kitt's throat broke apart. "Hello," he said, semblance of a relieved smile twitching on his lips, quieting the heartbeat that had thumped in his ears. "My apologies for startling you."

Mae hugged the darkly smudged towels. "You didn't startle as much as surprise me."

"The same way I did in New Mexico, when you thought I was dead?"

"Yes."

The remaining lumpy bits in his throat dissolved into relief and amusement. He'd spoiled her plans and she'd spoiled his surprise. "Forgive me. I didn't think. Well, I did think. I thought it would be a nice surprise, but you've had enough surprises. And so have I."

Mae swallowed, hand over her heart. "Jaysus, Kitt. *Jaysus*." She tossed the towels on the worktop beside the books. "I thought I was hallucinating from painkiller withdrawal." She rubbed the shoulder that had been pierced by a small-calibre bullet.

"Does it still hurt?"

"Mostly at night."

"That's common. Come here and kiss me. Or are you going to stand there looking like a chambermaid who's walked in on a man alone in a hotel room with his trousers bunched around his ankles, pitiful inadequacy in hand?"

"No. I'm not going to kiss you. One thing will lead to another, you'll wind up standing in this empty flat with your trousers nearly around your ankles, and we'll be back where we were in October, only without the bloody wet Christmas tree, Bryce and feckin' Llewelyn."

A rattling bang came from the rear entrance off the pantry. The pantry door swung open again. A lean black man in blue coveralls. "Leak was small. There's no real water damage."

"That's a relief."

"I'll get started replacing the old pipe. Wall will need a patch and lick of paint after," he said with a Jamaican accent, brown eyes looking Kitt up and down.

Kitt flashed a smile.

"Thank you, Mr Desmond," Mae smoothed her apron, "I'm quite capable."

Kitt chuckled softly, and head-shaking Desmond pushed the door, revealing a wet-dry vacuum and attached hose visible held by a chubby man with Elvis sideburns.

"Done, missus, I'll put it back downstairs for you," Elvis sideburns said.

"Thank you. Let me know if you need it again, Mr Kew." She nodded, the man and vacuum hurried through the kitchen, through the sitting room and out the front door, Hoover hose clattering against the wood frame. The sound of hammering filtered from behind the pantry door.

"Your timing, Kitt." Mae faced him, hands smoothing over the hips of her apron as she tried to smooth over her irritation and gave a soft, tetchy laugh. "Your timing has been off since you came home with that Christmas tree."

"I can see that. Decided to redecorate?"

"Just freshen things up."

A slab of alarm hit his gut. "Where am I to live while you freshen up?" Kitt rose from the stool. "Where am I to sleep, next door with you in your spartan home and pea-sized single bed?"

"You and your shite timing." She huffed all at once. "This really isn't how I pictured this moment."

"It's not how I pictured it either. There was supposed to be kissing. And furniture I could kiss you upon."

"Kew and Desmond are here, Bryce is coming, and I have a new tenant to accommodate."

"New tenant?" Fear rippled up his spine, a chunk of concrete settled on his chest. Desmond shuffled back into the kitchen, a drop cloth over his shoulder, tin of undercoat paint in hand. Kitt watched the man go into the butler's pantry. Relationships, entanglements that were murky with emotion and expectation, where feelings were hurt and bitter tears were shed, he'd avoided those all his life, never stopping once to consider he'd ever wind up being the one hurt and full of bitter tears. Oddly, he was numb. "New tenant?" he said again, the weight on his chest making breathing calmly arduous.

Irritated, Mae began folding the dirty towels. "*Walk away*, you said. *It would be safer*. Safer. It's funny what we think of as *safe*. I had hoped you'd be released. I know you well enough. I ought to have guessed you'd find a way, especially after having missed Christmas so spectacularly. I'm rather disappointed with myself for not moving faster, for needing help with this."

Safer. New tenant. Oh, Christ, she *had* heeded his advice. She was leaving. "Is this what you want, Mae?" Kitt said, looking around the empty kitchen. Why was it people always converged in kitchens to talk or argue or hash out ideas? They'd been in this kitchen last July, when he'd confessed he'd been in love with her for years and here they were now, and he was still in love with her while she, quite sensibly really, was leaving him.

He decided he hated kitchens.

"You know it makes the most sense." She stopped fiddling with the soiled towels.

Hammering began again. For a ridiculous second Kitt thought it was his heart, until his brain told him it was construction-related. He looked out into the vacant sitting room and brought his gaze back to her. "You walking away makes perfect sense, but it has dropped my trousers around my ankles."

A furrow appeared in her forehead. "Why would you think I'm walking away?"

A similar furrow rumpled Kitt's brow. "My flat is empty and you've said there's a new tenant. Is someone moving in here or did Stephens move out of your flat next door?"

Briefly, she pressed her lips together, suppressing a grin with her veneer of professional calm, her eyes locking on his. "In the process of freshening up this flat, I...found a leak. To fix it I had to expose a pipe running along the staircase between floors. Hence Desmond the plumber-handyman and all the hammering."

"You've exposed the staircase?"

She nodded, proudly. "This was once one house, not two flats."

In half a second, he realised what it meant. Kitt laughed, suddenly weightless. "That is brilliant."

"It is, isn't it? The stairs are hidden. It lets us go on as we were, only with more space and without having to clear it with your employer." She put a hand on her hip. "Did you think I was leaving you?"

"Of course not."

Mae tipped her chin and shot him the look that said he was full of shite. How he'd come to adore that expression.

"Yes, yes I did. It was something of a shock when I walked in and found my home empty. You mentioned you disposed of my clothes the morning we met Bryce. I was prepared for the clothes but not *everything* to be gone. It's caught me with my trousers down." Kitt frowned. "Have I any trousers left?"

She made a face. "No. I got rid of everything, shirts, trousers, jackets, underpants."

"My underpants?"

"I believed you were dead, I couldn't bear to have your shirts, your trousers, or underpants—"

"Yes, I see, underpants are far too intimate a reminder of someone you loved."

"I'll replace them."

"Yes. You will. My Wedgewood and Minton china, my atlases, my bourbon, where are those things?"

"Downstairs for now. I thought I could have it all back in place before you returned from being held in prison, but you surprised me. I know this is not the homecoming you expected. It's not what I wanted to happen either. Expectations for homecomings are *so* ridiculous. You're cross, I'm cross, and we're at cross purposes." With a *pfft*, she gathered the books and left the kitchen, soles of her Mary Janes squeaking softly on tiles and polished wood as she went to the window seat in the sitting room.

"I'm not cross." Kitt went after her and halted in the doorway. Kew had returned with a box of power tools and a roll of wiring. He sang along with the music coming through grotty-looking earbuds and stretched out a measuring tape along the built-in bookcase near the window seat.

Irritated with Kitt, with herself, Mae set the paperbacks in the window seat, watching the portly handyman crouch. She stared at the crack of the man's arse. Unexpected, unpredictable, that's what Kitt was, what he'd always been, chaos in her ordered world. There was something about having his chaos in her life, and everything pointed to why his chaos couldn't, *shouldn't* work, pointed to being practical and safe and alone, pointed to her walking away. She had to do what was right, despite every indication it was as wrong as seeing Mr Kew's arse crack.

Kew rose, knees popping. He pulled out his earbuds, the music emanating from them tinny. "The TV will just fit, Missus," he said. "If that's what you want, I'll have to take out these two shelves."

"Thank you, Mr Kew."

Kew hitched up his trousers, looking Kitt up and down. "Tell her. No intelligent person would put a TV there."

"He's right," Kitt said, his nod matter-of-fact. "No intelligent person would put a TV there."

"Why is that?"

"Too much glare from the window." Kitt moved into the sitting room. "And I don't have a television."

"You do now. I've subscribed to a satellite package." Mae looked at the window and the rain pattering against the glass, and back at the shelf. "I suppose you'll have to run the line where you said, Mr Kew."

Kew hitched his trousers again, shoved his earbuds in, and dug around his toolbox, while a tinny David Bowie *wham-bam-thank-you-ma'med*.

Mae lifted the stack of paperbacks, moved them across the cushions, and sat down. "Are you back at work now, Kitt?"

"Yes. Llewelyn's apologised and put me on the duty desk. Indefinitely I believe."

"I'm very sorry for your paperwork. I had very little paperwork."

"Were you debriefed?"

"M-mm, by a man named Dexter. I was told my observational reports on Taittinger were valuable and then I was thanked for my service. Llewelyn was present, watching. He didn't say a word. If that's debriefing, then yes, I was debriefed." She gave a half-snorted laugh. "Here we are then, at the resolution of this somewhat gritty cosy romantic spy thriller that tried hard to be amusing. What was it that exonerated you and led to your release?"

"Perhaps we can talk about this elsewhere?" Kitt slid his hands into his trouser pockets and flicked his gaze to Mr Kew.

"If we can hear Bowie, Kew can't hear us."

She had a point. Kitt nodded. "Tanner's people got him at the Mexican border. Foley, as the Americans say, rolled on Ruby Bleuville. It only ever takes one weak or loose thread to create opportunity and Ruby, a well-respected and knowledgeable fine art expert, saw an opportunity. She discovered a client, a very well-connected, wealthy client, had left a thread hanging at his freeport storage unit. Rather than take advantage of him, she drew Walter Molony's attention to the matter. He pulled the thread."

"What about Dalton?"

"He's very dead, but there's evidence he'd aided Molony, misdirected information regularly and fed him information. That's how Ruby knew about Grant. How she found out about you. How am I doing so far?"

Mae slipped an apron string between her fingers. "It seems plausible. So what was the thread Molony pulled?"

"Somehow, this client was issued a master pass security key fob to the Geneva Freeport. It could override the security systems, the fingerprint and retina-scan, facial and voice recognition of every location owned by FreeSuissePort in the world. Ruby said that it was Molony's idea to exploit this flaw, that he mapped out and created a network, using one or two individuals working inside a government foundation, a museum, a university, or charitable foundation. They tested it on several pieces of art Molony had access to—one of which was a piece owned by HRM. Items had a stopover in freeport for a few months before being packed and shipped on to museums and galleries in smaller American cities, like Albuquerque and Healdsburg California, in Sonoma County—an area well known for wine. That's where Ruby first met Milton Foley, at a tasting hosted by Taittinger."

Mae sighed. "It's easy to pin all this on a stupid, idealistic man like Taittinger."

Kew fiddled with a spade bit on his drill and smiled at them both. He was missing a front tooth.

"Yes. But Taittinger was a pawn. According to Foley, Ruby and Molony started small, but then she saw another opportunity in Foley. Foley had already been on Molony's radar. Taittinger had been on Ruby's. He was a wine collector, an activist for refugees as well as a cultural conservationist. Molony knew Foley had been smuggling in pieces of art for his Bible museum, under the guise of decorating samples. Foley already had ties to a network set up in Mexico, through Hector Rodriguez's wife's less than savoury relatives who moved drugs and people across the border."

"Tzin and Popo?" Mae ran her palms along her apron.

Kitt nodded. "Foley had been getting things past customs by packing artefacts with furniture and decorating samples. He turned to an already-existing route, one the Coyote brothers used for the Enrico Cartel, to smuggle pharmaceuticals and counterfeit handbags through Mexico to a warehouse in Las Cruces, New Mexico— where Taittinger and Felix were headed by the way. There's a tunnel running between Mexico and Las Cruces, it goes right under the warehouse. It was dug by the Coyote brothers and exceptionally well-hidden."

Mae untied apron strings, slipped off the white cotton, and tossed it beside the paperbacks. "They dug Taittinger's wine cellars, didn't they?"

"They did. The cellars are what made Taittinger so attractive. Ruby orchestrated things so that he never knew who *Chichiltic* was

—he was unaware Hector Rodriquez unveiled a vintage after Foley since he missed the man's Drunken Rabbits lecture."

"Was that a surprise to Foley as well?"

"Quite. Everything was carried out online. We traced a message trail that included photos of you, some came from Coyote's phone, others were ones Derek took of party guests. They were sent to an account Molony set up for 'Lou Ellen,' meaning Molony knew you were there from the start, Mae."

"And then he knew you were there."

"Yes."

"How did it all work?"

"When Ruby or Molony found a piece, they moved it through Taittinger since he knew who had an interest in wine and an interest in artefacts. He'd host a tasting and always include one or two collectors who were only interested in the wine to give a more legitimate feel to his auction. He was a stopping ground for artefacts he believed were going on to preservation and safe storage with Foley in his museum or warehouse. When a piece or pieces arrived, Taittinger had copies made and he was careful, but he wasn't aware the originals were being sold. The scam's been going on for years until someone, Nash we think, realised he'd been duped. Things began to unravel when Dalton decided to try for himself, but panicked and left a Byzantine icon on a tour bus outside Paris. Then it really started to disintegrate when Molony and Foley decided to take over and cut out some of the troublesome middlemen, like Ruby."

She rolled her eyes. "One can almost understand Ruby's murderous rage. Why do so many men think they can just take over?"

Kitt gave a sheepish grin. "Ego. Insecurity. A sense of entitlement. Stupidity."

They fell silent for a moment, looking at each other until her mouth rumpled and she laughed. "I think I miss the cowboy hat. Did you keep it?"

"Good, God, no."

Mae clucked her tongue. "There was never any counterfeit wine, was there?"

"No. Molony was covering his tracks by suggesting suspicion lay elsewhere, with several individuals who had wine and other items stored in freeports, like Taittinger, and intelligence officers like Gettler and Springer."

"And you. And then you actually showed up."

Kew's drill whirred, *zzzt-zzzt*, then emanated a high-pitched whine and puff of smoke. The man released a stream of obscenities and turned. "Sorry. Sorry for the language, Missus. Be right back." He jerked up his trousers and went to the kitchen.

Mae chuckled. "You were never going to be incarcerated, were you, Kitt?"

"It was a very real possibility."

"Because you'd gone rogue?"

"Because I wasn't *authorised*."

She laughed. "Because you went rogue."

"The bottom line is Agent Tanner preferred cooperating. As did Interpol."

"Was Tanner the 'distant relation' Bryce mentioned, the person monitoring me?"

"Yes, but on the periphery. Tanner had Rodriguez and family under observation, not for wine, but for ties to the Enrico Cartel— the Coyote brothers had connections. It was kind of Isabel to remember we're all on the same side, fighting for the same cause."

"Isabel." She smiled faintly. "You knew her?"

"I know her twin sister, she's FBI. Agent Tanner made a case in my favour. Llewelyn was more than pleased with the outcome."

"I bet he was." Mae squinted. "Tell me what 'the cause' was all about."

Casually, he lifted one shoulder and let it drop. "I can't. You don't have clearance."

"The least you could do is make up something."

The left side of his mouth rumpled. "It was all a matter of...greed."

"That's it?"

"Isn't that enough?"

"These things are always about greed, about money, aren't they?"

Kitt shrugged again. "Sometimes it's about revenge."

"That basic human need." Mae looked down at her hands. "Come sit here."

Kitt shoved aside the paperbacks and sat in the cushioned cubby. Sun poked through rain clouds and lit the space, warming their backs. "Do you know what the eggs were like in prison?"

"Probably powdered."

"I hoped we'd get back to where we were, but this homecoming without scrambled eggs and coffee is just so...unnatural, Mae."

"More unnatural than powdered eggs?"

"Yes."

She repositioned the books on the cushion. "I've had a lot of time to think about getting back to where we were, about how to best do that," Her elbow brushed his and she laughed. "In these last weeks, when it seemed likely that you'd spend your life eating powdered eggs in Leavenworth, or wherever it is the Americans put international assassin types and foreign intelligence officers gone rogue—"

"I did *not* go rogue."

Mae smiled contritely. "Do forgive me. In the last weeks when it seemed likely that you'd spend your life in Leavenworth, or wherever it is the Americans put supposedly dead international assassin types and foreign intelligence officers who are actually alive and breaching international laws without authorisation, I realised you were right about something. It's far simpler than I thought. I lost sight of what was important." She heaved a sigh of resignation. "I accept what you do. I accept what I've done. Nothing says I have to like it, or that it doesn't trouble me, or that I have to pretend it doesn't matter. It does matter. I don't like it. It does trouble me. However iniquitous my actions, I'm done pretending or trying to convince myself this would work any other way. I don't want to live my life focused on fear." She set a hand on his thigh. "Maybe there's something else we can do."

"Yes, find a hotel. A very quiet hotel where no one is hammering or drilling *walls*."

"Subtle innuendo, Kitt."

"I do try." His gaze settled back on her. "What do you mean by *pretending*? Is that what you've been doing this whole time, pretending?"

"If I've learned anything from you it's the importance of improvising. Life is nothing but improvisation. You're here when I didn't think you would be, so I'm improvising, and I'm not doing it very well, but I think you're mighty and you—"

The door buzzer rang, the sound thundering in the emptiness of the flat.

"That may be my new tenant—or Bryce. He's been instructed to buzz from now on. He's quite curious to see how this all goes."

"I should have killed him when I had the chance."

"Are you ever going to stop wanting to kill Bryce?"

"I'm plotting his demise right now."

"Well, please don't murder him here. I don't want to scare off my new tenant."

"I wouldn't dream of killing him in my home." The door buzzed again. Kitt stood and strode across polished wood. He reached the door and yanked it open. A silver-haired woman smiled at him She held a dog's lead in her hand. Felix pulled against that lead, long tail wagging as he sniffed Kitt's shoes.

"Forgot the upstairs door code," the woman said, removing the dog's blue coat, handing it to Mae.

"Thank you for the obedience training, Mrs Rigg."

"He's getting there, love." Mrs Rigg gave Kitt the once-over, mouth pursing.

Kitt mirrored her actions.

"He looks like he could use a bit of training."

"Well," Mae glanced at Kitt and leaned close to the woman. "I do have trouble getting him to stay."

Mrs Rigg chortled heartily and Kitt watched her disappear down the stairs with bewilderment rattling his bones. He faced Mae. She tossed aside the damp dog coat, cuddling Felix like a baby, and Kitt burst out laughing.

"I *really* liked the bit about the dog," she shrugged.

"Clearly. Please, explain how it is I'm looking at Felix."

"Reed."

"My brother did you a favour?"

"You're bully, I'm honey. You demand, I ask. Felix went to a shelter. He needed a home. I needed company while you were incarcerated."

"Has he been sharing your bed?"

"Yes, my pea-sized single bed." With a grin, she pulled the collar and lead from Felix and set him on his feet.

The dog darted around the empty flat, head down, sniffing a trail into the kitchen.

Mae moved back to the window seat. "I really should have waited until you came home to discuss it, but I thought organising a new home was more important."

His mouth pursed. "Do you really think a spy can have a dog?"

"No, but a spy's butler can have a dog. I didn't know when, or if, you'd be coming home, but Felix seemed like a good idea."

"I told you I'll always come home to you."

"Which brings us to your last postcard." Mae snorted, head shaking.

"You received it. I'm delighted. After the previous occasion I wasn't certain you would, but this time I posted it myself. Did you like it?"

"Shall I be honest?"

"Always."

"A text message would have cleared up any confusion. There could have been scrambled waiting eggs for you. And the card was a soppy choice."

"How I love your honesty."

Her expression, the one that told him how full of shite he was, combined with a nuance that implied he scored high on the scale of idiocy, which did nothing to temper his asking, "Did you keep it, or..." he glanced about the empty room, "...dispose of it as you did my underpants?"

"I'm not sentimental, but..." Mae reached into a pocket at the side of her dress. "*Be mine, Valentine.*" She dabbed her nose with a tissue. A tear rolled down her cheek. "It was sappy, but quite sweet. You're a thoughtful and rather romantic man."

"Yes. No one is more surprised about that than I." Kitt hadn't expected tears, yet another one trickled down to her chin. "But the point is, you were moved. I moved you."

"Obviously."

He smiled, knowing exactly how smug that smile was. "I thought it an improvement on *Quando*, particularly with how that turned out."

With a sniffle, she shifted the paperbacks again. "So here you are, and here we are."

"I'm home now."

Felix raced into the room and hopped up onto the cushion beside Mae, knocking over the stacked books as he turned one way then the other, two volumes falling to the gleaming floor. "Yes, you're home now. I've been thinking about our circumstance, the surreptitiousness of it," she said, scratching the dog's long neck when he plopped his narrow head on her lap.

Kitt retrieved the novels and made a new pile. "What matters is I'm here, with you, and—" he glanced at the titles, all spy novels: *The Day of the Jackal, Eye of the Needle, Where Eagles Dare.* "Was this your research?"

"Of course not. They belong to the new tenant."

"Felix isn't the new tenant?"

The dog put his head on Mae's thigh. "No," she said, absently rubbing soft fur. "If our only safe option was to go on as we were, I thought restoring the rear pantry staircase between downstairs and up made sense. The staircase is quite narrow, but it is hidden. You simply press a panel beside the washer. Think of all the fun you'll have creeping down the back stairs to my pea-sized bed."

"You're moving in downstairs?"

"And you're staying where you were."

"My, aren't you clever."

"Yes, clever enough to be a spy."

"Let's not get full of ourselves, Mae."

With a laugh, Mae picked Alistair MacLean's *Puppet on a Chain* from the pile of books and drew out the postcard she'd used to bookmark a page. "No one's ever given me a Valentine before." She gave an amused airy chuckle and held it out to him.

All in soft pastels, the postcard showed a Victorian-era gentleman on one knee before a woman, her hand in his. It was sappy and sweet and Kitt was surprised. "Why did you keep this one, but not the others?"

"You're alive this time, and hope has a strange way of making one hold on to silly things." She tapped the picture. "Is this supposed to be you with the moustache and me with the rather ample bosom?"

"That was the idea. I picked the soppiest, most saccharine Valentine I could find so you could mock me and I could revel in that mocking."

She knocked away another tear. "You succeeded."

"Not quite."

Mae gazed at him flatly. "Have I not mocked you since you arrived, am I not mocking you still?"

"Indeed, you are, you've done nothing but mock me since I got here. Shall I propose again, so that there's no confusion about my intention, so that you know I am serious about our very long engagement?"

"I've been thinking about that."

"I'm aware there are a few things that need to be sorted."

"Such as a ring."

"I have a ring."

"Let me see it."

"You've seen it. You've worn it."

"I gave it back to you and you gave it to Simon, didn't you?"

His head slanted to one side. "I'd very much like to take you to bed to continue this, but there is no bed and the place is full of tradesmen, dogs, and obedience trainers."

"I have an idea," she said.

"I have several," he said and door buzzed again. Felix scrambled off the window seat and ran about, barking. Kitt swore, strode across the room and yanked open the door, ready to give Bryce a blast, but a man built like a welterweight boxer stood on the other side of the threshold, a suitcase in his hand.

A tinge of pepper sprinkled the salt of thinning hair, and the man regarded him, a small smile, a crease in his brow, and narrowed, very blue eyes casting immediate judgment. He set down the suitcase. "You're the killer," he said.

"You're the priest." Kitt stared at a man whose brow-line and nose bore a resemblance to the woman behind him.

Very blue eyes flicked over Kitt's shoulder. "Keep that humpin' canine away from me."

Kitt half turned. Mae stood behind him, Felix in her arms. "Your new tenant, Mrs Valentine?"

Padre Sean Vincenzo had a boxer's cauliflower ear and an Irish lilt, the kind his sister had when she was angry. "I'm here for your confession, Major Kitt."

"I'm not Catholic," Kitt said.

"She is." The padre squinted. "And if I'm to marry ya, ya best be convertin' for her."

"What?" Kitt squinted back. And then he understood. He turned to Mae and watched her set Felix on his feet. "Yes, yes, you're very clever."

"No, she's not. It may not be a legal marriage," Padre Sean muttered, pushing the sniffing dog away from his leg, "but it was *my* idea.'

Mae ignored her brother's grumbling and looked up at a slightly crooked nose and blue-grey eyes, at features that were cold and ugly and warm and beautiful, at a man bound by a lethal profession, at a man she loved. Life, however they lived it, would always sit beneath a shadow, but there was no sense in not being together any way they could. She took his hand and kissed two truncated, stubby fingers. "Are you afraid, Hamish?"

Kitt's mouth quirked ever so slightly. "My love, I'm terrified."

"I'm not," she said.

ACKNOWLEDGMENTS

I am ridiculously grateful to Ainslie Paton for her patient hand-holding, video-making skills, sharp eye, and kindness to me when she should have been focusing on her own writing. There would be no book without Rebekah Turner's amazing patience, coffee-drinking, and graphic design skills. Thank you to my editor and tall little love Belinda Holmes and her little love Charlie. Every blessing on earth to Anne-Marie Scoones for wanting to read and finding a 'Kiss in Kitt.' My gratitude to dear reader Susan Garbanzo is overwhelming and I am thrilled she likes the book as much as the last. Thank you to my beta readers Lily Malone, Cindy Siverly Hollabaugh, Ann Cleary, and Annette Christianson. Love and thanks to Elle Gardner for wanting more of Kitt and Mae, to Lisa Barry who was so excited that there was going be more Kitt and Mae. I am indebted to Megan Whalen Turner—who knew where all the serialised high school fan fiction and adventure stories would lead?

I am forever beholden to my big, bearded Sicilian husband, who supports and encourages me, and finally read one of my books—and loved it nearly as much as he loves me.

ABOUT THE AUTHOR

All my books present women over the age of forty as lead characters. I am so interested in dispelling the myths and 'Hollywood' stereotypes of older women you often see (or don't see) in fiction and film I did a doctorate on the subject! You can call me Dr Sandra.

Although I live in Australia, please note I use both UK and US English spelling depending on the characters and setting of the book. My US-based novels, *A Basic Renovation*, *For Your Eyes Only*, *Driving in Neutral*, and *Next to You*, are romantic comedies and romantic-comedy-mysteries published through Escape, a Harper Collins imprint. My UK-set books that are part of the *In Service* series, *At Your Service*, and the origin short story, *Your Sterling Service*, are cosy and gritty romantic spy mystery-thrillers.

All my books are available via www.sandraantonelli.com.

I am not the fastest writer, but I aim to have *True to Your Service*, the third and final book in the *In Service* series, ready for publication in 2020.